SUMNER ISLAND

Michael Cormier

PublishingWorks, Inc.
2010

PublishingWorks, Inc.,
151 Epping Road
Exeter, NH 03833
603-778-9883

For Sales and Orders:
1-800-738-6603 or 603-772-7200

Cover Design by: Justin Manteuffel & Anna Pearlman
Layout Design by: Anna Pearlman

LCCN: 2009907337
ISBN: 1-935557-01-7
ISBN-13: 978-1-935557-01-2

Printed on recycled paper.
Printed in the United States.

SUMNER ISLAND

To Dad, who was always there.

What'll I do
when you are far away
And I am blue
what'll I do?

—Irving Berlin

PART I

PROLOGUE

July, 1924

S he never heard the intruder until he was standing over her, hammer raised, ready to swing.

The young woman had fallen asleep on the divan. Nearby, an Atwater Kent radio set played soft static, its exposed vacuum tubes giving off a dull glow. The only other light in the room came from an oil lamp on a small table beside the divan, which cast the intruder's shadow against the far wall.

It wasn't so much that she heard him as sensed his presence. She had been reading a new novel by Agatha Christie when she dozed off. In her sleep, she dreamed of a young man dressed in strange clothes. He seemed to know her, and in an odd way she felt she knew him, too. Yet in her dream the surroundings were unfamiliar: a quadrangle of buildings in a style like nothing she had ever seen before.

Then somehow the dream just stopped, like the end of a moving picture film running off its spool, leaving the screen blank. She opened her eyes and there, beside the divan, stood the man with the hammer.

In the instant before he swung she saw in his eyes that he realized his mistake. He had obviously meant to kill her in her sleep but hesitated too long. And then the hammer came down, claw end first. But she was quick and moved her head to one side just in time to avoid a killing blow. Instead of her skull, the claw sank into the pillow where her head had rested a fraction of a second earlier, making a dull *puff*.

In her haste to get away she rolled off the divan onto the carpet and crab-walked backwards into an alcove where she ended up against a wall, cornered and cut off from the rest of the room. The man followed slowly like a big cat cornering its prey. With no means of escape the young woman screamed for her father, unaware that he lay dead in a pool of blood one floor below.

The intruder lunged at her and swung, but she dipped her shoulders to one side and he missed her again. In lunging, he upset the small table on which the oil lamp stood. The lamp fell to the floor and the glass shattered, spraying oil in every direction. The oil caught fire and the flames spread quickly, forcing him to back away. Seeing his momentary distraction, she sprang to her feet and tried to dart past him, but he grabbed onto her dressing gown and pulled her to him. She struggled to break free, but he was too strong for her diminutive frame and he got his arm around her neck and squeezed. He swung the hammer sideways, but she got her elbow up just in time, blocking his wrist and causing the hammer to pop out of his hand.

"Damn you," the man growled. In spite of her small size the woman was putting up a much better fight than he'd anticipated. No matter, he thought, one good punch to the temple ought to do it—

Suddenly something—a movement or sound, he wasn't sure which—caught his attention. He swung his head to the right where a spiral staircase wound down to the floor below, but saw nothing out of the ordinary. Whatever he thought he had seen was no longer there, or never had been. Satisfied that he was safe, he turned his attention back to the woman, but by now the lack of blood flowing to her brain had weakened her and her body had gone slack. Realizing she would soon lose consciousness, he pulled his elbow in tighter to cut off the blood flow altogether. Before long, she slumped forward in his arms and he let her fall to the floor. She was still breathing, but quite unconscious. The man looked around for the hammer. One quick blow would finish her off.

The fire had spread, surrounding the hammer where it lay in the alcove. He tried to reach it but had to pull his hand back from the licking flames. At the rate the fire was growing the room would soon be completely engulfed. Certainly, it would surround the woman in a matter of seconds. There was no need to use the hammer now—the fire would take care of the rest. He had to get out before he became trapped himself.

He moved around the flames over to the staircase. Before taking the first step down he paused to look back, making sure the woman was still unconscious. She was, although he knew the smoke would soon cause her to cough herself awake. No matter. The fire had crept even closer to the staircase and now she was all but cut off from the only escape route.

He turned back to the stairs and took a step, and as he did, he heard a loud bang then he was falling head-first. He landed partway down the stairs and tumbled the rest of the way to the floor below, landing in a heap, unconscious. He remained that way for only a moment before coming to. Slowly, he got to his knees and looked up, trying to figure out what had just happened. Burning embers had started floating down through the hole in the ceiling from which the stairs descended, and he knew the fire would spread to this floor before long. He was hurt in the fall, but nothing was broken. He rose to his feet and stumbled off in the direction from which he had come.

July, 1984

The little boy in the green swim trunks walked beside his mother on the gravel-covered trail. Her pace was maddeningly slow for the boy, and if not for her tight grip on his hand, he would have broken away and left her behind. He had been promised ice cream at the snack bar up ahead and wanted to get there just as fast as his flip-flops would allow. But his father, laden down with most of their beach gear, lagged far behind.

The day was hot, humidity off the charts, and the thick layer of sun block on the boy's naked back felt sticky and uncomfortable. All afternoon his mother had slathered lotion on him over and over again. With his fair skin protected the boy had hardly given a thought to the heat. His parents, on the other hand, had succumbed to it rather quickly and finally decided to cut their excursion short and take an earlier boat off the island. The boy had protested until he was bribed with a farewell ice cream cone.

Curiously, even as his parents wilted in the New England heat wave, the boy's senses had actually sharpened. While other beachgoers trudged about lethargically, brains half-functioning in the life-draining humidity, the boy's senses had gained the alertness of a predatory animal. His eyes were so sharply focused he could make out the expressions on the faces of people a hundred yards away. His ears picked up the tiniest sounds. Scents were more pronounced and varied. But the boy hadn't really noticed, so distracted was he with building sand castles and catching hermit crabs. He did notice, however, when all these sights and sounds and smells began to be accompanied by others unfamiliar to him. Like the strange, narrow white tents that appeared on the back of the beach. And the occasional child playing nearby, dressed in an odd bathing suit that looked like black tights. And the lady he saw walking up on the boat dock dressed in a long white dress and wide hat covered with flowers. Yet he gave little thought to even these things. To his young mind these were all just quirky things that Mom or Dad could explain, just like all the other oddities in the world that crossed a young boy's senses.

Now, as he walked hand-in-hand with his mother, he saw the woman in the flowered hat again. She appeared up ahead about ten or fifteen yards, walking in the same direction in which he and his mother trudged. He hadn't noticed her on the trail before, and he wondered where she had come from. Walking this close to her he could see white boots with tall heels sticking out from under the long dress material. The boy giggled and his mother asked him why.

"That lady," he said, pointing with his free hand.

His mother followed his outstretched arm and saw two teenage girls, maybe twenty yards up the trail, shuffling along in sandals and wrap-around beach towels. "What lady?"

The boy watched the woman hike up the bottom of her lacy white dress away from the dusty trail, revealing the many buttons on the sides of her shoes. He giggled again.

"Mitch? Tell me," his mother said.

"The lady has funny shoes," the boy said.

He watched the woman stroll up the trail behind the two girls. The girls stopped to look off at the swimming beach to their left, but the lady kept going straight at them. When she was a mere step away the boy gasped, expecting a collision, but to his great surprise she passed right through them as though they weren't even there. His eyebrows went up and his mouth dropped open.

"What is it?" the boy's mother demanded, alarm in her voice.

"She just walked through those girls."

The boy's mother stopped, took him by the shoulders, and stared into his eyes. Behind them, the boy's father caught up and set the beach gear down. "What's the matter?" he asked the boy's mother.

The mother ignored him, her attention focused completely on her son.

"Do you still see her?"

The boy squinted up the trail. After the lady in the hat had walked through the girls in the sandals she seemed to just vanish. "Nope," he said, shrugging and turning his palms up. "She's gone."

Up to now the boy had felt more curiosity at what he saw than anything resembling fear. Concern never registered in his mind until the next thing happened.

One moment he stood in the blazing sun, squinting up the trail, trying to see where the woman in the hat had gone. The next moment he was surrounded by the dark of night, looking up the same trail. Only the trail wasn't quite the same. In the faint light of a bright moon it appeared narrower, the bushy growth on the left side bigger and scruffier. Otherwise, it was the same trail.

He was aware that his mother still stood close beside him. She was saying something, but he didn't hear it because a commotion to his right distracted him. When he looked that way he saw an expansive lawn rising up to an old hotel. It was the same lawn they'd been walking beside a moment ago. The same hotel, too, although something about it looked a little different, just like the trail looked a little different. People were hurrying out the front doors onto a wide veranda and down some steps leading to the lawn. All of them were dressed in strange clothes. The boy's gaze was drawn to a mansard tower sticking out of the roof at the center of the hotel. Behind a round window in the tower a fire blazed.

That's when a strange feeling came over the boy, one he'd never experienced in his young life. It was a feeling that made his stomach convulse, a sickening mixture of horror and desperation and great sadness. Somehow, he knew someone was dying up there behind that round window.

Then, mercifully, the feeling left him just as quickly as it had come. In the blink of an eye it was daylight again, and only a few people were on the lawn, all of them dressed in shorts and sneakers, casually moving about on their way to or from the hotel. The boy heard his mother talking at him in a near-shout, the same way she had the time he fell off a swing and broke his arm. He looked at her and realized they were both standing on the grass and that she no longer held his hand. Yet he didn't remember leaving the trail.

"Mitch, *please* tell me what you're looking at!" his mother pleaded.

He gazed up at her face. It was red and her eyes were wide and moist.

The boy looked back at the hotel, trying to recall what exactly he had been looking at. But, try as he might, he just couldn't remember. For many years after that day he would try from time to time to dredge up the memory, but he would be well into his adult years before he ever did.

CHAPTER ONE

Present Day

Ten miles off the southern Maine coast the eighty-foot passenger ferry, *Narwhal*, chugged along the rocky shore of a small island. Designed for short cruises within sight of the mainland, the *Narwhal* could carry up to sixty passengers and crew on her two decks, and on this sunny July morning, as with most summer mornings, her decks were filled to the limit.

On the open top deck, Mitchell Lambert leaned against the port rail as he had for most of the hour-long cruise out from the mainland. Directly in front of him, just a couple hundred feet to the east, the Maine State flag stood straight out atop a lighthouse rising from the rocks at the western tip of Forges Island. Mitch watched the tall, whitewashed structure slip by as the boat continued south, and out of habit he ran through its long history in his head. He could have recited that history better than any tour guide. For that matter, he could have gone on about the whole history of Forges Island if anyone cared to listen. But he was happy to remain alone with his thoughts, quietly enjoying his first trip out to the tiny Angels Islands since he was a little kid. Besides, Forges' sister island, just a quarter-mile to the south, interested Mitch far more and it was just about to come into view.

The lighthouse stood at the entrance to a body of water known as Longboat Harbor. Not a natural harbor, it was really an enclosure formed by three of the Angels and two connecting seawalls to keep out the churning north Atlantic sea. As the *Narwhal* turned into the harbor's mouth, the object of Mitch's growing excitement finally began to show itself on the southern horizon. This was Sumner Island, the second largest of the Angels, the one Mitch had waited more than twenty years to see again.

Once its westernmost tip came into view, Mitch made his way over to the starboard bow to get a better look. He found an empty spot at the rail and leaned against it, feeling familiarity wash over him like *déjà vu*. Considering he hadn't been here in so long, and that he was a small boy the last time he stood at this rail, the sensation took him by surprise. Yet the sound of passengers coming to life and gathering up baggage, the rumble of the diesel engines, the sight of the dock growing closer—all of this could have been a repeat from just last summer. Even last week.

When the ferry was fully within the harbor, the entire expanse of Sumner Island became visible on the horizon. Just two hundred acres in size, the western end was dominated by the hotel and grounds of the Smythe Resort where Mitch would be staying for the next three days. The hotel stood at the crest of a low hill, surrounded by an acre of perfectly groomed grass, one of the last of the grand hotels from the high Victorian era. Three mansard towers—two small ones at either end and a larger one in the middle—rose from a salmon-colored roof, and a wide veranda ran all along the front, turning at the western end toward another, plainer wing connected by a breezeway. In spite of the nor'easters and occasional hurricanes that had battered the old building every winter for a century and a quarter, today she gleamed like new in the brilliant sunlight.

The captain cut back the engines and pointed the *Narwhal* toward the Smythe's dock where a couple of young men in tan caps with red bills—the Smythe colors—sat on folding chairs, watching her approach. People had already begun making their way down the trails and walkways to the dock. Some carried baggage, but Mitch knew that a lot of them were just coming down to greet passengers. Guests often stayed at the Smythe for a week or two and sometimes invited friends and family out for the day. Other people owned summer cottages on the island, so there was always a crowd greeting the arriving boat.

The *Narwhal* slowed more when she got to within fifty yards of the dock, then the captain expertly swung the stern around and floated the port hull up dockside. On the main deck two sailors threw coils of thick rope off the bow and stern. The dock boys tied the boat snug against the rubber bumper, then ran a gangplank to the port side of the main deck. When it was securely in place, Mitch grabbed his duffle bag, wrestled it down the steep stairs to the main deck and waited his turn to go ashore.

Minutes later, he stepped onto the dock and gazed around. The last time he had been here he was too young to pay much attention to anything besides the boat trip and the beach where he had spent the day with his parents. Yet in recent years he had devoured mountains of books and magazines containing innumerable photographs of the place, enough that he recognized everything he saw as though he had been here a dozen times or more. There, at the eastern end of the resort, were the tennis courts where East Coast Brahmins and celebrities had played in charity tournaments throughout the 'thirties and 'forties. To the far west, the hotel's unofficial mascot and subject of a million postcards—the famous gazebo known as Lover's Lookout—appeared to teeter precariously on the rocks above the churning surf. Directly to the left of the dock, two swimming beaches, where the likes of Barrymore, Crawford, Bogart, and Kelly had posed for movie-land photographers, spread out in front of the harbor. A steep bluff huddled over the beaches, topped by a bathhouse and snack bar. At the foot of the dock, a walkway wound its way up the lawn to the hotel where a topiary dolphin and harbor seal stood in greeting just below the veranda steps. Everything within view had been here, almost exactly the same as it was today, for a hundred years or more.

Mitch slung his duffle bag across his back and started walking along the dock with the rest of the crowd. He only made it a few steps before a female voice called out, "Professor Lambert!" Startled because he hadn't expected anyone out here to know him, he looked around and saw a heavyset woman with snow-white hair and wrap-around sunglasses hurrying his way. He didn't recognize her, but the hardcover book she held over her head he recognized well: *American Princess: Maria Boudreau Remembered*. By Mitchell I. Lambert, PhD.

"Can I get you to sign my book?" she asked, stopping in front of him.

"Of course." He set his duffle bag down on the dock and the woman handed him the book and a Sharpie marker. "How did you know it was me?"

"Your picture. On the back cover."

Mitch smiled. It was one thing to know his name—after all, he had become a minor celebrity for a while when his book climbed the bestseller lists a couple of years back. But knowing his face just from the back cover? That felt a little weird, although not in a bad way. "What's your name?"

"Maria." The woman beamed. "Just like *your* Maria."

"Maria," he repeated, thinking *now she's* my *Maria.* This he didn't mind at all—his Maria had been good to him. He only hoped he had been as good to her, with her biography.

He flipped the book open to the first blank page opposite the cover. There he wrote, "To my friend, Maria. A lovely name, indeed," and signed it "Mitch Lambert." Corny, yes, but he knew from experience that she would love it.

He handed the book and pen back. "There you are, Maria."

The woman read the inscription and hugged the book to her chest. "Thank you, Professor Lambert."

"Mitch." He knew she would like this, too. Actually, he preferred being called by his first name over "Professor" or "Doctor" or even "Mister." At twenty-eight, he didn't feel old enough or wise enough to be referred to so formally.

"I loved the book," the woman went on.

"I'm glad."

"Nobody else could have written more . . . *affectionately* about her," she said with great earnestness. "Can I ask a question, if you don't mind?"

"Go right ahead."

"Do you think those sightings—you know, the ones people've been having . . . "

"Do I think they're real?" He had been asked the same question numerous times in the past few weeks. He answered the same way he always did. "Not really."

The woman's smile faded to a disappointed pout, making him feel guilty. Obviously, she was looking for a firm "yes." Like so many others caught up in the romance of the story, she wanted to believe in the supposed encounters with Maria Boudreau's ghost. The newspapers had hyped up the ghostly encounters so much it was a wonder ten other people weren't swarming around him right now asking the same question. He said, gently, "But I certainly hope I'm proven wrong."

The woman's smile returned as she puffed herself up. "Well, Professor Lambert, I think you will be."

He smiled back and picked up his duffle. "Enjoy your weekend, Maria."

He stopped at the end of the dock. The wind was little more than a breeze here, so he took off his windbreaker and stuffed it in the duffle. He wiped the salt spray off his sunglasses, then looked up at the dirt trails running east and west. This conjured up another factoid he'd learned about the island: one of its quaint oddities was the lack of any cars, at least gasoline-powered ones. Automobiles had never been allowed on the island, so there was no exhaust to foul up the air and no paved roads to cut up the landscape. But electric golf carts were allowed, as well as the electric-powered trucks used by the Smythe, and he saw a few of them puttering around. The carts shared the same hard-packed trails used by pedestrians who were required by island rules to step aside and let them pass whenever they approached. And before him were the beginning-and-end points of the two main trails, which joined at the dock. He was supposed to follow one of them, but couldn't remember which. *Left or right? East or west?* He just couldn't remember, so he fished in his pocket for the sticky note he had written the directions on. His scribble told him to take the cart trail to the left if he was facing the hotel. *Okay, then, left it is.*

The trail took him past the swimming beaches, which were crowded on this warm day. The trail itself was fairly crowded with people coming to and from the beachfront and others just out for a walk. He wound in and out of the ones who were in no big hurry to get anywhere. Not that there was much of anywhere to get to on this little island.

He started past the wooden stairs descending the bluff to the beach, the snack bar and bathhouse now visible around the corner—

—and stopped short in the middle of the trail.

A vision like a series of short movie clips had suddenly jumped into his head: a woman in a gray uniform holding an infant, a boy in an old-fashioned bathing suit playing on a beach, a man laying face down in a pool of blood in a dirty alley, a locomotive coming on fast in the dark of night. None of the scenes meant anything to him. He was sure he had never seen any of these things before. But the stew of emotions that accompanied them—joy and contentment followed by horror and despair—felt familiar in an old and faded sort of way.

Gradually, he became aware of a voice close by that seemed directed at him. He turned and saw a young woman in a Smythe cap. She stood beside him, peering closely at his face. She was asking him a question: *Sir, are you okay?*

He nodded vaguely at her.

She bent down to pick something up off the trail. He watched her lift up his duffle bag. *You dropped this.* She pointed behind him. *I thought you might want to throw it on the baggage truck.*

He looked back. An electric truck filled with luggage was stopped on the trail right behind him. The driver was waiting for him to get out of the way.

All at once the fog in his head lifted and he drew in a deep breath and shook his head at the girl.

"No—I'm fine—I'm—not at the hotel." He took his bag, thanked her, and continued on his way.

CHAPTER TWO

His directions told him to look for the first cottage on the trail as he moved east past the beaches. He trudged along with the duffle on his back, beginning to think he would never see it. Behind him, the bathhouse and the beaches disappeared around a bend, and now there were only trees on either side of the trail. Not a house in sight.

He was thinking about stopping to check the directions again when the trail took a sudden turn to the right, and there it was, a small cottage with a green tin roof on the right side of the trail, exactly as its owner had described it. The house stood at an angle to the trail facing Longboat Harbor, a square, one-story structure covered in layers and layers of white paint, most of it chipped and peeling. All around it sumac and berry brambles, and God only knew what other things, grew thick and tangled, some climbing up the sides of the house. He could even see a few swallows' nests tucked here and there under the eaves.

Coming around to the front, he was surprised to see a man on the porch, sitting in the most rickety old rocker he'd ever seen. The man looked about a thousand years old. His head was bald and covered in skin cancer spots and his ears stuck out, but the rest of his features were soft and kind. In spite of the warm weather he wore green work pants and a blue flannel shirt over a t-shirt. Underneath he appeared thin, but not frail.

As Mitch came closer, the old man picked up his pace in the rocker and gave a little wave. "Hello, young man," he called out in a sharp voice.

"Hello," Mitch answered from the bottom of the porch steps.

The old man went on rocking and smiling down at Mitch who stood there feeling the duffle bag growing heavy across his back. After a long uneasy moment, Mitch asked, "Is this the Arndt property?"

"Yes, sir."

Mitch nodded. In his head he ran through the conversation he'd had with one of the hotel clerks less than a week ago. He had called for reservations at the Smythe and was told the hotel was completely booked and the waiting list was long. When he mentioned who he was and why it was so important for him to be there that weekend, the clerk had asked for his phone number. A few minutes later the same clerk called back and offered him the "Arndt cottage" for the weekend at a very reasonable price. Of course Mitch jumped at the opportunity. While his credit card was being processed, they chatted about Mitch's book and the ghost hunt to take place that weekend, so there couldn't possibly have been a mix-up about the dates. The cottage was supposed to be his for the weekend. Including today. "I rented Mr. Arndt's cottage for the weekend," he told the old man in the rocker.

"That you did."

"Am I early? Should I come back?"

The old man shrugged. "If you want, but there's no need to. The cottage is ready for you now if you want to go in and unpack."

"I assume you're staying up at the hotel then?" Mitch said, hoping for the answer he wanted to hear.

"What for? I've got my own place right here. Put that bag down before your back starts to look like mine."

Mitch obeyed, letting the straps slip off his shoulders and swinging the duffle to the ground. He went up the steps and the old man stuck out his hand to shake. "Theodore Arndt, your landlord," he said brightly.

Mitch shook his hand, which was all bones and paper-thin skin but had a strong grip nevertheless. "Mitch Lambert, nice to meet you." He hoped the uncertainty he felt wasn't obvious in his voice.

The old man looked about five-eleven, Mitch's height, if you didn't count the stoop in his shoulders. In spite of his advanced years, Mitch peered past thin eyeglasses into a pair of clear, lively eyes—much livelier than he would have expected in a body so aged everywhere else. Something else about the eyes struck him, too. Something about the way they moved, maybe? The unique way in which they followed Mitch's own with great attention and (what was the word, empathy?). A manner Mitch would swear he had seen before. But that was impossible, of course. He was certain he'd never met this man until now.

"Likewise." Mr. Arndt flashed a smile and squinted, breaking Mitch's focus.

An uncomfortable silence passed, during which the old man seemed to be waiting for Mitch to say something. He finally did—exactly what was on his mind. "Did I tell you the wrong weekend I was coming out?"

"Nope." Mr. Arndt went on smiling, or squinting at the sunlight, Mitch couldn't tell which.

"I didn't expect you to be here."

"I'm here all summer. Come on. The cottage is all ready for you. Grab that bag of yours."

He walked over to another set of steps at the far end of the porch, gripped the rail and stepped down gingerly using his cane on each step.

Mitch followed and soon understood. On the other side of the porch a narrow trail ran through more growth than he had seen on the harbor side of the house, right up to a tiny cabin. It looked like one of those old one-room structures, the kind you can still rent along roadsides in some tourist spots. It, too, was painted white with a green tin roof.

"Your cottage," Mr. Arndt said, stopping outside the door.

Mitch nodded and let out a quiet sigh. Now he knew why the rent was so cheap.

They went inside what was, indeed, a single room furnished with a full-size bed, dresser, end table and lamp. It had a tiny bathroom in one corner, thankfully, but no kitchen. Seeing the look on his face, Mr. Arndt asked, "Is there a problem?"

"No, no, it looks comfortable," Mitch answered quickly, not wanting to offend his host. It was either stay here or take the next boat off the island, and he had no intention of leaving. "It's just that I was hoping to have a kitchen. I brought some food with me. Eating at the hotel can get expensive, so I thought—"

"Problem resolved," Mr. Arndt interrupted with a wave of his free hand. "You can cook at my house if you want, but you don't need to. Unless, of course, you're on some special diet."

Mitch shook his head. "I don't understand."

"You get all your meals for free up at the hotel. With me. As my guest."

Mitch waited for him to laugh and say "gotcha!" But the old man's face was serious. Mitch said, "I do?"

"Yes, sir."

Once again the old man was staring, making Mitch uncomfortable. Only this time it was a different kind of stare, the kind you might get if you had a piece of food dangling off the corner of your mouth and didn't know it. Yet his eyes didn't linger for long on any particular part of Mitch's face. They wandered around, starting at his mouth then climbing upward along his nose to his eyes, even up to his hairline. Then they seemed to appraise the whole face, taking it in all at once.

"Excuse me, am I—" Mitch started to say.

"*Remarkable.*"

The comment was barely a mumble, but the cabin was so quiet Mitch heard it clearly.

"Excuse me?"

Mr. Arndt blinked and turned away briefly. "I said 'remarkable.'"

"What's remarkable?"

He turned back to Mitch. "That you're here. I mean you told the clerk up at the hotel you had to be here this weekend, and here I was with a vacant cottage—"

"Cabin."

"—and it's just remarkable how things work out sometimes, don't you think?" The old man grinned at him. "So tell me, Dr. Lambert, did you come for the spook show like everyone else?"

"In a way. Probably not for the same reasons as everyone else."

"Meaning?"

"I'm interested in the historical part of it."

"I see." Mr. Arndt shifted his cane from one hand to the other. "So I take it you're a history professor?"

"American history, to be exact." The duffle had begun to feel heavy again and he set it on the linoleum floor. "I've studied the life of Roger Boudreau and his daughter."

"You seem awfully young to be a professor," Mr. Arndt appraised his face again.

"I haven't been at it long."

"I'm not doubting you. I'm just saying you look young—baby face and all that. But that's not a bad thing. It'll work in your favor someday." He grinned again. "I had a real baby face myself, you know."

Yeah, a hundred years ago. As for himself, Mitch couldn't deny having a young-looking face. With a rounded jaw and smooth cheeks that barely grew whiskers, soft gray eyes, and hair as thick as a schoolboy's, he was often mistaken for a student around the Fowler campus. "I thought I might learn something about the Boudreaus by being here this weekend," he said, changing the subject.

"Like how many nuts are out there thinking ghosts are around every corner, waiting to pop out and go *boo!*"

"As I said, I'm not interested in the ghosts, just the history."

He was lying, of course. Ever since he had heard about the sightings of Maria and Roger's ghosts, and the Smythe Resort's plans to bring a famous psychic out to the island to verify the haunting, he had made up his mind to be here. Would he have come out for some dull historical society lecture about the same pair? Definitely not. But this was different. So different, he couldn't pass it up despite his skepticism about the ghost sightings. After all, this was about Maria returning. In some form anyway.

But he was an associate professor at a small but reputable New England college, trying to earn tenure. And his biography of Maria and Roger Boudreau had been well-received in the academic world, which went a long way toward making that tenure. He wasn't about to blow his chances by admitting how badly he hoped his skepticism would be dashed to bits that weekend. He preferred to just get off this subject entirely. "So, you aren't kidding me about the free meals?" he said.

"Sure. Well, look here, I'll prove it to you right now 'cause it's getting near lunchtime and I missed breakfast. So let's go eat." He raised an eyebrow mischievously. "My treat, but you get to leave the tip."

Mitch left the duffle bag on the floor and followed him through the door. They started down another trail that wound between overgrown sumac and scruffy short trees and brush. It was slow going, and not just because the path was narrow with tree branches growing across. Mr. Arndt's way of walking was maddeningly slow and halting. He would plant his cane, step with one foot, step with the other, scrunch up his lips like Yoda then do it all over again. In this manner the old man made his way through the growth with Mitch just ahead, holding back the branches for him while he passed.

Along the way Mr. Arndt said, "So, how did you come to be an expert about the Boudreaus? No one's paid much attention to them in seventy years, at least."

A fair question. And not the first time he'd been asked it. "I sort of ran across their story while I was researching my doctoral thesis."

"Really? Tell me about it."

"My original thesis was America's attitude toward royalty after the Revolution. You know, the transition from kings to presidents. I thought Americans stayed fascinated with royalty and aristocracy—only it was the moneyed classes they admired, not dukes and earls."

"I would agree with that." Mr. Arndt stopped to catch his breath. "The gilded age, Newport society, Vanderbilts, Kennedys."

"Exactly. In fact, it was the gilded age I was studying at the time I ran across the story of the Boudreaus. They were just the example I was looking for. Do you know anything about them?"

Mr. Arndt shrugged. "A little." He had caught his breath and began walking again.

"Then you probably know Roger married a Russian princess and that Maria was their only child. So Maria wasn't just a rich kid, she was real-life royalty. America loved having its own little princess."

"She grew up to be a real beauty too, didn't she?"

Here Mitch hesitated. To him, Maria was more than a beauty. She had grown into the most exquisite young woman ever to grace this island—or any other place as far as he was concerned. He couldn't say this out loud, though. If he ever opened his big mouth to describe Maria he knew it would be obvious how deep his admiration went, and that wouldn't be very professional. So he replied, simply, "That's what they say."

"And these sightings—this haunting, or whatever you call it—would you say it's wishful thinking? I mean, you see what you want to see. Someone must have wanted to see Maria and Roger."

"Maybe." Mitch tried to sound casual—the old man was treading on sensitive ground again. The truth was that the sightings had begun shortly after his book hit the bestseller lists. It started with an adolescent boy who claimed never to have heard of the Boudreaus. He had awakened one night last summer and looked out his hotel window to see Roger's yacht, the *Tasha*, tied up to the Smythe dock. He described Roger and Maria to a tee, and said he watched them come up the walkway toward the hotel, and even heard them and others talking and laughing. They had evaporated just before reaching the veranda.

Several more sightings followed in rapid succession. The most famous was reported by a couple who also claimed not to know anything about the Boudreaus. They had been walking by Lover's Lookout and saw a young woman dressed in 1920s fashion sitting with a young man in a tuxedo. The apparitions had faded to nothing, but not before the couple got a good look at the girl. Later, they saw a portrait of Maria in the hotel lobby and swore it was her. Several other reports came from folks who said they didn't know anything about the Boudreaus, and who had no reason to lie. So Mitch couldn't say he agreed with Mr. Arndt's theory, although the coincidence of his book's publication, and the sightings coming on its heels, couldn't be ignored.

"Well, I hear the so-called experts coming out to investigate are world-class," Mr. Arndt went on. "Seems so many people tried to join in, they had to turn most of them away."

"That's what I heard."

The old man stopped and looked at Mitch. "Seems you had to get a personal invite from the head ghost hunter himself if you wanted to get in on the action."

Mitch had not only heard the same thing, he had tried to become one of the invitees. Several times he emailed that same "head ghost hunter" with his resume, hoping to get an invitation, but he never heard back. He was too embarrassed to admit this, so he just said, "I read that in the papers. So, what about you?"

"I read the same thing."

"I meant will you be involved in the ghost hunt?"

Mr. Arndt ducked under a low branch that Mitch held up for him then stopped. Just ahead, the trail widened and the edge of the Smythe lawn was visible through the trees.

"At my age, Dr. Lambert," Mr. Arndt said, squinting at the hotel standing atop the lawn's gentle slope, "it's better to spend your time paying attention to *this* world."

They started across the grass, which was cut low and even, and Mr. Arndt's pace picked up. "I didn't realize your house was so close to the resort," Mitch commented as they went.

"Next door neighbors," Mr. Arndt replied proudly.

"How long have you been coming out here?"

The old man stopped, leaned on his cane with both hands and looked skyward. "Well, I'm ninety-three this coming October, so I guess ninety-three years."

Mitch realized with awe that his companion had once stayed here at the very same time as Maria. Maybe even brushed up against her once or twice in the course of, what, ten summers? He could barely contain his excitement. "So I suppose you saw Maria—the Boudreaus—from time to time when you were small."

"Time to time. Hard to miss them. Roger was the cock-o'-the-walk, and Maria—well, it was hard to miss *her*."

"I guess it would be."

"Sure. Well, that should be obvious in my book."

"You wrote a book?"

Mr. Arndt frowned. "You mean you did all that research and you didn't even read my book?"

"Sorry, I—I didn't know about it."

The old man cracked a devilish grin. "I'm just razzin' you. I self-published it. Not many copies around. But I'm going to make sure you buy a copy up at the gift shop." He winked. "I'll even throw in my autograph, no extra charge."

Mitch laughed. "What's it called?"

"*Sumner Island: Then and Now.* I know it's kind of bland, but at least it isn't cute. I can't stand cute titles."

They continued on, the sun beating down on them from a cloudless sky. Some small kids ran by, heading in the direction of the tennis courts where a doubles match was going on. The beaches were crowded and so were the walking trails; the resort was at peak capacity that weekend. He hoped they wouldn't have to wait long for a table at the restaurant. He was famished.

After walking over the grass for what seemed like hours, they finally arrived at the veranda stairs. Looking up the eight steps, it dawned on Mitch for the first time that Mr. Arndt might prefer to take the wheelchair ramp at the east end of the hotel. He asked.

"I've never gone up that ramp before and I'm not going to start now," Mr.

Arndt snapped, waving him off.

Mitch held his breath as the old man started up, carefully negotiating each step the same way he had back at his cottage. It took him a while but he made it up safely. Once on the veranda he turned, using little shuffle steps, and frowned down at Mitch on the walkway. "Are you coming, or do I have to find someone else to eat with?"

Mitch hurried up and stopped on the wide gray deck, looking around. One of the things the Smythe was famous for was its dozens of Kennedy rockers all lined up in front of the veranda railing. Most of them stood empty this time of the day, but a few were occupied by guests relaxing with a newspaper or book or chatting with their neighbor. Mitch took in everything: the veranda, the lawn, the ocean, the sky, the other islands. It might have been the quality of the light, but the scene around him appeared in sharper focus than he expected. The sunlight seemed too brilliant, the colors unusually vibrant, as if he was looking at a picture postcard taken with expensive lenses and filters. Of course, the Smythe hotel and everything around it looked like props from Disneyland's Main Street or a Hollywood back lot. Maybe stepping into a place created a long time ago, which had barely changed over the years, was playing on his senses, making things seem a little surreal.

Keep your eyes peeled, it gets even brighter.

"Huh?" Mitch swung his head around and looked back at Mr. Arndt, but the old man was already halfway to the doors. He couldn't have said it, he was too far away. Yet the voice had sounded just like his.

Mr. Arndt stopped, made a shuffling half-turn and gave Mitch an admonishing look. "Come on, slow poke. You're keeping an old man from his nourishment."

CHAPTER THREE

Mitch followed him to a set of double doors with the trademark Smythe Resort flying angel etched into the glass panels. Two cheerful attendants—young men dressed in tan shorts, red polo shirts and boat shoes—held the doors open for them.

The lobby was small by modern standards. Two white pillars framed the entryway and a crystal chandelier hung from the high ceiling in the center of the room. To the right stood an ancient registration counter, its varnished wood darkened by the years but otherwise in perfect condition. Behind it, a young man and woman stood at attention. Their uniforms were more formal than those worn by the door attendants: crisp white dress shirts with the angel logo on the pocket and navy blue pants with a red stripe down the outer leg.

Off to the left, a small waiting lounge was tucked away in a corner. Red leather chairs stood among Chippendale tables and potted palms on an oriental rug, and a camelback couch faced a fireplace built into a wood-paneled wall. Above the fireplace hung a large portrait illuminated by a brass lamp. The portrait's oversized gilded frame, and the way the furniture was arranged around it, gave the sitting area the appearance of a shrine.

Mitch stared at the painting while following behind Mr. Arndt's slow shuffle-step across the lobby. In it, a middle-aged man stood behind a wingback chair in which a teenage girl sat. The man's hair was dark, his close-cropped beard and handlebar mustaches just starting to gray, and his clothes were in the fashion of early twentieth century aristocracy. He stood proudly, almost defiantly, with his chest forward and shoulders squared. One hand rested on the shoulder of the girl who filled the middle portion of the painting as though she were its main focus. Indeed Mitch, who was familiar with the painting (though, until now, he had only seen it in photos), agreed she belonged as its focal point. Though no older than sixteen, she was a classic beauty. Her dark red hair, tied on top with a wide blue ribbon, cascaded over her shoulders and down a satiny white dress. Her eyes were a green hue that defied description—a color as rich as pea soup, but with the shine of an emerald. Not only was she beautiful, she looked incredibly vibrant, ready to step out of the portrait and light up the room with *joie de vivre.*

"You *know* you're slow when *I'm* beating you."

Mitch turned his gaze from the portrait to Mr. Arndt who stood twenty feet away. Only then did he realize he had stopped walking. "Sorry." He caught up.

The Sea Star Room on the other side of the lobby was almost as familiar to Mitch as Maria's portrait, though, like the portrait, he had only seen it in photos. The décor was pretty much the same as in pictures going all the way back fifty years or more: a tasteful nautical motif. Another restaurant down the hall—the Sandpiper Room—catered to simpler tastes and budgets, so it surprised him when Mr. Arndt walked into the Sea Star. A man his age, probably on a fixed budget like most retirees, should be dining cheaper.

The hostess seated them at a square table covered in crisp white linen standing directly under a rotunda. Measuring twenty feet across, the rotunda was painted to resemble a sky of cottony clouds with cherubs ringing the edges.

Mr. Arndt noticed him admiring the fresco. "It was done by Louis Almquist in 1904. Impressive, isn't it?"

"Yes."

"Notice anything about the angels? As in which one doesn't belong?"

Mitch knew the answer but decided not to spoil the old man's fun. He studied the ceiling for a while then pointed at a cherub with wavy red hair. "They're all blonde except for that one."

"That's right. Do you know why? A little Smythe trivia for you."

Mitch gave in. "It's the one modeled after Roger Boudreau's daughter."

The old man's eyes twinkled with pleasure. "You *did* read my book."

Mitch shook his head. "Honestly, I haven't. I must have read about it somewhere else."

The waitress interrupted them. She took their drink orders—a cranberry juice and soda for Mitch and a scotch on the rocks for Mr. Arndt. Mitch cracked the menu and instinctively looked for the cheaper choices: chicken, pasta, salads. This was his habit whenever he ate at expensive restaurants. On his meager associate professor's salary he had to watch what he spent, even without a wife and kids to support. He found a pasta entry at a relatively reasonable price and closed the menu. When he looked up, he noticed Mr. Arndt hadn't even opened his.

"Let me guess—you know the menu by heart," Mitch said.

"Nope. Don't need to. I always order the same thing for lunch."

As if to confirm this, the waitress came back with their drinks and the first thing she said was, "Usual, Ted?" to which he answered, "Yes, Mandy," and winked.

Mitch ordered and the waitress went away, leaving them alone again. Mitch had never seen such fast service. Mr. Arndt didn't seem to notice at all, which got Mitch's curiosity up again. It was none of his business, and he might be treading on sensitive ground, but he decided to brave a few questions anyway. "If you don't mind me asking, do you eat every meal here at the hotel?"

"Yes, sir. Unless I sleep late."

"I take it you don't cook," Mitch said, edging closer to what he really wanted to know.

"Don't need to." He wasn't biting. Mitch gave him an inquisitive look and this worked. "I can cook but I hate cooking, so the hotel takes care of my meals."

"Doesn't that get kind of—"

"Nope. It's all free. Except for the tip, but I won't mind if you offer to pay that."

Mitch raked his fingers through his hair. "That's some senior discount."

"Senior discount? I don't know if I'd call it that. My father was the unofficial on-call doctor for the Smythe for thirty years. They appreciated his service enough to give his only surviving heir a few bennies." He smiled a crooked grin and raised an eyebrow. "They didn't count on me living so long."

They chatted about the island, mundane things like fresh water and plumbing issues, emergency evacuation plans, boat traffic. Eventually, Mr. Arndt got around to some history, especially maritime history. He seemed to know a great deal about local shipwrecks. Mitch also knew a little about the more famous ones, but he was surprised to learn there had been so many others over the centuries, terrible disasters on the shoals surrounding these islands. He listened, enrapt, as Mr. Arndt told one sea tale after another. Eventually the old man settled back in his seat, took a long swallow of his scotch, and said, "Maybe you know about the pirates who came around here."

Like the shipwrecks, Mitch knew a little but not enough to speak of. "I heard something somewhere." He leaned over the table on his elbows. "How much do you know?"

"Know? I'm almost as old as the pirates!" He winked, then added proudly, "I'd say I know as much as anyone, dead or alive. Why, my—Maria Boudreau is probably the only person who knew more local pirate stories than me."

"Really? Maria?" Like the story about the cherubs, Mitch already knew Maria had a thing for pirate stories, but he didn't want to discourage the old man.

"Yes, sir, she loved pirates. Sometimes she even liked to poke around the island for buried treasure."

"It doesn't surprise me, her being a tomboy and all," Mitch commented, hoping to elicit a little more information about Maria. Unfortunately, it went right over Mr. Arndt's head, because he just looked over Mitch's shoulder and said, "Here comes chow."

Lunch was first rate. Mitch had a seared tuna steak and it was marvelous. Mr. Arndt's "usual" turned out to be a crock of tomato soup and half a roast beef sandwich. The waitress put it all on some tab they never saw and Mitch left the tip.

Back in the lobby, Mitch headed straight for the front doors. He was looking forward to unpacking his bag and maybe relaxing for an hour or two before the afternoon boat arrived. But before he got to the doors, Mr. Arndt called out from the middle of the lobby, "Where are you going?" Mitch stopped and looked back at him. "I bought lunch, now you buy my book," the old man grumbled.

Mitch smiled. Actually, he was curious about the book anyway, so he gladly followed him down the corridor to the gift shop. Among shelves of souvenirs, snacks and toiletries stood a rotating display rack of paperback books. Copies of *Sumner Island: Then and Now* filled two sections. Mitch took down a copy and looked it over. A paperback of quality design, its front cover showed a photo of the Smythe hotel taken from a distance, probably just outside the Longboat Harbor limits. On the back cover, a black and white photo of Theodore M. Arndt, M.D. smiled up at him. The old man looked twenty years younger, with more hair and clearer skin. The bio below the picture described him as a retired professor of medicine at Harvard University and longtime summer resident of Sumner Island. Mitch flipped the book open and skimmed the table of contents. The book was thorough, starting with the geological history of the Angel Islands, moving on to prehistoric times, then their discovery by Captain John Smith and other explorers. Next, it covered colonial times, followed by the Victorian era and the Smythe years, which took up the most chapters. By the chapter titles it was apparent that Mr. Arndt had written a fair amount on the Roger Boudreau years.

A flash of something familiar made him look up. Mr. Arndt was holding up a book of the same size, also paperback, the front cover facing Mitch. Emblazoned on the cover in an elegant script was the title *American Princess: Maria Boudreau Remembered,* and at the bottom, Mitchell I. Lambert, PhD. "I knew you looked familiar, Professor Lambert," the old man said.

Mitch looked over at the book display and saw that Mr. Arndt had rotated it. There on one of the middle shelves, squeezed between copies of a James Patterson novel and a Dr. Phil book were several copies of *American Princess.* "My cover's blown," he said, smiling.

The old man shook the book at Mitch like a schoolmaster shaking a switch at a naughty schoolboy. "You *did* come out here. You *did* see the cherubs, you fibber."

Mitch shook his head. "Honestly, I haven't been on this island since I was a little kid. I must have read about the cherubs somewhere when I was researching the book."

"You mean to tell me you wrote all that detail about Maria's time on this island, and you never once came out to have a look around?"

It sounded odd even to Mitch. But it was true. Not only had he not set foot on Sumner Island while researching *American Princess,* he hadn't come out even after it was published. The reasons while researching the book were easily explained: all work had been done in the fall and winter when the island was shut down and inaccessible. This hadn't been a problem since he was able to find everything he needed to know about the island—narrative descriptions, histories, photographs, maps, illustrations—from library archives and on the internet. After that, his absence was harder to explain, even to himself. He had often thought about coming out for the day, but every time he made plans something else seemed to come up; in truth, he had been skittish about being at the place where Maria had died so brutally. Then all the ghost stories began floating around, and his curiosity—and something else he couldn't define—had overcome his apprehension.

The girl behind the counter caught their conversation. She said, "Two authors, here at the same time! Is there a book signing this weekend?"

"Just for me—Mr. Arndt owes me his autograph." Mitch set the book he held down on the counter.

Mr. Arndt set Mitch's book next to his. "Ring this one on my account, Hannah."

On the veranda, Mitch stared out at the lawn and the water beyond, remembering the words he thought he'd heard earlier outside the front doors: *it gets even brighter.* Mr. Arndt shuffled up beside him and gazed in the same direction, as though trying to see what was so interesting. Mitch noted the questioning expression on the old man's face, but he said nothing, just kept repeating the same words in his head until an impulse made him turn and ask, "Is it always so clear and bright out here?"

Mr. Arndt tapped his cane lightly on the wooden deck. "Out here," he said slowly, "the rest of the world doesn't matter . . . it's a whole environment unto itself." He grinned. "I should have been a poet."

The grin then faded and his face took on a grave expression. "The atmosphere can be exceptionally clear some days. But when the weather turns, no place on Earth gets more *un*clear. And vulnerable."

CHAPTER FOUR

Back at the cabin Mitch unpacked his clothes, threw on a fresh pair of cargo shorts and t-shirt and flopped on the bed. He lay with his hands clasped behind his head, thinking the little cabin wasn't so bad after all. The room was bright and sunny with everything he needed within easy reach. Except for a kitchen, of course, but that didn't seem to matter now.

He read Mr. Arndt's book for half an hour before dozing off into a deep, dreamless sleep, and woke to the sound of a clanging bell. He slipped into some flip-flops and went outside, following the trail to the edge of the lawn. From there he could see a crowd of people making their way down to the dock. The *Narwhal* had just pulled in and some kid was ringing a ship's bell hanging on a hook at the land end of the dock. So the afternoon boat was here. He didn't take naps as a rule, yet he had been asleep for two hours.

He strolled down to the dock behind what seemed like a much larger crowd than the one that had greeted the morning boat. From a spot close to the bell, he watched the dock crew run the gangplank up to the lower deck. When it was firmly in place, a motorized wheelchair filled with the largest woman Mitch had ever seen rolled out of the main deck cabin and pulled up to it. Its occupant used a joystick to steer the wheelchair down the ramp to the dock. There, she had to stop for a throng that surrounded her and her companion, a tall, lanky man with a bald pate and severe stoop. People stuck books and pens in front of their faces, and the two patiently autographed every one. While they did, a television crew unloaded equipment and a few other passengers who appeared to be part of the same entourage exited the boat.

Mitch moved down the dock a little ways and waited for the wheelchair to come by. When it finally approached, he stepped forward and said, "Hello, Mrs. Church, Mr. Leeds. I'm Mitch Lambert."

They stopped and stared at him with blank expressions. Realizing they had no idea who he was, he quickly added, "Professor Mitchell Lambert … Fowler College." Still their faces showed no recognition. He said, "I emailed you. I wrote the book about—"

"Excuse me," the tall man interrupted, hurrying toward Mitch and shaking his hand. Behind him, the woman in the wheelchair pushed the joystick forward and headed up the winding walk toward the hotel. The tall man glanced over his shoulder then back at Mitch. "Horace Leeds, pleasure to meet you, Professor. I apologize for being rude just now, but you see, Phyllis mustn't know anything about why she's here." Mitch liked his accent: sort of London cockney meets Boston Brahmin.

"I'm not trying to be flip or anything," Mitch said, "but are you saying she came here all the way from England without knowing why?"

Mrs. Church had put enough distance between them, so they started up the walkway together.

"Of course she knows why she's here," Leeds said patiently. "To make contact with the spirit world—but that's all she knows. That way, no one can claim she was influenced in any way. She arrives a blank slate and whatever comes to her comes strictly through contact with the other side, not from previous knowledge of the place. You see?"

Mitch said he did, but what he didn't see was how anyone could prevent Horace Leeds himself from slipping her enough information ahead of time so they could pull off a hoax. He decided it was wise to keep these thoughts to himself.

"Well, it's good to meet you, but I should get back to Phyllis." Leeds patted Mitch on the shoulder like a small boy. He might as well have *been* a boy next to the older man who was easily six-foot-six.

Leeds hurried up the walkway, and Mitch suddenly remembered why he had stopped him in the first place: to get an invitation to the ghost hunt. And he'd blown it. "Damn!" he said out loud, watching the back of Leeds' head reflect the sun as he moved up the walk.

Mrs. Church had stopped in front of the veranda, waiting for him to catch up. All at once she jerked her head to the west and seemed to cock an ear to listen. She turned the wheelchair ninety degrees, moved a little over the grass and stared in the direction of the west wing. Meanwhile, Leeds caught up to her. He bent down and said something and she said something back, still staring westward. They spoke briefly, then someone in a hotel uniform came out a door in the latticework under the veranda and led them in.

He considered going up to the lobby to wait for them again, but thought better of it. After traveling all day to get out to the island, they wouldn't be in any mood to be pestered. Better to wait for another opportunity. Instead, he decided to head back to his cabin, dig his hiking boots out of his duffle bag and wander around the island a little.

He turned to step off the walk—and plowed right into someone who went down on the grass in a heap of luggage.

It was a woman around his age, dressed in white Capri's and a striped blue and white shirt. A straw hat had tumbled off her head and one of the suitcases had popped open, spilling clothing—underwear included—all over the grass. Mitch apologized profusely and reached down for a bra, intending to put it back in the bag. Then, realizing his *faux pas*, he apologized again, trying to hide his embarrassment. By then the woman had stood up and was brushing herself off, but the damage looked permanent, at least to her white pants which now sported a big grass stain on one knee. He steeled himself for a barrage of accusations and insults. The woman looked him in the eye and said, with all earnestness, "Do I tip you now or later?"

Mitch blinked. "I'm sorry? Tip me?"

The woman went on staring at him gravely. "For helping me unpack." Suddenly she was fighting back a grin, and then she burst into a loud belly laugh, causing her blonde ringlets to toss around. "Well, don't worry about getting my underwear all over the lawn for everyone to see."

Mitch felt his face flush. Seeing his distress, the woman said, "Please! I'm just kidding!" She started gathering up clothes and stuffing them back in the open suitcase. One pair of panties with a leopard skin pattern had landed off to one side and Mitch grabbed it and held it out for her, figuring he couldn't get any more embarrassed. She took it, thanked him and said, "That's what I get for using old suitcases with broken latches."

"If you want to get even, I'll go get my bag and let you empty my underwear on the grass."

The woman broke into laughter again, making him grin. People coming up from the boat stared at them, wondering what they'd missed.

When they finished gathering up her clothes, Mitch hugged the broken suitcase in his arms and they started up the walkway together.

"By the way, I'm Wendy Mayer."

"Nice to meet you, Wendy Mayer." A second later the name registered. "You're *Professor* Mayer."

"Yeah!" She flashed a big smile. "Was I in the press release?"

"Matter of fact, you were: 'Professor of Parapsychology at Longfellow College.' I was hoping I'd meet you. I'm Mitch Lambert. I teach history at Fowler."

She shook his hand. "Nice to meet you, Professor Lambert."

"Mitch."

"Then I'm Wendy. Are you here for the investigation?"

"Just observing. At least for now. I was hoping they'd let me hover around since I wrote a biography about Maria Boudreau."

"Really? Well, then, I guess that makes you the expert on the main subject of this ghost hunt. I would think they'd let you do more than just hover. Maybe you can help if something they don't understand pops up."

"Thanks, but I think you're the first one to figure that out."

They had reached the dolphin and seal topiaries by now. Wendy stopped and said, "I'm serious. You should be part of the investigation."

She peered at him with gray eyes capped by furrowed eyebrows. The eyebrows were all natural, no plucking or shaping, and Mitch thought they fit her just right. Her nose was longish, but that fit her too.

"Have you ever been involved in a ghost investigation?" she asked.

"What do you mean?"

"I mean like a séance. A real one, not a parlor game like with a Ouija board. A real séance with a legitimate medium. Or even a reading."

"I've never been at a séance. I don't even know what a reading is, but I'm sure I've never been at one."

She set her bag down and took the broken suitcase from Mitch. All the while her eyes stayed fixed on his. "Do you believe in ghosts, Professor Lambert?" she finally asked somberly, as though his very life depended on the answer.

Mitch shrugged. "I don't know. I guess I'm a skeptic."

"Then let me ask you this." She stepped a little closer. "Are you skeptical for 'A' scientific reasons or 'B' because you never actually saw one?"

Mitch thought a moment. "'B', I guess."

Wendy nodded just as gravely as before. "Then there's hope for you." Suddenly her face brightened. "Well, it was nice meeting you, Mitch. Maybe I'll see you around this weekend." She picked up her other bag and started up the veranda steps.

Mitch watched her go. When she had disappeared through the front doors, he shoved his hands in the front pockets of his shorts and started across the lawn, wondering what she meant about there being "hope" for him. By the time he reached the cabin he still hadn't figured it out.

CHAPTER FIVE

It was now late afternoon but there was still plenty of time to hike around the island before dinner. Mitch went back to his little room, grabbed Mr. Arndt's book off the nightstand, and set out on the cart trail.

The old man was nowhere in sight when Mitch passed by the front of the cottage. Mitch suspected he was staying out of the afternoon sun. Since he had arrived on the island, the weather had gone from pleasantly warm to a little stuffy to noticeably uncomfortable. The temperature hovered near ninety, but it was the humidity that made it so uncomfortable. Even in shorts and a t-shirt he broke into a sweat not long into his hike. The smooth, dark water in Longboat Harbor to his left looked tempting, but he kept to the trail, staying focused on a very specific destination.

He had a vague idea how to get there, thanks to his research for *American Princess*. The trail had been widened sometime in the 1950s to accommodate electric carts. It wound east-southeast, mostly out in the open, but at times also cutting through thick clumps of shade trees and tall sumac that offered temporary relief from the sun.

He walked into one of these shadowy spots almost immediately, and when he came out the other end he was farther away from the water. On his left, facing the harbor, two houses identical to Mr. Arndt's stood among flowering wild shrubs. The only difference between Mr. Arndt's cottage and these two was the roofs, which were covered in wood shingles instead of tin. To his right, a field thick with tall grass and wild flowers rose at a gentle grade against the horizon like a scene out of a Monet painting. It, too, was teeming with wildlife. The distinctive sounds of a variety of birds filled the air, as did butterflies, bees and dragonflies. Up ahead, a groundhog rooted around in the grass beside the trail, unperturbed by Mitch's approach, while to his left something scurried into the underbrush beside the trail. The whole world seemed in motion. And why not? It was a beautiful day in spite of the muggy heat.

Yet he was the only person on the trail.

In fact, he appeared to be the only human anywhere, at least within his field of vision. This seemed odd. There should have been at least a few walkers and joggers out here on a midsummer day, humidity or no humidity.

He looked around again, this time searching for a "No Trespassing" sign. In researching his book he had studied just about everything in existence about Sumner Island, and learned that all trails—hiking trails and cart trails alike—were open to the public. This research had been done within the past three years or so; he couldn't imagine the road rules, which had been in place for decades, had suddenly changed. And there were no warning signs anywhere that he could see.

So where was everyone?

The road turned slightly right again, heading due south. Up ahead, thick brambles formed a wall on the left side of the trail and a patch of small, scruffy trees on the right hung over the trail offering more shade. He ducked in, enjoying the momentary reprieve from the heat. Walking through this tunnel-like growth, which went on for maybe fifty feet before the sides of the trail cleared out again, it struck him as odd that the Smythe resort, or whoever was in charge of these trails, didn't keep the wild growth trimmed back for the electric carts. In fact, this whole part of the island seemed to have been neglected. Even the trail itself was bumpy, not groomed at all.

Emerging from the other end of the tunnel, he found himself at a higher elevation and could now see the southeast side of the island where the pines grew thick and tall. Just north of those pines was his destination: a rocky beach he had read about in old articles from nearly a century ago. To his right, a single tree stood at the crest of a hill, which, from Mitch's angle, appeared to be the highest point on the island. He couldn't tell the tree's genus, but from his vantage point two hundred yards away, it looked like one of those flat-topped trees you see in documentaries about the Serengeti Plain. It stood tall and proud, commanding a view of everything.

The trail descended toward the water before rising again to a bluff. From the top of the bluff, looking down over twenty-foot cliffs, Mitch saw the beach he had been looking for. To his left, a steep ravine jig-jagged down the hill all the way to the rocks. Thankfully, someone had built a set of crooked but sturdy-looking stairs down the ravine so all he had to do was walk down. He did, ending up in a half-dried tidal pool at the bottom.

This was the place where Maria Boudreau had come to spend time alone whenever the world had closed in too much for even her patient tolerance. Here, she could sit on one of the many boulders strewn on the beach and look out across the endless Atlantic, relishing her temporary solitude. She had been a little girl when she discovered the beach, which, apparently, no one else bothered with because it was so rugged. Over the years she had come back again and again, even visiting it on the morning of her last day on earth—the morning of her twenty-first birthday—in 1924. Here, too, she had played a kind of solitary game, searching for pirate treasure in the small caves tucked away in the cliffs. Mr. Arndt had been right about Maria's love of the tales about pirates burying their loot around the Angel Islands. Legend told of treasure hidden by the pirate John Quelch, and even Blackbeard, somewhere on the Angels and Maria had once admitted to a magazine reporter that she'd poked around for the treasure many times, just for fun. Just for fun, she said, because she never really expected to find anything. Mitch would have added that it was just for fun because, as one of the wealthiest children in America in her day, Maria didn't *need* to find treasure.

And there they were, right in front of him: the caves Maria had once explored. Really they were just cracks in the cliffs, but big enough for a single person to walk into standing up. He made his way over and around the boulders until he stood before one of them. As a small child Maria was famous for her tomboyish ways, and had been photographed doing the most unladylike of things like climbing trees in her Sunday best or dirtying her bare knees playing marbles. Somehow, she had always managed to escape the cameras when out at this beach. Mitch could only imagine her digging around inside this cave, soiling her dress and destroying her shoes, and not caring that she did.

He wedged his way into the cave, which went back only a few feet, reveling in his knowledge that Maria had once done the same. If he looked hard enough, he even imagined he might find something she had left behind. Maybe her initials carved into the rock wall or a rusted trowel she had used to dig for treasure. Maybe a ribbon or trinket of jewelry she had dropped and never found again. If he spent enough time exploring all of the caves he might eventually happen upon something, but there had to be more than a dozen of them, and what were the chances of finding something more than eighty years later, anyway? He turned and looked out at the beach. If nothing else, at least he could say he'd seen the world from the same place Maria once did.

Eventually, he emerged from the cave and began climbing from one boulder to the next, getting as close to the churning surf as he dared. Down at the edge the sea crashed against the rocks that dropped off to deep, dark water. When the tide rose, the water would just about cover the rocks he now used as stepping stones. He shuddered to think of young Maria wandering around on these slippery rocks all by herself.

One of the rocks he came upon was the perfect height and shape for a seat and he decided it was a good time for a rest. He sat facing the open ocean, watching the water churn against the rocky drop-off below, the seaweed clinging to the rocks looking like green dreadlocks waving with the rise and fall of the sea. A crab scurried out from under a patch of seaweed and sidestepped across a rock toward another patch. As Mitch watched its progress, a flash of white came out of the sky at an angle and a seagull snatched up the crab and flew off in the direction of the bluff above.

He pulled Mr. Arndt's book out of his pocket, figuring he would read until the tide came in. He hadn't read half a page before something warm and wet splashed on the back of his neck. Looking up, he saw a flock of gulls buzzing around directly overhead and realized with great disgust what had hit him. This wasn't such a good place to sit after all.

He left the rock and made his way back to the rickety stairs and up to the trail, cursing the gulls all the way. On the side of the trail he removed his boots and used his socks to wipe the crap off his neck, then stuffed the soiled socks in his pocket and put his boots back on. Following the trail up the bluff, he came to a spot where the lonely flat-top tree became visible again. He trudged through the high grass toward it until he finally stood under its canopy. From here he could see every corner of the island and far out to sea. A mile offshore a sailboat cruised along, its bow pointed toward the islands. He counted three masts with three long sails, a schooner. Its sleek hull appeared all white, the cabins and masts a dark color and the sails a light tan. The crew wasn't visible from this distance, but the yacht was big enough to imagine it required a few people to sail it.

Mitch sat against the tree on the western side of the trunk and opened his book. He read only three pages before nodding off for the second time that afternoon. When he awoke his neck felt stiff, yet the sun hadn't moved much so he couldn't have been out for very long. Even so, he was getting nervous about the time, not wanting to miss his free evening meal with Mr. Arndt.

He stood up and rotated his neck, trying to loosen it up, and as he did, something off to the right caught his eye. He looked down at Longboat Harbor and saw black smoke rising into the sky. The hill rose slightly about midway down, obstructing the source of the smoke, so he couldn't tell if it was coming from someplace on the island or out in the harbor.

He started across the grassy field, hoping he wouldn't cut through someone's private property on the way back to the trail. But no fences or buildings stood between him and the trail, and he rejoined it at a point close to the water. Although thick growth obscured his view, he could see smoke above the trees and he hurried down the trail toward it.

He had walked maybe fifty yards before realizing he was on a trail that was very different from what he remembered walking on earlier that day. That one had been much wider; this one was only a couple of feet wide. He stopped and looked around, wondering how he had ended up on a different trail. He must have gotten turned around when he left the trail back at Pirate Beach to go sit under the tree. But the hotel was in sight, so all he had to do to get back was use it as a beacon. He looked for it, determined that he was at least going in the right direction, and continued on.

He came to another place where the trees grew close to the trail, their branches meeting in a tangle overhead forming something like a tunnel. When the trees finally thinned out again and he could see the hotel, it was closer but still some distance away. Something about it looked different, but he couldn't place exactly what no matter how long he looked at it. Over to his right, the harbor was just visible beyond the tops of the short trees covering the hill he now descended. He found the smoke again, but this time it was fainter, the plume thinner. What he had seen was not smoke from a fire on shore, but smoke billowing out of a boat moving away from Sumner Island, probably nearing the mouth of Longboat Harbor by now. He couldn't imagine what kind of boat would be giving off so much smoke. His curiosity compelled him quickly down the trail, looking for a spot where he could see the whole harbor. At the western end of Forges Island, as he had suspected, a boat was moving northwesterly, away from the island, trailing a grayish-brown plume. The smoke came from a tall, black smokestack in its center. It appeared to have two decks and was good-sized. No doubt about it, this was a working boat, not a yacht.

When the smoking boat had disappeared around Lighthouse Point, Mitch shifted his gaze over to the interior harbor which was dotted with boats, most of them pleasure craft laying over for the night on a trip up or down the coast, or maybe just out for the day. A normal scene for a weekend afternoon at the height of the summer season. Yet something didn't seem right. When Mitch had started out that morning, most of the boats he saw were powerboats with an occasional sailboat mixed in. Now, he saw almost all sailboats and a couple of cabin cruisers. So where had the other boats gone? Had they taken off ahead of foul weather? He examined the sky for storm clouds, but the sky was clear with no weather front in sight.

It was getting late and he needed to get back to the cottage to shower for dinner. The trail followed a gentle, downward slope toward the water now, twisting and turning through sometimes rocky terrain, sometimes small trees and undergrowth, then one of those tree tunnels. Just to reassure his mind that he was still heading the right way (he still hadn't met up with the wide, groomed cart trail but remained on a narrow, unkempt one), he glanced up over the foliage to his left, looking for the hotel. It stood just where he had expected, looming much larger than before, so he was definitely traveling in the right direction. He walked into the tree tunnel, feeling the cool of the shade. He was thinking about dinner, wondering what kind of dress was expected, when it dawned on him what was odd about the hotel when he saw it from the hill. The roof was the wrong color. It should have been red, but when he had looked at it from the trail it was gray. This made no sense. Unless, his logical mind told him, it was an optical illusion like the glare from sunlight making it appear gray when viewed from an angle. Or maybe it really was gray in some places that he could only see from this easterly vantage point. But that theory seemed even weaker since he had been able to see the whole roof, even if from a side angle, when he looked up. The whole thing had been gray.

He hurried on through the tunnel, looking for a clear spot where he could see the hotel again. It only took a few moments to reach a place where the trees thinned out enough to see it. He was still at an angle and the sun, indeed, glinted off parts of the roof. The trees obscured it somewhat so it wasn't the best view, but the roof was definitely gray. In the rear of the building, around the middle of the main wing, it looked like an addition was under construction. So far, the top portion was only framed-out, and he could see right through it. Its roof was complete but only half-shingled. The shingles were gray.

He hurried on, tossing around possible explanations in his head, and finally decided only one thing made any sense at all: the roof *was* gray. He had only remembered it as red from all the old pictures of the Smythe he saw in his research, and had carried that vision in his head. He just hadn't noticed the new gray shingles until now. Apparently, the hotel was undergoing renovations in the back, and they probably had decided to replace the roof at the same time.

With that resolved, he forgot about the Smythe's roof and began thinking of dinner again. He also thought about Wendy Mayer—her blonde ringlets, the curve of her lips when she smiled, her long, shapely legs . . . He wondered what she was doing right now, and what she had planned for later. He wanted to invite her to dinner, but Mr. Arndt was footing the bill so he couldn't rightly invite her to dine with them. She probably had plans with the Leeds-Church entourage anyway. Well, then, maybe after dinner—

All at once, Maria's face was floating around in his head. He tried to get Wendy's image back, but couldn't. To the open air, he said, "Maria, are you—" He stopped short of saying what he often had thought these past months: *are you real or am I crazy?* Instead, he mumbled, "When will you get out of my head?" The sharp cry of a nearby bird was the only reply.

He came to the place along the trail that passed by the two identical houses overlooking the harbor, which told him he was almost back at his cabin. The trail was wide again, and groomed, with tracks made by golf carts. Somewhere along the way the trail he'd been on had merged with the trail he first followed out to Pirate Beach, and he hadn't even noticed.

Minutes later he came around a bend in the road and saw Mr. Arndt's cottage. And there was Mr. Arndt in his chair on the porch. The old man started rocking vigorously when he saw Mitch coming up the road.

"Almost missed supper," he called out. "I was getting ready to go on up without you."

CHAPTER SIX

They cut between the cottage and cabin again on their way to the hotel. While making their way through the tangled growth, Mitch told Mr. Arndt about his hike out to the other side of the island. Mr. Arndt chuckled when Mitch told him about the wet bomb dropped by the seagull. He looked surprised when Mitch described the gray roof and construction in the back of the hotel, and positively confused when he described the lone tree at the crest of the hill.

"Pretty tough to get lost on this little island," he commented after Mitch told him how he'd gotten turned around on the way back. "All trails lead to and from the front of the hotel, and they're pretty well-groomed."

"Except that one I was on. Maybe it was an old cow trail turned into a shortcut across the hill with that tall tree."

"I still don't understand about that tree—" Mr. Arndt started to say, but Mitch didn't hear the rest. They had stepped out of the brush onto the Smythe lawn, and as they did, Mitch happened to glance up at the hotel. What he saw made him stop.

The roof was red.

Mr. Arndt had taken a few more steps in the direction of the hotel. He turned and stared back at him with an odd expression that Mitch could not interpret, something between curiosity and amusement. Even more odd was what he said. Instead of asking Mitch what was wrong, or what he was looking at, he merely said in a gentle, encouraging voice, "Come along, Professor. The tortoise is beating the hare."

Mitch looked back at the hotel and remembered something from that afternoon. He said, "Go ahead without me, I'll catch up," and took off at a jog toward the tennis courts.

He ran past the green wood-and-mesh enclosure surrounding the courts, past the gardener's shed, to the back of the hotel where a section of the building stuck out from ground level to the roof. It measured about fifteen-by-thirty feet and the roof shingles capping it were red. He took a few steps southward to get a better look at the entire rear of the hotel. The whole thing was intact. There was no construction going on—not even minor repairs—that he could see.

He stood staring at the structure a long time before finally turning back to the lawn, in a fog of confusion. Had he hallucinated the gray roof and the half-finished construction at the rear of the hotel? A hallucination could have been brought on by the heat, which also would explain why he kept nodding off. Even now he felt groggy. Yes, this made sense: First of all, he hadn't brought a water bottle with him so he'd probably become dehydrated out on the trails. He wasn't much of an outdoorsman to begin with, so he wasn't used to a lot of sun. His eyes had simply deceived him, brought on by heat exposure—

—like the time Mom and Dad brought me out to Sumner Island when I was a little kid.

He stopped and gazed out over the harbor, his head suddenly filled with vivid pictures and bits of conversation he hadn't thought of in a long, long time. Up to that moment all he remembered of his first visit to Sumner Island was playing on the beach. Nothing unusual about that—he'd only been five years old at the time, and the intervening years had naturally dimmed his memory of everything else. But now he had a clear memory of their trip back to the mainland that day. His parents had told the captain of the ferry that their boy was suffering from heat exhaustion; he had been "seeing things" on the island, they said. Apparently they were right about the heat exhaustion because he had quickly recovered out on the cool ocean.

So he *was* prone to heat exhaustion. He would have to be more careful the rest of the weekend.

He cut across the lawn and met up with Mr. Arndt, expecting a few questions after his sudden detour. Thankfully, Mr. Arndt just gave him a long look, cleared his throat and walked on toward the veranda steps.

They ate in the Sandpiper since the Sea Star required a jacket and tie at dinner, which neither of them had. Mr. Arndt still wore the same work pants and flannel shirt, and Mitch hadn't even bothered to change out of his shorts.

As soon as they were seated—which was immediately, even though there was a long waiting line—Mitch excused himself and went to the men's room to wash up. He stood before one of the basins, staring in the mirror at a face that, at the moment, looked much older than its years. Dark circles hung under his eyes and his skin was drained of color except for his brow and nose, which glowed red with sunburn. He looked ill, but only felt tired.

He bent down and splashed water on his face. As he did, he heard the bathroom door open behind him and the sounds of the hotel flowing in. A moment later the sounds became muffled again. His head was still bent over the sink, so he didn't see who came in but heard footsteps that sounded like dress shoes: heavy heel followed by slapping leather sole. The shoes stepped casually across the ceramic floor and stopped in front of the next basin.

"Hello, Professor."

Mitch grabbed a towel from a box on the counter, wiped his face and looked up at Horace Leeds. The man was busy squeezing toothpaste from a small tube onto some kind of travel toothbrush. He was dressed in slacks, a tweed sport coat and wingtips.

"You look like you're dining at the Sea Star," Mitch said.

"Just did. Fine meal, too." He stuck the toothbrush in his mouth and went to work.

Mitch looked back in the mirror at his own face. Some of the color had returned, but his skin still looked waxy.

"Feeling okay?" Mr. Leeds said through a mouthful of toothpaste.

"Spent a little too much time in the sun."

Leeds bowed like a giraffe over the sink and spit. "Got to be careful in this weather. Bloody humid today, eh?"

"Yes." Mitch wiped his face some more, stalling for time while he debated asking what was going on with the ghost chase. He finally got up the courage and asked.

"You should come to the press conference," Leeds said.

"Press conference?"

"The news people have been asking us to explain how all this psychic stuff works. We thought it would be easier to have a question-and-answer thing for everyone, instead of them chasing us around for interviews all weekend."

"When is it?"

Leeds looked at his watch. "Half an hour. In the ballroom."

Mitch thanked him and started for the door.

"That book you wrote," Leeds said to Mitch's back.

Mitch stopped and turned around, surprised. He had no idea Leeds knew about *American Princess*. Of course, he had mentioned it when trying to get on the invite list for the ghost hunt, but until now he had no idea Leeds had even read his email.

"I was skimming through it in the gift shop," Leeds said. "Very thorough. Well researched."

"Thank you. I put a lot of time into it."

"It shows. You know this Maria Boudreau well."

Mitch considered for a moment. "As well as I was able."

Leeds studied him quietly, then said, "You really should come to the press conference."

Mitch promised he would and left.

Back at the Sandpiper, Mr. Arndt was drinking a scotch on the rocks and Mitch noticed another one on the table. "I hope you don't mind I took the liberty of ordering you a drink," Mr. Arndt said.

Mitch sat down heavily in his chair and took a swallow. It burned all the way down making his eyes well up, but the burn actually felt good in a weird sort of way. He sipped again, this time more carefully, while Mr. Arndt watched with what looked like mild amusement. Mitch caught the look and said, "What?"

"Are you okay?"

"Horace Leeds just asked me the same thing."

Mr. Arndt raised an eyebrow. "You were talking with Horace Leeds?"

"I ran into him in the men's room. He said there's going to be a press conference in the ballroom in a little while."

"I know," Mr. Arndt said. "I'm invited."

"You are?"

Mr. Arndt chuckled. "I get invited to everything around here. I'm like the resort mascot, I've been around for so long."

"I was thinking of going. Are you going?"

He shrugged and took a tiny sip of his scotch. "Why not? Might be interesting."

"And, yes, I'm okay," Mitch said. "I just got too much sun today."

Mr. Arndt leaned forward in his seat. "Would that explain your behavior on the way over here tonight?"

Mitch took another swallow, relishing the burn. "I thought I saw something, but I was wrong."

The old man smiled. "People forget that island living is very different from what they're used to. The sun gets to you just as much as the wind and rain. It's exposed out here." He sat back in his chair, folded his arms on his chest and stared at Mitch.

"What? Why are you staring at me?"

"You said you fell asleep under a tall tree today. Up at the highest point on the island."

"That's right."

"And you saw construction going on at the back of the hotel."

"What are you getting at?"

The old man gave a little toss of his head and looked away. "You fell asleep up there," he said, matter-of-factly. "No wonder you have heat exhaustion. You can't fall asleep out in the sun in the middle of summer. My Papa used to treat patients all summer long for heat exhaustion." He looked back at Mitch. "Say, did Horace Leeds tell you about what's planned after the press conference?"

Mitch blinked, wondering how he had gotten on that subject. But the old man sounded excited again. "No, what?"

"A reading."

"Reading?"

"I think that's what they call it. Phyllis Church is supposed to go around getting 'impressions.' Sounds Halloweenish to me, but it could be fun. 'Course, I can't go. I'd just slow everyone down. But you could go in my place if you want."

It sounded Halloweenish to Mitch, too, but he agreed it might be fun and thanked him.

CHAPTER SEVEN

By the time they had finished dinner and shuffled down the hall to the ballroom, the press conference was already in full swing.

Mitch had read about the ballroom, which was named for Paul and Marjory Hodgson, the Philadelphia Mainliners who bought the Smythe Resort in 1931. Not as charismatic as the Boudreaus, but equally loved, the Hodgsons had steered the hotel through the tough Depression years. They loved music, and all the great bands of the day—Artie Shaw, Duke Ellington, the Dorsey brothers, Glenn Miller—had played the ballroom.

It still looked exactly as it had in pictures from the 'thirties and 'forties, from the parquet floor to the maroon curtains. Up on the stage a conference table covered in white linen and microphones had been set up. Behind it, facing the room, Horace Leeds leaned forward in his chair, elbows on the table, hands clasped together. Beside him sat Wendy Mayer, looking crisp and pretty in a yellow summer dress and pearl necklace.

A commercial-grade video camera with the station's call letters on the side had been set up on a tripod thirty feet from the stage. On either side of the camera thirty or more people filled rows of folding chairs. Some held palm-sized recorders and reporter notebooks; others looked like they were just there to listen in. Right now they were hearing Horace Leeds go on about ectoplasm—what it was and wasn't. He sounded as matter-of-fact as a chemistry professor lecturing on protons and neutrons.

Mr. Arndt and Mitch made their way along the wall as inconspicuously as they could, and finally took seats at the end of one of the back rows. As they did, Leeds finished up his lecture on ectoplasm and fielded the next question from a reporter in the front row who looked fresh out of college.

"Would you agree," the young man said, "that this investigation has gotten an unusual amount of publicity?"

Leeds leaned into the microphone in front of him. "I agree."

"Then what I'm wondering is how anyone can be sure your medium hasn't been tainted. A few minutes ago you said she didn't come to this press conference because she didn't want to be exposed to any information ahead of time. What about the newspaper stories? What about the people around the hotel talking about it?"

Leeds went on nodding. "Good question, one I've been asked many times before. First of all, I assure you Mrs. Church has avoided any newspapers or TV news since we've been here. She's been mostly shut up in her room resting, like she is right now. We've been doing this together for a long time and she knows how to avoid getting 'tainted,' as you say."

"But there's no way for *us* to know that." The reporter motioned around the room.

Mitch got the meaning, as did the rest of the crowd judging by their faces. He winced, expecting Leeds to blow up or at least admonish the young man, but Leeds kept his genial demeanor.

"Phyllis and I have teamed up on hundreds of cases over the past forty-some-odd years," he said pleasantly. "We've never once been paid for our services. If we had, I'm sure we'd be accused of charlatanism. Before we retired we both held full-time jobs because we had to put food on the table. All the royalties I've made from my books I've donated to the Society for Psychic and Paranormal Research. I assure you, the purpose of our work is strictly scientific. Speaking for Mrs. Church, she has a gift she never asked for, never wanted, and which, in some ways, has been a great burden for her. We're fortunate she chose to share that gift with us, asking for nothing in return. Except open minds."

The reporter thanked Leeds and sat down. At the other end of his row another reporter, equally young but female, stood up. She said, "Can you tell us what she *does* know—your medium, I mean," and sat down again.

Leeds leaned into his microphone and answered, "She knows we're staying at a hotel called the Smythe. She knows the Smythe is on an island called Sumner, which is part of a cluster called the Angel Islands not far from the Maine coast. She knows we've come here because there were reports of possible paranormal activity recently that I thought were worth investigating."

There was a brief but uncomfortable pause, as though everyone in the room expected him to say more. Finally, the reporter said, "And that's *all* she knows?"

Leeds thought a moment before saying, "She knows the crème broulet at the Sea Star is divine."

This brought a chorus of relieved laughter. Mitch looked at Mr. Arndt beside him. He wasn't laughing, but wore an amused smile.

When the laughter died down, Leeds said, "Seriously, my dear, we do this work because we can, and for no other reason. We have no purpose for cheating. On the other hand, getting details ahead of time tends to cloud a sensitive's—a medium's—inner sight. Mrs. Church and I made one strict ground rule long ago: we don't discuss details ahead of time. Ever. Unless, by chance, she happened to be familiar with the Boudreau story, she wouldn't know much more than what she's been able to observe of her surroundings these past few hours since we got off the boat. Don't forget, Mrs. Church lives in London—she just flew into Boston last night. She hasn't had the opportunity to learn much."

The reporter thanked him and sat down.

Next up was an older man with white hair and horn-rimmed glasses. "How will you conduct this—this séance, or whatever you call it."

Leeds said, "Fair question. If you've never been at a sitting with a sensitive, then your only impression of how it works is probably what you've seen in the movies. Which, of course, is just Hollywood melodrama and bunk.

"Mrs. Church and I do not generally conduct séances, although we sometimes do. Maybe I should clarify something: Mrs. Church is not a *physical* medium, which is to say she doesn't produce any ghostly things floating around the room or make the table levitate. Our preferred method is an induced trance where she communicates with people on the other side with the help of her control, Seamus."

"Seamus?" The white-haired reporter all but sniggered.

Leeds caught the skepticism. He said firmly, and with just the slightest hint of hostility, "Yes, 'Seamus'. Seamus is the spirit of an Irishman who died of consumption—what we know as tuberculosis today—in 1851. He's sort of a personal receptionist to Mrs. Church; he brings forth spirits we wish to speak with, or who wish to speak with us."

"Who wish to speak with *us*?" the reporter repeated, his voice now dripping with incredulity.

"Does that surprise you?"

"Well, it just seems—"

"Don't you think those on the other side who left family and friends behind—don't you think they're just as eager to check up on us as we are them?"

The man looked positively befuddled.

"Seamus brings forth the spirits and they speak through Mrs. Church while she's in trance," Leeds went on. "This is how we'll conduct our sitting tomorrow night. With any luck, we'll make contact."

"You mean we won't be seeing any ghosts, just listening to Mrs. Church say what comes into her head?"

Judging by his expression, Leeds' patience was waning and Mitch didn't blame him. Yet he still kept his cool, speaking in measured words. "As I said, Mrs. Church is not a physical medium. Believe it or not, producing a visual entity is not what most mediums try to do. The best results are achieved through trance, where the medium acts as an instrument through which the spirit communicates. You may find yourself quite fascinated tomorrow night. Even without ghosts floating around."

"But might they materialize as ghosts we can see while talking through Mrs. Church?" This question came from someone on the other side of the white-haired reporter.

It was becoming clear to Mitch that these journalists—at least some of them—were determined to see and record some kind of spook show just to sell newspapers. They wanted the same Hollywood melodrama Leeds had scoffed at. For some reason this made Mitch angry, and before he knew what he was doing, he had stood up and was saying, "Everyone here seems to be looking for a ghost this weekend. But I understand you've never actually seen a ghost yourself?"

Leeds immediately caught on to where he was going with this. He nodded vigorously. "That's true. I've made that clear in all my books."

"Yet you still believe." Mitch glanced around the room to see the crowd's reaction. As he had predicted, they were enrapt.

"Of course, how could I not?" Leeds said enthusiastically. "With everything I've experienced over the years?"

Another spectator a few seats down from Mitch, who did not appear to be a reporter, jumped in, asking "What *have* you seen?" She then added, apologetically, "I'm sorry. I haven't read your books."

"It just so happens I brought some copies with me; I'll be happy to sell you one after the press conference," Leeds said. This made everyone laugh again, breaking the tension.

Leeds leaned back in his chair and waited for the laughter to die down. When it did, he addressed the whole audience: "I've attended hundreds of sittings with trance mediums. In every situation, in every kind of place. Every kind of spirit, too. I can't count the times my sensitive revealed information that couldn't have been learned ahead of time. I have countless tape recordings and films and videos to prove it. Often, the information was simple stuff even relatives and friends of the spirit had forgotten but which the spirit reminded them of. There's no way it could be faked.

"But I've never personally seen a fully formed apparition, which doesn't trouble me a great deal because spirits don't materialize for everyone. Some people are more sensitive than others—more 'tuned in' you might say. Just because you don't see doesn't mean you can't believe. Especially considering the other phenomena I've witnessed—and by the way, I'm not the only one. Many dedicated investigators of the paranormal never once saw a ghost, but like me, they saw, heard, felt, even smelled things that couldn't be faked."

"Please," the same person practically pleaded, "can you give us some examples?"

Leeds paused while everyone waited in silence. Mitch realized that everyone in the room now was expecting nothing dramatic that weekend, and were just trying to get some column filler ahead of time. He was sure Leeds sensed this too, but instead of accommodating them with spooky stories, he said, "I would rather stay focused on what we're dealing with this weekend." Then he surprised Mitch by pointing at him and saying, "Professor Lambert, perhaps you can help us understand what we're dealing with."

Mitch hesitated, not sure of what he was referring to. He knew nothing about ghosts and the paranormal, and Leeds had to know that.

"Stand up if you don't mind." Leeds lifted his hand in the air, palm up.

Mitch stood and felt all eyes in the room staring at him.

"You know more about the Boudreaus than anyone else in the room," Leeds said. "Come up here and give us a little background before we get started on our investigation."

Mitch made his way up to the stage, the polite applause behind him barely registering in his muddled mind. After two years of teaching he considered himself a pretty good lecturer no matter what size the audience. But he always came prepared with at least an outline, and this time he had nothing to go on except memory.

He took the steps up to the stage, catching his toe on the top one which, thankfully, no one seemed to notice, and sat in an empty chair beside Dorothy Poulin.

"Dr. Mitchell Lambert is a professor of American history at Fowler College," Leeds announced. "He wrote the book, *American Princess: Maria Boudreau Remembered*. For those of you who haven't read it, I highly recommend it." He turned to Mitch. "Professor Lambert, would you mind giving us a little background on the Boudreaus?"

"I'd be happy to," Mitch said into the microphone. What else could he say?

The room fell silent. Someone in the audience cleared his throat. They were all waiting for Mitch to say something, but he didn't know where to start.

Well, then, start at the beginning, a faraway voice in his head told him. For some reason he looked straight at Mr. Arndt who sat with his arms crossed on his chest, beaming like a proud father watching his kid perform at a recital.

"Forgive me if I repeat information you already know," he began. "I guess I should start with Roger Boudreau. You may know him from his image on cartons of copy paper." He glanced around and saw some of the crowd nodding. "Roger was a lumber and paper baron from Bangor, a self-made multi-millionaire—one of the country's richest young men at the tail end of the nineteenth century."

He looked around the room again as he spoke, gauging the audience's reaction. Everyone sat still. All eyes were on him. Some of the reporters were scribbling notes. All good signs.

"In 1899 Roger met the Russian princess Tatiana Obolensky. Tatiana was a distant cousin to Tsar Nicholas and something of a celebrity in European society. She was considered one of the most desirable debutantes of her time. Roger must have thought so because he met her only once before asking her to marry him and come to America. She agreed. Some say it was because her family's fortunes had dwindled, others say she was as taken with Roger as he was with her. Whatever the case, they married in St. Petersburg then settled in Boston where Roger bought her a townhouse mansion on Commonwealth Avenue. They became the toast of the Boston social scene. I suppose it had to do with more than just money and glamour—Tatiana was real royalty, and Americans loved their fairy tale story.

"They were the toast of the Smythe Resort, too. They were invited by friends to stay here on the way back from Russia after their wedding, and they fell in love with the place. During their four years together they stayed at the Smythe several weeks every summer and entertained the cream of East Coast society right here in this ballroom."

Mitch surveyed the room as he made the last comment and the audience did the same. The butterflies in his stomach had disappeared. He was in control.

"Unfortunately, Tatiana died in 1903 while giving birth to their only child, Maria. Roger was devastated; he never married again. All of his private time he devoted to his daughter, and although he was rumored to have enjoyed the company of several women over the years, he was never seen in public with any of them. Tatiana was his only real love.

"He also did not return to Sumner Island for ten years. Then in 1912 the west wing of the hotel burned to the ground and the resort was in serious danger of failing. The majority shareholder at the time was the shipping magnate, Malcolm Akers. Akers had done business with Roger over the years and he convinced him to buy in. Roger did more than that—he became the majority shareholder himself.

"After that he seems to have found his love for the place again. He immediately built an apartment under the middle tower, and he and Maria made it their second home every summer for the next ten years."

A reporter raised her hand and Mitch nodded at her. "Do you have a question?"

The woman stood. "I've been reading about the Boudreaus on the internet. Maria seems much more famous than her parents. Why is that?"

Mitch nodded. The reporter was right: more had been written about Maria on internet sites than Roger and Tatiana combined. Not only had Maria been famous when she was alive, her name and life story had been enjoying a kind of revival since Mitch's book was published. Which, of course, had led him and other observers to wonder if it was this sudden popularity that had caused some people to imagine her spirit wandering around the Smythe grounds.

"Maria became a celebrity in her own right," Mitch said. "She was like an early version of Shirley Temple—a cute kid with a big personality. They say she was photographed more than even the president's children, which is why so many pictures of her survive today. That allure never faded, even after she became an adult."

"What exactly was it about her?" the same reporter asked.

Here Mitch hesitated. This was the part that always made him terribly uncomfortable. At numerous book signings and publishing events he had been asked the same question, and he never quite knew how to answer it. For him, personally, Maria had a kind of magical quality, something that made him feel like a schoolboy experiencing his first serious crush. Pictures of her, even words written about her, made him want to be there with her in that time long gone by. But how did you tell people this? How did you explain that you had spent two weeks' salary on an old Victrola and played 78 RPM records from that era on it just to feel a little closer to her? How could you say how you really felt without coming across as some romantic fool, disconnected from your own time, infatuated with a woman who died more than eighty years ago?

"Well, she was—she was very attractive physically," he said, trying his best to speak in his academic voice. "Her personality, too. As a child she was spirited, even a little tomboyish. She charmed everyone. Roger probably had something to do with it, too. Newspapers and magazines loved to write about this famous rich man raising his impish little daughter all by himself. The attraction only increased as she grew up. While attending Radcliffe she and Roger founded two homeless shelters and a charity that sent food and medicine to Russia during the famine in the early twenties. They wrote endlessly about that." Mitch smiled. "Their angle was: Roger's good at making money, Maria's good at giving it away."

"I heard the apparition people saw was a woman, not a child." This came from the white-haired reporter who had sounded so skeptical when he was questioning Leeds.

"That's true," Mitch agreed. "All of the sightings, at least from what I understand . . . " He looked down the table at Leeds who was nodding," fit Maria's description as a young woman."

Leeds leaned into his microphone. "If I may put in my two cents' worth, there may be a good reason for that. People who die traumatic deaths often appear later at the place they died. Maria died here, on this island, the weekend of her twenty-first birthday."

"That's right," Mitch confirmed. "The apparition was seen coming off a yacht, playing croquet, sitting in a gazebo with a young man—Maria is known to have done all these things the weekend she died, except for the last, which no one can confirm but which certainly could have happened."

"Tell us about the murders," the white-haired reporter said abruptly.

Leeds crowded his microphone again. "What is it you'd like to know?"

The reporter pointed at Mitch. "If you don't mind, I'd like the history professor's version." Mitch glanced at Leeds out of the corner of his eye. Leeds smiled good-naturedly and Mitch's respect for the old ghost hunter went up another notch.

"No need for gruesome details," Mitch said, his voice firm. "They were out here one weekend in the summer of 1924 to celebrate Maria's twenty-first birthday. Someone broke into the apartment and killed Roger and his valet, Fenton, with a hammer while they slept. They both died in the main apartment. Maria died in the tower room. A fire broke out up there—probably started during a struggle between Maria and her assailant. The tower was destroyed along with parts of the apartment and the roof."

"I read that Maria's body was completely incinerated to ashes and they had to—"

"You heard right," Mitch cut the reporter off. He knew he was being rude and he didn't care. "As I said, the gruesome details aren't necessary."

The reporter, wearing a surprised expression, slowly sat down. Mitch felt a mist break out on his forehead. He had a sickening suspicion—one he had experienced before—that his true feelings for Maria had been found out. Thankfully, someone in the audience took advantage of the uncomfortable silence to ask another question. "Who do you think killed them?"

Mitch looked out at the crowd. The voice that had asked the question was unmistakable: Mr. Arndt. He still sat with his arms folded on his chest, but his expression was now serious, even grave.

Someone else piped in: "I heard it might have been a Russian plot—the Bolsheviks."

Mitch had to restrain himself from rolling his eyes. This was a popular theory, but not with him. In fact, he considered it downright silly. "I seriously doubt it. Maria was only half Russian, had never set foot in Russia, never showed any interest in politics even though she did express contempt for the Bolsheviks on a few occasions. Her mother was a princess from a minor lineage—second cousin to the Tsar—and came over to this country long before the 1917 Revolution. I can't see how the Bolsheviks would have considered Maria such a threat that they would go to the trouble to murder her."

"But wasn't it a Russian émigré who killed her?" This came from Mr. Arndt.

"A Russian was charged, yes, but even back then most people thought he was wrongly accused. In fact, he was never tried—he died in prison before he ever got a chance to vindicate himself."

"Then who?" another voice asked almost before Mitch had finished.

So now it's a parlor game, a whodunit, Mitch thought. He was tempted to give them the facetious answer, "the butler did it," but then the crowd would be thinking he meant Roger's personal assistant, Fenton. Instead, he told the audience, "It's as much a mystery to me as it is to you."

"Maybe Mrs. Church will get some answers," the same voice suggested.

This one Leeds fielded. "That would be nice, but don't count on it. Spirits aren't always anxious to talk about their lives. They tend to be more interested in what we're up to here on the earthly plane.

"Then again," he said, grinning down the table at Mitch, "seeing as we have Maria's historian here, maybe they won't be able to resist the temptation to reveal a thing or two."

There were a few more questions about the Boudreaus and then the press conference ended. But before it did, Leeds announced that Mrs. Church would begin her "study" of the Smythe Resort with a tour of the grounds in the next half hour or so.

On the way out the ballroom door, Mitch asked Mr. Arndt if he was sure he didn't want to join in Mrs. Church's reading.

"Too tired," Mr. Arndt sighed. "You go ahead and have fun. I'm heading home to catch the Sox on the radio."

Mitch walked with him as far as the lounge, and there they parted.

CHAPTER EIGHT

ike the lobby, the lounge had wood paneling from floor to ceiling. Thick red and gold carpet covered the floors on which stood the same pedestal tables that had been there since the hotel first opened. A white grand piano filled one corner, and a man with slicked-back hair and a white dinner jacket was playing something Mitch had heard before but couldn't quite place, something romantic and jazzy. Mitch headed for the bar, which ran along the wall opposite the piano, only to find that every stool was occupied. But someone was just leaving a stool at the corner, and Mitch slid his backside onto it as soon as the other backside had slid off. He ordered a Smuttynose and the bartender poured it so quickly he wondered if she knew he was staying with Mr. Arndt.

The beer went down surprisingly fast and he ordered another one.

He was thinking about the press conference. It seemed odd to hold a press conference about such a whimsical subject as a ghost hunt. You would have thought Leeds was some sports figure about to play in a major tournament, or a politician announcing his candidacy for office. But a ghost hunter? Whoever heard of such interest in a ghost investigation? This was the kind of story normally buried in a Sunday travel section; ghost hunts were not front page news.

On the other hand, people were naturally fascinated with ghosts, and a ghost story taking place at a local, much loved hotel should sell lots of papers. And also boost interest in the Smythe among families making plans for next year's vacation. So when you really thought about it, this whole ghost-busting thing made sense, at least from a marketing standpoint. Or was he just being cynical?

No, I'm not just being cynical.

There had to be some marketing design behind all of this. He could see the Smythe's P.R. honchos sending newspaper clippings of the recent ghost sightings to Horace Leeds, enticing him, maybe even paying him a visit. They also might have funded Phyllis Church's trip from England—certainly they had put her and Leeds up at the hotel for free. A few calls to the right media contacts and pretty soon you had a news event. And lots of valuable publicity.

Yet no matter how clever the marketing plan, the media still had to find the event newsworthy, right? So the interest must have been there to begin with. Still, this much interest had been shown in only a few ghost tales of which he was aware—what exactly had made this particular one so interesting?

A voice to his left interrupted Mitch's thoughts. He turned, and there stood Wendy Mayer. She had changed into a t-shirt with the words GHOSTS WERE PEOPLE TOO emblazoned across the front, and a pair of plaid shorts and white sandals. Between the shorts and sandals was a pair of pretty, slender legs.

"I'm sorry, I didn't hear you," Mitch apologized.

"I said, can you buy a girl a drink or am I being too forward?" Wendy grinned and batted her eyelashes.

"What would you like?" Mitch stood up from his stool and waved the bartender over.

"Whatever you're drinking is fine."

The bartender came and Mitch ordered two drafts. Remembering his manners, he offered Wendy his stool. They did the refuse–insist–refuse routine before she finally sat and he leaned against the bar beside her.

"You were great at the press conference," Wendy told him.

Mitch snorted. "I sounded like a talking encyclopedia."

"Well, at least you got to talk. Nobody was interested in anything I had to say."

"Be thankful they weren't. No one in that room gave a damn about the science or history of this thing."

Mitch turned and watched the piano man who was now banging out a jaunty rendition of "Tea For Two." Though he sat on a short stool, Mitch could see he had a tall, slim frame. He appeared to be in his early twenties but had the manner of an older, more experienced player. And he was good, Mitch decided. In his youth Mitch had taken piano lessons and could spot true talent.

The piano man caught Mitch looking at him and nodded in the direction of Wendy. Mitch got the message: Pay attention to the girl, not me. He turned back to her. "They'll be interested once this thing gets into full swing. I think right now they're just all goo-goo eyes over a real-life medium and ghost hunter."

She blinked. "Huh?"

"The press. They'll be interested in your interpretation of what happens over the weekend—if anything *does* happen."

Wendy stared at him for a long time, and he stared back, admiring how perfectly her dark blonde eyebrows went with her hazel eyes.

"Do you really think nothing will happen?" she said. "Of course something will happen. Phyllis Church is fabulous."

"Okay, but if something does happen how will we know it wasn't planned?"

Their beers arrived and Mitch took a hearty gulp. When he looked over at Wendy, she hadn't even picked up her mug.

"You're a cynic, aren't you, Mitchell Lambert," she said, shaking her head, ringlets wiggling on her shoulders.

"I'm a realist."

"Then look at this reality, buster. These people have investigated spirit activity all over the U.S. and Europe for decades. They do this for free. They have nothing to gain by being here, except maybe the off-chance they'll add something significant to the science of parapsychology."

" 'Buster' ?"

"Can't you open your mind just a *little?*"

Mitch sighed. "You're missing my point. You saw those people at the press conference. It's just entertainment to them—ghosts and ghoulies, *woooooooooooo!*" He waved his hands in the air for emphasis. "Don't you think there's a lot of pressure to turn up something?"

"And so Phyllis and Horace must be tempted to fake it. Is that what you're implying?"

"Something like that."

"Or are you saying it because you think it's *always* faked, that there aren't *any* real spirits?"

Mitch shrugged and took a long swallow. An occasional drinker, he almost never had more than a couple, but right now he felt like he could drink all night. "You've never seen a ghost yourself, have you?"

Wendy picked up her mug and took a sip of mostly foam. "No, I haven't. That doesn't mean anything."

"Neither have I. And it does mean something. It means we have to take the word of other people that they exist, even though there's a number of other explanations for what people *think* are ghosts. I respect what they're doing, I honestly do. In this case, I think it's all on the up-and-up because these two seem genuine. But I don't get this theory that some people are born with a power to see things, like they have this special antenna or something. I just don't buy it.

"On the other hand, people have been seeing ghosts throughout history. I just wonder if maybe it's more psychology than parapsychology—it seems that way."

He took a long swallow of his beer, thinking how badly he hoped he was wrong—and how problematic that was. Even before he booked his ticket on the ferry he had worried that his yearning to see Maria might cause him to get drawn into the ghost hysteria. The way he felt about her was unlike anything he had felt for any living woman; the psychology of *that* weirdness suggested to him that he was definitely susceptible.

Wendy's next comment sounded like she had been reading his mind. "So you think people just see what they want to see."

"Maybe. You have to admit it's the leading theory among skeptics."

Wendy gave an exaggerated nod and drank again, this time a hearty gulp. "I'm aware of that. But consider this: There are hundreds of reported cases of collective apparitions. Do you know what I'm talking about?"

He did. Before coming out to the island he'd researched everything he could about ghost sightings, including ones where groups of people had reported seeing the same thing at the same time. He knew the arguments for and against their authenticity. "Like Fatima or Lourdes. Collective apparition, or mass hallucination?"

Wendy stood up abruptly, glared at him and tried to brush by, but he grabbed her hand. "Where are you going?"

She shook him off.

"Hey!" he said, surprised at her anger. "Why are you being so sensitive?"

She studied his eyes as though searching for something only they could offer. As she did, he sensed her tension waning. The crisis was over.

She sat back on her stool. "You're right. I'm being too sensitive. You're entitled to your beliefs."

Now it was his turn to study her face. Something in her expression defied easy description. She looked bewildered and sad, all at the same time, but something else too, something he didn't understand. What was perfectly clear, however, was that he had hurt her feelings, and he felt mean and foolish. "I'm sorry. I didn't realize how strongly you felt."

"Well, I *have* made it my life's work."

They both fell silent for a few awkward moments, drinking and turning their attention to what was going on elsewhere in the room. Mitch watched the piano man who now played "Oh, Lady Be Good," his head swaying, eyes closed in total concentration. Wendy, meanwhile, eavesdropped on a couple at a nearby table. She still looked sad in a childlike, pouty sort of way. For some reason Mitch found the look appealing and he wanted to hug her. Instead, he asked a question that had been floating around in his head for a while.

"What made you get into teaching parapsychology, anyway? What did you study in college?"

She turned her gaze from the couple at the other table and gave him a quizzical expression as though he'd asked some random question wholly unrelated to their earlier conversation. Then familiarity slowly seeped back into her face.

"I was an economics major at Georgetown."

"Really? I would have thought you majored in psychology or something like that."

"Not at first—psychology was the furthest thing from my mind. I wanted a career in economics. I graduated with a perfect cum', got accepted at Harvard for their Master's program, went as far as moving to Boston and enrolled in my first courses . . ."

"And changed your mind?"

She downed the last of her beer and Mitch did the same and ordered two more. She drew a long breath and slowly heaved it out.

"My parents died a week before classes started—they were killed in a boating accident. We used to live on Chesapeake Bay and my parents had a sailboat. One Sunday afternoon they were out on the water and some drunk in a Cigarette cut their boat in half. Dad was decapitated; Mom got trapped below deck and drowned before anyone could get to her."

"Jesus, I'm so sorry."

"I dropped out of the Master's program. I'm an only child and I had to take care of estate matters and all that. Besides, there was no way I could concentrate on school."

"Of course."

"I went back to Maryland and lived in the house alone. Didn't work, didn't go to school. Just hung around, depressed, unmotivated. I was very close to my parents and there was no one else in my life at the time to distract me. I was all alone.

"Then, after several months like this, I woke up one night about three in the morning. I'd heard a loud bang, like someone lit off a firecracker downstairs. I couldn't figure out what it was—no one else was living in the house, and I didn't have any pets. I've never been so scared in my life. I thought for sure someone had broken in and I was going to be murdered in my own home. I would have called the police, but I was so paralyzed with depression I never even bothered to pay the phone bill and they shut it off. I didn't own a cell phone. Anyway, I sat there in bed with the covers up to my nose and listened. But I never heard another noise.

"I must have waited there half an hour, but the house stayed quiet. Not a sound. I finally crept out of bed and tiptoed downstairs with a wooden coat hanger for a weapon." She grinned and made swashbuckling motions with her hand. "Can you imagine? I got to the living room, and from there I could see the kitchen through a doorway. The light was on, and I always turned all the lights off before I went to bed. *Always*. I told myself I must have forgotten this time, but I knew it wasn't true. I tiptoed up to the kitchen doorway and jumped through, swinging the coat hanger, all chills and rubbery legs and my heart pounding so hard I thought I would have a heart attack." She laughed out loud. "God, I must have looked like a complete idiot."

Mitch laughed along, picturing her slashing at nothing with the coat hanger while whatever had made the noise—maybe a squirrel or raccoon that got in the house and knocked something over—watched this crazy woman from another corner of the kitchen. "So what was there? Some wild animal?"

She shook her head. "No, nothing like that. But what I saw almost made me faint."

Mitch watched her and waited.

She saw the anticipation on his face and cleared her throat. "It was Mr. Buddha."

About a dozen thoughts flew through Mitch's mind, the most prominent being that she'd had a hallucination and saw *the* Buddha sitting in her kitchen. "Buddha," he repeated and waited for her explanation.

"*Mr.* Buddha," she corrected.

Mitch nodded. "Mr. Buddha."

"Mr. Buddha's my stuffed mouse. He's about—" She held her hands eight or ten inches apart—"yea big. He's gray and sits on his haunches so his fat belly sticks out like the Buddha. That's why I call him that."

"I see. So he, like, made all this noise?"

"Of course not." She gave him an incredulous look. "How's a stuffed animal going to make a noise like that?"

Mitch rolled his eyes and drank his beer.

She ignored his look. "Mr. Buddha was a present from my mother when I went off to college. She gave him to me as a good luck charm and to keep me company while I was away. She even put a chain and locket around his neck with a little picture of my parents inside. I brought him to college and not a day went by when Mr. Buddha wasn't either in my dorm or physically with me.

"But when I moved back home from Cambridge after my parents died, I was so screwed up in the head I forgot Mr. Buddha. I left him on a shelf in my apartment. By the time I realized it, the maintenance people must have found him and thrown him away because he wasn't there anymore. You can't imagine how much I cried when I realized he was gone forever."

"Yet there he was that night, right in your kitchen."

"Yes, and with the locket still around his neck." She gave him a questioning look. "Don't you see?"

"Someone found him and put him in your kitchen?"

Wendy blinked at him. "Do you know what an apport is?"

"It's where you go to catch a flight."

"Very funny. *Apport.* A-P-P-O-R-T. Teleportation."

"Well, now that you put it that way." He smiled. "Isn't teleportation that 'beam me up, Scotty' thing on Star Trek?"

"Close enough. An apport is an object that's moved by way of the spirit world to the physical world."

"So they have some kind of teleport machine in the spirit world."

"Keep it up!" She shook a fist at him but managed a grin. A quiet pause followed, during which her expression grew serious again. "Mitch, my *parents* moved that stuffed animal."

"How?" Mitch had known she was going to say her parents did it. What he really wanted to know was how she thought they accomplished the feat.

Her answer disappointed him. "I don't know."

"You don't know?"

"Well, I have theories like everyone else in my field."

"Tell me your theory."

Wendy took a deep breath and gathered her thoughts. "Well, first of all, you have to believe space and time aren't necessarily linear, or at least not all the time. If that's true, then it's possible our souls don't go that far away when we die but stay close by, separated from our physical world by some kind of membrane we aren't aware of. Spirits are able to see through that membrane, even though we can't, like a two-way mirror. They can also pass through it into the physical world quite easily and quietly because they aren't made up of matter. But it takes a lot of energy to make a physical object pass through the membrane, and that's why there's a tremendous exploding sound when something does. I think of it as like a sonic boom."

Mitch nodded. "I think I get it."

"That explosion I heard that night was Mr. Buddha coming through the membrane. Popping through it, you might say. My parents found Mr. Buddha and returned him to me. Obviously, they were sending me a message: get back to school. Get on with your life. We'll be waiting and watching from the other side."

Mitch thought this over. The scenario she gave was so easily explained in psychological terms: young, grieving woman having trouble getting out of a funk, needs permission to get on with her life, imagines supernatural event using stuffed animal as a symbol of permission. This, of course, would require Mr. Buddha to have been in Wendy's possession all along. She would have set up the stuffed animal in the kitchen, turned on the light and created a loud noise or even imagined the loud noise, all while in some kind of semi-conscious state. It was possible, he supposed. Yet something didn't quite fit.

"When did you start learning about all this supernatural stuff?"

"That's what I was leading up to. It was that experience that made me get into parapsychology. I started working toward my graduate degree the very next semester and never looked back. Only, I dropped economics and studied psychology and philosophy, instead. I eventually got my Master's in psychology, but I never went for my doctorate.

"I signed up for the night school program in parapsychology that Horace Leeds was teaching at Longfellow. While I was studying with Professor Leeds, Longfellow decided to take the program to a higher level and offer it as a full-credit course to its day students. So now there was going to be a paranormal studies program in the Psychology Department, and it would be offered to degree-enrolled students instead of just continuing ed students. Professor Leeds was asked to head up the program. He declined because he was nearing retirement, so they asked me. Leeds told me later that he recommended me because I was such an enthusiastic student. In other words, I just fell into it by sheer luck. And that's how I became a professor of paranormal studies and parapsychology."

"So you never had a supernatural experience until this . . . Mr. Buddha incident."

Wendy looked off in the direction of the piano, but her eyes were fixed on some object outside the window that Mitch couldn't see. "I never even believed in ghosts until that night." She looked back at him. "Just like you."

"It's not that I *disbelieve*. I just haven't seen anything that would cause me to *believe*."

She nodded. "Let me ask you something."

"Shoot."

"Do you believe me when I tell you I never had any interest in parapsychology until the Mr. Buddha thing?"

"Yes."

"Honest?"

"Honest."

"Would you believe me if I told you I never read a ghost story in my life—except *Turn of the Screw* in high school English—before the Mr. Buddha incident?"

"Yes."

"Then here's something else for you to think about. In England, there's an old mansion called Charlton House where there've been numerous incidents of paranormal activity over the years. Back in the 1990s, a BBC producer and some well-respected parapsychologists visited the house and recorded the most amazing thing. Late at night, when the lights were off, there was a loud explosion. When they turned on the lights they saw a broken tea cup in the middle of the floor. The broken pieces were all neatly arranged in a circle. The cup wasn't from the house or from anyone who had been there. No one has ever been able to explain how it got there. This was all professionally recorded under highly secure conditions."

She looked at Mitch, waiting for a reaction. When none came, she went on.

"I never knew apports existed until after Mr. Buddha showed up on my kitchen table that night. But people have experienced them for centuries."

She searched his face as if looking for some sign that she had gotten through to him. Finally, she sat back on her stool and turned back to the bar and her beer. "The point is," she said over her shoulder, "unless I'm lying, these things did happen to me. Unless Leeds and Church are lying, these sorts of things have happened to them over and over again. It might be all psychology or tricks of the mind or phenomena that can be explained with normal, everyday science. But isn't it only fair to consider it from another point of view?"

Mitch remembered how angry the skeptics at the press conference had made him when they treated Horace Leeds like he was a nut. "You're right. It's only fair."

"And, my esteemed Professor Lambert." She spun around on the stool to face him fully. "You, who know history so well. What is the recurring human emotion that permeates every stage of the human saga, every era, from ancient Egypt to modern times?"

"Love?" Mitch guessed.

"Yes! A-plus for you!" She gave him a gentle high-five. "Love. Love moves mountains. It causes people to do things they otherwise might not be able to do. It causes a hundred-pound mother to lift a two-ton car off her child; it causes a lost dog to walk hundreds of miles to get back to its family. It's such a compelling force, why is it so hard to believe it can cause spirits to find a way to return and comfort us? Maybe even cause a stuffed animal to apport?"

Mitch considered this and its alternative implication. "Maybe that's why we get so frightened by things that go bump in the night."

"What do you mean?"

He shrugged. "What's the other emotion that's moved mountains, nations, *civilizations*, over the course of history?"

Wendy thought for only a second. "Hate?"

He nodded. "Hate."

CHAPTER NINE

I t was still light out when they gathered on the lawn to watch Phyllis Church at work. This was an invitees-only affair, but scores of people hovered nearby on the veranda and the lawn, curious about the gathering whose focus was obviously the lady in the wheelchair. The gathering consisted of eight or nine reporters, Horace Leeds, a cameraman with a video cam on his shoulder and Wendy and Mitch.

As Mitch and Wendy joined the group, Leeds made a point of asking Mitch whether Mr. Arndt planned on joining them as well. He seemed genuinely disappointed when Mitch told him he would not, but was glad Mitch had made it. "Keep your eyes and ears open, Son," he told Mitch. "Phyllis might pick up something that only makes sense to you since you know the history of this place." This comment gave Mitch a feeling of importance, which Wendy confirmed with a pat on the back and a congratulatory "Cool beans!"

He and Wendy were still a little intoxicated, but not in an obvious way. Not that anyone was paying much attention to them anyway. Even when Wendy stumbled off the walkway onto the grass they didn't seem to notice. She started to laugh out loud, but Mitch gave her a quick warning look and she stifled it with her fist.

Mrs. Church led the way across the lawn toward the westerly end of the island. At first it looked like she was headed for Lover's Lookout, but when she reached the end of the veranda, she made a sharp turn southward and wheeled over the grass toward the west wing.

Not as glamorous as the main part of the hotel, the west wing still had a fabulous view all the way to the mainland, and every season its guest register filled up as quickly as the east wing's. This weekend it was especially full, judging by the crowds out on the lawn and sitting in Kennedy rockers on the veranda. They watched the approach of Mrs. Church and her entourage with the same interest as the people over at the east wing. Mitch glanced at Mrs. Church to see if she noticed them, but her eyes were fixed straight ahead, half-closed, as though she were staring directly into a strong wind. She didn't seem to notice anything around her at all, let alone the people on the veranda. Yet she drove her wheelchair perfectly, even making an expert turn to avoid a sprinkler fixture.

As they approached the west wing's steps, she slowed and turned her chair ninety degrees to the left to face the building directly. Leeds bent his long torso in half and said something to her that Mitch didn't catch. What she said back Mitch did catch: "The screams, Horace . . . I can't bear them." She closed her eyes and shook her head side to side as if she could shake the sounds right out of her ears. "So . . . many of them."

Without thinking, Mitch said out loud, "Naw, there's no way—"

"Shhh!" Wendy whispered, cutting him off. "We're supposed to be quiet."

Meanwhile, Mrs. Church had opened her eyes and fixed them on the top floor, slightly to the left of the gable over the veranda steps. Mitch looked from the building to Mrs. Church and back again.

Wendy whispered in his ear, "What's going on?"

Mitch put his lips to Wendy's ear, breathing in the pleasant scent of her hair. "I'll tell you later; pay close attention."

Leeds bent down again and quietly said something to Mrs. Church, to which Mrs. Church replied, "No. I've seen enough here." She turned her chair in Mitch's direction, and he was surprised to see her eyes were moist and red.

"Did you see her? She was crying," Wendy said in his ear, taking him by the arm.

"I know," he whispered back.

"What is it? You know, don't you?" Wendy was practically nibbling his earlobe. Her hair smelled like strawberries and he wanted to bury his face in it. Instead, he looked back at the hotel, took a deep breath and closed his eyes, willing himself to sense whatever Mrs. Church was picking up on, but nothing came. Whatever gift Mrs. Church had, whatever internal apparatus she used, he didn't share it. Judging by the way the rest of the crowd around her looked, including the great ghost hunter Leeds, they were just as oblivious. Everything just seemed normal, ordinary, like any other summer evening out on the Smythe lawn . . .

And yet . . .

There was something about the air. The atmosphere surrounding Mrs. Church seemed somehow denser. Mitch watched her roll across the grass in the direction of Lover's Lookout and noticed the air around her even *looked* different. At first he couldn't explain how. It took a while, but he finally managed to come up with the answer: there were no insects around her. Not a single one within a good ten-foot radius. It was the beginning of the twilight hour, the sun was down and the mosquitoes and gnats had started coming out in droves to take advantage of the fresh supply of flesh out on the open lawn. The rest of the Church-Leeds entourage whacked at arms and necks under the attack, and swarms showed against the backdrop of the sky. With the air so still and humid that evening, the bugs were dancing around and taking turns lighting on arms and necks, trying their luck at any exposed skin. Not in the vicinity of Mrs. Church, though. It could have been that she had doused herself with bug spray, but Mitch doubted it. The bugs didn't even come close.

Mrs. Church led the way across the cart trail and wound through low trees to a rocky clearing in front of the gazebo. Lover's Lookout stood on the edge of a bluff that jutted out into the sea. From that point, the sea view was more than a hundred and eighty degrees. The gazebo's name derived from the romantic view it afforded at sunset, which attracted more couples than any other spot on the resort grounds. Right now it was empty.

Mrs. Church wheeled in front of the gazebo and gazed up at the flying angel weathervane. It pointed northeast without any movement. She looked back down and steered her wheelchair toward the opening in the rail surrounding the gazebo. When she reached it, she had to have the wheelchair lifted up six inches onto its platform by four volunteers. Mitch was one of them.

She rolled to the middle of the platform and looked across the water at the Maine shoreline ten miles away. Then she toggled the wheelchair halfway around, looked past the crowd to the resort grounds and closed her eyes.

Mitch heard a noise and looked up at the rafters overhead where a sparrow's nest rested in one corner. Three tiny heads, beaks pointed heavenward, moved and chirped. Apparently, the noisy arrival of Mrs. Church and her entourage had roused them and they expected their mother to deliver worms at any moment.

Mrs. Church, meanwhile, still had her eyes closed. Her chest heaved with deep breaths and her nostrils worked open and shut like she was smelling the air. She opened her eyes and said, to no one in particular, "The emotions here are strong; so many kinds; most of them happy." She closed her eyes again. "There's one that comes through stronger than the others."

"What is it?" Leeds asked.

She furrowed her brow and shook her head. Then her face relaxed and she opened her eyes and turned her head to the left. "There," she said, nodding in the direction of the bench seat that ran along the railing. "A man. His name is 'Ardmore' . . . or 'Swarthmore.' He died here. On that bench. He was elderly. His wife died. Cancer, I think." She paused and her eyes moved rapidly back and forth as though she were watching a tennis match being played in super-fast motion. "He came here to die. His wife died—Millicent, I think. That's what I keep getting: Millicent. She died the same year, but before him. He came to this spot. May . . . nineteen fifty-two. He's wearing a—what do you Americans call it? The Indiana Jones hat. "

"A fedora," one of the reporters suggested.

"That's it. A fedora. Brown. With a dark ribbon around it. He's in brown pants, white shirt, tie. His sleeve is rolled up past his elbow. He injects himself with a needle. I can see him do it. He died right there." She looked at Leeds. "I feel peace. This isn't sad. I feel relief. There's love and peace here. A sense of . . . reuniting."

Mitch glanced around and saw the news people scribbling in notebooks and holding up recorders. The cameraman had his videocam pointed over Mitch's shoulder.

Mrs. Church wheeled over to the bench seat. She looked at the spot where she'd indicated the man had died, and smiled. She said something under her breath then rolled her wheelchair past the onlookers to the edge of the platform where she waited to be helped down.

Mitch wasn't one of the lift-down crew. It seemed everyone suddenly wanted to help. He hung back, examining the bench, trying to sense something, anything. But nothing came. The air was still and smelled of seaweed. There wasn't a sound or movement . . .

Not a sound or movement.

He looked up. The sparrows' nest he saw when they first arrived at the gazebo had been just about directly over this spot. Although he couldn't see it from underneath, he should have heard the baby sparrows squawking for a meal. But no sound came from overhead.

He stepped up on the bench seat, grabbed the rafter and did a chin-up. There was nothing there.

No birds, no nest. Not only that, there was nothing to indicate the nest had ever been there—no stray pieces of straw, no bird droppings, no loose feathers. Nothing.

He glanced around the rafters nearby just in case he had picked the wrong one, but they, too, were empty. Finally, his arms gave out and he dropped to the floor. Wendy was standing in the entrance to the gazebo, her arms crossed on her chest, watching him.

"*What* are you *doing*?" she asked.

He looked up at the empty rafter and back at Wendy. "Looking for birds' nests."

"Birds' nests?"

"I thought I heard some baby birds."

"I see." Wendy unfolded her arms and pointed. "Mrs. Church is heading back to the east wing. I thought you'd want to know."

They left the gazebo and started up the path, and as they did, Mitch heard a sound behind him. There was no mistaking that squawking chirp. He slowed and looked at the gazebo, wanting to go back and have another look, but Wendy took his elbow and moved him along.

They made their way up to the lawn in front of the west wing where Wendy asked, "What was going on with Phyllis when she stopped over here?"

"I'm not sure you want to know," Mitch answered.

"Why?"

"If it was what I think, she tuned into something pretty gruesome."

"I'm a big girl. I can handle it."

Mitch glanced sideways at her, remembering that she had buried both her parents after a horrific accident not too many years ago. "There was a fire in 1912 in the west wing, the one I mentioned at the press conference.

Almost two hundred people died."

Wendy gasped. "Oh my God, *that's* what she was seeing?"

"Well, that's what she *would* be seeing if she really—"

"How'd it happen?"

Mitch recalled what he had read about the fire and the terrible pictures he had seen, some in archives not open to the public. If Mrs. Church really had "the gift" then she had just witnessed one of the most horrific visions any medium could have the misfortune of seeing. He preferred to think she had already known about the fire—the story was pretty famous—and simply reacted to her memory of the story.

"You might have noticed Mrs. Church was focused on the center of the wing. The fire started around there, in one of the second floor guest rooms. It spread so fast, no one had a chance. Of course, there weren't any exit signs or sprinklers in those days; there weren't even any fire escapes. Some of the victims were killed jumping out windows in the back. The wing is built on a hill, it's a forty-foot drop from the third floor back there."

"My God," Wendy said under her breath, then aloud, "How did it start?"

Mitch shrugged. "No one knows. It might have been a cigarette, an electrical short—electrical fires were pretty common back then. But the fire moved so fast it almost seems like it was set."

"Set?" Wendy sounded incredulous.

Mitch nodded. He didn't want to think about it anymore. "Come on, let's catch up."

By the time they rejoined Mrs. Church and the reporters they had already reached the corner where the east and west wings came together. Mrs. Church was quietly wheeling along in the front while Leeds hung back, talking to a couple of reporters. Wendy and Mitch joined the back of the group, trying to stay out of the way. They had no idea where Mrs. Church was headed, and from what Mitch could see of the expression on her face, she didn't seem to know or care. She was like a magnet being drawn to different spots at random.

As if to prove his point, Mrs. Church stopped suddenly, causing Horace Leeds to nearly run into the wheelchair. She had been going at an angle roughly in the direction of Mr. Arndt's cottage. Now she looked to her right, up the hill at the hotel. Wanting to hear what she said to Leeds, Mitch stole as close to them as he could without being too conspicuous.

Mrs. Church was saying, "It keeps drawing me. I have to go back in."

"Anywhere in particular?" Leeds asked.

"No. I won't know until I get inside." She paused, looking from one end of the hotel to the other. "It's so strong. I wonder why it wasn't there before. It's like whoever wants to talk to me just woke up."

"Then let's say 'ello, shall we?" Leeds said cheerfully.

CHAPTER TEN

Mrs. Church turned her wheelchair and headed straight for the opening in the veranda's latticework. Everyone followed her under the veranda to an entrance leading into the sub-ground level of the hotel where a service elevator took them up to the first floor in two shifts. Wendy and Mitch went up with Mrs. Church in the first shift, and they came out near the gift shop, just down the hall from the lobby. While waiting for the elevator to go back down and pick up the second load, Mitch studied Mrs. Church, trying to gauge her emotions. She sat silently in her chair, staring ahead at a point in space somewhere between her and the nearest wall. Her face was a blank. But he could tell something was churning inside her. He didn't know how he knew; he just sensed she was alert and focused on something the rest of them weren't.

When the others arrived on the elevator, everyone followed Mrs. Church down the short hall to the main corridor. There, they turned right and headed in the direction of the lobby. About halfway there, Mrs. Church stopped short. Her gaze slowly lifted to the ceiling. She stared at it a moment, blinked, looked back at her followers and said one word: "Upstairs."

Down the corridor, she turned into another short side hall where two elevators with ornate brass doors waited. The entourage crammed into both elevators and rode to the third floor. There, Mrs. Church's demeanor changed again. She looked completely tuned in, like some antenna inside of her had homed in on a signal. Turning right out of the short elevator hall, she moved quickly down the corridor. She was headed straight for the Boudreau apartment.

The Boudreau apartment was famous among people who cared about the Boudreaus and historic hotels. From 1913 until their demise in 1924, the suite of rooms had been reserved exclusively for Roger and Maria and their personal guests. No one had stayed in the apartment since. Except for the cleaning staff, no one ever went in. Mitch had read somewhere that the rooms were still kept the way they were back then—furnishings, art work, books, everything. The tower, which was completely destroyed the night of the murders, had been rebuilt to exactly the same specs as the original, down to the wallpaper and carpet. Why this was done, Mitch had never been able to learn. Certainly it wasn't a shrine to the Boudreaus as no one was allowed in to see it. While doing research for his book, he had run across a story from the 'sixties in Look magazine about the Smythe, and that same question had been put to the hotel manager of the time. His answer seemed reasonable enough: they kept it closed off out of respect for the Boudreaus. Yet to leave it vacant for three-quarters of a century seemed a poor business decision. The grandest of the quarters in the hotel, the Boudreau suite would have fetched a lot of great word-of-mouth publicity among its wealthier guests who stayed in it. Not to mention a very high guest fee.

Then again, maybe it wasn't such a bad business decision. Closing off that suite had created a sense of mystery about the Smythe. The knowledge that beyond those doors lay a world from long ago, preserved just as it was when the two most famous people connected with the Smythe inhabited it, was an alluring amenity that never had to be advertised in travel brochures.

Following Mrs. Church down the corridor, Mitch had to admit he felt that same allure. He had never been on the third floor of the Smythe, but was familiar with the layout through his research. Just ahead, the corridor ended at a wall with gold-striped wallpaper and a huge painting of an eighteenth-century hunt scene featuring Russian Wolfhounds. At this wall, the corridor turned right, then left twice, then right again, skirting around the Boudreau apartment. If you were standing before the picture and turned left, you would see a plain, unassuming door down a little entrance hall. A brass plaque on the door read, "Welcome" in Russian.

The painting had been brought over from Russia by Tatiana Boudreau in 1900. Thankfully, it had been spared in the 1924 fire as the flames never reached the outside walls. Encased in security glass and bolted to the wall, it had only been removed a few times over the years when the walls were re-papered. The entrance door, too, was secured with an electronic deadbolt and a security system to keep out anyone whose curiosity or penchant for theft got the best of them.

They reached the painting and Mrs. Church stopped to admire it like she was in an art museum. The painting was six feet long and four feet high and richly detailed, and Mrs. Church's eyes wandered back and forth over it, taking in the entire scene piece by piece. The left side of the canvas was filled with three huge dogs with bared teeth surrounding a wild boar backed up against a tree. On the right side, several horsemen in long, fur-lined coats and fur hats were leaping over a stone wall. The lead rider had just caught sight of the dogs; the others were busy negotiating the jump. The background was filled with tall mountains and virgin forest, what Mitch imagined the Russian countryside looked like a hundred years ago.

Mrs. Church put her head back and closed her eyes as if to rest them after taking in such a large and busy painting. Some of the people in the back who had been chatting with one another in hushed voices fell silent. The man with the video camera worked his way forward and focused on Mrs. Church. Everyone waited, knowing who had lived on the other side of the wall—and what had happened to them behind that same wall more than eighty years ago.

Eventually, Mrs. Church opened her eyes and spoke, but the words were so weak and garbled that no one could understand them. Leeds leaned close to her ear and whispered something. Mrs. Church replied with a few quiet words. Leeds then said to the crowd, "Mrs. Church isn't feeling well and would like to go back to her room to rest. We'll suspend for the night."

A few observers grumbled, and a man close to Mitch said, "Paid full price and they cut out Act Three." Their disappointment was understandable—Mitch was certainly disappointed himself. But in another way he was glad she hadn't tuned in to anything because it gave him more confidence in her. If she was a phony, she probably would have put on a show outside the Boudreau apartment just to satisfy the crowd.

The entourage shuffled back down the hall to the elevators. Mitch stayed behind, admiring the painting again, but only because he wanted to appear like he had a good reason to linger. He was really waiting for everyone to go away so he could have a moment alone outside the apartment where Maria had spent so much time. Feeling like a dopey schoolboy, he tried to imagine how many times Maria's eyes had gazed upon that painting on her way to the entrance door.

Once everyone was out of view, he turned to the apartment door. Walking over to it, he reached up and ran his finger over the Cyrillic letters etched into the brass sign. It had been Maria's idea to have the Russian version of "welcome" on the door. She had become well-versed in her mother's native language while in her teens, hoping to one day visit or even study in St. Petersburg, before the 1917 Revolution had squelched her dream. Still, her friends continued to call her by her Russian nickname, Mashka, with her encouragement. She collected Russian objets d'art, including some expensive Faberge pieces, all her brief life. She obviously had been interested in her heritage, which probably kept her connected to her mother as well.

The brass plate was screwed solidly to the door. The doorknob, on the other hand, looked as ordinary and flimsy as any doorknob found on a broom closet door. It, too, was brass but scratched and tarnished. The real security was in a keycard deadbolt situated just above the doorknob. The apartment would surely be rigged with a state-of-the-art security system, too. Still, that flimsy doorknob just looked so out-of-place on such an important door. Or was he just exaggerating its importance because of the young woman who had once walked through it regularly?

Worn and tarnished though it was, the doorknob tempted him like a boy with a sweet tooth reaching for a cookie jar. He put his hand on it, feeling the smooth, cold surface, imagining what it would be like to turn it and push the door open, walk over the threshold, and stand inside Maria's suite all those years ago . . . and, just as soon as he thought it, he was there.

He was inside the apartment, standing in a small foyer beside an empty wooden coat rack. He looked back over his shoulder and saw the inside panel of the entrance door, confirming where he was. To his right, a set of three steps ran up to a big, open living room filled with old but rich-looking furnishings. A red velvet camelback sofa in the center of the room faced a rectangular window overlooking the Smythe lawn and Longboat Harbor beyond. Surrounding the sofa stood three wingback chairs, all covered in a floral pattern, and a couple of floor lamps with frosted-glass shades. Bookcases covered one wall from floor to ceiling. Among the many books stood a variety of vases, a Faberge guilloche clock, and statuettes of various people—some famous, some not—the most prominent a bust of Theodore Roosevelt. Mitch had read that Roger Boudreau admired Roosevelt very much.

On a small round table stood a black candlestick telephone with a bell-shaped earpiece hanging on the side and a black cord running to the wall. The cord piqued Mitch's curiosity. Somehow, seeing it still attached to the phone suggested that the phone was live. A ridiculous notion, of course. Why leave an old phone active in a deserted room? But no more ridiculous than the fresh-looking flowers he now spotted on a tea table in front of the window. He went to the table and touched them. They felt real, too. And the table had no tablecloth, but not a speck of dust could be seen. In fact, the whole place was spotless—

—and there's that old phone with the cloth-covered cord running to the wall.

He sat in the chair closest to the little table with the phone. The chair stood at an angle facing the window. If this was the original furniture arrangement, then this was probably where anyone making a call had sat many years ago. From this vantage point, he had a great view of Longboat Harbor. In her day, Maria must have sat here talking on the phone and looking out the window. And here he was—

—and there's that phone …

That phone with its cord attached to the wall, maybe to a live connection. And now that he was closer to it he could see finger smudges on the earpiece. Maria's finger smudges maybe?

Come on, Mitch, it couldn't be. That phone has to be a replacement. The fire would have destroyed the original one … Then again, didn't I read that this part of the apartment wasn't destroyed? Only the tower room and the rear of the apartment? The phone might just be the original …

And that would mean Maria had once held that earpiece to her own ear.

He reached over and picked the receiver up off the hook. It felt heavier than he expected, like it had been built to last forever. Looking at the six tiny holes in the earpiece, he realized there was a faint sound coming from them. He held it to his ear and heard the unmistakable hum of a dial tone. The phone really was live! He examined the base of the phone, wondering how to use it because there was no finger dial. He had seen candlestick phones without dials in antique shops and old movies, but never actually used one.

As he sat there trying to figure out how to place a call, the buzz abruptly stopped and a male voice came on the line. "Operator. How may I connect you?"

He hastily cradled the earpiece and jumped up from the chair. Why in the world would an antique telephone be left operating in a room that was never used and never seen except by cleaning staff? Come to think of it, why were there fresh flowers in that same room? Unless he was mistaken and the flowers were actually a high-quality silk arrangement that looked real—

A flash of movement out of the corner of his eye stole his attention. He looked back to his right at a spiral staircase in the corner of the room. The movement he had seen was a dark object just starting up the stairs. Whatever it had been—if it had been there at all—it was now gone from sight.

He started over to the staircase, which was much like the spiral staircases in modern homes except that these were much more ornate and built entirely of cast iron. Each of the risers was in the shape of a fleur de lis on a stem, rising to a brass handrail. The stairs rose through a square hole in the ceiling into the hotel's middle tower, which had been built out into a small room. He could not see most of it from where he stood, so he took the handrail and started up. He only got as far as the bottom step when he heard someone call his name.

It was a female voice, coming from behind him. For a brief but thrilling moment he imagined he would turn around to find that the voice had come from Maria, standing in the middle of the room, smiling at him. He started to turn—and saw it again out of the corner of his eye: a dark figure moving overhead in the tower room. He swung his eyes upward in time to see what appeared to be a pant leg move beyond the stair hole out of his range of vision.

"Hello!" he called out.

No one answered. He listened for footsteps but heard nothing.

"Hello!"

"Mitch," came a voice behind him.

This time Mitch turned around and looked straight into the face of Wendy Mayer. She stood so close he could have kissed her if he craned his neck a little. Bright sunlight behind her set her face in shadows, but he could see her well enough to note the concern on her face.

"What?"

"What are you doing?"

He blinked, not sure what she meant. Then he looked back in front of him and saw the brass "welcome" sign written in Cyrillic. He was standing in the hall outside the Boudreau suite.

"Mitch!"

"Huh?"

"Why are you standing there?"

"Have I been here long?"

From down the hall came the distinct sound of elevator doors rolling together, followed by the hum of the elevator motor.

"Long enough to miss the elevator. Mitch, you must know this suite is off limits." She reached around him and tried the doorknob. "These rooms are kept locked all the time."

"I know that."

"It's too bad, too. I'd like to have seen what Mrs. Church could pick up inside there."

They walked down the hall to the elevators where Mitch turned to Wendy, wanting to tell her what had just happened. But the words caught in his throat. Wendy stared back at him with a questioning expression. An uncomfortable moment later, the floor indicator above the elevator doors dinged. The doors slid open and two adolescent girls with damp hair and beach towels wrapped around them stepped out.

Mitch and Wendy took the elevator to the first floor in silence.

CHAPTER ELEVEN

Mitch saw Wendy off in the lobby and left for his cabin. On the way, he pondered what he had experienced outside the Boudreau suite. Wendy would have interpreted it as a psychic vision, but he didn't see how that could be, even if he was willing to believe in psychic visions. If Mrs. Church really had channeled into the west wing fire, and a suicide out at Lover's Lookout, wouldn't she have picked up on something outside the Boudreau apartment? If *she* hadn't plugged into something there, nobody else was going to, including him. That meant he had imagined everything, which wasn't surprising considering how many pictures he had seen of the Boudreau suite.

But that telephone. The flowers.

The dark figure on the stairs.

All in his head. A vivid, waking dream of some sort. If Wendy hadn't interrupted him he might even have imagined meeting Maria in that apartment.

He stopped on the lawn and looked back at the rectangular window below the middle tower. In the last of the fading light it appeared dark and ominous. In strong daylight it always looked bright and cheerful because a thin white curtain hung behind it. But tonight, in the shadows of dusk, it looked almost sinister. Directly above it another big window, this one round, looked out from the center of the middle tower itself. Inside that window was the little room that the circular staircase in the Boudreau apartment ascended to. The tower room where Maria had met her fate so many years ago.

Staring at that round window, Mitch half-expected to see the figure from his vision go flitting by. But the window stayed empty and still, a dark, lifeless eye looking down on the island Maria had loved so dearly, and which eventually served as the stage for her death.

The porch light outside his cabin door was lit when he got back. A swarm of moths and other flying insects darted around its dusty globe, and when he got close he could hear the tiny *dit-dit-dit* of them bumping into it. A single enormous moth resembling a green stingray rested on the clapboards close to the light, its wings spread wide as though preparing to take flight. Mitch moved up close to examine it. Its bulging eyes seemed to stare right back. Meanwhile, all around it, the smaller insects went on flitting about aimlessly, as though performing some insane dance for their king.

"It's a luna moth," said a voice in the dark.

Mitch looked back at Mr. Arndt's porch and saw him sitting in his rocker. His own porch light was off, and in the pale moonlight, all Mitch could see of him were his white pajamas and the dark outline of his head.

He climbed the porch steps and sat beside the old man. "Why are you sitting in the dark?"

"More restful in the dark."

The old man's eyes were fixed on the horizon past Longboat Harbor and the seawall connecting Forges Island and Breakers Island. There, out over the open Atlantic, a beautiful, nearly full moon was on the rise. It would have been even more stunning if not for the hazy atmosphere.

"Damned hot tonight," Mitch said.

"Muggy. Muggy as hell."

Mitch nodded. Usually you could count on an ocean breeze taking the edge off, but not tonight. The air lingered thick and warm like you were wearing a damp wool coat on a warm day.

"Would you like a cold drink?" Mr. Arndt asked.

"Love one." He was dying of thirst. The beer he'd drunk earlier that night had dried him out.

"Me too. Why don't you get a couple sodas out of the fridge? It's right inside the door."

Mitch went in. The kitchen was small—perfect for a bachelor who hated to cook. Although the appliances were dated, especially the refrigerator (Mitch had never even heard of a "Kelvinator") they looked functional. He opened the fridge and saw that its shelves were mostly filled with drinks: cans of soda, a bottle of prune juice, a tall can of V-8. The soda was all Moxie. No Coke or Pepsi, not even root beer. Just Moxie. Mitch had never drunk Moxie before, but he would have drunk almost anything right then. He grabbed two cans and went back through the screen door, letting it slam behind him. "Some moon," he said, sitting back in his creaky rocker and handing the old man a can.

"Nothing prettier than the moon over the water." Mr. Arndt popped open his can and drank. "So how was the reading?"

"Reading? Oh. Fine, I guess. Hard to tell, though, unless you can be positive Phyllis Church never heard of the west wing fire before."

"She picked up on that, huh?"

"If she did, it shook her up pretty bad."

Mr. Arndt's mouth was set in a grim line. "I imagine it would. The horror of that night is indescribable."

"Apparently, she picked up on something else, too."

"Oh?"

"Out at Lover's Lookout. She saw the spirit of an old man who committed suicide."

Mr. Arndt turned to him quickly then back to the moon, which had risen a little higher over the water. "Arthur Moore. That one doesn't surprise me either."

"You know about that?"

"Sure do. I knew Art very well. He and his wife came out here every summer. Art was a surgeon, one of the best in Boston in his time. He retired and bought a place on the other side of the island. Back in the 'forties and 'fifties we had a tennis club going and my wife and I used to play doubles against Art and his wife."

Mitch remembered Mrs. Church had gotten another name in her head. "Who was Millicent?"

"That was Art's wife. 'Millie,' we called her. Hell of a tennis player, even in her later years when I used to play against her. She was at least twenty years older than me, but she kept right up. Strong legs. Pretty, too. Quite a gal."

"And Art killed himself?"

"For all her energy and great legs, Millie got lymphoma and died in '52. Not too long after that, Art was out here on the island and one morning they found him at Lover's Lookout, dead. He'd injected himself with something. Died fast. Poor ol' Art. He and Millie were inseparable. Only death could part them. Even then, Art chose to follow her instead of spending the rest of his years without her."

Mitch drew in a long breath and blew it out loudly. "Seems like so much tragedy for one little island."

"Well, we're looking at a lot of years here. Got to be *some* bad stuff going on."

"I suppose. But it still seems like a lot. Mass death, suicide, murder. They've had it all here."

"That reminds me. Was there anything about the Boudreaus tonight?"

Mitch's experience outside (*inside?*) the Boudreau apartment flashed in his mind. His next thought was of Phyllis examining the painting outside the same apartment, then turning away without even a twitch of recognition. "Nothing."

The speed of Mr. Arndt's rocking picked up a notch. "Really? Nothing?"

"Yeah. You'd think she would get something outside that apartment, huh?"

Mr. Arndt made a throaty noise. Mitch looked, and in the faint moonlight he saw he was grinning. "What?"

"You would . . . think it. How's the Moxie?"

Mitch took a swallow and smacked his tongue against the roof of his mouth a couple of times. It tasted like nothing he'd had before, but he was beginning to like it. "It grows on you."

Mr. Arndt went on staring and not saying anything, but the grin hadn't faded.

"What?" Mitch asked again.

"When you published your book on the Boudreau murders, did you pick the photos?"

He was referring to the center section of *American Princess* which displayed a dozen pages of photos. Mitch had, indeed, insisted on choosing them, and he told this to Mr. Arndt.

Mr. Arndt nodded. "Very nice choices."

"Thank you. Why did you ask?"

Mr. Arndt squinted at the moon, which was getting brighter as it floated higher over the ocean. In the hazy atmosphere it seemed to have a dull halo around it. "Funny the way fate finds its way." The old man swigged his soda.

"What do you mean?"

"I mean you probably never thought you'd find yourself researching a biography of two people who died eighty years ago. Yet you were the perfect candidate to do it, and that biography was well overdue."

"I agree it was overdue, but I certainly wasn't the perfect candidate. I had no writing experience when I started the book. I had no idea how to write a biography. I just stumbled into the thing, that's all."

"And researched the story so thoroughly the only details left out were Maria's bathroom habits. You even described the cake they made for her twenty-first birthday party. Hell, you listed just about everyone who was there that night."

He was right, of course. Mitch had worked exhaustively on the project, obsessively poring over documents and pictures for hours, trying to find descriptions of the smallest things. Like what shoes Maria wore to her last birthday party, whether she had danced and to what music, what the weather was like. Anything and everything. Including her birthday cake: chocolate with vanilla frosting, three-tiered, topped by a miniature replica of one of the swan boats she loved to ride in the Boston Public Garden. It had been a lot of work, but he would have loved to do even more. "It was easy. There was so much material from the murder investigation."

"True. But, for example, how did you know she accidentally wore a quarter-moon-shaped brooch backwards at a charity event in 1922? Where'd you come across something like that?"

In the merciful cover of dark, Mitch felt his face flush. Mr. Arndt had him cornered. "Actually, it was in a newsreel. When she walked by the camera you could see the brooch plain as day. The outside curve pointed to her right side and the horns pointed to her left side. A few years back I saw a picture of the same brooch in a Christie's auction catalogue. The horns were pointing left, which would be Maria's right side. I checked with Christie's and it was photographed correctly."

"Something that might seem insignificant, but adds color. Well done."

"Thanks, but I thought it *was* significant. Maria was an enigma. She had so much grace and charm about her, but she could be terribly clumsy and forgetful, too. She was a good sport about it. She had a good sense of humor. I think it was one of her most attractive qualities."

"Funny, I never would have guessed she was clumsy." Mr. Arndt looked straight ahead, moonlight glinting off his bald head.

"Not in her social graces—those were exquisite—but she could be physically awkward. She could play tennis like a pro, but she often tripped going up the stairs. More than once she spilled a drink all over the table at some posh event or another. Things like that."

"All of which is common knowledge, of course." This came out as half-question, half-statement.

"Oh, no! The press never printed that sort of stuff about her. I mostly got it from sons and daughters of people who were close to her in life. I interviewed a lot of that generation, since most of her contemporaries are dead now."

"A remarkable work."

"Thank you."

"Your love for your subject leaps off every page."

"It's a fascinating story. It was easy to tell it."

"Because you were *supposed* to tell it."

Mitch looked closely at him, but his face was turned away from the moonlight. "What are you saying?"

"Fate, my boy. Your fate found you. You wrote the book you were supposed to write."

The word "fate" struck Mitch as lofty for what he considered a pretty minor work. When you got right down to it, Maria Boudreau was an insignificant historical character, having died before she got the chance to accomplish much of anything. "Well, maybe it was my fate to write Maria's biography, but not to meet her ghost. She was nowhere to be found tonight when Phyllis Church went looking for her."

"The weekend's just starting."

Not long after, they said goodnight. Mr. Arndt promised to wake Mitch for breakfast and Mitch stumbled his way back to the cabin, thoroughly exhausted. Outside the door, the smaller moths continued to flutter around the light in their neurotic dance while the luna moth clung to the side of the cabin. By now it had moved closer to the doorway, at eye-level height, so that Mitch found himself staring at it from inches away when he opened the door.

"Hello, mega-moth," he said.

The moth just went on staring at him, or beyond him, or at nothing at all, who could tell? Mitch walked in the door and shut it behind him and the outside light went off. Through the window, he saw Mr. Arndt at his own kitchen window looking back at him. Apparently, the switch to the cabin's outside light was wired into the cottage. Mr. Arndt waved, Mitch waved back and Mr. Arndt's window went dark.

He flipped on the light switch next to the door and the lamp on the nightstand came on. In the shaded light the cabin looked cozy. He lifted his duffel bag onto the bed, unzipped a side compartment, took out three items and laid them on the bed. The first object was a framed sepia-tone photograph of Maria dressed in an elaborate white gown, taken in 1921. In the picture her auburn hair was up, showing off her long, slender neck made even prettier by curling wisps of hair where the top of the neck met the scalp. Her smile was warm, and she looked out at you as if you were the only person in the world—at least the only one who mattered. He had seen the photo on an online memorabilia auction and bid high, not just because of its full-length depiction of Maria in all her elegant splendor but because it was the only copy in existence. Even the negative had been lost. He owned a one-of-a-kind photograph of Maria Boudreau, which, in some small way, gave him a feeling of intimacy with her.

He set the picture on the nightstand and picked up a leather journal cover, which he unzipped and laid open on the bed. It contained a black velvet display pad, the type that jewelers use. Fastened to the pad was Mitch's most prized possession in the world: the quarter-moon diamond-and-sapphire brooch worn by Maria at the charity golf tournament on Long Island in 1922. The horns pointed right, just the way Maria had worn it. Maybe it was weird for a man to be running around with a lady's brooch in his duffle bag, but it could have been a safety pin for all he cared. It was the fact Maria had been filmed while wearing it that made it valuable to him. He also had a copy of that five-second film clip, which he had found on a web site about the champion golfer Walter Hagen.

The brooch had cost him a small fortune, but, like the photo, he had to own it whatever the price. It was serendipitous that he'd found out about it to begin with. After purchasing the photo of Maria online, he had somehow ended up on an email list among auctioneers of memorabilia of the rich and famous. In this way he learned about the brooch being auctioned off by

Christie's, and the film clip in which Maria wore it.

He ran an index finger over the curve of the moon, feeling the roughness of the stones. This little souvenir had taken up a good chunk of his book royalties, but to him it was worth every penny. Admiring the brooch in the soft light of the cabin, he replayed the film clip in his head. In it, Maria was dressed in a long, light-colored skirt and matching summer jacket with lapels. On her head she wore one of those bell-shaped cloche hats so popular at the time. It is late afternoon as the film begins, and she is outside in bright daylight, walking away from a party tent toward the camera, accompanied by an older man in a stark white suit and straw hat. In the middle of the clip the man stops, but she continues on, saying something over her shoulder to him as she moves closer to the camera. Then she turns her head forward again and smiles for the camera as she passes. In the last of the frames her jacket lapel, with the brooch attached, fills the frame.

And here it was, that priceless brooch, here with him on Sumner Island, the place Maria loved the most.

He looked over at her picture on the nightstand then through the back window behind the bed. The three towers were mostly visible above the bushes and weeds growing behind the cabin. External lighting at the base of each tower lit them up, showing off their gingerbread-tiled splendor. He went to the window and stared at the middle tower, remembering the vision he'd had that evening. The spiral stairs were still vivid in his mind, as was the dark pant leg moving out of view at the top of those stairs. He did not know what the tower room looked like before the fire engulfed it the night of Maria's death; he'd never seen a "before" picture of it, and he wasn't sure any existed. But the furnishings he saw when standing close to the top of the stairs in his dream vision (the name he had given to his mental tour of the Boudreau apartment) had made the room look pleasant and inviting. As part of the renovations, the walls had been papered in a light, airy landscape scene. The skylight in the tower roof had been replaced—

Just then something clicked in his head.

All night long he had been telling himself he re-created the Boudreau suite in his mind from photos he'd seen in old archives. Yet he was certain he had never seen a single photo of the spiral staircase rising to the tower. How had he re-created that?

Well, you must have embellished the vision. You assumed what the staircase once looked like and sketched it in.

That took care of that.

Yet little thorns continued to prick at the edges of his thoughts. In spite of sheer exhaustion, he lay in bed staring at the darkened ceiling, unable to sleep. Beads of sweat dripped from his temples down his sideburns and around the bottoms of his ears, finally dropping to the pillow. Not even the slightest of breezes blew through the open windows. The humid air was stifling.

After a long while he did manage to fall asleep, but his dreams were no less disturbing than his waking thoughts. He dreamed the big moth by the door was now inside the cabin. It had positioned itself on the ceiling directly over his head, and seemed to be staring down at him, sizing him up, waiting for something. Some signal or stimulus. In the dream, he lay on his back staring up at it, not blinking for fear of what the creature might do in that split-second of vulnerability. And then something very odd happened: the moth started to grow. It slowly doubled in size, then tripled, then seemed to grow more rapidly until it took up Mitch's whole field of vision. At the same time, he gradually became aware that he was no longer on the bed but floating above it. And then another realization came to him: the moth hadn't really grown at all. Mitch had floated up to it until he was eyeball-to-eyeball with the thing. From his vantage point he could see its leaf-like antennae and the big, dark brown eyes. As he gazed straight into one of those eyes he saw something amazing: a big room filled with dancing people. The moth seemed to be watching a party going on behind Mitch.

He started to look down and found himself back on the bed, quite awake, lying on his side. He turned over and looked up.

There on the ceiling, just barely visible in the moonlight, the moth clung to the same spot where Mitch had seen it in his dream. It remained there only a second or two then took flight, disappearing through a crack in the window screen, out into the night.

CHAPTER TWELVE

He slept dreamlessly the rest of the night, and when he awoke, the sun sat low in the eastern sky. It was not quite six o'clock. He tried to go back to sleep, but a pounding headache at the base of his skull prevented that, so he decided to shower, and head up to the hotel for coffee and the morning paper.

Twenty minutes later he sat in the hotel lobby, the *Boston Globe* in his lap and a coffee mug in his hand, feeling refreshed and a lot better all around. The headache was going away, thanks to a couple of Tylenol he bought in the gift shop, and the air conditioning felt invigorating. He hadn't realized just how smothering the air outside was until he came through the hotel doors. This was the place to be in this weather. Mr. Arndt would just have to meet him here when he came up for breakfast.

He was thinking he should have left a note on the cottage door for the old man when Wendy Mayer walked up to him, accompanied by an elderly woman.

"Good morning," he said to Wendy. He nodded politely at her companion who gave a shy smile in return.

"I'm sorry, Mitch, this is Dorothy Poulin. Dorothy Poulin, Mitch Lambert."

Mitch hurried to his feet, letting his newspaper slide to the floor. Dorothy Poulin was Maria's last living cousin who had been only five or six when Maria died. She looked great for her age. Her thick white hair was stylishly groomed, her figure trim. Her cotton dress was up-to-date, and she even looked a little preppy with a white cardigan draped over her shoulders. "Very nice to meet you." He offered his hand and she gave it a quick squeeze.

"Nice to meet you, Mr. Lambert."

"I wrote a book about your cousin, Maria. There's a picture in my book of you as a baby, sitting in Maria's lap."

Mrs. Poulin beamed, which took twenty years off her face. "I know the picture. I've matured a little since then."

They all laughed and Mitch realized he was still holding the old woman's hand. It felt good to hold the hand of someone Maria had once cradled in her arms, and he let go with great reluctance.

"Where are you headed?" he asked.

"Breakfast," Wendy answered cheerfully. The look on her face suggested she knew what he was thinking. "Why don't you join us?"

They ate in the Sandpiper. The longer he spent in her presence, the more Mitch liked Mrs. Poulin. Her manner was gentle, even for someone of her years, and she spoke in an accent that hinted of Scandinavia. Her mother hailed from Norway, she explained, and as a small girl she had taken on her accent to a degree. Her father Guy (she pronounced it "Gee," as in "geese") was Roger Boudreau's much younger brother. Hence, in spite of fifteen years' age difference, she and Maria were first cousins.

Mitch pressed her for memories of Maria, but unfortunately there were few. She had been just shy of six years-old when Maria died, and in that brief span, she saw Maria only a handful of times. She vaguely remembered being at Maria's twenty-first birthday party; thankfully, her parents were able to keep her oblivious to the events of later that night so she was spared that memory. Other times she recalled with great warmth, especially one particular Christmas.

"I think it was the Christmas before Maria died," she said, holding a cup of tea in one hand and a saucer under it. "I remember being in a big house with big rooms and ceilings that seemed to reach up to the sky. There were chandeliers everywhere. I was fascinated with the crystals." She paused to sip her tea then continued. "It was my Uncle Roger's house in Boston. I remember the stone steps and the big arch over the front doors. And there was a Christmas tree in the middle of one of the rooms. It was the biggest Christmas tree I'd ever seen. I don't think I've seen a bigger one since, not inside a house anyway."

She paused to sip again, and Wendy said encouragingly, "It sounds like your uncle's house was pretty impressive."

Mrs. Poulin set down her cup and nodded, her eyes wide. "It was. My father was fairly successful himself—he was an architect—but nowhere near as successful as Uncle Roger."

"What do you remember about Maria?" Mitch asked impatiently, drawing a look from Wendy.

"Only that she was very beautiful and kind."

Mitch was in agony, waiting for anything unique about Maria that Mrs. Poulin could tell them. What did she wear? How did she walk? Was she really as clumsy as they say? Were her eyes as big and shiny as they say? Anything. But he could see in Mrs. Poulin's eyes that there was nothing else. It was too long ago, and the poor woman had been so young. How could she be expected to remember anything? And so he smiled a "thank you" at her and sadly turned his attention to his omelet.

"Oh, how could I forget?"

Mitch looked up and saw Mrs. Poulin holding up her right hand, admiring a ring on one of her thin, wrinkled fingers.

"What were you saying?" Wendy asked.

"My ring." She held it out for them to examine. "This was my Christmas present from Maria that same year."

Mitch looked closely at it and almost choked on his eggs. It was a white-gold ring with a cluster of diamonds and sapphires in the shape of a crescent moon. The largest stones were at the fat center part, growing smaller toward the horns. It was the spitting image of Maria's brooch, only smaller.

"It's beautiful," Wendy said.

"It is," Mitch agreed.

Mrs. Poulin beamed. "It's always been my prize piece of jewelry."

Mitch, of course, knew it was part of a set, and that the provenance of his own piece from that set didn't include Dorothy Poulin. So he knew the answer to his next question before he asked it. "Did she really buy that for a little six year-old girl?"

Mrs. Poulin grinned from ear to ear. "No, it was hers first. But I loved it so much she wanted me to have it. She put it in a little wooden box, wrapped it up and gave it to me that Christmas."

Mitch held her hand and ran a finger over the ring. Though smaller than the diamonds on the brooch, they felt so familiar. "Wouldn't it look good in a set."

"Oh, it *was* part of a set. There was a pendant and a brooch, too, but she kept those. I don't know what became of them after she died. I imagine one of my aunts ended up with them, but I never asked."

One of her aunts *had* ended up with the brooch. Maria had died without a will, and with both her mother and father dead, and no siblings, her extended family inherited whatever she had. This included a valuable jewelry collection, much of which had once belonged to her mother. The pendant was never found, and it was assumed Maria had lost it. One of her aunts elected to take the brooch from Maria's collection as part of her share of the estate, and when that aunt died in 1966, the brooch passed to her daughter. The daughter was the one who auctioned it through Christie's.

Mitch let go of her hand, and as he did, something made him glance at Wendy. She was staring directly at him, a questioning look on her face. He wanted to tell her about the brooch. He wanted to see the reaction on their faces when he told them that he now owned it, and what a small world it is when the ring and the brooch were back together all these years later, sort of. But he didn't. No one knew he owned it, and something told him he should keep it that way. "It's a very beautiful ring," he said to Mrs. Poulin. "I'm glad you ended up with it. I'm sure Maria loved you very much."

This last comment brought another bright smile to Mrs. Poulin's face. Looking at her, all aglow with pride, Mitch thought he could see the little girl back at Christmastime 1923 underneath the sagging skin and liver spots.

He happily picked up the check for breakfast, after which he and Wendy walked Mrs. Poulin to the veranda where she wanted to rock for a while "to digest her food." That left Wendy and Mitch standing at the top of the steps, looking out at Longboat Harbor. It wasn't quite 7:30, and Mitch hadn't a clue what to do with himself the rest of the morning. Mrs. Church's sitting wasn't scheduled until that evening, so he had the rest of the day to kill. And so, it suddenly occurred to him, did Wendy.

"Feel like going for a walk?" he suggested. "Might help digest our food just as well as rocking."

Wendy gave him a crazy grin, the same kind she'd given him the day before when he knocked her over. She hooked her elbow in his. "Lead the way, guide."

They went down the steps to the walkway where Mitch hesitated for a second, thinking he would turn left and head in the direction of Lover's

Lookout. He wanted to search again for the sparrows' nest in the gazebo rafters. But he quickly reconsidered and turned right, instead, thinking if he brought Wendy to the gazebo she might think he had a romantic notion. Actually, the truth was he did. He liked Wendy quite a bit. He just didn't think he could romance anyone here on this island where Maria had walked and breathed. He decided to retrace his footsteps from the day before and show her the places he had dubbed Pirate Beach and Lone Tree Hill.

They met up with the trail around the corner from Mr. Arndt's cottage. As they passed in front of the house, Mitch looked for the old man but he was nowhere to be seen. He pointed out his little cabin to Wendy and told her how Mr. Arndt had hoodwinked him into renting a one-room shack instead of a real cottage. She told him it looked "cozy." He told her she sounded like a real estate agent.

On they went, following the trail with the harbor to their left. The trees on either side became denser the more they walked, until they reached the first tree tunnel. The shade felt good, even more so than yesterday. The branches actually came together in a thick tangle up above, cutting off the sunlight enough to cast an unbroken shadow on the trail.

Wendy, too, noticed how comfortably shady it was under the tree branches. "We should pack a picnic lunch and eat under here later. It's the coolest spot on the island."

"The coolest spot on the island is the hotel. I'd rather picnic under one of the fichus trees in the lobby."

They came to the place on the trail where the overhang began to thin out, and now they could see the water again. No boats were moored at this end of the harbor, as the water was shallow and the bottom strewn with boulders. In the distance, Breakers Island rose between the two seawalls. Directly to their left stood the two small houses Mitch had seen the day before. The shrubs in front of them had been trimmed back since the last time he came this way, revealing white picket fences.

Wendy's eyes were focused on the open ocean beyond Breakers. "Look at the size of that ship." She pointed at a huge tanker, its hull long and black, white bridge tower rising in the center. It was fairly close, probably on its way into Portland or maybe Portsmouth. The seawall obscured part of it, making it hard to tell the exact direction it faced.

Mitch suddenly remembered the three-hundred-sixty-degree view from the top of Lone Tree Hill. "Let me take you where we can see it a lot better." He turned to his right to look for the flat-top tree.

It wasn't there.

The day before, he had looked up the gentle slope of that hill to the right and saw the tall tree standing sentry over all four corners of the island. Now he was looking at a wide, neatly carved cart trail rising up the hill to a perpendicular one, and beyond that, houses. Five or six of them, all with wood shingle siding and carefully designed landscaping, including semi-mature trees. The largest of the houses stood at the top of the hill where the flat-top tree should have been.

"What are you looking at?"

Mitch turned and saw Wendy peering closely at him. He opened his mouth to explain, but quickly changed his mind. Just last night she had seen him standing in front of a hotel door, clinging to the doorknob, frozen in some kind of trance. It must have been quite a sight. So now he was going to tell her that someone had built a bunch of houses where only a tree had stood less than twenty-four hours ago? Not a good idea. "Come on, let's get a better view," he said as nonchalantly as he could.

He led her on the cart trail up the hill, and when they reached the junction with the perpendicular trail, they turned left, skirting around the hill past smaller houses. These really were houses, not just little vacation cottages. They even had garages for golf carts. He walked fast now that they were on a more level trail, and more than once Wendy told him to slow down so she could keep up. He was anxious to get to the crest of the hill and see for himself if there was another hill somewhere on the island with a single tree, thereby proving to himself that he wasn't crazy, only mistaken.

They continued on the trail until it ended at a driveway. The driveway did an s-turn, up through the tall grass and wild bushes, ending in front of the big house at the very top of the hill. At the entrance to the driveway stood two posts topped by lanterns. On one of the posts, a small sign read "Private Property." Wendy said, "I don't think we're supposed to be going up there, Mitch."

"It's okay," Mitch said impatiently. "I just want to see something real quick then we'll go."

Wendy followed him up the crushed-shell driveway which crunched noisily under their feet. Mitch was sure the house's occupants heard them long before they got to the top. When they did reach the top, he stopped to observe the view. From there, as he suspected, the whole island was visible. If there was another hill on the island as high or higher, with a certain peculiar tree, he should be able to see it. But there wasn't any. He now stood on the tallest point of the island and it had no tree even remotely resembling the one he saw the day before. So that was that. The tree had been just another illusion.

"Okay, I saw what I wanted, we can go now." He managed a confident smile that said *don't worry, I'm not crazy, everything's cool.* He turned to go back down the driveway, and what he saw didn't surprise him at all. There were no signs of construction in the rear of the Smythe hotel. The addition he saw yesterday was not just framed out, but completely finished. And the color of the roof? Red, of course.

From a point partway down the driveway, he heard Wendy say, "What are you doing now? I thought we were leaving." And then a door opened somewhere behind him and a man's voice called out, "Can I help you?"

Mitch didn't even turn. He heard Wendy say, "I'm sorry. We thought we were still on the trail."

"There's a sign on the post, this is private property," came the man's response.

"We're leaving, sorry," Wendy said nervously, and then she was at Mitch's side, whispering, "Come on, Mitch, we have to go!"

She nudged his arm and he started down the driveway beside her, hearing the crunch of the shells, but not really aware of anything else. They were halfway down the driveway before he became conscious of anything besides that repetitive sound. And then they were at the posts at the bottom of the driveway, and he suddenly got an overwhelming urge to turn around. He half-expected to see a grassy field running up to the crest of the hill where his tree would be standing alone. But the hill was covered by the same houses.

"What's going on, Mitch?" Wendy asked.

He shook his head. "I'm feeling a little sick. Maybe we should head back."

Wendy agreed, and that's what they did.

CHAPTER THIRTEEN

Wendy pressed Mitch for an explanation only once after that, but he still wasn't ready to give her any answers. They made their way back to the hotel where he told her he would probably feel better in the air conditioning. There, they sipped Bloody Mary's in the lounge with about a dozen other patrons. Mitch had never been a Bloody Mary fan, but that morning he tossed back three of them.

Wendy left him after her first one, saying she wanted to get ready for the sitting. Mitch took this as a weak excuse since the sitting was hours away, but he didn't blame her for wanting to leave. He hadn't expressed a single coherent thought since they got back to the hotel, and he hardly paid attention to anything she said. He told himself he was just preoccupied; in reality, he was downright terrified that he was losing his mind. Up to that point, he had been able to explain away most of the odd things he had experienced on the island. The waking vision of the Boudreau suite, the dream of floating up to the moth on the ceiling—both he blamed on an overactive imagination, and in the case of the Boudreau suite, too much prior knowledge for his imagination to build on. But the more he thought about the hill and the flat-top tree, the less success he had explaining it. He knew he had taken the same exact trail the day before and there had been no houses on that hill. No structures of any kind. Not one. He would have remembered that. Especially a cluster of modern suburban-style houses, which looked so out of place on the island. He felt as if his personal reality had become amorphous, changing at will, and there was nothing he could do about it.

Then he thought: What if my walk with Wendy this morning was the unreality? What if I dreamed *that*? Maybe the tree *was* there, and the houses—even Wendy—had been a dream? Did it make any difference?

He was pondering these things over his fourth Bloody Mary when in walked Mr. Arndt, looking ridiculous in a turtleneck and sweater.

"Well, hello," Mitch said in a slightly boozy voice.

"Hello, yourself." Mr. Arndt leaned on his cane with both hands like a schoolmaster about to lecture his pupil.

"I've been looking for you," Mitch beat him to the punch.

"I've been looking for *you*."

"Good. It worked. See? We found each other."

"Actually, you found me an hour ago."

"Huh?"

"You walked right past my cottage with that nice-looking girl and you didn't even so much as say good morning. Were you worried I might move in on your dame?"

Mitch blinked and furrowed his brow. He hadn't seen Mr. Arndt when he and Wendy walked by the cottage. Maybe the old man just hadn't been on the porch. Maybe he had been somewhere else on the property, out of view. "Sorry. I didn't see you."

"Yeah, well, I'll forgive you but only because you had a good reason to be distracted. Nice looking gal."

"She is."

"Did you have breakfast?"

"Yes," Mitch admitted, feeling guilty like a kid who has spoiled his appetite.

"Well, I did too. Alone." He grinned and cocked an eyebrow. "I had no one to pay the tip."

Mitch gave a feeble smile, just to be polite.

"Feel like walking with me? That is, if you've had your fill of tomato juice." He nodded at the half-empty Bloody Mary in front of Mitch.

Mitch paid the tab and they left the hotel. Walking through the entrance doors, which a young girl with freckles and a Hollywood smile held for them, he regretted leaving. The sun was now at a good height and warming up all the humid air, making it steamy outside. He started sweating right away. Mr. Arndt, on the other hand, didn't seem to mind the heat at all. Despite his sweater, Mitch never saw a single drop of perspiration on him. Even as he struggled down the veranda steps, clutching the rail with one white-fisted hand and working his cane with the other, he stayed dry and cool-looking.

At the bottom of the steps he turned left and started across the grass in the direction of Lover's Lookout. Mitch followed, chatting about anything that came to mind: the weather, the condition of the hotel lawn, the species of a bird hovering overhead. Mr. Arndt didn't say a lot, just "Mm hmm," and "Yes," and "Could be." And then they were at the trail running past Lovers' Lookout, along the side of the west wing and out behind the hotel.

Mr. Arndt stopped for a moment on the trail, looking out at the waves crashing on the rocks off the south side of the island. "Let's walk a little ways. I haven't walked this trail in quite some time."

He seemed to pick up his pace a little now that they were off the grass, as though the hard surface of the trail was easier to shuffle on. They made a wide turn behind the southwest corner of the west wing, through some trees and down along the bluffs above the crashing surf. The trail then took them inland again, out behind the tennis courts and through thick blueberry bushes. It was slow going; even with his newfound energy Mr. Arndt's pace was excruciatingly slow. But they kept on steadily. Then they came to a little rise in the trail and Mr. Arndt stopped again.

"I'm tired," he announced. He looked northward and sighed. "Oh, to be young again." His gaze remained steady in that same northward direction, as though he were watching something. "There was a time when I'd just walk off this trail and cut across that hill, jogging most of the way."

Mitch finally followed his gaze to see what he was looking at. And there it was: the flat–top tree standing on the crest of a gentle hill near the middle of the island, about a quarter mile away.

While Mitch stared slack-jawed at the tree, Mr. Arndt started back in the direction from which they'd come. Mitch turned to watch him go, realizing as he did that this was the very reason Mr. Arndt had walked with him out this way. After the old man had disappeared around a bend in the trail behind some tall blueberry brambles, Mitch hurried off in the direction of the tree.

The hike up the hill wasn't easy but not because of the slope, which was even gentler from the south approach than the north. It was all the wild blueberry bushes and brush growing thick and tangled all over the hill that made it so difficult. Every now and then he would come upon a gull's nest tucked beside a bush, or a young gull or two wandering in the grass, and that was perhaps the biggest obstacle. Though the new gulls were well-grown that late in the season, in the eyes of their mothers they were still babies, and if he got too close he could count on an adult dive-bombing him out of nowhere.

Eventually, he stood at the summit of the hill under that familiar tree. He touched it and it felt real, rough bark scraping on the pads of his fingers, a piece of it falling away when he dug at it. He reached down and plucked some of the long grass growing under the tree, feeling it snap as it broke from its roots. The flying insects buzzed about in numbers he hadn't seen before on the island. The whole hill was alive with activity. And the air seemed cooler up here and less humid. In fact, a breeze kept the leaves rustling up in the tree—the first breeze Mitch had noticed since arriving on the island.

He sat against the tree trunk as he had yesterday and looked out over the expanse of Sumner Island to the Smythe hotel. Her roof was gray, not red. In the rear, an addition was going up. It was still mostly in its skeletal stages, framed-out, wide wood slats forming the outside wall structure most of the way up to the third floor. The day before, its roof had appeared only half-shingled; today, gray shingles covered the entire roof. This fact he found fascinating: he was actually seeing the progress being made on something that didn't really exist except in his own head—

Stop it, Mitch! Dammit, you can't keep saying that! It's not in your head. Somehow this is all real, as real as the houses on the hill in your own time. It's just not ... there all the time. It waits nearby for the right—what? Right time? Right circumstances? Right person?

He sniffed the air, smelling flowers and grass and the faint scent of the sea. No, there was just no way it could be his imagination, for all of his senses were informed in every detail. To confirm this, he ran his hand over the bare ground next to the tree, feeling its rough texture and the moist dirt gathering against his fingers. As he did, his little finger ran over something sharp which cut the flesh where the joint meets the palm.

"Ow!"

He jerked his hand back and looked at the ground. What appeared to be a bent rusty nail stuck out of the dirt. The cut wasn't long but deep enough to bleed pretty fast. A drop of blood fell on his sneaker and he held his hand away from his body to avoid bleeding all over himself. He reached into his front pocket with the other hand and pulled out a small wad of bills. Having nothing else to sponge up the blood, and meaning no disrespect to George

Washington, he wrapped the cut in one of the older, worn bills.

Somewhere in the distance he heard a hammer pounding. He focused on the back of the hotel again and saw two men perched on scaffolding. They wore long pants and white shirts, sleeves rolled up to the elbows. One of them was swinging a hammer while the other held the board in place for him.

Mitch stood and looked around the island. No question about it, he was at the high point and there was no cluster of new houses anywhere. He could see the twin waterfront houses off to his right. Mr. Arndt's house was there, too, though mostly obscured by trees.

He had seen enough. It was time to get back. He started in the direction of the harbor, and as he did, a thought occurred to him: what if this didn't end when he got back to the harbor area as it had the day before? That thought quickened his step.

But he needn't have worried because everything was back to normal as soon as he got through the last tree tunnel. When he arrived at Mr. Arndt's cottage, the old man was sitting in his chair on the porch, rocking slowly, a can of soda in one hand, his ever-present cane in the other. Mitch climbed up the porch steps, sat in the rocker beside him and was immediately handed a can of Moxie. He popped it open and chugged half the can with the hand he had cut. Except it wasn't cut any more. It wasn't even dirty.

He stared at Mr. Arndt. There were so many questions in his head, but for some reason he couldn't get his voice started. So he just sat there, staring at him like an idiot, rocking slowly and deliberately without saying a word. They went on like this for a good while. Then, without breaking his rhythm, Mr. Arndt glanced down at Mitch's feet and said, "You cut yourself."

Mitch looked down at his left sneaker. On the tongue, just above the laces, a splotch of dried blood spread out in a star pattern.

PART II

CHAPTER FOURTEEN

When he was seven, Mitch's grandfather took him to a magic show. The show was really geared toward adults more than kids; the tricks were sophisticated, and some were even a little scary. One trick involved a pretty lady in a French-cut leotard who stood inside a black box while swords were thrust through the sides and front. Mitch sat in the audience, transfixed with horror, as the magician shish-kabobed this pretty lady who inexplicably smiled throughout the ordeal. He was amazed when she eventually stepped out of the box without a scratch. After the show he demanded that his grandfather tell him how the magician did it. He had to know, and he had to know right now. Gramps, of course, knew that the lady was somehow tucked inside the box out of harm's way, or that the blades were made to look like they passed through the box when they really didn't. But he didn't want to spoil Mitch's fun, so he just answered, "Magic, Mitchell. Magic."

Mitch was left to ponder the mysteries of physical impossibilities all the rest of that day and long into the night. He lay in bed replaying the sword trick in his head over and over again, seeing the lady's grinning head through a door at the top of the box while the magician slid shiny blades through her midsection. He never did figure out how it was done. Even now, well into his adult years, he mulled the secret of the trick from time to time. He knew he could probably find the answer somewhere on the internet, but he never bothered looking. Pondering the mystery had become more fun than knowing the answer.

That day out on Sumner Island, after his second trip to the top of Lone Tree Hill, Mitch found himself in an eerie state of *quasi-deja vu*. The circumstances may have been different, but the feeling it gave him was the same he'd had when he was seven. Playing the role of Gramps was Mr. Arndt who, you might say, didn't want to "spoil the trick." The old man had known what Mitch would see when he took him on the south trail behind the hotel; the only question was whether he saw it himself. Yet in his shell-shocked state Mitch couldn't quite find the courage to ask him. He fumbled around for a while, hinting and dropping clues, but Mr. Arndt cunningly evaded the subject every time. He was Gramps all over again, and Mitch was seven years old and would have to learn in his own time if it was all an illusion or if the lady really got skewered.

Without any answers from Mr. Arndt, Mitch was left with two clues that seemingly cancelled out one another: a drop of blood on his sneaker and a hand without a cut. Being too old and wise to accept that things you can't explain are "magic," but realizing he was dangerously close to hysteria, Mitch decided he needed to talk with someone who might understand this. He went looking for Horace Leeds.

The desk attendant said he had seen Leeds walking down to the beach with snorkel gear, so that's where Mitch headed. When he got there Leeds was just coming out of the water, mask over his eyes, flippers flopping about. The beach was crowded, and Leeds had to snake his way through the throngs to get up to dry sand. By the time he reached Mitch he had removed the flippers and mask and carried them in one hand. In the other he held a mesh bag with a live lobster inside, which he lifted up for Mitch's inspection. "What do you think, is it legal?"

Mitch frowned at the creature. "Looks a little small to me." He really had no idea what the legal minimum size for a lobster was, but he felt sorry for it.

They walked down to the water where some little kids watched Leeds free the lobster beside some rocks.

"You look hot, my friend," Leeds told Mitch. "Lose the shoes and shirt and come swimming."

He didn't have to ask twice. In a second, Mitch had stripped down to his shorts and waded into the water beside him. It was damned cold. Though he had been swimming at New England beaches most of his life, he had never gotten used to the icy Atlantic. On the other hand, it was refreshing on such a hot day if you didn't mind your feet cramping and your loins burrowing up into your torso.

They stood there in chest-deep water, talking about boats and baseball while the sun burned their necks and Leeds' bald head. The conversation flowed easily, which surprised Mitch. He had pegged Leeds for a stuffed-shirt whose only passion outside of ghosts might be Masterpiece Theater. But he actually had a lot of interests, chief among them women. Younger women. Despite being a lifelong bachelor, by no means was he some cloistered monk. All the while he and Mitch stood in the water chatting, Leeds' eyes wandered about, observing the "talent." Every now and then he said something like, "Ten o'clock, green two-piece, in front of the blue umbrella," and Mitch would look and see the young woman Leeds wanted him to check out. Mitch always agreed with Leeds' assessment, even though he was in no mood for this game.

But he played along to make Leeds happy, and all of their idle chat and girl watching loosened both of them up to the point where Mitch finally felt comfortable telling Leeds about his experience with Lone Tree Hill. He described all three of his hikes—the one the day before and the two that morning—and ended with a description of Mr. Arndt's peculiar behavior on his last trip out to the hill. Leeds stopped his talent search shortly after Mitch started into his story, directing all his attention to him. When Mitch mentioned Mr. Arndt, something flickered in Leeds' eyes. For the second time in two days, Mitch was left with the impression that Horace Leeds and Theodore Arndt were somehow acquainted.

He finished his story and fell silent, waiting for Leeds' reaction. Leeds just kept nodding and looking in the direction of the hotel. After a moment, he sat on his haunches so that he was submerged over his head. When he came back up, he looked straight at Mitch and said, "That book you wrote about the Boudreau family . . . "

"Yes?"

"When you were doing your research, did you get some history of development on the island? I mean real estate development. Something about what the island looked like in the past compared to now."

Mitch thought about this. "No, I don't think I did. Other than the Smythe hotel and its grounds."

Leeds nodded. "You know it wasn't a dream or heat stroke, don't you?"

"Then what?"

Leeds held up an index finger, indicating "wait a minute," then dunked under the water again. He crouched at the bottom for a good half-minute then surfaced, shaking the water off his face.

"Come on," he said. "I've had enough sun and surf for one day."

They retrieved his snorkel gear and went up the steps past the snack bar and bathhouse to the trail. Mitch wanted to stay cool as long as he could so he didn't bother drying off, letting the cold water gradually dry on his skin.

Leeds led the way down the trail to the dock. They walked all the way out to the end before stopping.

"Look." Leeds pointed past the swimming beaches to the middle of the island. "Is that the hill?"

Mitch looked at the hill, clearly the highest one on the island. It was covered with houses. He started to say "I think so," but before he could, a voice in his head said, *You know so.*

Leeds answered for him. "Of course it is." He gave Mitch a stern gaze then put his hands on his hips and stared back at the hill. "I've seen this a few times before. Let me tell you about one of them.

"There's this old tavern—the Heath Tavern—in New York. It was built in the early eighteenth century, and during the Revolutionary War it was a favorite spot for Hessian soldiers. About thirty years ago, I got a call from the caretaker. It was still being used as a function hall, and the caretaker had just been hired to manage the place. Within a week of coming on the job, something happened that made her call me. It seems she'd come to work on a holiday when the place was closed, thinking she'd get caught up on some paperwork. She walked in the front door and immediately noticed the place smelled peculiar. There was a scent of fresh tobacco smoke, yet smoking hadn't been allowed in the building for years. The next thing she noticed shocked the be-jazzis out of her: the door to her office was missing. It should have been there to the left just inside the foyer, next to the stairwell going up to the second floor. But all she saw was a wall with a mirror. Later, we found out her office was in a part of the building that was added on just before the Civil War.

"So there she was, trying to figure out all this weirdness, when she noticed some noise coming from the original section of the building to the right. There were two doors and a small hallway separating the main dining room from the foyer, and both were closed. As soon as she opened the first one, the noises became louder. When she opened the second one, she now had a view of the dining room. Only it wasn't the dining room she was used to seeing. The room was filled with men in old uniforms—blue jackets, long white pants, vests with lots of buttons—all sitting around old tavern tables, smoking pipes and drinking from tall mugs. Their dress was clearly colonial-era military, and so were their hairstyles and the muskets that stood in some of the corners. There was a fire in the hearth and a big kettle of some kind of stew boiling over the fire. But the hearth hadn't been used in decades.

"At first she thought some local historical society had hired out the tavern for a Revolutionary War reenactment. But then a woman in a white duster cap, long skirts, apron—the works—passed right by without so much as a glance, and set down some mugs and a plate of bread and some sort of fruit mash. One of the soldiers spoke to her in a heavy accent, and she told them what they owed in British currency. Now the manager knew something was really wrong. She started to approach the waitress, thinking she'd ask what's going on, and the whole scene faded away to nothing, just like a scene fades in a movie. The hearth was empty, the people were gone, even the tables were gone. The smoke smell was gone, too.

"She called me on the suggestion of a friend of hers, and Phyllis and I agreed to investigate. Phyllis had no idea where we were going—just somewhere in the Hudson Valley to do a reading. The tavern had no signs in front, but it was obviously very old so Phyllis's only clue was that she was dealing with something possibly dating back to the colonial era. Anyway, the manager sees us pull up, comes out and greets us. Phyllis shakes her hand and immediately senses something about the woman. She knew right away this woman had the gift. But the woman didn't even know it—she just thought she was going crazy. Until Phyllis looked up at a second story window and told her she saw a soldier dressed in a blue coat and pointy brass helmet looking down at them.

"Phyllis didn't have the same experience this woman had in the tavern, but she picked up enough information to describe the building's original use and its original customers."

He stopped and held Mitch's gaze. "I think what you experienced was something I call passing behind the time curtain. It's pretty common, actually. Documented for centuries."

"So you don't think I'm imagining all of this." Mitch said. "I mean maybe I'm just caught up in all the hype over this ghost hunt."

"Actually, it's precisely because it happened to you on this particular weekend that I think it's real."

Mitch stared blankly at him, waiting for an explanation, but he didn't get one. Instead, Leeds said, "Dr. Lambert, would you like to join our sitting tonight? Mr. Arndt, it seems, has declined and he suggested you as an alternative. Personally, I think you might be an asset."

CHAPTER FIFTEEN

They parted ways and Mitch watched Leeds head toward the hotel, towel draped over his shoulders, flippers and mask in hand, looking every bit the shameless tourist interested in only sun and fun. But Mitch knew better. Just being in the man's presence, he had sensed the depth of his experience with things beyond the scope of what most three-dimension dwellers understand or even know to exist. But not just that. Leeds quite definitely was holding something back. He knew something about the island, or the Smythe, or Maria and Roger, and he wasn't telling.

In researching Horace Leeds and Phyllis Church before that weekend, one of the things Mitch had been most struck by was their innate skepticism. Contrary to what one might think, the two approached every case of possible paranormal activity with great caution. Each subject was treated as guilty until proven innocent. Leeds' approach to every case over the past forty years had been to first rule out a hoax then search for a natural explanation. Only after ruling out these possibilities would he consider paranormal explanations. In fact, Leeds once estimated that three-quarters of the cases he had investigated over the years proved to be duds. It was the other quarter he could point to as true evidence of incarnate existence beyond this world.

Yet just now he had accepted Mitch's story about Lone Tree Hill without question. This seemed out of character, and could only mean one of two things: he was humoring Mitch, trying to brush him off because he was too busy dealing with the Boudreau case, or he had other reasons to believe Mitch's story involved the paranormal. Something told Mitch it was the latter. Leeds knew something Mitch didn't know. And he wanted Mitch at the sitting that night.

Mitch watched Leeds bound up the veranda steps. After he had disappeared inside the front doors, Mitch turned his eyes to the round porthole window in the center tower. He didn't know what drew his attention to it, except that he had looked up that way a lot since arriving on the island. He thought about the room up there, the little haven Maria had created for herself. It had been her favorite room in the world, and her father had owned many rooms in several houses and apartments. From up there, Maria had commanded a view of the open ocean to the south and the harbor to the north. Whenever she was there, she would have been able to see her father's sailing yacht, the *Tasha,* moored in the harbor.

As he gazed up at that window, a shadow flashed across the wall inside the tower. He had been trudging casually along the trail above the swimming beaches, glancing up at the window every once in a while as he went. Now he stopped and turned to face the hotel—

—and saw another flash of shadow.

The white lace curtain that usually hung in the window either had been taken down or pulled aside because the view through the window was entirely clear. What he had seen was a distorted shadow in the elongated shape of an upper body and head spread across the wall nearest the left side of the window. He took a couple of steps onto the lawn in the direction of the veranda. The grass had been cut sometime that morning, leaving an up-and-down-and-across pattern that reminded him of a huge chessboard. This made him think of Alice and the Mad Hatter and the white rabbit. Just like Alice, he was starting to feel as though he'd fallen out of the real world and into some fantastical tale. Why, just in front of him stood a hotel with a penthouse suite that was never opened to the public, but left as a shrine to people who died over eighty years ago. And when you went for a walk outside the resort limits you sometimes—but not always—crossed a time zone. But you didn't lose just an hour. You lost decades.

And now he was walking in the direction of that empty shrine, tucked beneath a brooding tower with a Cyclops eye for a window … and inside that tower a phantom lurked—

Stop it, Mitch! Just stop!

He managed to push the thought away, but didn't stop moving. He was already halfway across the lawn to the hotel, barely aware of people moving around nearby. People in bathing suits, carrying towels and beach bags and umbrellas on their way to or from the beach. All completely unaware. Not the least bit conscious that they had all fallen down the rabbit hole together—

There again!

It *was* a man. This time he had seen him standing at the window. Not a shadow, but the real thing. A man in a white shirt. He couldn't make out much else because the figure had only remained at the window for a fraction of a second, just long enough to peek out.

At me!

The man had seen Mitch staring up at him, he would swear it. And as their eyes had connected for that brief moment, Mitch sensed the man had wanted to be seen.

He wants me to know he's there.

Mitch took off at a sprint toward the veranda steps, leaped up them three at a time and pushed his way through the front doors before the doorman had a chance to open them. Inside, he hurried up to the front desk and interrupted a clerk who was helping another guest.

"Is someone in the Boudreau suite right now?" he gasped.

The clerk, a middle-aged woman with a tight bun, looked taken aback at first, but she recovered quickly. "That suite is not in use."

"No, no, I know that. Is someone cleaning or fixing something in there?"

The clerk glanced quickly over Mitch's shoulder, then met his gaze again. She said, calmly, "Housekeeping goes in every two weeks, but I don't believe this is their week."

"Could someone else be in there for some other—"

"Can I help you?"

The question came from behind him. He turned and saw a hotel guard dressed in a navy blazer and khaki pants. A security badge hung off the breast pocket of his blazer, and he carried a two-way radio in his hand.

"Yes, you can. I think I saw someone up in the Boudreau suite. A man. In the tower window."

The guard was silent for a second or two. Then he asked, "What's your name, sir?"

Mitch gave his name. The guard glanced at the desk clerk then back at Mitch. "Come with me, sir."

They took the elevator to the third floor. On the way up, Mitch explained who he was and how he knew the tower was part of the Boudreau suite. The guard stayed quiet the whole time.

On the third floor, Mitch wanted to run down the corridor to the front door of the apartment, but his companion sauntered along, in no hurry. They arrived at the entrance door and the guard took a card-key out of the side pocket of his blazer. He took his time swiping the card in the electronic reader while Mitch sweated and wished he would hurry up. It wasn't until the guard turned the doorknob that it occurred to Mitch that he might not let him in for fear he was a thief, or that there really was a burglar and he might get hurt. But he just swung the door open and casually stepped over the threshold without a word. Mitch followed.

They walked into a small foyer and took the steps to the right, the same way Mitch had in his vision the day before. At the top of the steps the sitting area spread out before them, also looking a lot like it had in Mitch's vision. But not exactly. The wallpaper was similar in color, but the pattern was not quite the same. Some of the furniture looked a little different too, although you really had to look hard to notice. What was really striking, though, was what was not there: the candlestick phone and the fresh flowers. But that made perfect sense. His mind could not have recreated the interior exactly as it looked in the modern day since the only pictures he had ever seen were pre-1924 ones. The candlestick phone his mind had put there because such a phone would have been common in that period. As for the flowers, well, there must have been a reason his mind placed those there, too. Whatever it was, this was the reconstructed version of the apartment, the apartment as it looked after the burned portions were torn out and rebuilt and some of the furnishings replaced. Working antique phones and fresh flowers certainly did not belong in this room, which remained perpetually vacant.

Yet, knowing part of what was in this room had been there when Maria was alive, Mitch was thrilled to think where he now stood. For a brief moment he forgot why he was there, until he saw the security guard starting up the circular staircase to the tower room. He hurried to follow him up. Once again the guard took his sweet time, making Mitch want to push him off the steps and sprint the rest of the way up. They reached the top and looked around the small room. Nobody was there. Only a long couch and one overstuffed chair stood in the room.

"No one here," the guard said in an I-told-you-so tone.

"The bathroom, the bedrooms, we didn't check there."

The guard gave Mitch a look and brushed past him down the stairs. Mitch followed him down to a short hall leading to three small bedrooms and two bathrooms, all with few furnishings and no decorations or windows. They poked through all of them, but found no one.

Back in the living room, the guard said, "Are you satisfied, Dr. Lambert?"

Mitch shrugged. What could he say? Whoever had been in the tower had gone out before them—or hadn't really been there at all. He had to admit it seemed the latter, considering the apartment had been locked when they arrived. "I'm sorry," he said, "but I really thought I saw someone."

"Maybe the sun reflecting off the window. No harm done. I appreciate you alerting us, just in case." He looked around at the sitting area and out the big rectangular window. "I don't know who would want to come in here, anyway. Nothing all that valuable to steal. Unless you were some Boudreau fanatic. There are some Boudreau nuts out there, you know. Just like Elvis nuts."

That last comment stung a bit, but Mitch kept quiet.

"Well, tour's over. Let's go"

He led the way down the steps to the foyer. Mitch descended one step then stopped and looked back at the spiral staircase. It looked exactly as it had in his vision the day before: wrought iron *fleur de lis* balusters painted black, rising up to a brass handrail—

—But he had never seen a photo of those stairs.

"Can you give me just a second?"

Before the guard could answer, he went to the staircase and stood at the bottom, running his hand along the handrail and down one of the balusters while looking up into the tower room. *Well, I could have surmised that a spiral staircase was used to reach the tower room.* But there was no way—just no way at all—that he could have known the stairway would have a brass handrail, black iron steps, and those exact *fleur de lis* balusters.

"Time to go," the guard said behind him.

Mitch turned. The guard stood close by, looking at him a little suspiciously, probably thinking he had made up the story about the man in the apartment just to get a look inside.

"How long has this staircase been here?"

The guard shrugged. "Far as I know, since the apartment was put in by the original owners."

"What about the fire?"

"Well, you can see it's made of iron. I'm sure it survived the fire."

He was probably right. Mitch made a mental note to double-check this. He ran his fingers over the handrail once more and turned back to the guard. "Why do they keep this apartment closed off from everyone? Don't you think that's a little strange?"

The guard made a noise in his throat, which Mitch took to signify agreement. "Maybe out of respect for the Boudreaus. Maybe superstition."

"Superstition?"

"Could be. A terrible murder took place here. Maybe they don't want to put guests up in a suite like that. Bad karma or something."

Mitch nodded. "Maybe."

The guard motioned toward the foyer with his two-way radio: time to go. They left the apartment and the guard radioed someone at the security office somewhere in the hotel and reported that everything was clear. Then he and Mitch took the elevator to the first floor.

Mitch introduced himself to the concierge at a desk in the corner of the lobby. He asked about the staircase and was told it was the original, which had been repainted and re-bolted and put back in its original spot. Mitch then asked if he might rent the apartment, and what would it cost, and received a curt answer: The Boudreau suite is never rented out.

"Why not?"

The concierge gave a muted smirk. "You would have to ask the Hodgsons."

"You mean the Hodgsons who owned the hotel in the 'thirties? Aren't they dead?"

The concierge went on smirking. "Yes, sir."

"So it was their idea to close it off?"

"I don't know if it was their idea, but they're the ones who renovated it and closed it off."

"Would you agree it's a little weird?"

"No, sir." The concierge shifted in his seat.

"You could get an awful lot of money renting that apartment out as the Admiral Suite or the Commodore Suite or something."

"You can also profit handsomely by *not* renting a room where a well-loved man and his daughter met their end." The concierge measured his words carefully. "It's about respect, and it engenders goodwill with the guests when they see that we care."

The concierge stared Mitch down until he finally had to turn away, feeling small and petty. How could he argue with that? He thanked the man and went on his way.

While crossing the lawn to his cabin, Mitch concluded that there definitely was more to the closed-off Boudreau suite than he was being told. Turning this thought over in his mind, a sudden urge made him look up at the middle tower. He knew what he would see even before he looked. In the big round window, leaning against the frame, the dark man in the white shirt stared out across the lawn. Something in the harbor seemed to have caught his interest.

Mitch looked that way, too, but saw nothing unusual. When he turned back, the man was gone.

CHAPTER SIXTEEN

That evening, even after the sun had dipped behind the mainland, the mercury was still climbing. Earlier, the big dial thermometer nailed to Mr. Arndt's porch had read ninety-six degrees. When Mitch left his cabin for the hotel just before nine, the needle pointed at ninety-eight.

After spending much of the afternoon sweating in his little room, he hoped to feel a breeze off the water, but there just wasn't any. The only place to get any relief was inside the hotel, and he hurried in that direction in a short-sleeve shirt, light chinos, and topsiders with no socks.

The sitting was set to take place in the Pink Parlor, and he knew just where to find it. After the center tower, the Pink Parlor was the most famous room in the hotel. A relatively small room compared to the other function rooms, it was also one of the most out-of-the-way, tucked in a corner of the easternmost end of the wing. Victorian-era women had once gathered there to crochet and gossip and even smoke out of view of their husbands and children. Its name derived from the pink patterned wallpaper and all the variations of red—dusty rose, maroon, and of course, salmon—found in the carpet and most of the furnishings. Remarkably, the room was almost the same as a hundred years ago, down to the original floor lamps and chandeliers, all rewired to meet twenty-first century standards. Overstuffed chairs and elegant settees—most of them original to the room, reupholstered from time to time in their original colors and patterns—stood among occasional tables and ornate planters. A huge oval table, polished to a mirror–like sheen, dominated the center.

People had already begun gathering in the room by the time Mitch arrived.

He recognized a couple of reporters from the press conference. On the side of the room farthest from the doors, the camera guy was busy setting up his equipment. He had extended his tripod high, with the video camera on top pointed at the corner where an armchair stood beside a brass floor lamp with a crystal-beaded shade. A dozen folding chairs stood in a neat semicircle facing the armchair, with one more folding chair next to it at an angle.

Mitch didn't know anyone in the room, so he bided his time wandering around examining paintings. A jumble of landscapes, marine-scapes and portraits of people once important to the Smythe Resort graced every wall. One particular painting near the entrance door caught Mitch's eye: a portrait of a peasant girl in a blue dress with a white bandana over her long brown hair. She stood on a rural road beside a fence, and carried on her back some sort of cloth bag filled to the top with a red vegetable, maybe radishes. The scenery and the girl were simple and pretty, and the painting gave off a feeling of wellbeing when you glanced at it casually. But when you looked closer, as Mitch now did, the mood quickly turned to a disturbing sense of danger. Off in the distance, on a portion of the same road on which the girl stood, half a dozen soldiers with rifles could be seen poking and taunting a bound man. Mitch had never seen such a contrast of moods in one picture.

As he puzzled over what the artist might be trying to convey, in walked Wendy through the open doorway accompanied by Horace Leeds and Phyllis Church. Leeds and Wendy were engaged in an intense conversation, complete with excited gesticulations and exaggerated facial expressions. Mitch recalled Leeds checking out the babes on the beach, and felt a twinge of jealousy. Then he remembered Leeds had mentored Wendy at Longfellow College, and he tried to convince himself that any attraction to her was merely intellectual. It didn't work, of course.

He turned to face them, and Wendy gave a quick little wave. In her usual cheerful way, she said, "Hey stranger, I hear you're our guest of honor."

Leeds smiled and stuck out his hand at Mitch. "Glad to have you aboard."

Mitch shook, but his feelings toward the man were not all good at the moment, and not just on account of jealousy. He was wondering if Leeds told Wendy *why* he was the guest of honor. Specifically, had he blabbed about what Mitch told him down at the swimming beach that afternoon. "I'm looking forward to it," Mitch said to him with as much enthusiasm as he could muster. "Very much," he nodded at Mrs. Church.

"I have a good feeling," Mrs. Church said.

They made their way to the rear corner where Leeds and a hotel employee helped Mrs. Church out of her wheelchair into the armchair. She shifted and made herself comfortable as Leeds plunked himself on the folding chair next to her. The rest of the crowd, other than the cameraman, filled the seats arranged around Mrs. Church's chair. Mitch sat in the second seat from the right, with Wendy and Dorothy Poulin on either side of him.

The hotel staff now left the room and closed the doors behind them. Before they did, Mitch caught a glimpse of a dozen or so hotel guests hovering around in the corridor outside trying to see what was going on. Everyone in the hotel must have been talking about this evening's event; it had certainly been advertised enough. He wondered if all those curiosity seekers lurking about the halls might somehow send interfering vibes that could jam up Mrs. Church's mental antenna.

Leeds pointed at the cameraman who went over to a light dimmer on the wall and turned down the chandelier. Now the room was lit dully, but not so dull that Mitch couldn't see the people around him. Everyone was focused on Mrs. Church whose hefty body had sunk deeply into her chair, and whose head rested against the top of the backrest, tilted to one side, her eyes closed. Leeds spoke to her in low tones that Mitch couldn't make out. He leaned over and whispered to Wendy, "What's going on? What's he saying?"

Wendy whispered in his ear, "She's going into a trance. Shush!"

Leeds continued speaking to Mrs. Church in his low voice for several moments. Then he turned and said, just loud enough for everyone to hear, "Phyllis is now in a trance but she can hear my commands." A couple of book lights came on around the semicircle of chairs, and reporters began scribbling notes.

Mrs. Church made a half-groan, half-whine in her throat and tossed her head over to the other shoulder. Leeds turned back to her. "Is someone with you, Phyllis?"

"Hello, friend," a voice answered.

The words seemed to come from Mrs. Church, but the voice was unmistakably male. The accent was thick, maybe Scottish or Irish.

"Is that Seamus?" Leeds asked out loud.

"Aye," the male voice answered.

It was definitely not Mrs. Church faking a brogue. The voice was too strong, too deep for Mrs. Church to fake. Yet the idea that a spirit was speaking through her in its own voice struck Mitch as a cheap parlor trick. Instinctively, he glanced around the room for an extra person hiding behind something, or maybe a speaker that had been set up when nobody was paying attention.

"Seamus, Phyllis and I are here with friends," Leeds said.

"I see and I approve," Seamus replied. Mitch had to admit the voice didn't sound like it was coming out of a microphone. If it was, then Phyllis's lip-synch was perfect. "There are more here who would like to join us," Seamus added.

"Tell them we would be delighted to have them," Leeds said.

As if on cue, Mrs. Church straightened her back and lifted her head attentively, but her eyes remained closed. A new voice came out of her mouth, a different male voice, higher-pitched with a different accent. American. Possibly New England. It said, "You aren't supposed to be here."

"Who says? Who are you?" Leeds asked.

"The parlor is reserved for Mrs. Frye. You can't be here."

"Who is speaking? What is your name?" Leeds demanded.

"I'm Nick Barber, sir, and I'm setting up for Mrs. Frye's tea. I have to ask you to leave. Mrs. Frye will be terribly sore with me." The boyish voice was almost pleading.

Leeds leaned a little closer to Mrs. Church. "Mrs. Frye will not be sore with you, Nick Barber," he said, gently. "My name is Horace Leeds. I'm a friend, and Mrs. Frye doesn't mind me being here. Nick, are you confused about why my friends and I are here?"

"No one is supposed to be in here. Mrs. Frye will be upset if the room isn't ready by three."

"Nick, Mrs. Frye will not be needing this room today," Leeds said slowly. "Nick, do you know what year this is?"

"Sir, I don't know why you're talking this way. I've been ordered to prepare the Parlor for Mrs. Frye and her group, but you won't leave. Now you insult me by asking if I know the year."

"I assure you, I don't mean any insult. Please tell me the date. If we're not supposed to be here, we will go."

"It's June 29, sir. Mrs. Frye has reserved the Parlor for tea at three. I have to get to work."

"What *year* is it?"

There was a short pause then the voice, sounding rather cross, said, "Why would you ask such a thing—it's 1938, of course."

Leeds looked at the floor between his shoes, thinking. He lifted his head again and said, "Nick, Mrs. Frye is not having tea today. Her tea date was seventy years ago. Nick, you have passed on but your spirit has stayed here for some reason. Do you remember anything about that?"

Mrs. Church sat very still, eyes closed, mouth hanging open. For a few moments the room was perfectly silent. Even the reporters had stopped writing. Mitch thought Nick Barber had gone, but then Mrs. Church's mouth began to move, and a few seconds later the voice of Nick Barber came through again. He said, softly, "It was the fall," in a tone that could have been a comment or a question.

Leeds said, "Yes, Nick, it was the fall. But you didn't know it. Now you do. I want to help you now. You have performed your duties for the Smythe hotel exceptionally, but now it's time to be with your family and friends on the other side. Do you understand, Nick?"

There was a pause during which Mrs. Church's mouth worked again. Mitch found himself feeling sad for this Nick Barber who couldn't find his way. He hoped he would now.

Everyone waited in silence. Finally, Leeds said, "Nick, do you understand what I've told you?"

Another short silence, then out of Mrs. Church's mouth came the words, "Lucy is here. She says I should trust you."

"She's right, Nick. You should follow Lucy. Go with Lucy." Leeds was now excited, his voice rising in triumph. "Go with Lucy. Our prayers are with you."

Mrs. Church heaved a long sigh then fell silent again. Her eyes stayed closed.

Nick was gone to wherever he was supposed to be. Lucy had helped Nick do this, whoever Lucy was. A sister? A friend? Or were Lucy and Nick just figments of Phyllis's imagination coming through as voices? Then again, Mitch had to go back to his original question: How could Mrs. Church perform such voices even if it was just her imagination?

And now another voice completely unlike Mrs. Church's own voice was coming from her mouth. This time it was a woman speaking in French.

"Monsieur, pardonnez moi, mais je suis à la recherche pour ma fille."

"Comment vous appelez votre fille?" Leeds asked in an impressive French accent. "Do you speak English?"

"What are they saying?" Mitch asked Wendy. Wendy shushed him and whispered, "I don't know."

"Oui, but not very well. Her name is Adele."

"That is very pretty—très jolie," Leeds said, and in his voice Mitch heard something he hadn't heard from Leeds before: pity. No longer was he all business. The famous ghost hunter, who had tracked every kind of spirit and poltergeist throughout the world, who had devoted his life to raising parapsychology to a mainstream science, felt sorry for this poor spirit who couldn't find her child. A child that, for all he knew, had already died of old age.

"Merci, yes, she is pretty!" the woman said with pride. "She is nine. I cannot find her."

"What is today?" Leeds asked.

"Today?"

"Aujourd'hui."

"Mm, oui, it is Saturday."

For a second Mitch thought the woman was aware of the earthly time in which the living guests in this room existed. Today was, indeed, Saturday.

"What year is it?" Leeds asked.

"Nineteen ninety-five."

So he was wrong. The woman had been dead a little over a decade. Her daughter would be in college now. Mitch watched and waited, wondering how Leeds would handle this one. He was quietly thoughtful for a moment or two. Then he did something that surprised Mitch. He called Seamus again.

"Seamus, I need your help. This unfortunate woman you've brought to me is looking for her daughter. Her daughter would be a young woman now. Can you please explain to her? My French isn't good enough."

Seamus spoke up immediately. "Aye. She is telling me she was staying at the hotel. Her daughter wandered off. She couldn't find her for a full day. I'm getting the impression this lady, in her anguish, had a heart attack. She doesn't know it and she doesn't know what happened to Adele."

"Can you call on anyone she knows who passed before her? I dread the thought, but did Adele pass that day?"

"She did not," Seamus answered.

"Can you explain to her mother what happened? Can you help her cross over?"

"Aye," Seamus said. "But she wants to see her daughter first. I'll arrange it."

"Thank you, Seamus," There was genuine relief in Leeds' voice. "But before you do, I have other business I'd like you to help me with if you would be so kind."

"I will do what I can, yes," Seamus said.

"I wish to make contact with three people who died in this hotel in 1924. I am speaking of Maria Boudreau, her father Roger, and their friend Harold Fenton."

It seemed up to now Leeds had been coming up with only the fish that were biting. Now he had decided to ask the captain to take him straight to the fish he wanted. For this, Mitch was grateful. Not that he wasn't sympathetic to the plight of other spirits. He just had reached the end of his patience, having waited all afternoon for the main event. All he had of Maria were a grainy five-second silent film and a lot of black and white photos. He didn't even know what her voice sounded like because it had never been recorded and none of her contemporaries had ever described it in print. In Mitch's mind, Maria remained incomplete because he couldn't put a voice to her. In other ways, too, he'd been denied a complete picture of her: her handshake, her laugh, her cry, how she chewed her food, how her dimples formed when she smiled.

As they waited in silence for Seamus to speak again, Mitch closed his eyes and concentrated on Maria's face as it appeared in the painting in the lobby. In his head he chanted, "Maria, please come to us," over and over. No longer did he look around the room for signs of tricks. Skeptical or not, this was his once-in-a-lifetime chance to make contact with Maria, and he had to give it every effort.

A noise came from the corner of the room. Mitch opened his eyes and saw Mrs. Church shifting uncomfortably in her chair and making a low groaning sound. She opened her mouth wide like a vampire about to strike. Suddenly, out of her throat came a noise Mitch was sure he would never forget if he lived to be a hundred: a low, guttural sound like the warning growl of a cornered jungle cat. Slowly but steadily it rose in pitch to a more human level, then words began to form in a male voice.

"Go away!" the voice shouted.

Leeds wasn't deterred. "We have no such intention. We merely wish to speak with either of the Boudreaus or with Mr. Fenton. Do you know them?" His voice was measured, each word spoken clearly and a little louder than usual.

Mrs. Church's mouth opened wide and she leaned forward as though to vomit. But what came out was a loud and long bellow, like the protest of a large, wounded animal. She jerked back in her chair and her jaws came together again in a grimace. "This is not your place, this is not your business," her voice said between clenched teeth.

In the semi-darkness, Mitch could see concern in Leeds' face. Yet he pressed on, leading Mitch to believe his concern was for Mrs. Church and not out of fear of this spirit. "What is your name?" Leeds demanded.

"That doesn't concern you," the voice answered. There was a brief pause, then the voice added, "Don't interfere."

"We're not here to interfere with anything," Leeds insisted in a calm, but firm voice. "The spirits we seek left our carnate world many years ago. We only want a word with them."

At that, Phyllis's body jerked forward again and out came another great bellow, only this time it was a bellow of words: "Then why do you bring *him* here?"

Leeds hesitated, seemingly unsure how to respond. He quickly regained his confident demeanor and said, "It's not your place to be the gatekeeper. Please move on and let us continue with our—"

A loud roar, more like the screech of big machinery than anything produced by a living thing, came out of Mrs. Church. It caused the floor to vibrate and the crystals on the chandelier to clink together.

Off to his right, about a dozen feet behind Wendy, Mitch caught movement out of the corner of his eye. When he looked that way he saw what appeared to be faint white smoke hovering over the floor. His first thought was that the room had somehow caught fire, yet he couldn't see flames anywhere.

He started to stand up, but Wendy grabbed his arm and sat him back down.

"Look!" he whispered out loud, pointing at the hovering smoke.

Wendy looked in that direction then back at him. "I don't see anything. Pay attention to Horace."

But Mitch kept focused on the spot behind Wendy. The loose smoke or mist or whatever it was had pulled together, forming a column that rose toward the ceiling, and now there were what looked like tiny firefly lights blinking within the column. He couldn't believe Wendy didn't see it. He tapped her on the forearm again, but she just shushed him and kept her gaze on Leeds.

Mitch looked back at Phyllis Church, and what he saw nearly made him leap to his feet again, this time to come to her aid. She had sunk back in her chair and her eyes were closed but her mouth hung wide open. She worked her mouth like a fish out of water, gasping, making wheezing sounds as if her breath was being cut off. Leeds had pulled his chair closer to her and was saying something in a low, absurdly calm voice.

A moment later, Leeds motioned to someone standing by the door who opened it, letting in light. The cameraman turned the dimmer up and the chandelier glowed brightly. Mitch glanced behind Wendy and saw that the mist was completely gone as if it had never been there.

Over in the corner, Phyllis Church leaned forward in her chair, breathing deeply. Her face was pale. Everyone had gathered around her, and Mitch heard Leeds telling them she would "be all right," "not to worry," and so on.

All at once Mitch felt nauseous. The room kind of teeter-tottered back and forth. Although the air conditioning was icy cold, he felt beads of sweat forming on his forehead and his hands were aflame, too. His knees had gone weak, and the rest of him was drained of energy. All he wanted was to get outside in the fresh air, stifling hot as it was outside. He said a quick goodnight to Wendy and hurried out the door.

Outside, he settled into a rocker in a dark corner of the eastern end of the veranda near the wheelchair ramp. The air felt heavy and thick, yet somehow it reinvigorated him. The nausea faded and his strength gradually came back, although not completely. He decided to rest in that chair in the dark for a while before venturing back to his cabin.

He sat staring out at Longboat Harbor, enjoying the solitude and feeling a little better as the minutes passed. He mulled over what had happened in the Pink Parlor. Mrs. Church's voice inflections, her distress at the end. The mist, which nobody else—certainly not Wendy—seemed to have seen. He wished it had continued to thicken and form whatever it was trying to form. The more he thought about it, the more he believed it might have been Maria trying to materialize, since Leeds had just asked Seamus to bring her to them. If only that other spirit hadn't interfered.

He was still mulling these things when he heard a familiar voice call his name, and looked up to see Mr. Arndt coming his way. The old man walked in a straight line, forcing other guests on the veranda to step aside for him. Eventually he reached Mitch's end of the veranda and took the rocker next to his.

"Some fun, huh?" the old man said.

"Did you go in there?"

"I wanted to see how it went. I heard Phyllis didn't get through to Roger and Maria."

"We sort of got waylaid by a spirit with a bad attitude. But it was interesting."

"Glad to know someone appreciates Phyllis's work," Mr. Arndt said bitterly. "Those newspaper people in there, they all think she's doing those voices with hidden speakers like the wizard in *The Wizard of Oz*."

"I have to admit the same thought crossed my mind." Mitch paused. "At first, anyway."

Mr. Arndt looked at him. "You saw something, didn't you?"

"How did you know?"

"Wendy told me."

"Well, whatever I saw, she didn't see it and I didn't notice anyone else picking up on it. It might have been my imagination."

In the semidarkness, Mitch felt Mr. Arndt's eyes studying him. The old man stayed silent for a long time. Finally, he said, "Why do you keep doing that?"

"Doing what?"

"Trying to deny what you know you see."

"It's not so much I deny it—I just don't know what it is. I don't trust my mind. When I was a kid I had a wild imagination. I saw things sometimes."

"Really? What kinds of things?"

A vivid memory formed in Mitch's head, one he hadn't thought about in years. "It was usually at night, just when I was falling asleep. I remember there was this lady in a white gown I used to see in the corner of my room sometimes. She'd just stand there, facing me, but she didn't say anything. It was too dark to see her face. At first I thought it was my mother checking up on me. I asked her once when I was about sixteen or seventeen and she said it wasn't her, that she hadn't come in my room at all. Besides, my mother always wore pajamas. Of course she pressed me about it, and when I told her I had been seeing the same lady for a long time, she sent me to a shrink. She must have thought I was nuts. The shrink thought I was just going through one of those weird changes teenagers go through. So he sent me back to my parents with a clean bill of health and a rational explanation. I never saw the lady in the white gown again."

"I see," Mr. Arndt rocked slowly three times then asked, "So you think you're having a second adolescence?"

"No," Mitch ignored the joke. "I know I saw something. I just don't know what, and I don't understand why I'm the only one who saw it. I just keep thinking back on how I stopped seeing that lady in my room as soon as the shrink explained it in clinical terms."

Just then a voice called from down on the lawn. It was Leeds, standing ten feet below the veranda, looking up at them. "I've been looking for you two."

He came around to the wheelchair ramp and up to where they sat. "I was heading down to your cottage just now and I heard you talking". He leaned his back against the rail and stared at Mitch. "What did you think of the sitting, professor?"

"Cool." Mitch didn't have any other adjectives in mind just then.

"Cool," Leeds repeated. "I had hoped for more. Since you saw an apparition."

"Wendy told everyone, huh?" Mitch tried to sound disgusted even though he really wasn't.

"She told me, but she didn't have to. I already knew. It may look like I'm too busy with Phyllis, but I keep my eyes and ears open for anything else going on in the room. I heard you trying to get Wendy to look at whatever you were seeing."

"I don't know what it was—it disappeared before it could fully form."

"Too bad. But I had to bring Phyllis back. She wasn't doing too well at that point."

Mitch recalled the tail end of the sitting. It seemed when the angry spirit couldn't get Leeds to stop trying to reach Maria, it had made Mrs. Church choke. He wondered out loud if the apparition he had seen was that same spirit trying to take form.

"Could have been the ornery chap," Leeds said. "Could have been one of the Boudreaus, too. What do you think, Ted?"

Mr. Arndt had been quietly rocking with his face straight forward, chin up. He didn't change his pace or turn his head when he answered, "Could be."

Leeds watched him for a second or two as if waiting for him to say more. When nothing came, he said, "I was talking to Phyllis and we both think a séance might produce better results. But only if Mitch and Mrs. Poulin are there. I don't think we'll get what we want without you, Mitch. So how do you boys feel about a good old-fashioned séance?"

Mitch told him it sounded good. His curiosity was way up, and now that Leeds had suggested the apparition he had seen might be Maria, he was more than agreeable.

Leeds nodded at Mitch. "Good." He turned to Mr. Arndt and said, "Ted?"

Mr. Arndt turned his face toward Leeds and said something Mitch hadn't expected based on his past noncommittal attitude toward this whole project. "If Professor Lambert is there, I want to be there, too."

Leeds nodded vigorously. "We'll do it tonight. At 10:30. I'll go arrange it." He walked away toward the front doors.

Mr. Arndt was facing the harbor again. His expression was hard to read, but if Mitch had ventured a guess, he would have said the old man was feeling anxious. Why, he didn't know. But he was determined to find out.

CHAPTER SEVENTEEN

Mr. Arndt told Mitch he didn't feel like walking back to his cottage only to make the hike back up the lawn to the hotel at 10:30, less than an hour away. But it was hot as Hades, as Horace Leeds aptly described it, and most of the hotel's guests had wandered inside to stay cool. Mr. Arndt and Mitch decided to do the same and have a drink to pass the time until the séance began.

In the lounge Mitch looked around on the off-chance Wendy might be there, but he didn't see her. She'd probably gone back to her room to rest and wait for 10:30 to roll around. He couldn't imagine she would miss the séance.

They found a table in the middle of the room. The lounge was crowded, but a waitress came over almost before their butts touched their chairs. "Good evening, Mr. Arndt, you're out late."

"It's Saturday night, Annie, I'm partying." Mr. Arndt gave her a wink. "I'll have a scotch on the rocks."

Mitch ordered a beer and she went away. He knew she would be back just as fast as the bartender could fill their orders. "How do you do that?" he asked Mr. Arndt.

"What?"

"Get everyone to hop for you around here."

"One of the perks of staying out here ninety summers."

"You already told me that once. I'm sorry, but I don't buy it. Nobody gets service like that, not even people who've been customers for ninety years."

"Have you ever been a customer for ninety years?"

"My generation's lucky to stay a customer for ninety minutes."

"In that case, you don't know how you would get treated." Mr. Arndt's tone was pleasant, yet Mitch detected a little annoyance.

"How do you know Horace Leeds?"

Mr. Arndt rolled his eyes thoughtfully, and Mitch knew he wasn't going to finesse this one. "I've known Horace Leeds a long time."

"Really?" Mitch was genuinely surprised. "How?"

"I dabbled in parapsychology for a short time myself. I met Horace back in the late seventies."

"Did you ever investigate a paranormal event together?"

"We did."

The waitress returned with their drinks in record time, just as Mitch predicted. Judging by his face, Mr. Arndt was grateful for the interruption. Why was the old man so reluctant to talk to him about these things? "Did you know ahead of time that Leeds was coming out this weekend?"

"Know? Hell! I'm the one who got him to come!"

This answer didn't just surprise Mitch, it floored him. He had known someone connected with the island contacted Horace Leeds, but he didn't know who. He never suspected it was Mr. Arndt. "Why?"

"Why not? I knew him."

"Well, yes. But did you believe in all this ghost stuff going on?"

Mr. Arndt paused thoughtfully then said, "Some."

"Some? As in some of it? Or as in you partially believed?"

"Both."

Mitch sighed. "Look. A few minutes ago you told Horace Leeds you didn't want me at that séance tonight unless you were there."

"I did."

"And there's a good reason, I would imagine."

"There is."

"So . . . " Mitch stared him down. "Come on, what's this all about?"

The old man sipped at his scotch. "I'm not sure. But I didn't like what I heard from the people coming out of that sitting a while ago."

"You're copping out on me." Mitch's frustration bordered on anger.

"No, I'm not, " Mr. Arndt said sharply. "I honestly don't know exactly what's going on. But I suspect we may run into Horace's 'ornery chap' again sometime soon. I don't want a novice dealing with it alone."

"Why me? Why do you think it'll involve me?"

"Isn't it obvious? You're tuned in. Nobody else is, at least so far. Who do you think would get messed with, besides Phyllis?"

Mitch drank and looked off in the corner. The piano player was on the job again tonight. He saw Mitch looking at him and nodded recognition. Mitch nodded back.

"You know someone over there?" Mr. Arndt asked.

"The piano guy. He's a real character—likes to know what's going on around the room."

Mr. Arndt looked in the corner then back at Mitch. "Was he doing that just now?"

"No. He was just saying hello." He drank and got back to the subject of angry spirits. "You know, I find it surprising you would be concerned about me. I thought ghosts couldn't hurt you."

"I used to think that, too."

"What do you mean by that?"

"Just what I said."

"What changed your mind?"

"Something we can talk about later, not now."

"No, I want to know now." The old man's evasiveness was really getting to him.

Mr. Arndt looked patiently at him. "No. Not now. Not before the séance. You don't want any distractions. You also don't want your judgment affected by old stories, true as they may be. I need you fresh and focused."

The phrase, "I need you," didn't escape Mitch's attention. He found himself repeating it in his head. It wasn't just a figure of speech, not the way Mr. Arndt had said it. He was beginning to realize that he wasn't just a spectator on the sidelines anymore. He had become one of the players—maybe a key player—in this ghost hunt. Two days ago he wasn't even sure he would be allowed within spitting distance of Phyllis Church and Horace Leeds. Hell, a couple of weeks ago he thought he would be pitching a tent somewhere off the Smythe grounds because the hotel couldn't find him a room. Now he was going to be a V.I.P. at the séance. He should have been surprised. Yet almost since the moment he stepped off the *Narwhal* onto the dock, things had happened that he couldn't explain. Why should this surprise him?

Mr. Arndt had been looking off in the corner of the room. Now, he gripped his cane with both hands and pushed himself to his feet. "You should pay close attention to things around you. That piano player, for example. How many people have you seen go up to him tonight and request a song?"

Mitch looked over at the piano man. As a matter of fact, he hadn't seen anyone make a request tonight. Or the night before, for that matter. "None," he shrugged.

"And you won't. Now, I'm going to wait in the Pink Parlor. There's a chaise in there I can rest on until we get started." He glanced at the corner one more time and left.

Mitch watched the piano player for a minute or two, thinking about what Mr. Arndt had just said about him. The young man was jangling out a song Mitch didn't recognize, something not pop but not classical either. A little jazzy, but also not. On his piano sat a large jar for tips. It was empty.

Looking around the room, Mitch saw that no one in the crowd was paying any attention to the piano player or his music. This wasn't unusual in itself—like in any other bar, the patrons were more interested in the people at their own table—but this was a little different. Not a single person tapped a foot to the tune, which had a jumpy, fun rhythm. They didn't watch the piano man, either. They didn't even glance his way.

As Mitch surveyed the room, the music stopped and the piano man stood up from his stool. Piped-in soft rock came through ceiling speakers, replacing the piano tunes. Mitch got up from his chair, intending to go pay his compliments and maybe see if he did take requests. He might even request a song. Maybe "Bewitched, Bothered and Bewildered."

The piano man went in the direction of a narrow hall where Mitch assumed a men's room must be located. He moved that way too, thinking he would wait near the hallway for him to come back. In his path stood a wide wooden column that he skirted around. As he did, the column obscured his vision for a split second and he lost sight of the piano man. When he came around the column and looked for him again, he was gone.

Mitch stopped and looked around the room. It didn't seem possible the piano man had gotten to the little hallway, or anywhere else for that matter, in that brief time. He did a complete turn, looking around at the tables in case the man had stopped to talk with some guests, but he was nowhere in sight. People looked up at Mitch with questioning eyes so he moved on to the little hallway, thinking the piano man must have gotten by him somehow. The hallway led to a small storage room with a sign on the door: "Authorized

Personnel Only." Mitch doubted he had gone that way. He started back to his table. On the way, he happened to glance in the direction of the doorway to the main corridor. And there he was.

The man leaned against the wall directly across the corridor from the doorway, one hand casually stuffed inside the pocket of his white jacket, the other holding a cigarette. His tuxedo looked impeccable, neatly pressed and perfectly tailored for his tall, slim build. His hair was well-groomed, the bangs long and slicked back to the sides. He had a certain poise, the confidence of good breeding. He looked young, maybe mid-twenties, and that confidence didn't seem to fit his youth. Yet it was there in abundance. In fact, he looked cocky smoking a cigarette in a luxury hotel where smoking clearly wasn't allowed.

Mitch moved through the tables toward the doorway, and as he went, he realized the piano man was watching him. As if he had been waiting there for him all along. He reached the doorway, stepped into the corridor, and said hello. The piano man took a deep drag on his cigarette and blew the smoke out.

"Break time?" Mitch said, pleasantly.

"Your girl, the blonde."

Mitch had no idea what the guy meant. He waited for an explanation, and when it didn't come, he said, "What about her?"

"You're ignoring her again."

He motioned for Mitch to follow him and started down the corridor toward the eastern end of the wing. Mitch hesitated, still puzzling over what this was all about. By the time he made up his mind to follow, the piano man had turned a corner. Mitch hurried to catch up, smelling the cigarette smoke as he went, wondering where this fellow got the chutzpah to smoke inside a luxury hotel. He was thinking this as he turned the same corner where he'd seen the man moments ago.

He was gone.

The hall had taken a sharp turn to the left for fifteen feet then turned right again, and now Mitch was facing down a long corridor with potted fichus trees and palms and nothing else. The piano man was nowhere in sight. The elevators were halfway down that corridor in a tiny hall on the right, yet even that distance couldn't have been covered so quickly unless the guy ran. But why on earth would he run in the first place? Was this some childish game? If so, Mitch refused to play. Instead he took his time, knowing chances were he would have to wait for the elevator to arrive anyway. But when he came to the hall with the elevators, the man wasn't there. The "up" button was lit but the elevator was on its way down, so he hadn't gone up yet.

What the hell's going on?

Mitch stood in the hall, smelling cigarette smoke and thinking about what the piano man had said: "You're ignoring her again." What did he mean by that? Since arriving, Mitch had spent more time with Wendy Mayer than anyone else, even Mr. Arndt. He hadn't ignored her at all. And so what if he had? Why was this guy nosing into his affairs?

A woman in an evening dress turned into the hall and stopped to wait for the elevator. Mitch could hear live music coming from the ballroom nearby, and deduced that she had just come from a party going on in there. She gave him a quick smile, the kind you give a stranger you suddenly find yourself alone with, and he gave one back. She looked a little tipsy and her perfume was a little stronger than it should have been, but not strong enough to mask the smell of cigarette smoke.

"Do you smell cigarettes?" Mitch asked, making conversation.

The woman's nostrils flared as she breathed in. She smiled again. "No."

"Really?" Mitch was genuinely surprised. It seemed pretty obvious, like the smoker was standing right beside them puffing away.

She shook her head. "No. I really don't smell anything."

Well, how could you with all that perfume . . .

The elevator dinged and the doors opened. Two more people in formal evening wear came around the corner and got on the elevator with them just before the doors closed. They all took the car to the third floor.

Sometime in the course of the past two days Wendy had told Mitch her room number, and it had stuck in his head for no particular reason. Room 323E. He wandered down the hall, following the directories, and finally came to it. The room was close to the far end of the corridor. Although the door frame was the original carved wood frame of a hundred years ago, the door itself was a modern steel door with an electronic key-card slot. The little light on the device glowed red—the door was locked.

Mitch stood in front of the door for half a minute, though it seemed like ten minutes, wondering if he should knock and what he would say if Wendy answered. A scene played out in his head: Wendy answering the door, Mitch saying hello, Wendy asking why he was there, Mitch saying this musician downstairs had told him he was ignoring her and he thought he'd better come up and would she mind if he came in . . .

The scent of cigarette smoke suddenly filled his nostrils again. It hadn't been there a moment ago. He breathed deeply through his nose and looked around, wondering where on earth it was coming from.

Suddenly, from behind the door there came a shrill scream.

CHAPTER EIGHTEEN

"Wendy!" Mitch shouted, grabbing the door handle. It was locked. "Wendy!" he yelled louder.

"Mitch!" Wendy shouted back from inside the room.

He tried the door handle again but it was useless. Like all modern hotel doors, this one was designed to lock automatically when you closed it behind you. The little red light still glowed. He put his shoulder into the door, hoping to break the latch, but it held fast. "Wendy!" he shouted again, and listened for an answer. This time there was none. Not a sound.

He stepped back a couple of paces, intending to use a running kick to break the latch on the doorjamb. As he gathered his strength and looked at his target spot next to the card-key reader, the red light went out and the green light glowed. Just like that, the door was unlocked.

He grabbed the handle before the light could turn red again, turned it down and shoved the door open. Inside, the room was dark. He flipped a wall switch next to the door and a ceiling light in the entranceway came on.

"Wendy?" he called out. Letting the door swing shut behind him, he took a few steps and saw a king size bed off to the right and an armchair in the corner near the window. In the chair, Wendy sat straight upright, staring at him with wide eyes that were moist from crying. A book lay open on the carpet beside the chair.

"Wendy, are you okay?"

She whimpered softly, but didn't answer. He walked over to her, glancing around the room and under the bed as he went in case an intruder lurked in some shadowy corner waiting to jump him when his guard was down. But he saw nothing.

"Are you okay?"

"Mitch," Wendy managed before breaking down in sobs. A floor lamp stood beside the chair and he clicked it on to get some more light in the room. Wendy had buried her face in her hands. She was dressed in a white hotel robe over powder-blue pajamas and matching fuzzy slippers.

"What happened?"

She took her hands away from her face. "Hold me, please," she said, reaching for him.

Mitch sat on the arm of the chair and held her. Her face was hot and soggy against his shirt. It felt wonderful.

"I was reading and I fell asleep," she said once she was finally able to get the sobbing under control. "I don't think I was out long. I woke up and the room was dark, but I hadn't shut the light off. At least I don't remember shutting it off. There was this man—" She stopped, shuddering against Mitch's chest and burying her wet nose deeper into his shirt. "His face was . . . *hovering* over me. But he had no body. Just a head. There was nothing below the neck."

"You were dreaming," Mitch said to reassure her, but he was thinking of the piano man.

Wendy pulled her face away from his chest and wiped at her eyes with her hand. "No, I wasn't. I was as awake as I am now."

Mitch looked around again. There was a closet in the corner, but it was small and the door was open. If someone was in there he would be able to see him. He had already glanced into the bathroom, which was just inside the door, and saw nothing.

"No one's here, Wendy, and I would have seen him leave. I was just outside your door when you screamed."

"I *saw* him."

"What did he look like?"

Wendy looked straight ahead, as if envisioning the face. She shook her head and buried her face in his chest again.

"Was he in a tuxedo?" He was thinking the piano player might have somehow gotten in and out of her room just before he arrived.

"I didn't see a body. There was no body."

"Maybe you just didn't see the body in the glare of the lamp."

"No. Listen to me: *He had no body.*"

She sounded more exasperated than frightened now. Mitch tried another tactic. "What did his face look like? Hair? Eyes?"

Wendy thought for a moment. "I can't remember. Except for the eyes. Light-colored, piercing eyes. Shiny, like polished marble. The kind that make you feel like your mind is being undressed."

He hadn't expected this description at all. The piano player had dark eyes. "Did he . . . *do* anything?"

"Oh, for Pete's sake, Mitch, he didn't have a body." She rolled her eyes. That was the Wendy he knew. She was coming back around.

"Well, did he say anything?"

Wendy thought a moment. "Just before you started yelling to me, he said something."

"What?"

"I don't know." She furrowed her eyebrows. "He said it kind of soft. But it didn't sound friendly, that's for sure."

Mitch thought of the sitting earlier that night and the pissed-off spirit. Maybe Wendy hadn't been dreaming. But what purpose would a ghost—belligerent or not—have for visiting Wendy and scaring the living daylights out of her? Whatever the reason, Mitch didn't want to leave her alone. "Do you know we're having a séance in a while?"

She shook her head.

"Mrs. Church wants to give it one more try. Leeds thinks I'm some sort of magnet, and maybe we'll conjure up the Boudreaus."

"Am I invited?"

"You must be. You were at the sitting. Besides, I want you there."

Wendy gave a quick smile. Her eyes were red and her nose was runny, but right now she looked more attractive than she had all weekend.

"I think I should stay with you 'til then," he said, feeling a little bashful.

She smiled again. "I'd hoped you would."

CHAPTER NINETEEN

They talked in Wendy's room until it was time for the séance. They talked about everything—childhoods, careers, whatever came to mind—and Mitch discovered she was a good conversationalist when he wasn't busy arguing with her.

The best thing he heard was that she had broken off an engagement just before coming out to the island. So she was single. He liked her and she seemed to like him. And there they were, in her room, a couple of lonely souls hitting it off . . .

But their time together remained entirely conversational. She stayed in the chair the whole time while he sat on the edge of the bed. It was obvious she was still trying to get past her broken engagement and needed a little space. As he was leaving the room so she could get dressed, she took his shoulder, pulled him down to her level and kissed him on the cheek. "You're a good sport," she said. Good sport, Mitch thought with a sardonic grin. Any other guy spending an hour with an attractive woman in her hotel room would have been a *lucky* sport.

They took the long way down to the first floor, opting for the elevators near the lobby. This was Mitch's idea. He wanted to walk past the Boudreau suite once more before the séance to see if he picked up on anything. For a moment or two they stood outside the entrance door, concentrating with all their might, but nothing happened. If the Boudreaus were around this Saturday night, they sure didn't seem to be in their apartment.

Downstairs, they found Mr. Arndt in the Pink Parlor laying on a chaise lounge as he had said he would be. Everyone else had arrived before them, and Mitch noticed several of the crowd stealing glances in his direction. He asked Mr. Arndt if he knew why.

"You're the man of the hour, Professor Lambert," he winked.

As if to confirm this, Phyllis Church toggled over to him and took him aside. "I'm glad you came."

"Wouldn't miss it."

"Professor Lambert—is that what you prefer? Or is 'Doctor' better?"

"Mitch is better."

"Mitch, then," she said with enthusiasm. "I understand you wrote a book about the Boudreaus."

"I did. It's easy to find—it's the only one written about them in seventy years."

"And you chose all the photos for it?" She peered at him over frameless reading glasses.

"Uh, yes." Mitch was taken aback. This was the second time that weekend he'd been asked that question. What did it matter that he had chosen the photos? "Why do you ask?"

She went on staring at him over her glasses. It reminded him of his grandmother's look when he was a child and about to get lectured. "Because I'd like to know," she said in a tone that also could have been his grandmother's.

"I picked them because I had access to archives that hadn't been opened in decades. I figured I could choose them better than some editor who didn't know all the available resources. I also knew which photos really meant something."

"Thank you." Mrs. Church gave him a quick smile. "The reason I asked—" She stopped and considered a moment. "I think you may have a connection to Maria." She peered closely at Mitch again as though looking for a reaction, which she didn't get. "Maybe you developed it in the course of your research. Anyway, the point is, I think Maria is *aware* of you. It's more complicated than that, but it's the best way I can explain it in short order."

Just hearing that Maria might be aware of his presence was enough to make Mitch's heart pick up speed. If it were true—if Mrs. Church wasn't just playing with his head—the trip had already been well worth it.

Mrs. Church must have seen the joy on his face because she added, "Unfortunately, I don't think Maria's the only one who's aware of you. You were at the sitting, you heard that intrusive spirit."

"Who was that?"

Mrs. Church shrugged. "I don't know yet. But everyone's waiting for us, so I suppose we'd better get started." She did a quarter-turn in her wheelchair. "I'd like you to sit next to me, and I want you to concentrate like you never have before. I'll squeeze your hand when I feel we've reached the right atmosphere. When I do, I want you to call to Maria with your mind. I want you to whisper her name." She paused then added, "I think she's here, Mitch, but she needs your help to come through. She needs to be able to find you."

"I'll do my best."

She reached for his hand and squeezed it, then turned her wheelchair and rolled over to the head of the table. Mitch followed and sat in an empty chair to her right that had a note card on the seat with his name scribbled on it. Everyone else had already been seated around the table in an organized fashion. Dorothy Poulin sat on the other side of Mrs. Church, looking a little tired but excited. Next to her sat Wendy and next to Mitch was Mr. Arndt, also looking tired.

The various reporters and observers filled up the rest of the seats around the table. The chair directly opposite Mrs. Church was taken by Horace Leeds. The cameraman had set up his tripod to shoot over Wendy's shoulder, which meant Mitch would be in the picture with Mrs. Church at all times. He wondered if Mrs. Church had directed this.

When everyone looked comfortable, Leeds asked a hotel worker to come over and light a tall candle that stood in the center of the table. Once it glowed with a healthy flame, Leeds instructed the cameraman to dim the chandelier until it was out altogether.

Now everyone sat quietly, listening to Mrs. Church's instructions as the cameraman started recording.

"I'll ask each of you to relax and let all the tension flow out of your body so you can concentrate," Mrs. Church began in a slow, quiet voice. "Then I would ask each of you to put all thoughts out of your mind. Discard them, one by one, leaving a blank slate. On that slate, I want you to begin drawing a picture, a picture of the Smythe hotel in 1924. Picture Maria Boudreau here at the hotel. It's a lovely evening. Her friends are waiting for her in this room."

She paused to let everyone do this, then continued.

"Please put both hands on the table," she instructed. After everyone had done so, she said, "Now take your neighbor's hand on either side." She waited for everyone to hold hands. "I want you to hold hands throughout this séance. Do not let go until I say so. We'll need our collective thoughts and energy. Now I'll ask you to think about Maria Boudreau again. Her friends are waiting for her in the Pink Parlor. We are her friends."

Mitch kept his gaze on Mrs. Church who closed her eyes and jutted her chin forward a little. In the dim light, her face looked tense with concentration. A moment later it relaxed and she even smiled. "Maria, dear," she began in a gentle, loving voice. "You have friends waiting for you in the Pink Parlor. Maria, we are here waiting for you to join us. We ask that you honor us with your presence in this room."

She paused, letting her chin drop. The candle flickered. Mitch looked around the table to see if someone had let out a heavy breath.

"Maria, you are among friends," Mrs. Church continued. "We know how you have made your presence known recently. We also know of your past efforts with Dr. Arndt."

Mitch jerked his gaze in the direction of Mr. Arndt. The old man looked back with an expression of acknowledgment. Somehow, Mitch had known all along that his friend was deeper into this thing than he'd let on. He was itching to ask him what Maria's "past efforts" with him were, but it would have to wait.

"Maria, there are three very special people here tonight. We have your cousin, Dorothy Poulin, who hasn't seen you since she was five years old and wishes to see you again. We have Theodore Arndt, who is here to complete a conversation you might also wish to complete. We also have Dr. Mitchell Lambert who gave us a loving biography of you, and whose acquaintance I believe you have already tried to make." She paused, breathing regularly and rhythmically, her face totally concentrated. "We ask that you make your presence known. If you so choose, we ask that you appear for us as it would bring joy to so many around this table."

As she said the word "table," Mrs. Church squeezed Mitch's hand and he obediently closed his eyes, bowed his head and began picturing the newsreel of Maria at the golf tournament in 1922. He played it over and over again, focusing on the brooch on her lapel each time. Then he began whispering, so low that only Mr. Arndt and Mrs. Church could have heard it, "Maria, please appear for us, Maria, please appear for us." After a while the chant became "Maria, appear for *me*." After maybe half a minute he heard a tiny gasp. He looked up and saw Dorothy Poulin staring wide-eyed at the candle. He followed her gaze and saw the candle flame swaying back and forth in a little dance as though two people were taking turns blowing at it from opposite sides.

He looked back at Mrs. Poulin and saw that her expression had changed from shock to pleasure. Her eyes were closed, her head tilted back a little and she wore a peaceful half-grin. She made a soft moaning sound then opened her eyes and watched the candle flame again. The flame had increased its to-and-fro tempo.

The room was quiet, but to Mitch the air seemed alive. Around the table the reporters and observers all looked bored. They sat with their eyes open, hands still clasped to their neighbors', looking doubtful and impatient. The energy at Mitch's end of the table would have to make up for the lack of it elsewhere if anything was going to happen.

He closed his eyes, bowed his head and began the chant again. "Maria, appear for me." He concentrated on Maria's face and said the words as earnestly as he could. But nothing happened. Still, he kept trying. And then, all at once, he understood what it was that Mrs. Church had tried to get him to do. He hit a stride. It was like when you were jogging and you reached a point where your breathing and your leg strides and arm pumping all got in sync and you relaxed and just let the rhythm take over. His chanting became less deliberate, more automatic.

Before long he sensed something and opened his eyes.

There, standing behind Dorothy Poulin, he saw Maria Boudreau.

She had not fully formed, so her body was quite transparent, but her face was easily recognizable. She wore a cream-colored dress, simple in its design yet elegant in its features, one of those straight, shapeless dresses with the dropped waist that were popular in the twenties. On her head she wore a headband with sequins. The hair itself was parted in the middle and hung to her shoulders. He could see all of this, even though she was as transparent as a photo slide. Her movement was fluid, alive, not at all like a movie or even a video clip. If her image had been more solid she could have been mistaken for another of the séance guests.

After his initial shock wore off, Mitch glanced over at Phyllis Church, searching for some indication that she had seen Maria too, but her eyes were still closed. He looked around the table for the same indication, but not a single other guest gave any hint of seeing her.

Something told him he should try communicating with Maria in his mind. He told her that he seemed to be the only one at the table who saw her. Immediately, a voice in his head answered, "I know. It's okay." The voice was girlish. He had never expected Maria's voice to sound that way and it fascinated him.

In answer to this thought, Maria said, "Yes, that's my voice."

A smile spread over Mitch's face. "It's beautiful," he replied with his mind.

Maria thanked him. Then she put her hands on Dorothy Poulin's shoulders, bent down and kissed the top of her head tenderly, as though her cousin were still a child. Mitch watched for a reaction from the old woman, and he wasn't disappointed. Just as Maria kissed her, Mrs. Poulin's face lit up and her shoulders went back. This was followed by a soft giggle of delight.

He wanted to ask Mrs. Poulin what she felt—he wanted to know what it was like to be kissed by Maria—but he knew he couldn't speak up right now. Besides, at that moment Maria turned her face to him and started moving his way.

This surprised him. If Maria was going to move around the room, he naturally assumed she would avoid the furnishings. Instead, she came right through the table. She appeared to be walking, but her body cut through the table as though it wasn't even there. Indeed, Maria didn't seem to notice the table at all. She came over slowly and stood in front of Mitch, hands clasped in front of her, head bowed a little.

In all his dreams Mitch had never imagined she would be so beautiful. She had taken on a more solid form by now, and her hair appeared thick and three-dimensional. From the bottom of her headband it cascaded down just past her shoulders in thick, auburn waves. Her eyes were that same deep green so often described by her contemporaries, even lovelier than the portrait in the Smythe lobby conveyed. Her lips were childlike, a cherubic bow, but the jaw line was strong and firm. Although her body lacked any defining shape under that loose-fitting dress, it was easy to see that she had a small, slim frame.

Mitch didn't know if she had paused to let him drink in her form, or if time just stopped momentarily, but it seemed he looked at her much longer than a gentleman should. Maria showed no sign of annoyance at this. Only kindness, and something else Mitch hadn't expected: affection. Emotion welled up in his gut and he felt compelled to say something to express how he felt at that moment.

"You're an angel," he whispered, this time with his real voice.

Out of the corner of his eye he saw Mr. Arndt turn his head and look at him. Others around the table had heard him whisper and they, too, were looking in his direction. Mitch could tell they were struggling to see whatever he appeared to see. But he knew they couldn't, sensing this was his own private meeting with Maria.

"There's danger in this," Maria's voice said.

"What danger?" Mitch whispered. To his left, Mrs. Church lifted her head and he felt a little squeeze of her hand: keep it going.

"I'm close by," Maria said to Mitch. "Stay close to me."

Then something distracted her. Mitch could see it in her face. Her eyes drifted up and away to some spot behind him. But she quickly looked back at him and smiled warmly again. "You were there for me," she said.

"I'm here for you now," Mitch answered through the lump in his throat.

She leaned forward and Mitch felt her arms around his shoulders and her cheek against his own. Her skin felt warm and pliant, like real skin, yet thinly composed. He realized that these sensations were in his head, too, like their conversation. It didn't matter much, though. He now knew the feel of Maria's cheek, and that was enough.

And then the feeling was gone, and so was Maria. She had faded away while holding him. Mitch didn't see her fade, but felt a sort of tingle then a lightening of the atmosphere around him, and he didn't have to look to know she was gone. He relaxed in his chair, relishing his contact with her. All eyes around the table were focused on him. Mrs. Poulin and Mrs. Church had warm, happy smiles on their faces.

Suddenly, Mitch felt something like a burst of air around his torso and he flew backwards in his chair, skittering along the carpet on the back two legs. The chair stopped abruptly when it had gone a dozen feet, twisted to the left and dumped him violently on the floor. So suddenly was he thrown that he landed squarely on his nose. For a second or two he saw stars, but was able to get to his knees fairly quickly and start to shake it off.

Through the haze in his head, he heard chairs around the table being pushed back and people talking excitedly. Someone had turned up the dimmer so the chandelier now shone brightly. He felt his nose, and when he pulled his fingers away, they were covered in blood. In a daze, he watched the blood drip on the rug.

Now people were all around, helping him to his feet, asking if he was all right. Wendy was examining his nose and telling people to move back and let him have some air. They did, and Mitch walked back to the table and sat in a chair, all the while keeping his head tilted back on Wendy's instructions. Someone produced a handkerchief and Wendy pressed it to his nostrils, making his nose sting. She ordered someone to go get ice.

Until now, he hadn't had a chance to really think about what had just happened or even to be frightened. As he sat, waiting for the ice to arrive, it occurred to him that Maria had tried to warn him.

"Guess I'm not popular with everyone," he said to Mrs. Church.

That sent a wave of nervous laughter through the crowd, even though no one, except maybe Phyllis Church and Horace Leeds, understood much about what had just happened or how it had happened. Mitch could see in their expressions that most of them realized they had just witnessed an event maybe more significant than anything else they would witness the rest of their lives. Some of the reporters had out notebooks and digital recorders, busily taking notes. Finally, they had their big ghost story.

A hotel employee arrived with a champagne bucket filled with ice and some small white towels. Wendy wrapped ice in a towel then dipped it in the bottom of the bucket to soak it. She held it to Mitch's nose while he tipped his head back. He stared at the ceiling because there was nowhere else to stare, and in his head he could still see Maria's face as though she were looking down at him.

When the bleeding stopped, Mitch was left with only a sore nose and a slightly bruised ego. He felt like he had just got bested in a schoolyard tussle in front of all of his friends. Everyone was back around him again, asking questions. What did it feel like? Did you fight back? Did you sense anything else? Did the ghost say anything to you? One of the reporters used the word "poltergeist" and Leeds corrected him, saying this didn't really fit the poltergeist model.

"So what was it?" the reporter asked.

Leeds grinned and winked at Mitch. "A really pissed-off ghost."

CHAPTER TWENTY

Mitch said goodnight to Wendy and left with Mr. Arndt. In spite of the late hour, people milled around the lobby, giving them a lot of stares as they passed through. Most of them were paranormal nerds who had come to the island to be near their heroes, Horace Leeds and Phyllis Church, and maybe glimpse something of the afterlife in the process. But hotel staff had kept them far away from the Pink Parlor so they wouldn't interfere. Now, they stared at this man coming from the séance with blood smeared all over his shirt, accompanied by an ancient man hobbling on a cane. They must have been wondering what on earth had just happened in that room. Judging by their expressions, some of them already knew. He guessed that the reporters coming out of the Pink Parlor ahead of them had described his little chair ride.

Yet the reporters couldn't have told them the most important thing that had gone on in there because they didn't know he had seen and even touched Maria. He wondered, as he and Mr. Arndt walked through the crowd, just how much any of them would have cared about that. It seemed to him that these people would find his tussle with the angry ghost much more appealing. Then he remembered how well his book about Maria had sold, and all the other interest in her after it was published, and he changed his mind. A lot of these folks weren't just fascinated by ghosts. They were fans of Maria Boudreau.

Nobody got up the courage to ask questions, and Mr. Arndt and Mitch were able to make their way across the lobby and out the doors unmolested. On their way down the veranda steps, Mitch told Mr. Arndt he deserved some answers after that scene in the Pink Parlor. This time Mr. Arndt didn't try to evade him. He said, "Let's go somewhere quiet."

They went down to the dock and stood at the same rail where Mitch and

Leeds had gazed at Lone Tree Hill earlier that day. The moon was up pretty high, still bright in spite of the haze. Out on the water a few lights burned on boats moored in Longboat Harbor for the night. Conversation came from one of the bigger boats, the loudish, slurred talk of people who'd had too much to drink. It all felt surreal, this familiar, everyday scene juxtaposed with an incarnate world able to seep into it at will. Mitch pictured the partiers in that forty-foot yacht, oblivious to the goings-on in the hotel a thousand feet away. Common folks drifting through their mortal lives while another world went about its own business close by. Before this weekend, he had been one of those oblivious people. Not anymore. Most mortals would never have an experience even close to what he'd had that night. It didn't matter how long they lived, or how much they exposed themselves to the right circumstances. This included the paranormal nerds loitering in the hotel lobby right now who believed fervently in that other world. Yet he, who had never in the past suspected he had the "gift," who only half-believed in a spirit world at best, somehow had plugged into that other place with a high-voltage cord. Why him? More important, how?

He needed answers and he knew Mr. Arndt had at least some of them. So while they stood at the rail, elbows resting on the top bar, Mitch tried to find the right words to open the conversation. As it turned out, Mr. Arndt opened it himself.

"This is where she always came ashore," he said, looking over the water in the direction of Forge's Island. "The *Tasha* always docked right here. The plank was put out right there where you're standing, and Maria was usually the first off the boat."

"I know," Mitch said impatiently. After all, he had written the book on her.

"There's a lot you don't know, Professor Lambert," Mr. Arndt snapped. "You wanted to hear what I know, right?"

"Yes."

Mr. Arndt looked at him briefly, then back out over the harbor. "The *Tasha's* bow stretched to . . . " He pointed at a spot in the air diagonally away from him, "right about there." He swept his arm back to another spot at a northwest angle. "And her stern was back there. She was beautiful. Three masts, white and tan hull, sleek lines. I last saw her in 1924. But it could have been just yesterday, I remember that magnificent boat so well.

"Maria would come ashore first, but she was always followed by either Fenton or her father or one of the *Tasha's* crew who stayed close by. There had been death threats and kidnapping scares—not uncommon for a famous heiress, unfortunately—so no one on the dock was allowed to get too close to her. By that summer, she was being accompanied by a bodyguard a lot of the time. He would be mixed in with the friends or relatives who sailed with them. Roger and Maria were generous with their good fortune, you know. They liked to share it with people they cared about. Even though they were very private people, they looked forward to having their closest friends around them and they often brought them along.

"I was just a boy when I knew her in the flesh, but I got to see her up close a lot. There were dinners hosted by Roger that my Papa got invited to, and Papa always brought me along. Maria liked me and I liked her and she always had me sit close to her. And she was always kissing me on the cheek just to watch me blush. Oh, my God I blushed! She was so pretty." Mr. Arndt touched his face and smiled, but the smile quickly faded. "The last time I saw her was that terrible weekend. They arrived on a Friday. Late afternoon, just before dinnertime. The bell rang—that same bell you see hanging by the dock. I ran out there and watched the *Tasha* tie up like I did every time the Boudreaus came out to the island. I loved that boat and I loved to see Maria." He paused, looking out over the water as if envisioning the scene. A smile spread over his face again. "I was wearing gray shorts, a blue-striped shirt and suspenders. I wasn't quite ten years old."

"You really liked Maria," Mitch said, getting him back on track.

"Most people did. Only the ones who were jealous didn't like her. She had one of those rare magnetic personalities. It wasn't just her pretty face. It was her . . . way." He looked at Mitch. "I thought only Dorothy could understand what I mean by that. Now I know you can, too." Mitch waited for an explanation but never got one. Mr. Arndt just went on without skipping a beat.

"She came off the boat with her papa, and of course Fenton and a bunch of other people. There was a young man in the crowd. Good-looking, athletic, obviously well-bred. For some reason I was struck by him. I waited next to the walk, and as she came up, I said, 'Hello, Mashka.'" He held up his hand in a shy wave, the way a little boy might. "She stopped, bent down to my height, and said, 'Hello there, Teddy, how are you today?' Just like that. She had on a straw hat with a red band around the brim. She smelled like Coty La Rose Jacqueminot. That was her favorite.

"I saw her again at dinner. My father was invited to Mr. Boudreau's table. All the big wigs around the hotel that weekend were at the table. I was the only child, but Papa would not have sat at that table without me. He never dined without me, and Roger and the rest of them knew it. Besides, I always behaved impeccably, so Roger didn't mind me being there at all. And, of course, Maria liked having me there to tease and coddle. I wore a little tuxedo and everything; it was all very impressive sitting with all these high-brows dressed in tailcoats and long dresses."

Mitch already knew most of this from his research. Roger Boudreau had been joined that weekend by his partner in the Smythe Resort, Malcolm Akers. They had sailed aboard the *Tasha* together and dined at the V.I.P. table that night.

"I don't remember much else about that night. Everything seemed fine. I remember everyone had some sort of torte for dessert and I wanted strawberry ice cream and everyone got a kick out of that." He added, "I was a cute kid, you know."

"I don't doubt it."

"I didn't see Maria again until the next night. In those days, there was a playground up by the tennis courts and I spent most of Saturday up there. My dad always had an arrangement with a schoolgirl to babysit me. That summer it was a girl named Susan Sharpe. Nice girl. I spent part of the day up at the playground and some of it down at the beach with Susan while Papa worked. There's a picture of me in my swimsuit taken that day. Full-body swimsuit, like you see in cartoons. Boy, I hated that suit. But I had light skin and I had to be careful. So even though some kids wore short suits, I had a full one. Anyway, enough of that. It's not important.

"That next night was the night of Maria's party," Mr. Arndt went on. "It was her twenty-first birthday and the ballroom was reserved for a couple hundred of her closest friends and relatives, plus a lot of Roger's business associates and society people. A lot of eligible young men were there. I think Roger was trying to use the party as a matchmaking thing. Here was Maria turning twenty-one and she still showed no interest in settling down with one guy and thinking about marriage. In those days, parents worried their daughters would turn out old maids if they weren't at least thinking about marriage by that age. Roger had one particular young man in mind for saving her from spinsterhood: Robert Akers, Malcolm's son."

"Huh?" This caught Mitch off guard. In all his research he had never come across any such information.

"Not a well-known fact. Remember that young man I told you I saw coming off the dock with Maria's crowd? That was Robert."

Mitch knew Robert had sailed with his father and the Boudreaus aboard the *Tasha*. But he had no idea Robert was hand-picked by Roger to date Maria. "Are you sure it wasn't just a rumor?"

"Oh yes, I'm sure," Mr. Arndt said convincingly. "Robert was being groomed to eventually take over his father's business interests, so he was shadowing Malcolm a lot around that time. He was twenty-four, not long out of college. In the course of Roger's and Malcolm's dealings, Maria and Robert were introduced and encouraged to spend time together. Eventually they began carrying on some kind of romance, though it was pretty guarded so it's hard to say just how deep the romance went."

Mitch shook his head in wonder, still not sure if the old man was speculating or just flat out making the whole thing up. "How do you know all this?"

Mr. Arndt turned and faced him. He hugged his cane to his chest with both hands, drew a deep breath and let it out slowly. "Doctor Lambert, you may know Maria pretty darned well from your research, but some of us knew her pretty darned well in the *flesh*."

Mitch started to say something, but Mr. Arndt spoke again before he could get a single word out. "You're also not the first one to speak to Maria after her death."

CHAPTER TWENTY-ONE

For several seconds they stood looking at one another, unblinking. Mitch had no voice. Finally, he managed two words: "Tell me."

Mr. Arndt leaned on the rail again and looked out over the harbor. "It was a few months after Maria died. I was back in Cambridge with Papa. She found me there the way I suppose they do when they have business to attend to. I was actually in school when she came to me. I was out in the schoolyard playing marbles with my friends, and I happened to look up and there she was, over by the schoolyard fence. I could have easily mistaken her for any other woman—she was dressed like she was on her way to a business meeting—but it was Maria all right, and I knew it the instant I saw her. I went over to her, and she said, 'Hello, Teddy, I'm so happy to see you,' and I said, 'I'm glad to see you, too, Maria.' Just like that. Like any other time we'd seen each other.

"She told me she needed my help. She said there was a 'complication'— that's the word I remember her using. 'Complication.' She needed me to help her straighten something out. I thought it was strange for a grown-up to need *my* help, let alone a dead one, but I told her I would do what I could. She said, 'Teddy, some of what I'm about to say you won't understand, and some of it you won't even remember until you're much older.' Then she told me how she had been separated from a man who was very important to her, a man who had recently died. At first I thought she meant her papa, but she told me it wasn't, that her papa was always close to her even now. She never told me who the man was, only that she couldn't be with him and it was a mistake. This wasn't supposed to have happened and it needed to be fixed.

"She wanted me to remember that she would need my help at some point in the future, many years from now. She said I would know when the time came—she would let me know. She said goodbye, and then she faded away. I never saw or talked with her again, at least not like that."

"But I thought she said she would contact you when the time came," Mitch reminded him.

"She did. But as time goes by and we get older, some of us who had the ability as children lose it. I'm not sure why. I think it's like a skill that gets rusty if you don't use it, or a window that gets all cloudy with dirt if you don't keep it clean. As we get older, all of life's cares just seem to clog up that part of our brain, or dull it. By the time that 'time' had rolled around, I was in my sixties. By then I wasn't tuned in to anything but retirement. In fact, I had come to think that I just imagined my encounter with Maria in the schoolyard."

"So did you see her again?"

"Not exactly. But I heard her and smelled her. At first I thought it was my wife coming to me because she had died a couple years before that. But after a while I realized it had to be Maria."

"How did you realize it?"

"Well, as I've told you, when I was a little boy I got to know Maria pretty well. For example, I told you she wore La Rose Jacqueminot perfume when she was alive. I hadn't smelled that perfume in years. Then all of a sudden I'm smelling it in my house all the time. Another thing: Maria played piano. Not real well, but she loved to play. Sometimes she played the grand piano in the ballroom, and one of her favorite songs to play was "Ain't We Got Fun," one of the popular songs of that time. Well, one day I came home in the afternoon and heard "Ain't We Got Fun" playing on the piano, kind of haltingly, the way Maria would have played it. The thing is no one was in the house at the time. Better yet, I didn't own a piano!

"That was the final clue that convinced me Maria was around. I hadn't thought about her in years, but now I found myself thinking about her all the time. One day I went into Boston and walked by her old house thinking I might tune in, you know? But nothing came. I realized I needed help getting through to her or her to me, I suppose. I called the Parapsychology Society in Boston and they recommended Horace Leeds."

"I *knew* you knew each other," Mitch interrupted.

"We do. He and Phyllis helped me contact Maria. Nearly thirty years ago."

"How did they do it?"

"Same as tonight. Horace put Phyllis in a trance and Maria came right through. Spoke to me through Phyllis's own mouth."

"What did she say?"

"She said, 'Hi Teddy, do you still like sardines on rye crackers?'" He smiled and shook his head. "I'll never forget that. She asked if I remembered our conversation in the schoolyard when I was a child, and I told her I did. She said, 'I told you I would need your help, and I do.' I thought she meant right then and there, but I was wrong. She told me to just wait. So I said, 'For what?' She said, 'Something important has happened, but you won't understand it for many years to come.' And I'm thinking to myself, *many years?* I'm in my middle-sixties now, how many more years do I have! Anyway, she said, 'Watch for me at the dock, Teddy, like you used to.' And that was it. Later on, Horace made me promise to tell him if I ever saw Maria again."

Mitch quickly put two and two together. "So, Horace came here this weekend because of that contact with Maria." He thought a moment. "He waited all those years for your call and finally got it."

"That's right."

"Which means Maria contacted you again."

Mr. Arndt nodded. "She kept her promise, although I never expected it to happen so many years later. Thirty years is a long time to watch the dock, especially when you're an old man. But I did. Every summer I went out there almost every day. Usually early in the morning when the sun had just come up and no one was around. I'd walk out to the end of the dock and stand pretty much where we're standing now. I came to call it my 'morning constitutional.' I never doubted she would be there one day. That contact with her back in the late seventies had reawakened something from my childhood. 'Faith' I guess you'd call it. Anyway, I never once doubted she would return. My only worry was that I'd croak before that day came. After a while I realized *she* knew I wouldn't die first. Kind of a weird feeling, by the way, knowing your life is measured by the appearance of a ghost. Kind of like how Mark Twain was born the year of Halley's Comet and died the next time it returned. All I knew was that I wouldn't die until she came back. Sort of a brief gift of immortality when you think about it. Anyway, now I know I can die anytime and that's perfectly fine with me. I've lived long enough."

"So you saw her recently." Mitch said.

"First week I was out here this summer. Out on the dock, just like she promised. It was a beautiful morning. Sun just up, no noise except for the gulls. I walked out to the dock and saw the *Tasha* tied up there, looking as solid and real as I remembered her from eighty years ago. I walked the length of the dock before I realized Maria was standing on the gangplank. I didn't see anyone else, just Maria. She was dressed the same way as the last time she came down that gangplank, the summer of 1924. I said, 'Your little Teddy's not so young anymore, Mashka.' She smiled—even dead, she could light up the whole planet with that smile. She said, 'I only follow the program, just like you, Teddy.' Then she told me there was a man she needed to meet. The time had come and it could now be arranged, but she needed me to make sure it happened here on the island. Of course I asked her how exactly I was supposed to make it happen. She said, 'I told you, I only follow the program. Your part in the program is yours.' Then she said goodbye and told me she'd see me soon. Next blink, she and the *Tasha* were gone. I never even got a chance to ask the name of this man I was supposed to bring to her.

"Well, I sat in one of the rockers up at the hotel all morning long, trying to figure out how I was going to 'do my part' without knowing what my part was. I knew that some hotel guests had been seeing Maria's ghost around the island. I also remembered one little comment in a recent *Atlantic North* magazine article. It said that the Maria sightings began shortly after the publication of your book. I had read it, and I knew a little about you from your biography on the back cover, the one with your picture—nice picture by the way. I remembered the same thing about the sightings. Only, the magazine implied they were somehow psychologically induced by the book's popularity. I agreed that your book might have something to do with it, but not because it was causing people's imaginations to run away with them.

"So I dug your book out of my reading basket next to the john." He caught Mitch's look and winked. "At my age you spend a lot of time there— helps to have something to occupy you. Anyway, I spent the day on my porch reading it again. I read the whole thing, thinking maybe you or your book had something to do with Maria's little riddle. Not only did I read the book cover to cover, I examined every picture, looking for a clue. Nothing came to me. Problem was I was looking too hard. Finally, I'm flipping through the picture section one more time, kind of randomly, and there was the answer staring me in the face. I knew you were the one."

"Me?"

"You."

"What made you think it was me?"

Mr. Arndt studied his face. "I don't think you'd believe me if I just told you. You need to see for yourself."

"See what?"

"Remember last night I asked you who chose the pictures in your book?"

Mitch nodded. "Phyllis Church asked me the same thing."

"Look at the next-to-last page. Top picture. Look at it carefully."

"Why?"

"Just look at it."

He turned, set his cane firmly in front of him, and began shuffling back toward the land end of the dock. Mitch followed.

"I knew you were coming out to the island," the old man said, staring straight ahead at the hotel whose lights were now mostly out as the last of the late-night guests retired. "I didn't know if I was supposed to get you out here or just be here to help when you did get here. I really didn't know what my role was. Truth is, I still don't know. When it got close to this weekend, I checked in with the hotel to see if you were on the guest register. Just by sheer luck—or maybe it wasn't luck at all—I happened to speak with the same girl who took your call when you asked about a room. I told her I had a cabin for you."

"Cottage."

"Huh?"

"You said you had a *cottage*."

He gave a little chuckle. "That's right. I asked the girl to call you back and offer my cottage."

Mitch nodded in the dark. Some things were falling into place, but a lot of others hadn't yet. He wasn't sure he even wanted to know all of them. One question came to mind immediately. "What if I hadn't been the one Maria spoke to you about?"

Mr. Arndt stopped abruptly. In the moonlight Mitch saw his eyebrow go up, followed by the corner of his mouth. "I guess I'd still be cheating the grim reaper then, huh?"

They walked some more, this time in silence. Mitch sensed Mr. Arndt was thinking pretty hard and he finally asked what about.

"There's one more thing I wanted to tell you," the old man said, still three-stepping with the cane, but a little slower now. "I'm starting to think there's more going on here than either of us understands. And I think it has something to do with that sitting I had with Horace and Phyllis years ago."

Mitch waited for him to explain.

"You see, Maria wasn't the only one who came through to us that day," he went on. "Just as Horace had started to bring Phyllis out of her trance, another spirit came through. But it wasn't just a voice; it actually took possession of Phyllis's body. It shouted something in gibberish, and Phyllis—who's been a paraplegic since childhood, by the way—stood up, grabbed Horace by the throat and flung him across the floor. Thank God Horace kept his cool and just went on bringing her out of her trance. Just before she woke up, the voice shouted something in a terrible screech. Then she came out of it and fell on the floor in a heap. Fractured her elbow in the process."

"Jeez," Mitch said, picturing it. "What did it shout?"

Mr. Arndt stopped and stared off into space. "Well, it wasn't clear. Back then I thought I heard 'fever.' That's what it sounded like to me. I thought maybe this spirit was trying to get across that it died of a fever, or some kind of fever was making it violent, something like that. But I just wasn't sure. I've thought about it a million times since, but I couldn't come up with it." He looked at Mitch. "I thought about it again tonight after that first sitting, and I think I finally got it right."

"What do you think it was?" Mitch asked.

"'Leave her.'"

CHAPTER TWENTY-TWO

Mitch saw the old man off at his porch and went out back to the cabin. As he fumbled in his pocket for the key, the outside light came on. He looked back over his shoulder and saw Mr. Arndt waving from his kitchen window. He waved back, turned around, and there was the luna moth clinging to the same piece of board where he had been the night before. The smaller moths flitted about the burning light, but the king of them all just sat there facing down, watching Mitch. Or so it seemed.

He went inside where it was so sweltering he knew he would have trouble sleeping no matter what he did. He turned on the little table-top fan and went in the bathroom, removed his shirt and splashed cold water all over his face and torso. While drying off with a towel, he remembered what Mr. Arndt had said about his book: Next-to-last page of pictures, top of the page. What the hell was he trying to get across?

He tossed the towel aside and stepped from the tiny bathroom into the bedroom. A copy of *American Princess* was tucked inside his duffel bag and he dug it out. Sitting on the edge of the bed, he flipped open the book to the photo section and thumbed to the next-to-last glossy page. The page contained two black-and-white photos, both of them horizontal shots. The one on top had been taken at the Smythe Hotel the weekend of Maria's death. It showed a group of people gathered in a corner of the ballroom, all of them dressed in the formal wear of that era. The men wore white tuxedo jackets, shirts with wing collars and bow ties, their hair slicked back with Brilliantine or whatever hair tonic was popular at the time. The women were clad in light summer dresses, loose and strappy, and some wore headbands decorated with feather plumes or jewels. To the far left of the photo the stage steps were visible as well as part of the stage curtains. In the foreground stood Maria surrounded by friends. They were all young and vivacious and appeared a little intoxicated. Some were seated but mostly they stood, arms around shoulders and waists. In their time they had been well-known by the public for the surnames they bore, names their fathers and grandfathers had built into symbols of power in politics and business. But this young set was still at that stage in life where easy money means instant pleasure more than power and status. For some of them the money would be a past memory in a few years as the stock market crash and the Great Depression overtook them like a tidal wave. But for now, at the height of the Roaring Twenties, that seemed an impossibility judging by their faces.

Mitch studied the photo, wondering what Mr. Arndt had tried to alert him to without actually spelling it out. The picture had held no special significance for him when he chose it out of the hundreds he saw in collections at two local universities and the Boston Public Library. His only reason for including it in his book was that it was the last known photo taken of Maria. Fortunately, it was excellent. Maria appeared sharp and clear in the foreground and you could almost count each individual bead on her dress. Of course, the figures behind her were a little fuzzier due to the focal point being Maria. For this reason, the caption did not list the names of anyone in the picture other than Maria, as Mitch had feared incurring the wrath of some modern-day descendant if he misnamed any of them. So the "extras" in the photo remained anonymous to anyone not knowledgeable about Jazz Age society.

Mitch examined all of the faces surrounding Maria, wondering what on earth could be contained in the photo that excited Mr. Arndt so much. The only thing that stood out for him was the grand piano, which looked like the one now standing in the hotel lounge. The man seated at it would have looked familiar in the lounge, too; his appearance was strikingly similar to the piano player Mitch had followed up to Wendy's room just that evening. In fact, he was the spitting image . . .

Mitch looked closer. The resemblance was remarkable! Same tall, slim build, same tuxedo, same slick hair . . .

But everyone wore their hair slicked back in those days, Mitch thought. Why, when you looked closely, the guy next to him also had his hair slicked back in the same style . . .

Mitch blinked twice and stared hard at the figure beside the guy at the piano—

And nearly dropped the book on the floor.

It's me!

He was staring at an image of himself in a photograph taken in 1924. Though the grease in the man's hair made it look darker, the hairline was his own. The shape of the eyebrows, the nose, the chin, all his. Even the smile. It was exactly the same face.

My face.

He stood beside the man at the piano, one hand on his shoulder, stooped over in his direction with his head turned back toward the camera. Judging by their smiles, which were wider and more devilish than anyone else's, they had just shared a good joke.

What was just as remarkable, now that he looked closely at the picture, was that the guy at the piano and Mitch's doppelganger appeared clear and well-focused, just like Maria and the other people in the foreground. Yet everyone else in the back appeared slightly out of focus. The only way this could have happened was if the photograph had been doctored. But that would mean someone had played a rather odd, not-so-funny joke on him before the book was published. Besides, he had picked the photo himself and never noticed those two figures in it before. Then again, he hadn't really had a reason to pay attention before. So, he thought, if a man had existed at that time, who just happened to look a lot like him (okay, identical), couldn't it just be a coincidence? Couldn't it? No, he decided. Not someone who ran in Maria's crowd. Not with everything else he had experienced that weekend.

So, if my double lived eighty years ago, what does it mean?

He looked at the photo one more time, awestruck at his likeness, but also curious about the man at the piano who appeared to be the same one from the lounge. He mulled it over as he took off his clothes and slipped between the warm sheets. Laying there with his hands clasped behind his head, he pondered things that could never be explained with simple physics. After a few minutes of this, something finally clicked.

He got dressed, hurried outside and jogged across the Smythe lawn up to the hotel. Inside the quiet lobby he rushed past the front desk, turned left in front of the painting of Roger and Maria and stopped at the entrance to the lounge. The glass doors were locked; closing time had come and gone. The bar patrons had retired to their rooms and no one was inside. He would have to wait until tomorrow. *Damn!*

Then he saw a shadow cross in front of the frosted glass door. He knocked loudly. A moment later the doorknob turned and a man in coveralls pulled the door open. "The lounge is closed," he said.

"Please," Mitch pleaded, "I just need to come in for a second."

"Did you leave something? I can let you in to look."

"Yes. I think I left my cell phone."

The man let him pass, and he went straight to the corner where the piano man had played earlier that evening. The piano wasn't there; in its place stood a round table.

The man in the coveralls was wiping down another table nearby. Mitch asked, "Was there a grand piano in this corner earlier tonight?"

The man looked up and said, "Nope. Only piano in this hotel's in the ballroom, and they wouldn't move it unless they had to. It's pretty old."

Mitch hurried down the hall and poked his head into the ballroom to verify that the piano was there. It stood in the corner near the stage steps, just like in the picture. Mitch hadn't even noticed it when he sat in the ballroom during the press conference. Its white surface shined like new, although it had a crack or chip here and there as a reminder of its age. Mitch ran a finger over it then stepped back to where he thought the photographer had stood when he took the picture of Maria and her friends. He imagined her there, and he imagined this phantom man in the back who looked so much like himself. Walking back to the piano, he stood beside its stool and imagined the piano player sitting there. The man next to the piano player would be standing just about where Mitch now stood, looking straight ahead. And there would be Maria, straight in front of him. He would be looking over her shoulder at the photographer. Mitch stood with his hand in the air about chest height. Maria's shoulder would have been at about the same height.

A thought, maybe a revelation, came to him. Something else in the picture.

He left the ballroom and hurried back to his cabin. He had hoped to talk with Mr. Arndt, but the cottage was completely dark. Now he understood what the old man had been trying to tell him, but what he now knew only raised a thousand other questions. Hopefully, some of them would be answered for him in the morning. For now, he would have to endure the torment of his excitement.

—◆◇◆—

The moth came to Mitch in his sleep again. Only this time it wasn't on the ceiling but on Mitch's belly. He watched it grow to the size of a turtle, then its legs began to move and it crawled toward his head. When its face was inches away it stopped and stared at him, making no movement at all. The round, bugged-out eyes reflected what it saw, which should have been Mitch but wasn't. Instead, in one eye Mitch saw a room crowded with people dancing and milling about, and in the other he saw flames leaping from a roof.

He awoke at that point to find himself sitting straight up in his bed, naked, the sheets tossed aside. He was covered in sweat, which was no wonder considering the room temperature had to be a hundred degrees. He sat there, panting like a dog trying to cool off, until an urge made him turn and look out the window. Outside, through a gap in the underbrush and trees, a small patch of the Smythe lawn was visible. On that patch of grass, bathed in moonlight, stood a man. He was little more than a shadow, but Mitch was certain the man faced directly his way, staring back at him.

Mitch jumped out of bed and ran out the door. He followed the little path to the edge of the lawn, but by the time he got there the man was gone.

Only then did Mitch realize he was still naked. He hurried back to his cabin, this time being careful not to step on rocks or hurt anything delicate on a low branch.

On the way inside he looked for the moth. It was gone.

CHAPTER TWENTY-THREE

The sun was high when Mitch woke up the next morning. He dressed without showering and headed out the door to grab some coffee and see if the Sunday newspapers had arrived on the early boat. He wanted to see if any reports about the séance had reached the mainland.

Coming out of the trees, he spotted Mr. Arndt halfway across the lawn to the hotel. It didn't take long to catch up.

"You didn't get me up for breakfast," Mitch said, pulling up beside him.

"You wouldn't wake up. I banged on your door."

"Oh. Well, I have a lot of questions for you."

"Good morning to you, *too*."

"Sorry. Good morning. I do have questions."

"I'll bet you do."

The newspapers had arrived, and Mitch picked up copies of the *Boston Globe*, the *Portland Messenger* and the *Portsmouth Gazette*. Of the three, only the *Gazette's* reporter had managed to beat the Saturday night deadline and file a story. Mitch read it in the Sea Star over a sumptuous breakfast of eggs benedict with steak, sliced fruit and a bagel. Most mornings he ate a lot less, but for some reason that morning he was ravenous.

The newspaper article was entitled *Smythe Guests Who Never Checked Out.* The by-line listed Jennifer Yost, Assistant Features Editor, as the reporter. It read:

LONGBOAT HARBOR, Maine – The next time you stay at the Smythe Resort, keep an eye out for a non-paying guest or two.

It seems that some of the guests who checked in back in the roaring '20's never checked out. And it doesn't appear they'll be leaving anytime soon.

The Smythe Resort on Sumner Island was the site of an old-fashioned séance Saturday night. And judging by some weird occurrences, which this reporter personally witnessed, the séance was a success.

Candle flames danced and flickered without any wind, a shadow appeared to hover over two of the guests. And one guest's chair slid backwards and dumped the startled man onto the floor.

If there was any trickery going on, it was well-hidden. No one present has been able to explain these phenomena as anything but supernatural.

Last night was just the latest in a string of ghostly happenings at the resort.

For months now, hotel guests have been reporting spirit sightings, strange shadows and strange scents. One guest even saw a phantom ship docked in Longboat Harbor, directly in front of the resort.

The subject of most sightings seems to be Maria Boudreau, a socialite and heiress to a lumbering fortune who was murdered at the hotel in 1924. Guests have seen her wandering the hotel's corridors and the resort grounds. One guest saw her playing croquet on the hotel lawn.

But no one has actually come in contact with her. That is, until last night.

Dorothy Poulin, 89, a cousin of Miss Boudreau and the last living relative who had contact with her in the flesh, described "feeling" Maria at the séance.

"At one point, I could feel hands on my shoulders and what felt like someone kissing the top of my head," she said. "I never saw her, but I know it was her."

Maybe Ms. Poulin didn't see the spirit, but a video camera did.

Steven Pepperell of WHCV television was there taping the séance for a feature that will appear later this month. Pepperell's camera seems to have picked up something not easily explained.

"The camera was focused on [medium] Phyllis Church," Pepperell explained. "But it picked up the people on either side of her, too. I didn't see anything myself, but when I played back the tape, there was this sort of gray shadow behind the old lady [Poulin]. It moved across the table to the college professor."

The college professor was Dr. Mitchell Lambert, a history instructor at Fowler College. Dr. Lambert recently wrote a biography of Maria Boudreau.

He is also the one whose chair flew back and dumped him on the floor.

Asked what it was like, Dr. Lambert said, "It felt like I got hit in the chest with a burst of air. No solid feel to it, but I was helpless to resist. I just moved backward and next thing I knew I was on the floor."

A rude greeting from a spirit that has outstayed its welcome, to be sure.

But if the shadow that kissed Dorothy Poulin on the head was, indeed, Maria Boudreau, who was the prankster? Maria Boudreau hardly seems the type to get tough with college professors.

"It definitely wasn't Maria," said Horace Leeds, the world-famous ghost hunter who also attended. "Earlier, we had made contact with a male spirit and I think it was the same one. We tried pumping him for some information about himself, but he didn't cooperate much."

Judging by the hotel's tragic past, it could be the spirit of any number of people.

The Smythe resort was built in …

Mitch stopped there. "Well, this story's not so bad," he said to Mr. Arndt, who was busily carving a grapefruit.

"Good. I'll read it later."

Mitch watched him use his butter knife to slice each triangular section with a surgeon's precision. After he had traded the knife for a serrated grapefruit spoon and started eating it, Mitch said, "I saw the picture in my book."

"You did?"

"Yes."

"So what do you think?"

"I was about to ask you the same thing. I don't know what to think."

Mr. Arndt looked up at Mitch and said, through a full mouth, "He's a dead ringer."

Mitch rolled his eyes. "Whew! I thought you were going to say it's *me*."

"I didn't say it wasn't." He hunched over the grapefruit again and dove in with the spoon.

"So what are you telling me?"

"I'm saying I don't believe in coincidences. Your presence here today is somehow connected to the presence of someone from back in the summer of 'twenty-four who looks just like you."

"Then who the hell can it be?" Mitch said, his voice rising.

"Shh! This is a respectable establishment," Mr. Arndt said good-naturedly. "I don't know who it is. Maybe it *is* you." He spooned another chunk of grapefruit into his mouth.

"Or my doppelganger."

"Or your doppelganger."

Mitch studied his eyes. "You really think it's me."

"You saw the picture."

"It *is* me. No one could look that much like me."

"Unless, of course, the reprinting process caused a change to the image and it just coincidentally looks like you."

"I'd rather bet my money on the lottery."

"Yup. Me too."

"So it's me."

"I didn't say that."

Mitch threw his arms in the air. "Okay, I give up. Tell me what you're really thinking, Doctor."

The old man went back to carving fruit. "That's right, I'm a physician by training. I taught forensic medicine for years. My mind runs on reason and logic. When I see a dead body, I see a nonworking slab of meat and bones that once worked but doesn't anymore. It's a broken-down machine, that's all it is. Never to run again, of course, because the engine can't be re-started. I respect the theories of Einstein and all the rest, but I don't believe we can go back and forth in time."

He drank from his coffee cup and looked across the room at something that seemed to have distracted him. Impatiently, Mitch said, "And?"

"Patience, boy, I'm collecting my thoughts." He went on sipping coffee for a while then started in again.

"After I saw your face in that old photo, I remembered something I once read in one of those New Age psychology magazines. Seems there are some theorists who believe in a thing called transprogression. It's sort of a variation of reincarnation, best as I can tell. The belief is that sometimes we're born into a time and place where we don't belong. A mistake of birth, or maybe not a mistake, just the timing was wrong. Maybe that very particular person was needed elsewhere or else-*when*. Whatever the case, the person's life *transprogresses*, they say, to a different time and sometimes a different place. Instead of being reincarnated into a brand new life, a brand new form, the same life is reborn someplace else or some*time* else into the same person. Got it?"

"So you don't come back as a water buffalo or a grasshopper."

"Same person, same personality. Same soul, I suppose, if you believe in that sort of thing."

"Because of a mistake."

He shrugged. "That's what the theory suggests. If it were true, it would explain why some people have past-life memories."

"You sound like you believe in it."

"Oh, I don't know. It's a reasonable alternative to reincarnation where you keep being reborn into different random forms. What for? Transprogression is about progress, correction, even conscious placement for a specific purpose."

That last part got Mitch's attention. "Conscious? As in God?"

"Or something like that."

Mitch snorted and shook his head. "I don't buy it. Too much divine intervention stuff for me."

"Oh, there are even bigger problems with it in your case. See, in your case the person you theoretically were back in the early twentieth century seems to be the very same *physical* person you are today. It doesn't take a doctor to see the genetics problem. Yet there you are in that picture."

Mitch shrugged. "I agree, but I can't even prove the genetics problem—I was adopted. I have no idea who my real parents are."

Mr. Arndt sipped his coffee thoughtfully. "Of course, I see lots of physics problems with your chair moving by itself, or Maria's ghost walking off a phantom yacht. But that didn't stop it from happening."

Mitch still wasn't sure he bought into this transprogression thing, but he certainly had the feeling he wasn't in control of his own life, that he was being jerked around by someone or something. That was the only intervention he was concerned about. He said, "I'm starting to feel manipulated."

"I expect you would. But only because you've had the benefit of seeing first-hand how the other side has had a hand in your fate. Who knows? Maybe all of us flesh-and-blood types are being pushed around on a great big chessboard and we're just not aware of it. The difference is, in this case you *do* know it."

"That's the problem—I'm *not* entirely aware of it." Mitch shook his head. "I know I'm here on this island on this particular weekend for a reason. But I don't know what that reason is, or what's going to happen next. And so far, all I've gotten is a bloody nose caused by some spook with an anger management problem. I don't like this at all."

"You don't have to like it. But if I were you, I'd feel privileged. You're now a member of Maria Boudreau's inner circle."

He was right, of course. Underneath his consternation, Mitch did feel privileged. And excited, too, because he knew there was a good chance he might encounter Maria again. In fact, he intended to ask Mrs. Church and Leeds if he could have a private sitting sometime that day. Maybe Maria would come to him again.

But his hopes were dashed as soon as he and Mr. Arndt left the Sea Star and walked out into the lobby. There, they found Leeds and Church, surrounded by luggage, checking out.

"You're leaving now?" Mitch said to Leeds.

"We've done what we can here, professor." Leeds extended a hand to shake. "I'm speaking at a symposium on Wednesday in Atlanta. Gotta go home and get ready."

"Goodbye, Dr. Lambert," Mrs. Church said from her wheelchair. "It was nice to have met you."

"And you too." Mitch shook her hand. "I just wish you two could stay another night."

"Dr. Lambert wants one more contact with Maria Boudreau," Mr. Arndt explained.

"You do?" Leeds said.

"I want to, but I also think I'm supposed to," Mitch told him.

"May I talk with you privately?" Mrs. Church interrupted, looking at Mitch gravely. She toggled her wheelchair over to a corner and Mitch followed. When they were out of earshot, she said, "You think you're *supposed* to?"

Mitch shrugged. "Mr. Arndt told me about your meeting with him back in the seventies. He thinks I'm supposed to be here. To communicate with Maria."

"Is that what he told you?"

"And showed me," Mitch said. When she furrowed her eyebrows again, he added, "The photo in my book."

Mrs. Church nodded. "I must tell you, I've been doing this for the better part of a half-century, and I've never seen anything like what I saw in that picture."

"What do you make of it?"

She shrugged and said, matter-of-factly, "Maria will let you know."

Another non-answer. Mitch could barely contain his frustration. "What makes you think Maria will let me know?"

Mrs. Church took his hand and pulled him down so he was face to face with her. She smiled and whispered out loud, "Intuition. No hocus pocus. Just intuition."

Out at the dock, the ferry boat blew its horn, indicating ten minutes to departure. They said goodbye to Mrs. Church and Leeds and left the hotel.

PART III

CHAPTER TWENTY-FOUR

Mr. Arndt and Mitch parted at the bottom of the steps, and the old man headed back toward his cottage while Mitch wandered off in the direction of Lover's Lookout for no particular reason. He had no idea what to do with himself the rest of the morning. Nothing really appealed to him. Up at the tennis courts, guests in expensive tennis garb panted in the excruciating heat. Down at the beach, mothers played in the sand with the younger kids, while the dads and older kids snorkeled and rafted. The ice cream stand at the beach pavilion wasn't open yet. The walking trails held no interest for him (he would just as soon stay off them for now, thank you very much). The health room inside the hotel sounded good. At least it would be cool in there. Of course, if he wanted to cool off there was plenty of ocean nearby for that. But he just had no motivation for it.

So he walked out to the edge of the island between Lover's Lookout and the dock to climb around on the rocks. The wet rocks close to the water would be dangerously slippery, so he stayed up high where the view was unobstructed for miles. White sails dotted the water everywhere, and here and there a powerboat trailed a white wake behind it. A casual summer weekend in New England. Maybe hotter than usual, but normal in every other way. If he were back on the mainland, he probably would have been driving with some friends up to the White Mountains to escape the heat. Not one to get bored easily, Mitch could always find something to occupy his days. Yet today he just couldn't get himself going. At first he couldn't figure out why. Then it occurred to him that he was in a waiting mode. Waiting for something to happen, or maybe waiting for a sign. A signal telling him what to do next. He hoped Maria would give him a clue about when and where he could make contact with her again. Even though Phyllis Church was leaving, he believed he could make the connection without her. He just had to figure out how.

A commotion near the hotel brought Mitch back up on the grass. Halfway down the walkway, Leeds and Mrs. Church were moving slowly toward the dock, surrounded by reporters and television crew getting in their last questions and video footage. Today the reporters seemed much more eager, probably because of Mitch's chair ride the night before. Mrs. Church—with Mitch's unwitting help—had made believers of them at last.

Then he saw Wendy, and his heart sank. She walked just behind the crowd, wheeling two large suitcases behind her. It hadn't even occurred to him that she might leave the island before him. He watched until they were all the way to the bell by the dock, then he climbed back down on the rocks and sat staring out to sea. He couldn't bear to watch them go.

The sea rose and fell on the rocks below. After a while, he spotted something tangled in the seaweed attached to the rocks: a dead animal. He hadn't noticed it before because it was roughly the same color as the rocks. The water rose and fell a couple more times before he realized what kind of animal it was: a harbor seal. He saw no signs of trauma, yet it was definitely dead and its body appeared deflated. Probably a power boat prop had sliced its underside open and he just couldn't see it from this angle. Seeing it all deflated like that reminded him of the legend of the selkies, the seal creatures that come ashore, shed their skins and become human, only to return to the sea if they find their skins again.

Mitch stood and began leaping from rock to rock, back up to the Smythe lawn. He jogged across the grass and down to the dock. The Leeds-Church entourage had reached the end of the dock and was saying its last goodbyes as everyone prepared to board. Mitch ignored them. They weren't the ones he had come to see.

Wendy had her back to him when Mitch came up to her and lightly touched her on the shoulder. She turned and smiled at him. "Hey, Mitch."

"Don't go," he blurted without even thinking.

She gave him a quizzical look then glanced down at the two suitcases resting upright on their wheels. "Oh. I'm not leaving. These are Phyllis's. I just volunteered to bring them down to the boat for her."

Beneath his relief Mitch felt stupid, and he began searching for an explanation for his sudden display of emotion. Finally, he said, "Good. I need a dancing partner tonight and Mr. Arndt's a little slow."

Wendy frowned. "I'm booked on the afternoon boat."

Mitch's heart dropped again. "Well, then, maybe we can spend a few hours together before you go."

"Okay."

They watched the last of the passengers board. Then the boat crew came and got the two suitcases and the gangplank was pulled away. The rope lines were unraveled from the cleats and tossed aboard. The *Narwhal* backed up, did a 180-degree turn to port and started out of the harbor, its passengers yelling goodbye and waving to the people on the dock who waved back. When the ferry was a good distance away, the crowd on the dock began walking back in the direction of the hotel, leaving Wendy and Mitch alone.

They stood there, quietly watching the *Narwhal* disappear around the western point of Forge's Island. When its stern finally went out of view, Mitch said to Wendy, "So, what do you feel like doing? Swim? Tennis? Kind of hot for tennis. We can go back inside if you'd like."

"How about we just find a shady spot and talk."

They turned and began walking off the dock. Halfway along, Mitch's head began to feel light, and a picture danced in his brain, seemingly just behind his eyes. In his mind he was looking behind him, as though he had proverbial eyes in the back of his head. He slowed and Wendy asked what was wrong, but he ignored her. He was too busy watching the vision in his head. It had blinded him to what was in front of him and so he stopped, turned around and blinked hard. Out across Longboat Harbor, a thousand feet away, Forge's Island spread out in roughly the shape of a salamander seen from a side view, the western end serving as its tail. Halfway up the tail stood a woman. From this distance it was hard to make out much more than her outline, but she appeared to be wearing a long, dark dress and a wide-brimmed hat, the kind a woman might wear gardening on a sunny day.

"What are you doing?" Wendy asked from Mitch's side. When he didn't answer, she added, "Mitch, *what* are you *looking* at?"

"Do you see her?"

She followed his gaze. "Who? Where?"

"That woman over on Forge's. Directly across from us."

Wendy shaded her eyes with her hand. She shook her head. "I don't see her."

"Right there, plain as day. Just above the rocks, standing on the grass. She's in a long dress. It's flapping around in the breeze."

Wendy squinted. "Mitch, there's no breeze. And there's no woman over there. Are you sure you see her?"

He tore his gaze away and stared at Wendy. "Yes, I'm sure. I really am, Wendy, just like you were sure about Mr. Buddha."

Wendy searched his eyes for a moment as if looking for the source of his vision. Mitch stared back, hoping she would find it, wanting her to share it. But she didn't. She just blinked and turned her eyes back across the harbor. "I wish I could see her, Mitch, but I can't."

He looked back at Forge's, and there stood the woman, this time beckoning to him with an outstretched hand.

"Is she still there?" Wendy asked.

"Yes."

"What's she doing?"

"She wants us to go over there."

Wendy looked back and forth over the island, but she obviously didn't see her. "Should we go over?"

Mitch didn't even hesitate. "Let's go."

CHAPTER TWENTY-FIVE

Next to the main dock, a smaller finger pier stuck out into the harbor at a perpendicular angle. Tied to the pier were a dozen rowboats of all different colors. Mitch led Wendy out onto the pier where they met up with a young man in Smythe regulation shorts, polo shirt and dock shoes. He took their information and helped them into one of the boats.

Mitch had never rowed in his life, but he quickly got the hang of it. The hardest thing was steering with his back to the place they were headed. Every time he looked over one shoulder to see where he was going, he somehow managed to pull too hard on the opposite side and went the wrong way. They ended up weaving back and forth like a tacking sailboat, dodging the much larger boats moored in the harbor, until there was nothing but open water between them and Forge's Island.

After meandering this way for three hundred yards, the bow scraped through gravelly sand on the southern side of the island. The tiny beach on which they had landed lay at the bottom of a steep bluff, so it was impossible to see the dark woman who would be up high on the grassy part. Mitch helped Wendy out of the boat and they scurried up the soft, sandy hill until they stood at the top. From there, they looked across the grass at the spot where the woman had stood when Mitch first saw her from across the harbor. She wasn't there. He started to tell Wendy that they were too late, but then he caught a glimpse of dark blue out of the corner of his eye. He turned his head and saw the woman across the grass on the north side of the island. She had just started descending toward the northern shore.

"This way," Mitch said.

They walked northward until they reached the edge of another bluff overlooking a muddy, rock-strewn beach. Down on that beach, close to the water, the woman stood looking out to sea. Her back was to them and her straw hat obscured most of her head, but not enough that Mitch couldn't see her hair. It was dark red and wavy, falling to her shoulders.

They descended the bluff by letting the sand give way under their feet and sliding most of the way down. At the bottom, Mitch led Wendy from rock to rock. He had to look down at where he was stepping most of the time, and so he lost sight of the woman. The next time he looked for her, she had disappeared again.

They reached the spot where she had stood just a minute or two ago. At first, Mitch saw no sign of her having been there. But when he looked closer he saw two prints in the wet sand between the rocks that looked like they had been made by sandals. Forge's Island was owned by the Smythe Resort and few people visited it other than guests who rowed over for picnics and blueberry picking. Even they seldom came over to this muddy beach. Mitch had no doubt it was Maria who had stood there. Looking closer, he could see more footprints on the other side of the rocks going into the water. They seemed to just keep on going, right into the ocean. Mitch stepped over the rocks and followed the prints. Surprisingly, he did not sink in as he expected to in the mushy, clam flat-type mud. But when Wendy started to walk out beside him, she sank in halfway up her sneakers and retreated back to the rocks.

"That's odd," Mitch said. He jumped up and down lightly. "I should be sinking in."

But he didn't. Something solid beneath his feet kept him up. He scraped the side of his sneaker through the mud to see what it was. He didn't have to dig down far to reveal boards, half a foot wide, lined up close together. At first he thought he had dug up a sunken boat, but soon realized it was a dock. Maria had walked out on its mud-covered ruins before disappearing.

"Hey Wendy, come take a look. It's solid."

Wendy traced his footsteps, walking gingerly on the mud, until she realized she wouldn't sink in. She hurried over to where he stood.

"What is it?" she asked, looking at the planks that were the same color as the mud.

"There used to be a dock here."

"Where's the woman?"

Mitch looked around. "I don't see her anymore. But I think she wanted us to see this."

Wendy made a face. "Why? It's just a rotted old dock."

Mitch shrugged. "I don't know."

He looked around again, hoping Maria would appear. All he saw were gulls.

When it became clear Maria wasn't going to show herself again, they rowed back to the Smythe Resort. It was afternoon now, and with the sun at its peak and the humidity way up, it felt like a steam room. The sun burned bright in a cloudless sky, yet he could see the haze when he looked toward the mainland.

By the time they had rowed back to Sumner Island, they were both drenched in sweat. Mitch suggested a swim, and Wendy, who hadn't been in the water all weekend, thought it was a terrific idea. As Mitch watched her walk up to the hotel to change into a bathing suit, it dawned on him that they both had treated the past couple of days like work days. Today was their last day on the island together, and it would be a shame if they didn't get in a little fun. That's exactly what we're going to do, he thought as he watched Wendy's slender legs and bouncing blonde curls moving up the walk toward the veranda. But his next thought was of Maria, and his pleasure at watching Wendy turned to guilt. He said out loud, "Stop acting crazy, Mitch." But he knew it would do no good.

He changed into swim trunks and met Wendy in front of the pavilion by the beach. She had been given carte blanche as one of the Leeds-Church entourage and was allowed to go anywhere on the resort property, so they went down to the private beach. Normally, Mitch would have preferred the public beach—he just wasn't the private club sort—but it was a nicer beach, less crowded, and he figured, what the hell, how often do I get to do this?

They swam first and the cold Atlantic felt fabulous and invigorating. Wendy had brought down a pair of goggles and they took turns diving down to see what was at the bottom. Wendy found a sand dollar and Mitch found the handle end of an oar. He tossed that, but Wendy kept her sand dollar, vowing to bring it home and keep it as a souvenir of their afternoon together.

Up on the beach, they slathered sun block on each other's backs and lay on huge beach towels Wendy had borrowed from the hotel. All around, the wealthiest Smythe guests sat under red-and-white striped umbrellas, also owned by the Smythe. Their swim wear looked expensive, probably more expensive than any of Mitch's business suits. Their kids were little carbon copies of their parents, and several of them were being cared for by nannies while their parents sipped cool drinks under umbrellas or up at the little bar on the side of the snack bar facing the beach. Mitch had never been terribly comfortable around rich people, so he offered to buy Wendy an ice cream cone up at the snack bar. Wendy, maybe sensing his restlessness, feigned heat exhaustion and they went up together. They bought two cones and strolled across the grass, licking the rapidly melting ice cream and chatting about absolutely nothing. It felt good to have nothing to do or think about for a little while.

Their stroll took them up to the Smythe's veranda where they found two vacant rockers. They rocked slowly, saying very little, crunching the last of their cones and looking down the hill at the boats in the harbor. Seagulls flitted about, squawking and diving. An elderly couple nearby spoke in low voices. Off to their right, past the eastern corner of the hotel, the *bop!* . . . *bop!* . . . *bop!* sound of a tennis game floated their way. The day felt peaceful and lazy. Mitch rocked in rhythm, his head against the caned back of the chair, and felt all the tension drain from his body.

The next thing he knew, Wendy was rubbing his arm and telling him to wake up.

"What?" Mitch looked around. "How long was I out?"

"Only a minute or two. I started to doze, too. It's probably all the sun we got today. Maybe we should take a nap before dinner."

"You mean you're staying?" Mitch said, feeling like a little kid.

"Yeah. I'll just miss the boat and let the hotel pick up my tab for another night." She stood up and stretched. "I'll meet you and Mr. Arndt for dinner if you don't mind me joining you."

"Of course we don't mind. But be warned: he might make you pay the tip."

She placed her hand on one of Mitch's cheeks and kissed him on the other. "I had a great time today." She turned and left.

Mitch watched her go in the direction of the front doors. After she had gone inside, he headed for his cabin, feeling guilty again.

CHAPTER TWENTY-SIX

By the time he reached his little cabin, Mitch was feeling so relaxed and sleepy he wondered if someone had spiked his ice cream with something. He had never been so tired this time of the day.

He lay in bed on top of the covers, naked to the world if anyone cared to look in the window. Outside, the sounds of gulls and children down at the beach wafted in. He listened to the hypnotic sounds, trying to think of Maria but mostly thinking of Wendy. He wondered what she looked like sleeping in her hotel bed, if she slept naked even though she didn't have to because her room was air-conditioned. His last thought was of Maria, though. He knew she could come to him at will, but he wondered if there was any way he could summon *her* at will. So far he hadn't thought of a way.

Before long he was asleep on his back, arms thrown to the sides, and when he woke up he was in the same position. His sleep had been dreamless as far as he could remember, and the nap seemed to last just minutes. Yet as soon as he opened his eyes he knew it was morning. The position of the sun is what told him this: the light outside the window on the eastern side of the cabin was much brighter than the western side. If he was right, that meant he had slept sixteen hours or more, which didn't seem possible. Yet he was certain it was morning.

To confirm this, he threw on some clothes and went outside. Sure enough, the sun sat low in the eastern sky. He'd gone down for a one-hour nap and slept through the night instead. How could this have happened? What was the matter with him? He mentally checked for symptoms of illness—stuffy nose, ticklish throat, achy joints. But he felt fine except for a little haziness in his head, which he attributed to his extraordinarily long nap.

He stood just outside the cabin door listening to the sounds of early morning: chirping birds, squawking gulls, water lapping against rocks. The joggers weren't out yet or he would have heard the sound of feet pounding on the trails. In a moment he heard the sound of a loud, whining engine and looked up to see a yellow bi-plane pass over Longboat Harbor. It appeared to be an exact replica of a World War I fighter. The pilot dipped the wings as it flew low over the water, and when Mitch looked in the open cockpit, he saw the pilot was wearing one of those old leather flying helmets and goggles. Maybe there was an air show nearby. Or . . .

Mitch started out in the direction of the little trail running from the cabin to the Smythe lawn, and discovered that the trail wasn't there. Just a wall of wild shrubbery of some kind. A familiar sense of disjointedness rushed over him, and he turned and made his way back around the front of Mr. Arndt's cottage to the main trail. Something made him glance back at the cottage where he saw gray slate shingles covering the roof instead of green tin.

It was happening again.

He followed the trail toward the dock, wondering how he got here, what he kept doing to make it happen. On the beach to his right he saw tall white tents, the kind people once used for changing into swim suits. A little farther down the trail the bathhouse stood quiet, not open this early in the day. It looked the same as it had the last time Mitch saw it, only now it was painted a peach color instead of gray.

Over in the harbor, boats rested at anchor, and the scene was about the same as in modern times except for the look of the boats themselves. Every one of them was built of wood. No smooth fiberglass hulls, just wood slat over wood slat, wood cabins, wood masts. Most were sailboats, but there were a few runabouts and one big cabin cruiser that looked a lot like Hemingway's *Pilar*. The harbor looked like a floating nautical museum.

Up ahead, a bell began ringing. He looked up the trail and saw a young man in a striped shirt and gray pants jerking the clapper rope on the dock bell. Out in the harbor a huge, three-masted sailboat was just tying up at the dock. Its hull was painted white with a tan stripe around the top, and its cabins were a rich, dark brown. The *Tasha*.

On her deck, guests of the Boudreaus stood talking and waiting for the gangplank to be run up. After a minute or two, Maria emerged from a cabin door and Mitch's stomach did a flip-flop. She looked sharp and lovely in a long yellow dress and wide-brimmed hat. The spring in her step, the way she stood tall and poised as she walked, even the way she turned her head shouted out good breeding and the vitality so often ascribed to her.

Her father emerged next from the same door, followed by a shorter, stockier man: Fenton. They wore dark pants, gray knit shirts, and what looked like Greek sailor hats with gold trim around the brim. The three joined two men by the rail, one young, the other white-haired and a little heavyset. Mitch couldn't see their faces, but he thought they must be Malcolm Akers and his son Robert.

Mitch continued on the trail, drawing closer to the dock, never taking his eyes off Maria. By the time he reached the bell, the gangplank had been set in place and the passengers had started to disembark. He stopped and watched the procession. Nearby, an elderly woman dressed in an ankle-length dress and a huge, frilly hat leaned on a wooden cane, also watching. Mitch remarked about the beauty of the *Tasha*, just to make friendly conversation. The woman didn't react, just kept on watching. Mitch shrugged off the sleight, thinking she must be hard of hearing.

The Boudreau entourage approached on the dock, and suddenly Mitch realized how odd he must look. Every man on the dock wore long pants and a long-sleeved shirt, and here he was dressed in shorts and a t-shirt with the Nike swoosh emblazoned on the front. He hoped no one would ask questions.

It turned out that he didn't have to worry because none of the crowd gave him as much as a passing glance. One of the dock boys even walked right at him and Mitch had to move aside to avoid getting run over. Now he understood why the old lady hadn't responded. He was merely an observer, standing in the middle of something like a 3-D holographic movie.

Maria passed by him, and the first thing Mitch was struck by was her height. She was taller than he had expected, almost as tall as him. Beneath the straw hat her auburn hair fell to her shoulders in a cascade of waves, which glistened in the bright sunlight. Her body was slim, not curvy at all, yet delicate and feminine. She walked with her shoulders square, legs together, in a casual-yet-purposeful gait. Although she gave off an air of confidence, at the same time Mitch sensed an underlying awkwardness, even vulnerability, which all the charm school training in the world could not hide. It was one of the things that had made her so endearing to her contemporaries: this contradictory personality, the unsure little girl inside the determined woman's body. Seeing her up close in living color and fluid movement, Mitch was more taken with her than he ever imagined he could be. But she was just a vision. Or a ghost. He wasn't sure which. How could he be so taken with the equivalent of a hologram? Still, as she walked past, he felt nothing short of love for her. Before, he had thought he was just infatuated, but infatuation couldn't possibly feel so solid, so complete. And he didn't even know her. It made no sense at all.

He watched her progress up the walkway, accompanied by four women he did not recognize and two powerful-looking men in the rear—probably bodyguards. Then came the male guests, eight or ten in all. Roger was easy to spot: tall and regal, dressed impeccably, his thinning hair covered by his hat, his tsar-like beard perfectly trimmed. Beside him Fenton appeared short, though he was probably Mitch's height, and round like a barrel but with a regal air of his own. As the group passed, Mitch looked for Robert Akers and quickly found him. He was the youngest of the men by a good ten years, tall and slim in light-colored clothes. His long, thin nose and broad mouth fit well over a strong, squared-off jaw. His eyes were his most notable attribute— the color of glacier ice.

Mitch watched them go up the walk, laughing and chatting and shaking hands with some hotel management people who had come out to greet them. Caught up in the excitement, he was suddenly overtaken by an irrepressible urge. He cupped his hands around his mouth and shouted to Roger, "I'm just gonna take the boat around the harbor once or twice, I'll be right back!" He looked over at the little old lady with the huge hat who was also watching the procession go by, smiling like a kid who had waited all day for Santa Claus to arrive at the end of the parade. He walked up to her, gave a deep bow, and said, "May I have this dance? Let's see, you must have been born before the Civil War. We'll waltz." He reached for her shoulder and right hand and there was a sudden flash, not of light but of blackness like a film negative. The next thing he knew he was sitting on the ground looking up at her. The lady looked around, eyes wide open, her smile replaced by a bewildered frown. She had dropped her cane. Something had happened to her, too, when Mitch touched her.

Mitch stood up and dusted off the seat of his shorts. So this vision thing wasn't just a holographic picture. Though not solid, it had a substance nevertheless. An energy, a hum just like his own physical world. He wasn't sure he would call it life, but he had to call it real. As real as his own world.

And he didn't belong here. He was voyeuristically peeking through a two-way mirror, eavesdropping on the other side. And it was all wrong.

Except that Maria wanted him to be here.

She had *caused* him to be here, he was sure of it. He just had to remember that he was an awkward guest who had to respect this place, follow the rules and try his best not to disrupt anything.

Right now that wasn't a problem because he suddenly got an overwhelming urge to get back to his cabin and look at that photograph in his book again. He needed to decide once and for all if the face in the picture really was his own.

He hurried down the trail to his cabin, pulled out *American Princess* and turned to the photo of the crowd in the ballroom. This time it only took a glance to make up his mind. The man in the picture was definitely him. It was as though his own face had been superimposed on someone else's body by some jokester photo editor. The thought of such a practical joke crossed his mind again, as absurd as it seemed. Probably because the alternative theory seemed even more absurd.

Something made him look up. Nothing had changed in the room, but something was different. It only took a second to figure it out: the quality of the sunlight had changed again. He moved closer to the window. Outside, it was now dusk instead of early morning. The sun sat low in the west. In a matter of minutes the day had wasted away to evening.

He left his book lying open on the bed and went outside to get a better look at the sky. Indeed, the sun was setting over coastal Maine, casting long shadows.

A flash of movement to his right made him turn his head. On Mr. Arndt's porch the wooden screen door opened, and out walked a middle-aged man in a white tuxedo jacket, followed by a boy of about ten in a suit and tie with short pants. The boy looked uncomfortable, the way young boys do in formal clothes, and the grease in his hair couldn't hold down a rooster tail at the back of his head. The two walked quickly down the steps on the other side of the porch and out to the trail, so Mitch never saw their faces. He hurried after them, hoping to see them from the front. But when he reached the trail they were nowhere in sight.

He jogged down the trail until he reached the bottom of the Smythe lawn. Up ahead—way up ahead—the man and boy were just walking up the veranda steps on their way into the hotel. Time had skipped a beat again.

Mitch hurried up to the veranda, walking between guests in Gatsby-esque clothing, lots of them wearing hats, none of them in shorts or t-shirts, all looking unusually proper for being on vacation. Most of the younger women wore loose-fitting dresses with low waistbands and some wore cloche hats. The men wore linen shirts with Eton collars and light-colored jackets. It seemed as if he had walked onto the stage of a Broadway play about the Jazz Age.

Standing on the veranda just outside the doors, it occurred to him for the first time that he couldn't just stroll inside. He had to wait until the doorman opened the doors for some guests, then sneak in behind them. This took a few minutes of waiting, but he finally managed to accomplish it without touching anything.

Inside, he looked around the lobby. It didn't appear much different from the way it did in the twenty-first century. Except for some rugs and plants, and the color of the columns which were a light pink instead of white, it looked pretty much the same. The front desk was the same one, but the people behind it wore red bow ties. Bellhops in red pillbox caps and suits—uniforms Mitch had seen a thousand times in old movies but never in real life—scurried about. Over by the fireplace, the furniture seemed to be the same leather chairs and Chippendale style tables, but the most obvious difference was the absence of the portrait of Maria and Roger above the fireplace. What hung in its place was an impressionist painting of a landscape.

Directly in front of him, Mitch noticed one other stark difference he hadn't picked up on before. The sign above what should have been the Sea Star restaurant read, simply, "Dining." He was reminded of what he knew of the hotel's dining facilities of that time. What he should see if he went through that archway was one long dining hall comprised of all the space that today was divided into the Sea Star at this end and the Sandpiper at the other. Curiosity impelled him through the archway to have a look. His prediction was right. He stood in a long hall filled with tables covered in fine linen and fresh flowers. Waitresses and waiters bustled about in uniforms that reminded him more of butlers and maids. There seemed to be a servant for every function—a water-pourer, a wine steward, a head waiter, and several bus boys replacing dinnerware after each course. There was so much activity Mitch had to keep moving around to avoid being bumped into.

His dodging brought him closer to the middle of the hall where he had a better view of the Sandpiper end. Down that end, he could see a long table with sixteen guests in elegant dress seated around it. At the head of the table sat the hotel's manager, Terence Barkley, whom Mitch recognized from pictures he had seen in his research of the hotel. Roger Boudreau was to Barkley's left, and next to Roger were Maria and Fenton. To Fenton's left sat the man and boy Mitch had seen coming out of Mr. Arndt's cottage—Dr. Arndt and a very young Theodore Arndt. Across the table from Roger and Maria were Malcolm Akers and Robert Akers. Everyone else at the table Mitch knew only by name, having read the list from the police investigation of the murders. He couldn't put name to face, but he knew they were all V.I.P.'s of the time. Their expensive dress certainly fit the bill.

He made his way closer, being careful not to bump into anything or anyone. When he had drawn close enough, he could hear the buzz of conversation from their particular table. A few feet closer and he could hear Robert saying something to a much older woman seated beside him. She answered "Yes" then looked in the direction of the wall across the room. The wall was covered in a huge tarp, and a sign hanging on it read "Temporary - Renovations." Robert said to her—and this Mitch heard clearly—"A rat could get through that in a heartbeat." The lady looked alarmed. She said, "You know, you're right!" She leaned closer to Robert and said something Mitch couldn't make out. Robert chuckled and said something back, which made the woman break into polite, restrained laughter.

Seeing the tarp, Mitch was reminded of the construction he had seen from up on Lone Tree Hill. He went over for a closer look. The tarp was some kind of heavy white canvas treated with an oily substance to make it waterproof. One corner of it was drawn back just enough for someone to poke their head through, and Mitch did just that. Behind the tarp the addition, measuring about thirty feet by fifteen feet, had been framed out from ground to roof. The bottom framing was covered in twelve-inch-wide planks up to about the window level of the second floor. The rest of the way up, similar tarps covered the frame while it awaited planking.

A long wooden ladder leaned against the hotel wall inside the addition. It seemed a little odd that it stood inside the frame job instead of outside, but Mitch didn't give it much thought. He pulled his head back in and returned to the Boudreaus' table.

This time he stood near Maria, drinking in her beauty and grace, falling in love with her all over again. She sat tall and straight in her chair, hands resting properly in her lap, perfectly at ease among the cream of society. Mitch noticed that Robert kept looking her way, trying to catch her eye, but Maria kept her gaze elsewhere. Mitch was jealous of the man and thankful that Maria did not flirt with him, which would have made it even worse. He tried drawing on his rational side to keep his emotions in check; this was, after all, just a replay of something from many decades ago. He shouldn't feel jealous any more than he would watching an old movie. But he felt it just the same.

As he scanned the people around the table, Mitch was surprised to find one other little fellow who appeared to feel the same way: Theodore Arndt. Teddy, as they called him in those years, kept stealing glances first at Maria then at Robert, and if looks could kill . . . Mitch was surprised at this display of emotion in such a young boy until he remembered how Mr. Arndt had described his childhood relationship with Maria. Maybe he felt threatened by this new man in Maria's life, the way a young boy naturally might under the circumstances. Judging by the daggers firing out of his eyes right now, this was the case.

As a historian, it excited Mitch to see this whole scene playing out. The fact this dinner party had taken place was common knowledge among everyone who knew the story of the Boudreaus. But who else knew this boy had spent the evening giving his adult rival dirty looks? Or even the smallest of other details, like the fact Maria had a tiny mole on the back of her neck, or that the older woman sitting beside Robert Akers had a habit of resting her hand on his thigh as she spoke with him. Or that Terence Barkley, Malcolm Akers, Roger and Fenton were all half in the bag before the main course arrived. Only Mitch knew these things. A real scoop if you were a Boudreau-phile.

The more he came to know little nuances about each of these people, the more Mitch wanted to be physically closer to them. Without taking care to look around at who was nearby, he took a couple of steps in the direction of their table . . . and crossed the path of a waiter carrying a tray full of plates.

Next thing Mitch knew, he was on the floor beside the waiter, surrounded by a lot of broken plates and ruined food. He had done it again.

He got to his feet and looked around, certain everyone would be gawking at him, but all eyes were on the waiter instead. All except Maria's, that is.

Maria was staring straight at Mitch.

She sees me! She's aware *of me!*

He stared back, so thrilled to be in communication with her that all he could think to do was shrug and give a stupid grin. Maria's face softened and she stifled a giggle, causing Fenton to shoot an admonishing look her way. Apparently, he thought she was laughing at the waiter!

By now, the waiter had gotten to his feet and brushed himself off and was apologizing profusely to the guests at the table. He looked terribly distressed, and kept saying he had no idea how he had spilled the tray. Mitch could tell by their faces that the dinner guests thought the waiter was just plain clumsy and he felt bad for the guy. He wished he could help him.

The dining room floor was getting too busy and Mitch decided it was time to get going. He gave Maria a shy wave and made his way along the wall back to the entranceway and out to the lobby. As he went, he marveled at the contact he had just made with her. If this was some sort of not-so-instant replay, an image of something that happened more than eighty years ago, how could Maria be aware of him? How?

At the exact center of the lobby Mitch stopped abruptly, turned on his heels, and marched back through the entranceway into the dining room, thinking he would go back to Maria and see if he could get her attention again. But that wasn't going to happen. Because now there was a wall dividing the dining hall into the Sea Star and the Sandpiper. And the diners were dressed in modern clothes. Just to be sure, he walked back out to the lobby and looked up at the sign over the entranceway. It read "Sea Star."

He was back in his own time.

CHAPTER TWENTY-SEVEN

Mitch scrambled around looking for a clock, and finally found one hanging on the wall behind the lobby desk. It read 5:30. Still a little early for dinner.

Walking out the door and across the veranda, he tried to imagine how he had gotten up to the hotel in the first place. His first theory was that he had walked through a tear in the membrane—or whatever you called the thing that separated physical from ethereal—but somehow his physical self had remained in the present. Which would mean he had actually walked to the dock then up to the hotel even as his mind was seeing and encountering things that hadn't been there for decades. But if that was the case, why hadn't he bumped into something that was there now—a chair or table for instance—that hadn't been there in the past?

Then again, maybe he hadn't really walked up to the hotel at all. Maybe he had ended up there when he went through the tear in the membrane, like passing through an earthly wormhole. The thing that happened next convinced him that this was a more likely explanation.

He descended the veranda steps and started across the lawn in the direction of Mr. Arndt's cottage. Behind him, he could hear people playing tennis. In front, he heard beach noises. At first all these noises were loud and clear, but as he walked, he noticed all these sounds beginning to fade. Not the way sounds gradually fade when you walk away from their source, but the way they do when your ears get blocked descending in an airplane. He stopped on the grass and rubbed his ears and yawned, trying to unblock them. Then, all at once, they cleared up by themselves. He heard birds and voices again, and something new and completely baffling: the sound of traffic. Cars. Fairly loud ones, too. Something he knew had never existed on Sumner Island.

The sound seemed to be coming from behind him, and growing in volume. He spun around to see a pair of round, bugged-out headlights not twenty feet away, bearing down on him. He leaped to one side, landing on a hard-packed dirt surface, just as an early Model-T drove by. As it did, he caught sight of the driver, a man with round goggles and a white cap. He never slowed down, never even looked Mitch's way, as if he wasn't even there.

Which he wasn't, Mitch realized.

He stood up, looked around, and immediately recognized where he stood: Commonwealth Avenue in Boston, close to the Public Garden. He was standing in front of Roger Boudreau's mansion. The day was sunny, and a cool breeze ruffled the yellow and orange leaves in the trees lining the street and the wide, grassy median. The cars parked along the street and the clothing worn by the pedestrians confirmed that he was back in the early part of the twentieth century.

And there was Roger's home, right there in front of him, windows open to catch the breeze. Coming out the front door was a servant girl in uniform looking like she was on her way to run some errand or another. He ran up the steps and darted through the open door before the girl could close it.

He stood inside the entranceway, looking at a spacious hall with wood floors, wood-paneled walls and a fabulous curving staircase. The staircase rose to a landing with ornate railings, and a huge crystal chandelier hung above everything. Thick hand-woven rugs of obvious quality spread out from wall to wall.

To Mitch's left, an arched entranceway with French doors led to a parlor with a black grand piano. To the right, open doors led into a matching room with a fireplace and a wall-to-wall Oriental rug. The full-length windows on the far side of the room were open, and lace curtains fluttered in the breeze. Mitch heard voices coming from that room, but he couldn't see the people, so he ventured closer and stuck his head inside the doorway. Near the long windows facing the street, couches and chairs stood around a large coffee table. Roger sat in the largest of the chairs, a green leather one with brass tacking. In the other chairs sat two young women, one in the same navy blue uniform Mitch had seen on the servant girl leaving the house, the other in a gray uniform with white trim. The girl in the gray uniform held an infant wrapped in a white blanket. On a sofa covered in red velvet sat Teddy's father, Dr. Arndt. Judging by his hairline, this version of Dr. Arndt was younger than the one Mitch had seen in the Smythe's dining room. He kept crossing and re-crossing his legs, then leaning forward on his elbows. Whenever he looked at the sleeping child in the woman's arms, which was often, Mitch could see the fascination in his eyes. The girl in the gray uniform smiled back at him from time to time.

"Why do you ask me?" Dr. Arndt was asking Roger in a light German accent.

"Because I can't imagine giving him up to anyone else, Wolf," Roger replied. He held a snifter of brandy or something in his hand, which he kept swirling around but never drank.

"I've never taken care of a child."

"You've taken care of hundreds of children. I've seen you with your patients. You'll make a fine father." He added with finality, "I will trust no one else."

"He won't have a mother," Dr. Arndt said, still admiring the child who slept soundly.

"He'll have Clarissa." Roger nodded at the girl in the blue uniform who smiled acknowledgement. "She'll be his nanny. You will hire her and I will see to her stipend and any of the child's expenses."

"You don't have to do that, Roger." Dr. Arndt looked at his friend for the first time and picked up a snifter of his own off the table. "I have the means."

Roger sat forward. "I *insist*, Wolf." His voice softened when he added, "You know I also have selfish reasons."

Dr. Arndt nodded.

"I'll never interfere," Roger went on. "But I do insist on the boy knowing his sister, and enjoying her company and her love."

"Of course," Dr. Arndt said. "It's a sensible arrangement. I'm not arguing with you there."

"All that it requires is your acceptance of this child. I want him to have a father who loves him as I would . . . and do." His face still retained its proud sternness, but his eyes softened somewhat.

Dr. Arndt stood up and reached down to the woman in gray who handed the baby to him. He cradled the child in his arms, and Mitch could see in the man's eyes his obvious affection for the child.

But he didn't see much more because one of those dark flashes happened without any warning, and the next thing Mitch knew, he was standing on grass under a tall weeping willow tree. He looked around to get his bearings and immediately recognized where he was: the Public Garden, just up the street from Roger's home. The day was sunny and warm and lots of people were out strolling and picnicking. Their clothing—ankle-length skirts and wide-brimmed hats on the ladies, light-colored suits and straw hats on most of the gentlemen—told him it was still a long time ago.

He walked along a trail to the small bridge spanning the Garden's pond, which he had seen many times in his own era. As he stood on the bridge, people strolled by oblivious to his presence. Below, he saw the swan boats making their slow, lazy way around the pond. They did not look much different than in Mitch's time; only the passengers set a stark contrast. He watched first one then a second boat, powered by a man pedaling in the rear, pass slowly under the bridge. A third approached, and on the front bench sat Maria looking lovely in a white dress, her long auburn hair pulled back and tied up with a white ribbon. She looked about sixteen or seventeen, already as stunning as any young lady could ever be. She wore a beige-colored dress and white stockings and held a closed parasol in her hands. Beside her sat a boy of five or six in gray knickers and long black stockings. In spite of the boy's youth, Mitch immediately recognized him as Teddy. He had the same tousled brown hair and freckled nose as the boy he'd seen at the dinner party at the Smythe. He and Maria kept elbowing one another playfully, and at one point Maria tickled his sides making him laugh out loud.

The boat floated lazily under the bridge, and Mitch turned to follow it, but the bridge and pond were no longer there. In the space of time that it took to turn his head, the scene had become the private beach on Longboat Harbor. Another sunny day, another crowd enjoying the weather, just a different place. Mitch stood behind the bathhouse end of the pavilion in the shade of a small tree, and from this spot he could see the whole beach. In the sand, he spotted Maria and Teddy kneeling and digging together. Their long-legged bathing suits made Mitch smile—not much tanning going on there. But they looked comfortable and happy, concentrating on whatever they were doing in the sand.

"She's more like a mother than a sister, wouldn't you say?" a male voice commented.

Mitch looked around for the source, but nobody was nearby. Then it occurred to him that the voice hadn't actually come from outside his head, but from within. He said out loud, "Who said that?"

No answer came. All he heard were exterior noises. Gulls squawking, children laughing, the far-off sound of a powerboat.

"I asked who said that," Mitch repeated. Then he realized he was talking to someone in his head and he felt a little crazy. He said, "Never mind. I don't need to be hearing voices in my head on top of everything else."

"She's more like a mother than a sister, wouldn't you say?"

Mitch couldn't help looking around again, even though he was still pretty sure the voice came from within. "Who are you? *Where* are you?" he demanded.

"Don't you remember me? I know you do."

Mitch had to admit the voice did sound familiar. But he couldn't quite place it.

"You recognize my voice," the voice said.

Mitch replayed the words, and all at once a name came into his head: "Bertie." Then "Bertram Fletcher". And then a phrase swam through an open gate in his mind: "As Bertie played, so did you." These thoughts came as easily as if he were recalling names from his own past, yet he knew full well this couldn't be right. He had never known anyone named Bertie.

"*You're* doing that," Mitch said out loud.

"I don't have to," the voice replied.

This time Mitch tried a different tact. Instead of speaking out loud, he said with his mind, "I don't know those people."

And quickly the voice replied, "Of *course* you do."

In his head a picture of a piano keyboard flashed, followed by a black bow tie against a white shirt. Then another phrase: "Bertie tickled the ivories while Jerry tickled her fancy." It sounded like some semi-obscene inside joke, yet at the same time it sounded perfectly serious. He couldn't tell which it was meant to be.

A mini video clip played in his brain: Bertram Fletcher, dressed in a tuxedo, sitting on a piano bench, looking up from the piano keyboard to face the camera. Bertie was the piano man, the one Mitch kept seeing in the hotel's bar. "You're—"

"I told you, you know me," the voice interrupted.

Suddenly, Mitch's sight went fuzzy and he thought he was going to black out. Then came the familiar dark flash and he was standing on the cart trail in front of Mr. Arndt's cottage. Up on the porch the old man rocked lazily, still in a flannel shirt in spite of the blazing heat. He stared at Mitch with a look of expectation. Mitch couldn't imagine what he was thinking after seeing him pop into view out of thin air.

He walked up to the porch and stared back for a moment, not sure how to explain. The old man broke the silence first.

"Hotter 'n Hades," he said with disgust. "Want a Moxie?"

CHAPTER TWENTY-EIGHT

Mitch grabbed two cans of Moxie out of the refrigerator and joined Mr. Arndt on the porch. "What time is it anyway?"

"Oh, about 5:30 or so."

Mitch nodded and took a gulp of soda. "I suppose you're wondering how I came to be standing outside your cottage".

"Nope. But you can tell me if you want to."

Mitch looked at him. "Didn't you see me? You were looking right my way. Did you see me just—" He smacked his free hand against the soda can— "poof! Pop in?"

Mr. Arndt's eyebrow went up. "You didn't exactly pop in. Matter of fact, I thought you were walking kind of slow. Can't blame you, the weather's so darned—"

"Walking slow!" Mitch practically shouted. "Do you have any idea where I've *been*?"

Mr. Arndt looked up at the sky. "Let's see. You were in your cabin. Then I thought I saw you heading down the trail toward the dock. I lost sight of you after that until a minute or two ago."

"I did go down to the dock. To greet Maria Boudreau."

The old man didn't flinch, just took a swallow and belched quietly. "How did she look?"

"Not bad for a hundred years old. Do you believe me?"

"Why wouldn't I?" Mr. Arndt said, and Mitch instantly realized what a stupid question it was. After what the old man had seen for himself, including his own contact with Maria, this was routine stuff.

Mitch settled down after that, and rocked in rhythm with Mr. Arndt. The old guy was just toying with him. He wasn't going to make this easy. That was his way. "They called you Teddy when you were a kid," he said after a while.

Mr. Arndt grinned, stretching his liver-colored lips taut. "Teddy," he repeated to himself.

"She was very close to you. You loved her very much."

The grin faded, but the mouth remained tight, the jaw set. "Mm hm," he said with a slow nod.

"Like a sister," Mitch ventured.

Mr. Arndt sighed. "You *have* been hanging around with my girl, haven't you."

"I have."

"She wasn't just like a sister, she *was* my sister. You know that now, don't you?" Mr. Arndt shot a quick glance his way.

"Half-sister as I understand it."

Mr. Arndt shook his head. "Didn't matter if she was my half-sister, whole-sister or no sister. I loved her so much." His voice hitched and Mitch realized he was crying. "So much," he repeated quietly.

"Mind telling me about your mother? Who was she?"

Mr. Arndt drew a deep breath. "That point doesn't matter much, but I'll tell you anyway. I never knew her. Her name was Abigail. She was married to some Beacon Hill trust baby. Old money, bad habits, idle-rich drunk. Roger had an affair with Abby at a lonely time in their lives. I was a mistake, a big one. Abigail and her husband went traveling in Europe and the Middle East just before she started to show. By the time they came back—with yours truly secretly in tow—she was all slim and trim again. Beacon Hill was none the wiser. Roger refused to let me be adopted by a stranger so he asked my father. Roger and my papa knew each other from sitting on the board together at Mercy Youth Hospital in Boston. They'd become close friends. I think that's part of the reason he chose Papa—he could see how he loved children. I like to think he also chose Papa so he could still have some kind of place in my life. Uncle Roger, you know?

"Whatever the reasons, Papa was a great man. Just the greatest. He took me in, loved me, cared for me so well I hardly noticed I had no mother. But at the same time Roger played the role of a good family friend and I loved him, too. Maria, on the other hand . . ." His voice hitched again, and he wiped at his eye with an index finger and blinked hard a couple of times. "Maria was my—" He stopped and thought. "My angel on Earth. I didn't even know she was my sister. Maria did, but she never let on. I only learned after Maria and Roger were dead. Papa told me when I was a teenager, just before he died. It came as something of a shock, but the fact she was a blood relative isn't what mattered. She was already my best friend, and I loved her just so, so much."

"Do you remember riding the swan boats with her?" Mitch asked.

He smiled. "Yes."

Mitch fell quiet for a moment. Then he asked a question that had been floating around in his head for a while. "Why didn't you tell me before that Maria was your sister?"

Mr. Arndt's answer was immediate. "I never told anyone. What for? Abigail didn't die until 1962, and I wanted to spare her the embarrassment. After that, it didn't matter much."

"But it matters this weekend. You know that, don't you?"

"Only you know that," the old man said firmly.

"Huh?"

"This is your show now."

Mitch thought about this and decided he was right. Now that Phyllis Church and Horace Leeds were gone he was a hundred percent tuned in. It was as though the ghost hunters had actually interfered with the signal while they were here. Now, he could see that Maria wanted him to know something, or do something, maybe both. He wasn't sure yet.

"So, if it's my show," Mitch thought out loud, "then I guess I need to start interpreting these things she showed me."

"I wouldn't start yet," Mr. Arndt replied quickly.

"What do you mean?"

"I mean I don't think she's shown you everything she wants to show you."

"What else is there?" Mitch asked innocently.

Mr. Arndt glanced his way then quickly back at the harbor. He rocked a few times then leaned his weight on his cane to stand up. "I'm hungry. Time for dinner."

——◦◦◦——

They made their way up to the hotel in the sweltering heat that just wouldn't break. Mitch welcomed Mr. Arndt's company at that point. He had become weary of the visions, especially the way they came unannounced, leaving him feeling disoriented and ill. For some reason, which had nothing to do with logic or experience, Mitch believed the visions would not come if someone was with him. It turned out he was right, though it may have had nothing to do with Mr. Arndt's presence. For the next hour or so he remained vision-free.

Wendy was in the lobby when they got up to the hotel. She sat in a leather chair not far from the portrait of Maria and Roger—and even closer to some young guy in a striped polo shirt that hugged his muscled frame like Batman's suit. They talked in hushed tones, leaning over the arms of their chairs toward one another.

Mitch found himself fighting back a sudden urge to attack the guy. But then his eyes were drawn up to Maria's portrait, and just like that, the anger roiling in his gut evaporated. He took a deep breath and actually smiled.

"Hi, hon'," he said to Wendy, taking her hand. "Who's this?"

Wendy raised her eyebrows at him. "Mitch, this is Brad. I'm sorry, Brad, I didn't get your last name."

"Hollister," Brad told her.

Mitch had all he could do not to roll his eyes. He lifted Wendy's hand and she rose obediently. He said, "We're late for dinner, hon'." Then to Brad he said, "Nice meeting you, Mr. Hollister."

"Brad," Brad said, all friendly-like.

Mitch escorted Wendy, hand hovering lightly between her shoulder blades, to the Sandpiper where Mr. Arndt waited in the doorway. On the way, Wendy said, "*Hon'?*"

"He looked like a creep. Just looking out for you."

"He's not a creep. He's a skydiving instructor."

"He's a sub-primate."

She shook her head and gave him an amused look. "You're *all* sub-primates."

As soon as they got to the hostess they were escorted to an empty table in the otherwise filled-up room. Mr. Arndt ordered Scotch on the rocks all around. Mitch was glad he did. He needed a good stiff drink.

Any other evening the menu would have had Mitch salivating, but tonight it held no appeal for him. His stomach still felt queasy, as though popping in and out of the past caused a kind of motion sickness. He actually considered going to the gift shop and buying some Dramamine. But the queasiness subsided with a few sips of Glenlivet, and he decided if he just went light on dinner he would be all right. He ordered a Caesar salad and some bread sticks, and that was it. Mr. Arndt ordered prime rib and Wendy ordered a stir-fry. After the waiter left with their orders they all sat in silence, sipping drinks and looking around the room, ignoring one another. Mitch didn't know why, except that the oppressive weather had been sapping their strength and he thought everyone was just plain tired.

Eventually Mr. Arndt spoke up. "Mitch, did you tell Wendy about your travels this afternoon?"

He hadn't, of course, and the old man knew it. He was just trying to break the ice.

"No, but I should," Mitch said. "I think she could teach a whole course down at Longfellow based on what happened to me this afternoon."

Wendy had been quietly looking out the window. Now she turned back to the table and said, "What?"

"I saw Maria this afternoon," Mitch told her, barely containing his excitement.

"Maria?"

"Maria Boudreau."

Wendy looked at Mr. Arndt, her mouth slightly agape, pleading for an explanation.

"Don't look at me, let him tell you," Mr. Arndt said.

Mitch did, but only a heavily edited version. He left out the scene in Roger Boudreau's house, thinking it was for Mr. Arndt to decide whether or not to tell Wendy who he really was. He finished off by describing Maria in the full-bodied bathing suit. "She can make you keel over even in that get-up," he said. Then, thinking out loud, he started to add, "If only—"

"If only *what*?" Wendy snapped, and it really was a snap. The crack of a very sharp whip.

"Nothing," Mitch answered, taken aback.

"If only you'd been born around, oh, say, 1903?" Wendy spewed. "Mitchell, you're pathetic. You act like those bloggers in the Boudreau chat rooms. The ones with no life. She's dead, Mitchell. *Dead*."

It was Mitch's turn to look for guidance from Mr. Arndt, but the old man's attention seemed to have shifted to other goings-on in the room.

"She looked pretty alive to me."

"It was a dream. You're a little too caught up in this. You, of all people."

Mitch shook his head in wonder. "It wasn't a dream. Unless I was sleepwalking."

"Maybe you were."

He gave her a long look and she stared right back, making him blink first. "I assure you it wasn't a dream," he finally said. "There's no way I could have known what I saw, and it's all verifiable." He glanced Mr. Arndt's way, but the old man was still people-watching.

"You, of all people," Wendy repeated.

Her sarcasm touched off a nerve. "*Me*, of all people? How about *you* of all people? You, the great believer, the 'I've devoted my life to the science of the other world' queen. *You*, of all people, doubting my story without keeping an open mind, without checking into it to see if it can be verified, which, I assure you, it can."

Suddenly, Wendy was up on her feet and tossing her napkin on the table.

"Don't leave, this is just getting interesting," Mitch said.

"You stupid . . . *stupid* man. You just don't . . ." She hesitated, turned on her heels and left.

"Don't what?" Mitch called after her, but she kept on walking.

By then Mr. Arndt had turned back to the table. He said, "I believe she was about to say you just don't get it."

"Don't get what?"

The old man watched Wendy leave the restaurant, her pretty blonde curls bouncing with the rhythm of her hurried walk.

"It," he said, fighting back a grin.

CHAPTER TWENTY-NINE

Mitch went looking for Wendy in the lobby, but by then she was long gone. He figured she had gone up to her room and it was best to let her cool off before he tried talking to her. He went back in the Sandpiper where he and Mr. Arndt ate mostly in silence. After dinner he had Wendy's meal boxed up, thinking he'd bring it to her, but when he went up to her room and knocked on the door she didn't answer. He placed the Styrofoam box in front of the door and left.

On the way down in the elevator he debated whether she had gone off somewhere or just refused to answer her door. He thought of the lounge and decided it might be worth a look to see if she'd dropped in for a drink.

His guess was right, but he wished he had been wrong. She was seated at the bar next to the Abercrombie model again. Mitch started across the room, weaving between tables, his body tensing with the same adrenaline rush he'd had in the lounge before dinner. It frightened him to think what he might do when he got to the bar, he seethed with so much anger. Fortunately, he never got there. Mr. Arndt called his name sharply from somewhere behind him, making him stop and turn around. The old man stood just inside the doorway, leaning on his cane, pinning him to the floor with his eyes. Over in the corner by the windows the piano music started up. Mitch swung his head that way and saw the piano man, all decked out in his tuxedo and slicked-back hair, jangling the piano keys and wailing out some old love song.

Mitch wanted to go that way. He wanted to demand that the bastard stop playing. In his half-crazed mind the piano man's crooning was the reason Wendy was falling for that guy at the bar. But another sharp "Mitch!" from Mr. Arndt made him hesitate. Finally, he went to the old man instead.

"You see him, don't you?" Mitch said as soon as he reached him.

Mr. Arndt looked at the bar then at Mitch's eyes, which were still focused on the corner of the room. "Who?"

"The guy playing the piano. Over there." He lifted his chin in that direction.

Mr. Arndt looked again and said, "No. I don't doubt that you see him, though."

Mitch looked closely at Mr. Arndt. "There's no piano over there either, is there?"

The old man shrugged. "No piano." He glanced at the corner one more time. "What's he playing?"

Mitch listened to the lyrics. "I don't know . . . something about a girl named Margie."

Mr. Arndt nodded. "It's Bertie, all right. He loved that tune." Before Mitch could respond, he added, "Bertie was tall, thin, kind of a crooked nose. Chummed around with Robert Akers and his crowd in college. You saw him in the picture in your book, seated at the piano. Played pretty well, as I recall." He chuckled. "Kind of a ham—liked to do an Eddie Cantor impression."

"I've met him."

"I suspected. You've been making lots of friends this weekend."

"I'm not sure they're all friends," Mitch said dryly.

Mr. Arndt put his hand on Mitch's shoulder and squeezed. His grip was surprisingly strong for a man his age. "No question someone around here isn't your friend." He squeezed again and started out the door.

Mitch followed him. "What did you mean by that?" His stomach felt queasy again. Mr. Arndt's comment had only confirmed what he'd been feeling the past twenty-four hours: Maria's little historic tours had a purpose other than to show him her past. Somehow, they were connected with the angry entity that had thrown him out of his chair at the séance.

"I mean I may not see what you see, my boy, but I feel things when I'm around you. And I don't like some of those feelings." He whacked Mitch's back lightly with his cane as they walked. "Don't take that the wrong way. I interpret it as something negative hovering around you. Something bad. Not evil—that's a Hollywood word—just bad. You know, for some reason this island gives off strong emotions. They're either bad ones or good ones, but they're always strong. I've been coming out here all my life, and I can tell you that's how this place has always been. And I don't know why.

"In your case, I can see your joy in getting close to Maria. But I also sense something else. Fear, I think. You don't have to tell me you're scared. I know you're scared. And I don't blame you."

He took a few more steps before adding, "There's more coming, you know. You haven't seen everything Maria wanted you to see. Be careful, boy. Watch your back."

—◁◇▷—

Mr. Arndt left to go for a walk down by the beach, but Mitch had other plans.

He wanted to be alone for a little while to think. The weekend had changed everything for him. His whole belief system had broken down. It wasn't just that the existence of ghosts had been proven to him. It was their proximity, their accessibility, their very nature that had profoundly affected him. He had always thought that if ghosts really did exist, they were merely images, a picture imprinted on the atmosphere like light passed through celluloid film. Or leftover flickers of energy like the image left on an old television screen after it's been turned off. Now he knew they were as self-sufficient and purposeful as flesh-and-blood mortals. They stayed close by, watching, sometimes interacting with us, and we didn't even know it most of the time. Other times we might catch them when their guard was down, and they allowed us to see what they were up to. Maybe they did it on purpose, wanting us to know they were there, especially when we got too comfortable with the idea that we mortals exist exclusive of any other form of existence. How they must laugh to think we harnessed electricity, sent sounds and pictures through the air, split the atom, yet still refused to believe in a spirit world. Did they see the irony in their own disbelief when *they* were mortals? Yet even after they reached the other side, where they weren't bound to the earth by gravity or prone to sickness and pain, where they had achieved an enlightenment we could never achieve here on earth, they kept coming back. Why? Why would they want to?

Why was Maria here? What did she want?

What does she want with me?

So far she hadn't shown him anything that wasn't already known by someone living. The fact she had a half-brother was a surprise, but the one it mattered to most—the brother himself—already knew it and was just as happy to keep it a secret. Mr. Arndt also knew about Maria's romantic link to Robert Akers, and others must have known as well. Nothing terribly new. And nothing that meant a whole lot, unless she was pitching for an updated version of her biography, one with all new revelations for gossip hounds.

Yet Mr. Arndt was certain that Maria had more to say. What made him so sure? There could be only one explanation: the old man already knew what it was. So why didn't he just tell Mitch himself? And why had Maria waited to tell Mitch, rather than Mrs. Church or someone else?

He had wandered across the lawn and down to Lover's Lookout before the answer finally came to him: he was the only one Maria was able to show these things to. She'd waited all these years for the right person to come along, and it was him. He was plugged in; the energy of her world flowed right through him. Mr. Arndt had been right: it was no accident that he wrote Maria's biography. All that research had been just an introductory course, and now he was in graduate school. Maria had known all along that Mitch would be the conduit by which the rest of her story, or at least the rest of what mattered, was told.

He reached the gazebo and sat on the bench seat opposite where the old man, Arthur Moore, had committed suicide. He thought of the photograph, the one taken the night of Maria's death. If that person standing beside Bertie really was him, then that meant he was more than just plugged into Maria's spiritual world. Somehow, he had already been a part of her world when she was alive. And now her spirit was a part of his own earthly existence. The membrane had a door that swung both ways, and he and Maria each passed through it as easily as the other.

So why didn't this happen for Mr. Arndt, who had been as close to Maria in life as anyone else? To Mitch's thinking, the only plausible explanation was that this was *about* Mr. Arndt. Maria had something to show Mitch that concerned Mr. Arndt, something that he already knew, or that she didn't want him to know. But what? What else could there be, after the revelation that he was Maria's half-brother?

He draped an arm over the rail behind the bench and looked out to sea. A breeze coming off the water would have felt great, if there had been any breeze. But the evening air was perfectly still, and the humidity as thick and blanketing as warm syrup. He watched the sun dipping in the west over the Maine coastline and the boats moving into shore before nightfall caught them. Though he was no sailor, Mitch knew the Maine coast was no place to be out in a boat after nightfall unless you were an experienced boater. The rocky coast could chew up your vessel and spit it back out in pieces. Roger Boudreau had known this. An experienced sailor himself, he had always left the helm of the *Tasha* to his captain except in the open sea. Maria, too, had learned to sail and could handle the *Tasha*. She had loved sailing, just like her father. She also loved doing just what Mitch was doing now: sitting in this gazebo, watching boats sail by.

As he sat there, sweat beads dripping down his temples, Mitch imagined Maria sitting beside him, staring at the same sea, the same coastline, the same sun, the same flock of gulls passing over Tintagel Island a mile to the west. He watched the flock move northward, and it occurred to him that the gulls were flying in an odd pattern, jittery, flitting every which way in chaotic flight. Then he realized it wasn't a flock of gulls at all, but a swarm of some kind of flying insect just off this island, maybe a hundred feet away. He watched the swarm spread out, then come together, then spread out again before finally turning and coming in his direction. As it made the turn, the swarm came together one last time in a long, tight bar, seemingly gathering speed. Judging by its velocity, Mitch was certain now that it was just offshore. It wouldn't be long before it arrived at Lover's Lookout if it continued this way.

He watched and waited for it to waver and turn away, but it kept coming straight. The closer the swarm came, the more he realized just how many of the insects there were. A little closer and he could see the type of insect. Moths. He had never heard of moths swarming like bees or locusts but here they were, in a tight formation, still coming straight at him.

When they were about twenty yards away, he stood up, thinking they had to be getting ready to veer off. But they kept coming. Ten yards away and Mitch was saying out loud, "Shit, this isn't right."

Then the swarm was at the gazebo, but not inside it. The moths spread out in every direction as they reached the ocean side of the structure, moving up, down and sideways, surrounding the gazebo on all sides as though some sort of invisible shield kept them out of the gazebo itself. At first Mitch just stood there watching in wonder, marveling at how many there were. After a short time they covered every open space making the interior of the gazebo dark. He could see them crawling, moving around on the invisible force field, seemingly looking for a way in. But not a single one found its way inside.

Then, from directly above, Mitch heard a scratching sound. He looked up and saw the green luna moth from his cabin clinging to the gazebo's ceiling. It was huge like in his dreams, about four feet across. The creature scurried to the edge of the ceiling where it began crawling down the bellies of the thousands of swarming moths, all the way to the floor. There it stopped and stared at Mitch. Mitch stared back, frightened half out of his mind. He looked around for an escape route, but everywhere the teeming moths crawled about, a moving wall inches thick, leaving not even the smallest of spaces for sunlight to poke through.

The luna moth took a step toward Mitch. Mitch stepped back. Then it did something very strange for a moth: it reared back on its hind legs and leaped. Mitch fell back, screaming, as it landed on his face and upper body, its wings enveloping him like a hot blanket, forelegs hugging him like arms.

Suddenly, a hand grabbed his wrist and yanked, and he stumbled into the wall of moths. For a split second he felt their zillions of legs crawling all over him, and then he was outside the gazebo, standing on the grass, staring up at a dark night sky.

He looked back at the gazebo and saw nothing there, no moths of any size. It was deserted. Something was different about the gazebo, too, something he couldn't quite place at first. It took him only a second or two to figure out that it was the color. It was gray when it should have been white. He knew the gazebo had been gray up until the early sixties when some PR person decided it would look more attractive in postcards if it was painted white.

He'd gone back again.

CHAPTER THIRTY

Mitch looked at the hotel. A lot of people were milling about on the east wing veranda, sipping champagne and smoking. Everyone was dressed in expensive gowns and tuxedoes.

He walked along the bottom of the veranda, glancing up at the guests now and then, admiring their clothing and jewelry. He thought vaguely of his own sloppy clothes, grateful that he was no more conspicuous to these people than a movie viewer was to the actors on the screen. But somewhere along the way he became aware that he was no longer dressed in a t-shirt and sneakers. Somehow they had been traded for a tuxedo and patent leather shoes.

As in his earlier visit to the 'twenties, he waited for some guests to come through the doors, then neatly slipped through them without as much as a sleeve brushing against anything. Once inside, he headed straight for the ballroom. By now he had figured out that he was crashing Maria's birthday party. Only, he knew he wasn't really crashing it at all. He had been invited.

He walked down the east corridor, which looked very much like it did in his own era. The music he heard coming from the ballroom certainly wasn't the same. A live orchestra was playing a song that featured a lot of brass and woodwind instruments. A clarinet broke out in a light, jazzy solo, climbing up and down three octaves. The closer Mitch got to the ballroom the more he was struck by how loud and jumpy the orchestra played. He had never realized how much energy they put into their music back then.

He reached the ballroom doors where couples came and went freely, but under the watchful eye of a group of four men who Mitch took to be bodyguards or bouncers. Even they wore tuxedoes, as did the band—some twenty men on the stage, most of them with their hair parted in the middle and slicked back. A singer stood before the microphone, snapping his fingers and nodding to the beat of the music, his eyes fixed on the clarinet player wailing out the solo. All around the crowded room people stood with drinks in hand or sat at tables covered with empty glasses. Mitch recalled that Prohibition was in effect at this time, but that didn't seem to matter here. Like everywhere else in America, the law was being scoffed at—the government might as well have passed a law against breathing. On the dance floor, couples, mostly young but some older folks too, danced the Charleston and other fast dances, their moves frenetic and jerky. Hands, elbows, knees and feet flew about in seemingly mindless abandon.

The crowd was thick, and Mitch carefully wended his way through it and around it until he found an empty corner where he could watch the action without worrying about getting bumped. Without realizing it, he had made his way to the corner with the white piano where the group photo would be taken sometime that evening. Just to see how it felt, he stood next to the piano, striking a pose like the one in the picture. He looked in the same direction where he thought the cameraman had stood that night—and met the gaze of Maria Boudreau.

She wore a white, sleeveless dress with a v-shaped neckline. White beads covered the entire outfit, which reached to her mid-calf where fringes trimmed the bottom. Her hair was held back by a headband of the same color as the dress. She looked incredible. An unearthly light seemed to emanate from her, though it might have been his imagination.

As with his visit with her and her friends in the dining room earlier that evening, she was perfectly aware of Mitch's presence. She made a small motion with her head indicating he should come over, and he gladly obeyed, walking carefully between the guests. Fortunately, Maria stood away from the dancers so he didn't have to dodge too much.

When he reached her, she gave him a warm smile and said, "Hello, Mitch. I'm glad you made it."

Like a nervous schoolboy meeting his crush at a dance, Mitch found himself unable to speak at first. All he could do was look at her. After a brief moment he pulled himself together and croaked a response. "I am, too. Thank you for inviting me."

She raised an eyebrow in a mischievous expression that reminded him of her half-brother. "Why do you assume *I* brought you?" He never got a chance to answer, because she quickly added, "Will you do me the honor of asking me to dance?"

Me, honor you? Mitch thought. He tried to think up an appropriate response. Finally, he said, "The honor's mine," and immediately wanted to take the words back. He sounded like a character in a Jane Austen novel.

Suddenly he remembered what occurred every time he touched people in this place. "But I can't dance with you. I can't—"

"Try it," Maria smiled.

The fast music had stopped and now the band played a slow, wistful number. It was a song Mitch had heard before somewhere, but not being terribly sophisticated about old music, he had no idea what the piece was called. He only knew it was the kind of song that gives you a feeling of bittersweet longing, and it could not have been a better tune for the mood he was in. Maria took his hands, and for a second he waited for her to bounce off and the ensuing dark flash, but neither happened. Her hands felt warm to the touch, like real flesh. She led him around the floor in a waltz step, moving him through the other dancers expertly and gracefully. Much to his surprise, he followed her steps as easily as if he had danced like this all his life. It was an amazing feeling.

They moved around the dance floor for what seemed like hours, barely watching where they were going because their eyes stayed mostly on one another. Her beauty was so strong it almost hurt to look at her, like a dazzling gem glinting in the light. As far as Mitch knew she was only a vision, albeit one that he could feel as well as see, but real or not, she had him completely. Her deep green eyes of a color even her portrait could not completely capture, her hair with its girlish, curling wisps around the ears and forehead, her dimples when she smiled—everything about her made him feel like a thirsty man staring at a pitcher of ice water. He *ached* when he looked at her, a sweet, dull pain in the upper gut. He wanted to kiss her and he very nearly did, but his intentions were interrupted by a couple that bumped into them. The man was fairly large, so when his elbow went into Mitch's ribs, he really felt it.

"Pardon me," the man said, waltzing away as though swung by the momentum.

Mitch smiled and nodded. No problem. Then, realizing the significance of what had just happened, he turned to Maria and said, "He reacted like I'm really here."

"You *are* here," Maria said, drawing him closer.

Mitch's forehead broke into a sweat. He could smell her light perfume. He breathed it in deeply.

"Coty," she said. "Do you like it?"

"Very much. What did you mean, 'I am here'?"

"You're dancing with me, aren't you?" Maria said plainly. "You're touching me."

"But that's not what happened in the dining room."

"No, it's not."

Mitch tossed this around in his head but couldn't make sense of it. "Have I traveled in time?" he asked.

"Not exactly."

"Then what?"

As they whirled around the dance floor, their heads close enough to speak without shouting over the music, she tried her best to explain. Linear time, she said, was a fallacy invented by the organic brain which is unable to conceive of time the way it really is: like a liquid mass as infinite as the universe. There was no "then" and no "now" because every event, every time interval, had always existed, each one floating like a bubble in the liquid. And because of time's fluid nature, these intervals could be made to move around until they came into direct contact—the same way the twentieth and twenty-first centuries had come together for them this weekend. At Mitch's request she gave a long, technical explanation of just how this had occurred, but it was instantly lost on him just as she warned him it would be. But he shouldn't feel stupid. The only mortals who'd ever come close to understanding were the great theoretical physicists, and even they understood only a tiny bit. Some things were impossible to fully understand without experiencing them first-hand, she explained.

"So this one isn't a vision," Mitch summed up.

"No, it's very real."

"But won't people be asking who this guy dancing with you is?"

"Why would they? Everyone here knows who you are."

Mitch smiled, thinking it was a joke. But her expression was sincere. He asked, "Do *you* know who I am?"

"Mitchell Lambert, PhD, second-year professor at Fowler College in Massachusetts, born in 1979, etcetera."

Mitch stared at her, amazed. "Do these people know that?"

"No, silly, they know you're Bertie's college friend, Jerry, visiting for my birthday."

"Jerry? Where'd they get that?"

"I would imagine from Bertie."

Mitch reached up to push his hair back—something he habitually did whenever he was perplexed—only to find it was plastered to his head with some pleasant smelling hair oil. He left it alone and put his hand back on Maria's waist. "I've met Bertie, you know."

"I know," she said, and Mitch wasn't sure whether she meant in the future or now. Then she stopped dancing, and her eyebrows came together and her mouth turned down in a frown. "I'm hot. Can we go for a walk? I'd like some fresh air."

She led him by the hand through the dancers and over to the door. He followed obediently, aware that all eyes were on them. If not for the terrible events to come later that night, he wondered what the talk would have been among society gossips the next day.

They strolled down the hall, king palms standing at attention on either side like an honor guard. Maria did most of the talking as they made their way out to the veranda, describing, at Mitch's prodding, her quirkiest friends and relatives who were there that night. He especially enjoyed hearing about people with whom he was already familiar, comparing the dry facts he had found in old archives to the colorful details only someone with Maria's intimate knowledge could relate. Just before they reached the lobby, a small girl went tearing down the hall past them, the white lace of her knee-length dress tossing all around, shoes sliding on the carpet. Only when Maria called to her, "Dottie, slow down!" did Mitch realize who she was. He said, "I've met her," and Maria replied, "Of course you have."

Outside, they leaned against the veranda railing and gazed down at the lawn where a huge white tent had been set up. Party guests wandered back and forth and in and out of the tent, and danced to the music of a small band on the lawn. After watching quietly for a few moments, Maria did a quarter turn and looked up into Mitch's eyes. Her expression was almost pleading, but she said nothing. She just went on studying, first the right eye then the left then back again.

"What is it?" Mitch asked.

She took his hand and turned back to the lawn. "It's not fair, is it? It's not right."

A warm rush of adrenaline overtook him. Before, his love for Maria had felt pleasant, like youthful infatuation. Now it felt desperate. He realized they were being watched by some of the crowd on the veranda, but it didn't seem to matter much to her. Maybe it was because she knew what was coming. This thought made him terribly sad.

"No, it's not right," he said, and then a burst of anger made him squeeze her hand in a tight grip. "Isn't there anything that can be done? Isn't there some . . . way to make it so it never happened?"

She shook her head and drew one side of her mouth down in a lopsided frown. "We're incredibly fortunate that you can be here. But you can't change what has happened."

"Isn't *this*—right now, me and you—really happening?"

"Only for me and you."

"I don't understand."

"I know," she said patiently. "I'm sorry. It's just too hard to explain. Can we go someplace private?"

They walked down the veranda steps and across the lawn. As they went, Mitch fully expected the 'twenties version of paparazzi to be jumping out in front of them, snapping pictures. Maria was so famous, and such a draw for photographers, that it seemed natural the world would be curious about this gentleman accompanying her at this important event. But no one bothered them, not one flashbulb went off. Mitch asked Maria why, and she told him that only one official photographer had been allowed on the island for her party. Right now he was setting up his camera in the ballroom to take some photos before the party moved out on the lawn.

They made their way out to Lover's Lookout where they found the gazebo unoccupied. There they sat in thoughtful silence on the bench seat. Mitch thought about what Maria had said earlier about this being "real." When Mitch had first started researching Maria's life for his book, he remembered feeling an odd sense of familiarity about what he read. It wasn't so much familiarity with the events in her life as the emotions, as though he knew how it *felt* to be in her world. It was partly that feeling that had driven him to do the exhaustive research he did, and to put it all together into what one critic had called a "remarkably thorough first work".

"I *have* been here before," he said to Maria.

She nodded. "Yes."

"I fell in love with you. Tonight. In 1924."

Maria looked back with a bittersweet smile. "Actually, it was a little earlier. For both of us."

She slid closer to him, craned her neck, and kissed him lightly on the cheek. Her lips were full and moist, and the feel of them sent a warm surge through him. He turned his head to the left and faced her squarely, their faces separated by only inches. The next thing he knew, they were kissing and he was holding her in his arms as tightly as he could. For these brief moments everything was perfect. When they parted, Mitch saw in her eyes that she was right there with him, feeling everything he felt. He asked her if she was happy, and she told him she was. Then, without any forethought, without even knowing he was going to do it, he asked her to marry him.

Maria smiled that same bittersweet smile and said, "I'll always be with you." She held his cheek in her hand and looked straight into his eyes. "Always."

CHAPTER THIRTY-ONE

Before Mitch could ask Maria what she meant, a man on the lawn near the trail shouted, "Miss Boudreau, the photographer is ready."

"Come," Maria said standing and taking his hand.

He followed her out of the gazebo and back to the lawn where she started in the direction of the hotel. Partway across the lawn he took her hand and stopped her.

"Maria," he said, grasping her shoulders, trying to hold her there in that spot with him forever, "there *has* to be a way . . ."

"There's so much you can't understand, Mitch," she said calmly. "You were supposed to be here. With me. But now you have to be there, and that can't change." Then, to Mitch's dismay, her face brightened. "Remember what I told you. I'll always be with you. Please come."

She gently removed his hands from her shoulders, took one of those hands and led him up the gentle incline to the veranda. Inside the hotel, they made their way along the corridor with some other couples to the ballroom where a big, boxy camera atop a wooden tripod stood in the middle of the room. A mustachioed photographer ordered Maria to the front of a crowd gathered in front of the white piano in the corner. She obediently went to her spot and chatted with some of the other young ladies, a few of whom glanced in Mitch's direction more than once. Mitch stood off to the side, hurting terribly and feeling a little crazy after their conversation. After a while Maria came over and said, gently, "Can you go stand beside Bertie, please?"

Mitch looked and saw Bertie sitting at the piano, and it finally registered in his mind which photograph this was going to be. He dutifully took his place beside the piano and looked down at Bertie. The young man appeared exactly the same as he had in the bar that weekend back in Mitch's time. Mitch said hello. Bertie said hello back.

From the middle of the room, Mitch heard, "Everyone, look at the camera. All together. Now … hoooold!" The photographer bent down behind the camera, and as he did Bertie said, "You look better in pants than shorts." Mitch looked down at him and saw he wore a big grin. In spite of all his misery and desperation, the comment and the look on Bertie's face struck Mitch so funny that he put a hand on his shoulder and leaned down to say something back, like, "You should stop stealing the piano." But as soon as he leaned down, the photographer said, loudly, "Facing the camera now—you in the back by the piano, please!" Mitch looked up, still grinning, feeling for the first time that he was really a part of this crowd. "Hoooold!" the cameraman called out. A flash went off and the photo was done.

Mitch turned to Bertie again. "We know each other," he said, stating the obvious, he thought.

Bertie gave him a look that said, "Are you getting weird on me?" But underneath that look it was easy to see he knew what Mitch meant. Still, he wasn't letting on. He said, "Of course . . . Jerry."

"Mitch," Mitch said back.

Bertie stared. There was a twinkle in his eye. He opened his mouth, but before he could say anything a man interrupted them. Without excusing himself he just walked up to the piano, stood between Bertie and Mitch, and began talking to Bertie. Mitch looked off in another direction, trying not to eavesdrop. After a minute, Bertie politely interrupted the man and said, "Bobby, do you know Jerry?"

The young man turned, and Mitch instantly recognized him: Robert Akers. He gave Mitch the once over and a quick nod of acknowledgement. Standing next to him, Mitch could see that he was an inch or so taller and that his hair was a little thin for someone his age, though it didn't detract from his looks at all. He was handsome in a blueblood sort of way. He said, in a voice as disinterested as his gaze, "We haven't met."

"Jerry Sande, Bobby Akers; Bobby Akers, Jerry Sande," Bertie said. Mitch couldn't help feeling he was doing all this introducing with tongue firmly in cheek. There was definitely something going on in Bertie's head.

Mitch said, "Nice to meet you," and stuck out his hand. Robert took it in a firm grip and shook quickly, as though he was in a terrible hurry. Then, just as quickly, he turned his back to Mitch again and said to Bertie, "I'm being told the guy is romancing her all over this damned island, the son-of—"

Bertie cut him off by sweeping his leg out and kicking him in the ankle.

"Ow! Dammit, Bertie, what are you doing?" Robert protested.

"Sorry, it was an accident," Bertie said with no sincerity at all. He got to his feet. "Come on, Bobby, let's grab a drink outside."

Robert immediately started for the door, but Bertie hung back for a moment. He shook Mitch's hand and said, "I'll see you later, Jerry." Then he added something that convinced Mitch that he did, indeed, know much more than he was letting on. "Look for me."

As Mitch watched the two go out the door into the hall, he mulled what Robert had said to Bertie. The guy was pretty ticked off. Soon enough, he would find out who was romancing Maria. Probably he would come looking for Jerry to rough him up, but Mitch didn't care. It was worth every minute he had spent with Maria that evening.

He watched her over in another corner of the room, sitting at a table with some girlfriends, chatting excitedly and laughing. It suddenly hit him again how this night was going to end and his mood sank. He knew he was an intruder here, yet he was here, so why wasn't he able to affect the outcome? Why couldn't he find a way to stop it? Because you can't change events that already exist in time even when you can access those events—that's what Maria had taught him. This melding of two realms that he and Maria had somehow accomplished was only temporary, and quite artificial. Whatever he did tonight would make no difference. It would never find its way into history books because it would never have really happened.

And yet, the photograph . . .

The photograph that had just been taken included him. And that same exact photograph would find its way into *American Princess*. How? He tried to recall where he'd found the photo and drew a blank. He couldn't remember what archive, what source file. He couldn't even remember handling it, or looking at it outside of his book. He wanted to tell Maria this, but she looked so happy with her friends that he didn't have the heart to interrupt her and bring up this stuff again. All he wanted for her was to be happy, even if only for a little while.

He needed some fresh air. The Smythe ballroom of this era was not air conditioned, and it suddenly felt very stuffy.

He made his way slowly out to the veranda, hands stuffed in his front pockets, head down. Stepping out the doors into the warm but pleasant night air, he was met by the noise of the tent party. The band on the grass wailed away, dozens of people danced on the lawn, alcohol flowed from bottles on every table, intoxicated revelers chatted and laughed out loud. It didn't matter that Maria wasn't out there with them—it was the party that mattered. The Great War was a distant memory, the economy was booming, the American people felt confident, even invincible. Women were freer to express themselves than ever before, the youth of the nation was busy throwing off the shackles of the Victorian and Edwardian eras. Life was just a big, drunken party. Fitzgerald had yet to publish *The Great Gatsby*, suggesting an ugly underside to the roaring 'twenties. For now—and at least until the chill winds of October 1929 reminded the nation that there was a price to be paid for so much unchecked prosperity and debauchery—the present was too good to worry about the future.

Yet for some here tonight there was no future.

Mitch surveyed the crowd below and caught a glimpse of Robert and Bertie. They sat at a crowded table with other young men and women. Bertie was talking animatedly to the girl on his right, using his hands like a mime, while the girl nearly laughed herself off her seat. To Bertie's right, Robert sat with an arm draped across the back of his chair. His bow tie hung crooked and his tuxedo jacket was nowhere in sight. Even from this distance, Mitch could see the scowl on his face. He kept gulping from a glass and looking around. Eventually, he looked Mitch's way. He raised his head, stood up from his chair and started walking toward the veranda steps. Mitch thought, "Oh boy, here it comes, he knows it's me." But the closer he came, the more apparent it was that his focus wasn't on Mitch at all, but on a point near the entrance doors. Mitch looked behind him to his right and saw Maria standing beside the doors, talking with a group of young women. That was where Robert was headed.

He watched Robert come up the steps and walk casually over to Maria. Though he didn't sway or wobble, his slow and deliberate gait told Mitch that he was drunk. As he reached Maria, her friends stepped aside to allow him an audience with her, like a noblewoman's staff parting for the arrival of the crown prince. This was a man who was used to such treatment, the heir to a great fortune who, ironically, would meet his fate in a dirty alley behind a bar in Manhattan a decade later. But for now he was Michelangelo's David in a tuxedo: young, handsome, and as the quintessential American hero of the time, rich and powerful. He stood before Maria, erect yet casual, hand in one pocket, cigarette in the other. A lesser girl would have been putty in his hands. Not Maria. She regarded him from that place on the veranda, feet firmly planted on the decking, her expression unyielding.

From where he stood thirty feet away, Mitch couldn't hear their words, but he could easily see that the conversation wasn't light. Robert's demeanor was caustic—he spit his words out like he was blowing poison darts out of a tube. Maria's return was more subtle, lady-like, yet jabbing in its own way. Her arms were folded on her chest, her neck craned slightly forward, sure signs she wasn't backing down. Mitch was sure that Robert was interrogating her about the mysterious man she had been with that evening. This golden boy who had been born into privilege and handed everything, and who had taken what wasn't handed over just because his name was Akers, demanded to know the identity of his rival. And this American princess, with the blood and confidence of Russian nobles flowing through her veins, who cared little about being wealthy but whose wealth was apparent in everything about her, stood toe-to-toe with him, denying him, refusing to satisfy his ego. And Robert Akers wasn't handling it well.

Mitch could see in his expression how much Robert detested being challenged by a woman. This was a man who wasn't used to being challenged by anyone, let alone a woman.

Mitch took a step in Maria's direction. Maria saw him and made a "back off" motion with her hand. Robert must have caught Maria's signal because he looked straight at Mitch. "Here it comes," Mitch thought. But Robert quickly turned back to Maria, said something, and walked away. He joined a couple of young men nearby and they headed off in the direction of the tennis courts.

Maria started toward Mitch and he met her halfway. He started to ask about her conversation with Robert, but she quickly cut him off and told him to follow her.

They went down the steps onto the lawn and headed in the direction of the least populated part of the grounds, the croquet court. It was a squarish course in the lawn, surrounded by a low picket fence. Just beyond the court, the trail wound its way along the water and past the dock. They stopped there and Mitch reached for Maria, but she drew away.

"What?" he said, hurt.

"You're an observer now." There was concern in her eyes. She obviously saw the pained look on his face.

"What do you mean?" He touched his own shoulders and arms. "I don't feel any different."

"Mitch." Maria folded her arms across her chest and looked at the ground. She was quiet for a long time. When she lifted her head again, Mitch could see she had been crying. "You can only observe from now on. And I need you to do that. You have to know every bit of it—ugly as it may be."

Mitch thought about what she was saying and his stomach twisted in a knot. "How can you just . . . go willingly to your—"

"Remember what I told you. From here on you're just an observer. And what you will see is just a vision, a reenactment if you want to think of it like that."

"I don't think I can do this."

"Yes you can. You have to."

She started away in the direction of the hotel, leaving him with a breaking heart. After a few steps, she turned back to face him.

"I love you."

She turned again and continued toward the veranda steps. And that was the last time they spoke.

CHAPTER THIRTY-TWO

itch knew he would stay and observe because he would never let Maria down. Whatever reason she had for keeping him there, to see what he dreaded most in the world, he trusted that it was a good reason and he wanted to do it for her. But he still dreaded it.

He started in her direction with the idea of hovering nearby, but he didn't have to. As in his other visions, he moved through time and space involuntarily, guided by some force that seemed to emanate from inside his brain. Now he found himself standing on the lawn behind the tent, watching another confrontation between Maria and Robert. He could not hear any of what was said over the band, but the argument looked like a heated one. For a couple of minutes they went at it full bore, then Robert said something that made Maria suddenly stop. She stood there glaring at him, hands curled into fists. Judging by the look on her face, she might explode at any moment in a flurry of accusations and disparagements. Then all at once her shoulders fell, the fists uncurled and she leaned closer to him. Whatever she said, it seemed to come out in one long, measured sentence with no emotion attached. When she was finished she walked off as casual as you please, leaving Robert to watch her go, a look of barely controlled rage on his face.

Mitch followed Maria's progress up the lawn toward the veranda, and as he did, he noticed someone moving in the shadows near one corner of the tent. When Maria was out of view, the eavesdropper walked out into the open. It was Teddy, dressed in a little tuxedo, shirttails hanging out and hair starting to get rumpled. While Mitch looked on, unnoticed, the boy skittered away toward the hotel. Mitch got a good look at his face as he moved into the light from the veranda, and was disturbed at what he saw: contempt like nothing he had ever seen on the face of a boy his age before.

He didn't have much opportunity to dwell on it, though, because now he found himself on the Smythe dock watching Robert Akers board a Chris Craft runabout. Robert said goodbye to a couple of friends on the dock, swung a suitcase over the wide wooden gunwale onto a leather seat and hopped on board. The boat left with Robert waving to his friends, looking as nonplussed as he had when he walked away from Maria.

Another quick flash and now Mitch was standing in back of the hotel watching a dark figure climb through a hole in the boards covering the new construction. Mitch drew nearer without feeling his legs move, and poked his head through the same hole. He was just in time to see the dark figure pick up a hammer with a long, straight claw from the bottom rung of the ladder inside the addition. The ladder rose to just below the third floor window. The window was covered by a white tarp made of the same material as the one covering the hole in the dining room.

The figure climbed the ladder quickly and silently to the third floor and slipped under the tarp. Just like that, he was inside the Boudreau apartment. Despite all the fuss Roger Boudreau had made over the years about security, all this burglar had to do was slip under a tarp and climb a ladder someone had left inside the new addition. Incredible.

Just as Mitch lifted a leg through the hole in the wall, he found himself standing near the spiral staircase in the Boudreau apartment. All the lights were off and the moonlight coming through the windows bathed the rooms in an eerie, blue-gray light. He could hear heavy snoring coming from the first bedroom, Roger's room.

The dark figure moved down the short hall and silently opened the door to Roger's bedroom. It slipped in, and a moment later Mitch heard a noise he knew was coming, and which he had dreaded but was helpless to avoid hearing. It was a dull *thunk,* the sound of the hammer claw sinking through Roger Boudreau's sternum into his heart. That ended the snoring and the apartment fell silent. Seconds later, the figure emerged from Roger's room and quietly slipped through the door of the middle room, Fenton's room. Another dull *thunk,* followed a second or two later by a barely audible cracking sound, came from the room. Mitch knew from the autopsy report that the hammer hadn't hit the heart this time, probably because there wasn't much light in

Fenton's room and the murderer's aim was off. The second noise was the dull crack of the hammer claw driving into Fenton's forehead—the killer blow.

And now the dark figure emerged once again and went for the last room, Maria's bedroom.

The door to Maria's room was wide open, and the man with the hammer walked right through. A second later he came out again and hurried Mitch's way. He looked wildly about when he reached the living room, and Mitch knew why: Maria was elsewhere in the apartment. What had looked like a quick and easy one-two-three attack now had a serious complication.

He came in Mitch's direction and stopped directly in front of him. For the first time Mitch was able to see the man's face, a face which probably should not have shocked him but did nonetheless. It was Robert Akers. Robert Akers, who had left the island on a boat earlier that night. Somehow he was back on the island and in the middle of a killing spree. Mitch, of course, knew the history of that night better than anyone who wasn't actually there, and everything he had read indicated that Robert reached the mainland in the Chris Craft long before the murders took place. Yet here he was. The thought that he was watching a revised version of the murders came to mind, but he quickly dismissed the thought. He had learned from his earlier experiences that only factually accurate visions came through to him.

Robert dashed quietly about the rooms, silent as a cat. After he had checked every corner of the apartment, he arrived back at the spiral stairs where he stood so close to Mitch he could have reached out and touched him. Mitch thought of doing just that, remembering what it had done to the waiter in the hotel dining room, but before he could, Robert moved away and started up the stairs.

Maria had made it clear to Mitch that he couldn't interfere, that what had happened had happened and it wasn't for him to change it. So, Mitch thought, what am I doing here? What is her purpose in subjecting me to this horror? Couldn't she have just *told* me the identity of her killer? Does she really expect me to stand by and watch her be brutally murdered?

Robert moved slowly up the stairs, being careful not to make them creak. Mitch tried to follow, but couldn't move. The higher Robert went, the more the panic rose in Mitch's chest. Finally, he reached the top. Just as he did, Mitch heard a murmur from somewhere up there in the tower room. He tried again to release himself from the invisible bond holding him back, but he might as well have been encased in cement. He tried shouting to Maria, but no sound came out. Then, just as he thought he would go insane, the bonds fell away and he was in the tower room, standing next to the top of the stairs. An oil lamp and a radio set with exposed tubes illuminated the room enough for Mitch to see what was happening. Robert had already moved over to the divan where Maria lay in a dark blue dressing gown. She was just waking up, and as Mitch watched in horror, Robert swung the hammer. But Maria was awake enough to realize what was happening, and she moved her head just in time. The hammer's claw sank into the pillow where Maria's head had been laying just a moment earlier. Maria rolled off the divan onto the floor, so far unharmed.

Mitch yelled at Robert but he didn't hear. Neither did Maria, who was now crab-crawling backwards in the direction of the porthole window. There was a small alcove under the window, and she backed up right into it. Robert followed slowly. Neither of them said a word at first, and then Maria began screaming for help. Just how effective her screams were Mitch couldn't tell, but the tower room was well above even the third floor ceiling, so he doubted anyone could have heard unless they were standing on the lawn outside.

Robert came at her again. Mitch shouted, "Maria, move!" Maria rolled to her right, but it was impossible to tell whether she moved because of his warning. Robert swung the hammer and missed, and in doing so, he knocked over the oil lamp which stood on a small table next to the divan. The lamp fell to the floor and broke, spraying oil all around, which instantly caught fire and began spreading in every direction, including the alcove in which Maria now sat. Maria leaped up and tried to run past Robert, but he was too quick. He grabbed her by the dressing gown, nearly tearing it from her body. She struggled violently, and Robert wrapped his arm around her neck from behind, choking her. He swung the hammer, but her arm caught his wrist and the hammer fell to the carpet. He began tightening his grip on her neck, and that's when something inside Mitch broke free.

He found his voice and shouted, "Robert!" Robert seemed to hear him because he turned in his direction for a split second, eyes wide with confusion. But, seeing nothing, he regained his focus quickly and turned back to what he was doing.

By now the lack of blood flowing to Maria's brain had weakened her, and her body relaxed in Robert's arms. Robert pulled his elbow in tighter, cutting off the blood supply even more. A moment later, Maria fell forward in his arms and he let her crumple to the floor, still breathing but quite unconscious. He looked around for the hammer.

Realizing what Robert was about to do, Mitch tried to yell his name and distract him again. But this time nothing came out. He tried again, but it was no use—he was an unseen, unheard bystander again. An "observer", as Maria had called him earlier.

If only he could break free of whatever force held him where he stood, if only he could move across the room and cut off Robert, the force of their opposing energies would throw them both around like the waiter in the restaurant and the old lady by the dock. Maybe Robert would become frightened enough that he would forget about Maria and take off out of the apartment. But try as he might to get his legs moving, Mitch's body remained frozen in place.

Helplessly, he watched Robert go for the hammer. But when Maria had knocked it out of his hand it had bounced over by the alcove where flames surrounded it. Robert tried reaching over the flames to retrieve it and burned his hand. The fire continued to spread, and he finally had to back away from the alcove. The fire licked at the walls and the divan smoldered, giving off a thick white smoke that mixed with the black smoke filling up the room. Robert's eyes watered and he wiped at them with his sleeve. The room would soon be completely engulfed in the fire. It was already surrounding Maria. Apparently Robert decided there was no need for the hammer and he moved over to the spiral staircase.

Before taking the first step down, Robert watched Maria for a moment as if making sure she was still unconscious. She was, and the flames continued to encircle her. Soon there would be no escape, even if she came to.

Mitch still stood close to the stairs, unable to move. In his mind he screamed for Maria to wake up, but his mouth stayed silent. As Robert stopped on the top step to look back, a rage like nothing Mitch had ever felt before started in his belly and rushed up to his head. If he had been flesh and blood, he was certain the adrenaline rush would have given him the strength to throw Robert across the room like a rag doll. If only he had been flesh and blood . . .

And there lay Maria, still unconscious, the fire all but touching her. And there stood Robert Akers, the murdering son-of-a-bitch, ready to descend the stairs and make his way off the island and out of harm's way. It was more than Mitch could bear.

In his mind he screamed a string of obscenities at Robert, while tearing at the invisible encasement that held him. Then all at once, there was a bright flash that seemed to fill the entire room, and a screech like a train's wheels locking up at full-speed, and he was free.

He didn't have time to wonder how he had been freed. His only thought was to get Robert Akers out of the way and then somehow pull Maria out of the room before it was too late.

Robert had just turned back and stuck out a foot to step down. Mitch charged him and they collided in a black flash, but this time the flash was not instantaneous. For a while Mitch seemed to float in an endless dark void. Scenes began popping in and out of his vision, all of them cumulatively forming a story as fascinating as the one now playing out in the tower room: two boys arguing loudly just outside the gates to the Smythe tennis courts; one of them telling the other, "Your kind don't belong here"; the other boy walking away, but turning to shout one last vulgarity; the first boy standing in a hallway lined with doors and glowing wall sconces, a small bag hanging from one hand and something concealed in the other; the same boy kneeling in front of one of the doors, opening the bag, fanning something under the door, taking something out of the other hand and—*oh dear Jesus, he's not really going to*—

Suddenly Mitch found himself sprawled on the landing at the top of the staircase, watching Robert tumble down the stairs and land in a heap at the bottom where he lay deathly still.

Mitch got to his feet and started toward Maria. Until now he hadn't noticed it, but he felt no heat coming from the fire. He moved closer, testing it, waiting to feel searing heat blast the front of him. But he felt nothing. In this state, he either could not feel pain or was not affected in any way by such things as flames. He would just step right through the growing wall of fire in front of him, pick up Maria and carry her to safety. He didn't care that she had warned him against interfering. He didn't care that what had happened had happened and you couldn't change that. He had to try.

He stepped into the fire, reached for Maria's crumpled body, and—

—he was standing on the lawn.

He looked around. He was at the center of the Smythe lawn, just beyond the empty white tent, facing the harbor. Turning around, he saw orange flames licking at the round window in the tower room. It was fully engulfed now. Yet not a soul stirred outside. The fire hadn't been discovered yet. Maria was still up there and nobody was there to help, including him.

He let out a wailing scream, which, of course, nobody heard. Meanwhile, all he could do was watch as his dear, dear Maria died in the flames up there in the tower.

CHAPTER THIRTY-THREE

That should have been all. How much more could he take? How much more could *anyone* take? But it wasn't over.

Mercifully, he didn't have to watch the fire for long. The next black flash brought him to a spot on a dusty trail—one of the resort's trails. Looking about, he recognized the Arndt cottage, all white in the dull moonlight, its roof covered in gray shingles. Up above, to the southwest, flames leaped from the roof of the tower.

In the firelight Mitch saw people gathered on the lawn near the big tent that had been used for Maria's party earlier that night. A fire pumper in front of the veranda shot water at the tower. Next to the cottage, Dr. Arndt and a couple Mitch did not recognize walked toward the lawn. On the cottage porch a small figure stood watching Dr. Arndt go. It was Teddy, dressed in pajamas, holding a stuffed animal. He looked tiny standing there with the terrible flames as a backdrop.

The porthole window exploded outward and fell in pieces on the veranda roof, which quickly caught fire. Someone shouted at the guests, telling them to stay down by the water, but they remained on the lawn anyway, still dangerously close to the fire.

A noise, a slight rustling sound, came from some bushes near the trail. Teddy heard it, too, because he swung his head that way and peered closely, trying to see what it was. The sound only lasted a second, but Teddy stayed focused that way. He stepped quietly down the porch steps and moved, barefoot, down the trail toward the bushes. When he reached them he stopped and leaned forward, trying to see beyond the outer leaves.

Suddenly, Robert Akers leaped from behind the bushes and grabbed Teddy. He held him by the neck with one arm, much the same way he had held Maria up in the tower room, and clamped his free hand over the boy's mouth. Teddy, his eyes wide with terror, struggled and tried to shout through Robert's hand, but it was no use. Robert was much too strong for the small boy.

Robert said something and Teddy stopped struggling.

"That's better," Robert said in a menacing growl. "Now, you listen to me, boy. I know who you are, and I know who your father is. If you so much as sneeze, I'll snap your neck like a twig. Understand?"

Teddy nodded vigorously, eyes bulging from their sockets.

"Good." Robert took his hand away from Teddy's mouth. "Now here's the other thing. If you ever tell a soul you saw me tonight, I'll come for your father first. I'll slice him up into pieces in front of you. Then I'll slice you up. Understand?"

Teddy nodded again, rubbing his throat.

"No one will ever believe you, boy. My father's one of the most powerful men in America. They'll never believe you over me. Don't ever forget that."

Teddy nodded.

"Now, get back up to your house and get to bed. And when your papa gets back, pretend you're asleep."

Teddy obeyed and started back toward the cottage. When he was inside the door, Robert crossed the trail to the water side and made his way down to the harbor's edge. In the moonlight, he waded into the water and started swimming toward Forge's Island.

Another flash came and Mitch found himself in a dark place that he didn't recognize. He stood on a low, flat rock. The strong scent of tidal mud and the sound of lapping water told him he was beside the ocean. Aside from that, he had no idea where he'd gone. Looking around, he saw a light to his left. Someone with a lantern stood in a small boat tied to a dock jutting out of the rocks. Now Mitch knew where he was: the other side of Forge's Island where he had walked on the sunken dock with Wendy. Only, the dock was still above water in 1924. Farther to his left, a man moved on the rocks, picking his way toward the dock. He arrived at the boat and stepped over the gunwale. The other man held up the lantern and said something. The lantern revealed the man as Robert Akers, whose hair and clothes were wet. Robert said something back, and the man on the boat started the engine. The boat backed up slowly then motored away under low power, its engine cut back to keep the noise at a minimum, with no running lights on.

Mitch watched the boat until even the moonlight couldn't illuminate it enough to see it, and once it was out of sight, he looked back over his shoulder. The night sky still glowed above the bluffs behind him indicating the tower was still ablaze. He tried not to think of Maria in there, but it was impossible not to. He had to keep reminding himself that these events happened long ago—that Maria's suffering happened long ago. Still, it was heart-wrenching to think what had happened to her. He could only hope she had never regained consciousness after Robert choked her.

He stood on the rocks for a while, waiting for something to happen. Forge's Island was silent, but voices came from Sumner Island across the harbor where the guests must still be on the lawn watching the fire. The smell of smoke carried on the breeze in his direction. Soon the flames would be out, but not before the tower was destroyed along with parts of the Boudreau apartment and some of the roof. The bodies of Fenton and Roger would be found and removed. But not Maria's. Her body would be completely incinerated in the white-hot flames that consumed the tower room.

He had to push the thought away—it was just unbearable.

By now, having seen what he was supposed to see here, he expected to be whisked off that rocky beach in another black flash. But this time he found himself waiting, surrounded by near-quiet and mostly darkness, which gave him time to reflect. Somewhere out on the ocean a boat motored slowly toward the mainland where Robert Akers would disembark at a private dock owned by a friend whose name Mitch couldn't think of at the moment. In the inquest that followed, the friend and the owner of the Chris Craft would both say that Robert arrived hours earlier and was tucked in bed for the night long before the murders at the Smythe. The next morning Robert, supposedly unaware of the events in the early-morning hours, would take his friend's car down to Massachusetts where he was scheduled to play in a polo match. Anyone who saw him that day would say Robert looked a little hung over—not unusual for him—but otherwise normal. Upon being informed of the murders, he merely asked about his father's safety and never mentioned Maria.

Robert did not remain a suspect for long—Malcolm Akers' money saw to that. Without the most obvious suspect to point the finger at, a less obvious suspect—but a much more convenient one—emerged. His name was Vladimir Maliakov, and he was part of the construction crew working on the addition to the hotel that weekend. In those days, construction workers had stayed overnight in servants' quarters while working on the hotel, rather than riding the ferry back and forth each day. Vladimir Maliakov had slept in these quarters the night of the murders.

"Vlad the Impaler", as his coworkers had jokingly referred to him for the way he attacked nail with hammer, had escaped with his family from Russia during the Revolution. From a strain of aristocracy even weaker than Tatiana Obolensky's, he and his family nevertheless had barely gotten out with the clothes on their backs. In America they had been forced to become common laborers to survive. At age sixteen, Vlad had learned carpentry and was soon very skilled at it. His hammer—which Mitch now realized Robert Akers had used on Roger and Fenton—had been found in the rubble the next day, Vlad's carved initials still intact on the partially charred wood handle. In the ensuing interrogation, Vlad swore he had been in his bunk at the time of the murders. But his roommate, a young man with a sketchy past named Gilbert Roy, said he did not recall seeing Vlad come back to his room after the rest of the work gang finished up a late card game. Roy only recalled seeing Vlad in his bed later on when the hotel staff came down to evacuate the workers from the building. Without a solid alibi, and with the murder weapon clearly belonging to him, Vlad was accused and tried in the witch-hunt atmosphere that followed. It seemed he had once complained to a co-worker that Roger had done little to help the Russian émigrés following the Revolution, and this revelation at his trial sealed his fate. He was convicted and jailed for life, which turned out to be a short sentence, for, three years later, his throat was slit by another lifer for refusing to give up a half-smoked cigarette. Interestingly, Gilbert Roy ended up on Malcolm Akers' payroll as a full-time handyman at the Akers' Long Island estate—at twice the pay he earned before.

But that wasn't the end of the story of Vladimir Maliakov. Less than a year after Vlad's murder, a man named Henry Nason turned up out of nowhere and claimed he had seen Vlad stagger off to bed, quite drunk, before the card game ended that fateful night. Nason even helped Vlad remove his boots and got him under a blanket. Vlad was snoring by the time he left the room, Nason said. Nason was convinced Vlad was so intoxicated that night, he never could have found his way to the bathroom, let alone the Boudreau suite.

So, he was asked, why hadn't he told this to the police? He did, Nason said. It just never made its way into their report. Nason said he had spent the last few years working for an uncle down in Baltimore, but before leaving New England he had given police his forwarding address. When questioned about Nason, the investigating police said they not only had never interviewed him, they had never even heard of him. Yet hotel records showed that Nason, indeed, had been one of the construction workers on the island that weekend. In a story that caused a sensation—and sold a lot of newspapers—reporters reminded the public that the police had interviewed everyone on the island who was old enough to talk. How could they have missed Nason?

Mitch was thinking about the obvious implications of this as he started walking across the rocks toward the bluff behind him. What he now knew to be fact, many people had only been able to speculate about back in the 1920's. An innocent man had died because Maria was so popular and so loved, and Roger was so famous, that someone had to take the fall before the public's outrage could be quelled. That person was never going to be Robert Akers. Guys like him didn't take the fall. They went off and played polo and let their money and their lackeys take care of things. Only in Robert's case money couldn't insulate him forever. In 1933 he would be involved in a brawl at a seedy bar in Manhattan. The next morning, his body would be found in the alley behind the bar, a knife gruesomely embedded in his ear up to the hilt. His killer was never found. The other patrons involved in the brawl were still in the bar at the time he was murdered, and they later left in a taxi. Their alibis were airtight. Police detectives concluded that some vagrant probably had murdered Robert for his money, although Robert's wallet was still on his person when they found him. The case was eventually closed, never to be resolved. And yet, Mitch thought as he approached the high bluff on the north side of Forge's Island, something about that murder—most particularly the place and the year in which it happened—raised some interesting questions.

As he reached the bottom of the bluff Mitch felt the now-familiar sensation that the scene was about to change on him again, but no black flash came. Instead, his body rose up over the bluff and moved across the expanse of the island in the direction of Longboat Harbor. Passing over the water, he saw people standing on the decks of their boats, watching the fire.

On the lawn at the Smythe, hundreds of people, most of them in sleepwear, stood watching the firemen trying to put out the blaze. As he moved in the direction of his cabin, the scene began to fade.

Just before everything went completely dark, Mitch came up with the answer to what had been gnawing at him about Robert Akers' murder. And then he lost consciousness.

CHAPTER THIRTY-FOUR

When he came to, he was in his bed in the little cabin. Something was different from the last time he'd been there, and it didn't take long to figure out what it was. There was a breeze, a strong one, coming through the open windows. For the first time that weekend Mitch saw the curtains flutter and felt refreshing air flow over his body. Not cool air, just moving air, but he was grateful even for that. He would never take such a thing for granted again after that three-day spell.

He wanted to feel the air from out in the open, so he left the cabin and walked up to the Smythe lawn where nothing would obstruct the wind. There, he stood on the grass and felt the wisps of air blowing in from the west. He did a slow hundred-and-eighty degree turn to catch it on all sides. When he had gone full circle and looked to the west again, he saw a cloud bank forming in the western sky. Though it was full dark, the moonlight illuminated the clouds from without, and an electrical storm illuminated the clouds from within. Lightning flashes popped in random places inside the cloud bank, showing the breadth of the storm and the speed at which it was traveling. It appeared to be moving at a fast clip, but the most interesting thing was that the clouds seemed to be gathering in the middle, moving in from both north and south, growing denser in the center.

Up at the hotel a lot of guests had come out on the veranda to enjoy the breeze, and a stream of them began wandering down the steps to the lawn. Several people pointed to the west, and the chatter coming from the front of the hotel carried across the lawn in excited, slightly tentative voices. The reason for this nervous excitement was the light display in the cloud bank, which was even more active now. The storm had rolled off the mainland and was moving at what seemed an impossible speed. At this pace, the clouds would be over Sumner Island in just a few minutes. They were in for one hell of a storm.

He walked across the grass in a daze, mesmerized by the gathering clouds, not even thinking about the danger such a storm could pose. In the time it took to walk from the edge of the lawn over to the dolphin and seal topiaries, the cloud bank reached Tintagel Island a mile to the west, and lightning illuminated it like midday. The water around Tintagel was lit up, too, and Mitch could see it churning and pounding against the rocks. The storm was closing in on Sumner, and the hotel guests who had come out on the lawn were hurrying back inside.

Not Mitch. Still mesmerized by the storm, he felt a serene confidence like he had never felt before, a calm that fear could not penetrate. He was supposed to be out here, storm or no storm. Why he could not explain. He just kept on walking, in no hurry and with no particular destination, sensing the reason would find him, not the other way around. He watched the front of the cloud bank reach the western shore of the island, felt the wind pick up, felt the first big rain drop hit him on the forehead. Another followed close behind, and then another, and soon he was being pelted by stinging drops driven by the hard wind. In a matter of seconds he was standing in a driving, soaking rain storm, his clothes drenched to the skin. Then the lightning strikes began.

Until now the lightning had stayed in the sky, appearing as flashes totally contained within the clouds. Now Zeus unleashed his fury in jagged bolts that careened across the sky. Mitch looked to the west at Lover's Lookout during one of these bright displays and thought he saw the angel weathervane on top glow green. In the next flash, the Smythe grounds lit up like a ballpark under flood lights. Then all became dark again, this time even darker than before. The hotel went black, losing power in the last lightning strike. All the lights came on again a moment later as the backup generators apparently kicked in. Then a huge lightning bolt lit up the island in an eerie green, and the hotel went dark again. The generators themselves had somehow been knocked out. The island was dark to stay.

Mitch waited on the grass, bullets of cold raindrops pummeling his body, his clothes flapping furiously. It felt as if he could fly away if he just stuck out his arms. A clap of thunder set his ears ringing, and another lightning bolt followed a second later. In that flash, which lasted only a millisecond, Mitch thought he saw another man on the lawn about a hundred feet directly in front of him. He didn't get a good look at the man, but his clothes seemed familiar: white shirt, black pants. Mitch called out over the sound of the roaring wind, "Hello! Who are you!" He was answered by loud thunder, which made the whole island vibrate. The next lightning bolt touched down on the far side of Longboat Harbor, turning everything bright green for a moment, and when the harbor went dark again, a sailboat had burst into flames. Its occupants came running up from below deck and began spraying a fire extinguisher. Not long after, an explosion at the rear of the boat sent everyone leaping into the water.

Thunder rolled again, and the accompanying lightning bolt struck immediately, this time sending jagged fingers all over the harbor and setting other boats aflame. Two boats exploded, one after the other, shooting splinters of fiberglass and wood everywhere. Some of the pieces landed on shore. Mitch could only pray that the boats had been unoccupied when the explosions came, but he knew better.

Another thunder roll announced an impending lightning strike. Just before it hit, the wind died down to a stiff breeze and the drenching rain became more like a sprinkle. The bolt that followed wasn't really a bolt at all, but an intense flash of light that made Mitch feel like he was standing inside a light bulb. It seemed to electrify the whole island, bathing everything in a sickening bile color. Mitch's eye caught something to his right, and when he turned his head, he was staring into the dark, vacant eye sockets of Robert Akers' ghost.

"Jerry Sande from Chicago," Robert said matter-of-factly.

Other than the dark holes where his glacier-colored eyes would have been, he looked exactly the way he had the last time Mitch saw him in 1924 stepping into the hidden boat out on Forge's Island. His wet hair hung limp to the side, his damp tuxedo shirt clung to his skin. His feet were bare.

"Yeah, Jerry," Mitch said, startled and a little scared, but angry, too. "Bertie's college bud'."

Robert smiled, showing impossibly white, impossibly straight teeth. Behind the teeth was a pitch-black void, the kind Mitch imagined you would find in the deepest corners of the universe.

The flashing stopped briefly and the island plunged into darkness again. Mitch wondered if Robert would be gone now that the lightning had stopped, but Robert's voice, close to Mitch's ear, assured him he was still there. "You're shaking, Dr. Lambert."

Mitch was deeply aware that he should be afraid. He was no tough guy, not terribly strong or resourceful in a fight. But all he kept thinking was, *This son-of-a-bitch killed Maria.* He said to the darkness, "You'd better be, too."

Thunder roared, lightning flashed and Mitch no longer could see Robert beside him. He did a full turn, but Robert was nowhere in sight.

The next lightning strike hit the dock, making the steel rail glow white for a moment. Another bolt lit up the night and Mitch heard "up here." He looked back at the middle tower and saw Robert watching him from the round window.

He broke into a run, took the veranda steps in three leaps and raced through the front doors. Inside the lobby, guests were crowded around the windows, watching the storm and the damage being done to the resort. Many of them looked terrified, and a few children and women cried and spoke as if the world were coming to an end. Mitch had to admit it really did look that way out there.

As soon as he got inside, the rain started mixing with marble-sized hail, which rattled on the veranda roof. The wind picked up again, blowing debris all around. The grass lay almost flat at times, and all the rocking chairs on the veranda rolled violently back and forth. Inside, the staff ran around with flashlights, lighting up the hotel as well as they could, trying to calm the guests down, insisting the storm would pass soon and the lights would come back on. They weren't very convincing, and the guests hardly calmed down at all. This wasn't just a passing summer storm. It was a major assault.

Mitch snatched a flashlight off the front desk and made his way through the crowd to the elevator. He pressed the "up" button twice before remembering the electricity was down and the elevators weren't operating. He took the stairs instead, passing people who had to feel their way down without the aid of any light. He made it to the third floor and hurried down the hall to the wall with the painting of the Russian wolfhounds. The dogs looked even more menacing in the flashlight beam. Swinging the light to his left, he expected to see the door to the Boudreau suite closed and locked, and he felt foolish because he had no keys and couldn't get in. But the door was wide open. He approached it slowly, worried that Robert Akers would pop out from somewhere and surprise him. Once he reached the doorway, he wasn't willing to venture any farther without knowing Robert's whereabouts.

"Where are you?" he shouted into the doorway.

From a distance away, a cheerful voice called, "In the tower. Come on up."

Mitch stepped over the threshold, swinging the flashlight beam wildly around, but nothing moved and no face materialized out of the dark. He took the steps up to the living room and stopped again to look around. In the light of the flashlight, the room appeared the same it had when he came in with the hotel guard, only it was eerie and forlorn in the shadowy light. He briefly stood before the window watching the electrical storm, which seemed to have settled over Forge's Island permanently, its creeping lightning bolts occasionally finding their way to the ground.

"What are you waiting for?" Robert's voice called from the tower.

Mitch moved slowly over to the spiral stairs and started up. Looking through the hole in the ceiling, he saw a dull glow illuminating the room as though a candle burned up there. When he reached the top of the stairs, he saw it wasn't a candle but an oil lamp.

Over by the round window, Robert Akers stood with his back turned, arms folded on his chest. "Yes, it's the same lamp," he said, his voice world-weary.

"Great. Are you going to burn the tower again?"

Robert turned around. No longer were his eye sockets empty and black, but even the ice-colored eyes with which he now regarded Mitch looked dead.

"Or do you think you might burn down the whole place, like you burned the west wing when you were twelve?"

Robert went on staring, his face devoid of expression.

"You blew gunpowder under the door of that boy's room. You lit a match. They didn't have a chance—no one had a chance. All because some kid called you a name."

"Maria knew, didn't she? Somehow, she found out. She told you that night on the lawn when you argued with her. You thought she might have told someone else, so you killed her and the two people you thought might know." He shook his head. "It was never about me, it was about your sick, dirty little secret."

Robert unfolded his arms and stuck his hands in his front pockets.

"What I don't understand is how Maria found out when no one else did. No one ever would have suspected a twelve-year-old kid. Malcolm Akers' kid."

Robert turned to the window again. "You should be able to figure that out by now, Professor."

Mitch thought about it and came up with the answer in no time at all, like it had been there in his head all along. "She had the gift; she saw what happened, just like I did tonight."

After a long silence Robert turned from the window and looked around the room. "They did a pretty good job restoring the place. Almost looks real."

"No thanks to you, you son-of-a—"

"Leave it alone, Professor. You needn't concern yourself with things that happened a long time ago."

Mitch had to restrain himself from leaping at him. "You killed Maria. That concerns me very much."

"Maria lived and died in my time. Not yours."

"I loved her then, too."

"Oh, yes. That neat little trick." He grinned and shook his head in wonder.

Mitch shot back a smirk of his own. "That's right. Bertie's buddy, Jerry." Thinking of Bertie, he was reminded of his presence around the hotel, and he added, "I've run into Bertie a few times this weekend. How about you?"

"I know what Bertie's up to."

"Apparently he also knows what you're up to. You were the one in Wendy's room, weren't you?"

"The blonde girl? Cute."

"Stay away from her."

"Here's a deal for you: I'll stay away from your little blonde girl, you stay away from Maria."

"But Maria's dead. You said so yourself."

"Don't toy with me. You know what I mean."

He walked over to the round window, and Mitch moved closer to see what he was looking at. Outside, the world kept lighting up in flashes, but the lightning now seemed to be staying up among the clouds and not finding its way to any earthly target. The hail had stopped and the rain had tapered to almost nothing. The wind was just a strong breeze. The storm seemed to have mellowed, but it still hovered over the islands like it was waiting for a cue.

Mitch moved to one side and glanced at Robert's eyes to see where they were focused. He appeared to be looking over the treetops east of the swimming beaches. Although Mitch couldn't see much in the darkness, he knew Mr. Arndt's cottage was down there among those trees.

All at once a realization came to him. "You're not going to bother that old man are you?" But he already knew the answer.

"Little Teddy."

"He's not little any more. He's a feeble old man."

"I remember him following Maria around like a cute little puppy. He wasn't so cute when he grew up."

"It was a long time ago, you said it yourself."

Robert's smile could only be described as sinister. "Some things seem like just yesterday." As he finished the last word, a great drum roll of thunder rattled the window. It was the loudest thunder Mitch had ever heard, and it was immediately followed by a bolt of lightning like a jagged searchlight beam shooting down at the very spot on which Robert's gaze was fixed. Trees in the vicinity exploded into splinters and began to burn.

"You dirty—"

"What?" Robert cut him off. "So we're having a little summer storm—"

Mitch didn't hear the rest because he had taken off down the spiral stairs.

CHAPTER THIRTY-FIVE

Mitch raced through the Boudreau suite out into the dark corridor and stumbled his way down to the first floor. Just as he reached the lobby, a bolt struck the veranda to the left of the entrance doors. Rocking chairs flew, and parts of the veranda roof burst into flames, making the crowd in front of the windows retreat across the lobby.

Mitch dashed through the front doors and scrambled down the steps before the flames could spread in front of them. Out on the lawn, he could see tall flames leaping from trees near Mr. Arndt's cottage. In the harbor, boats still burned and shouts and cries could be heard. A bunch of people in a motorized dinghy were making their way to shore. The last of the people from the burning boats were being pulled up into a large sailboat moored nearby. Mitch couldn't tell if they were all right or if they had been burned in the explosions. Boat debris lay everywhere on the water, some of it still in flames. He wanted to help, but had to get to Mr. Arndt first.

He couldn't take the shortcut to the cottage because the burning trees were too close. Instead, he ran down to the cart trail by the beach and followed it around to the front of Mr. Arndt's cottage. Just before he arrived at the porch, lightning hit the roof, ran down all sides, and blew Mitch clear off his feet onto his back. For an instant the cottage glowed bright green. He thought it would explode and he would be killed by the flying debris, but the glow faded away and the sky went black again. He had dropped the flashlight when he was knocked down, and when he went to pick it up again it burned his hand. It was now warped and inoperable, and hot as hell. He left it on the ground and headed up the porch steps.

He went inside the kitchen door and called out for Mr. Arndt, but no response came. The house was silent and dark, and for a horrifying moment he wondered if the green lightning that hit the house had killed its occupant. In the living room, he turned to his left and saw two doorways that he presumed led to bedrooms. Both doors were open. He looked into the one on the left and saw Mr. Arndt standing in the center of the room, looking like an apparition in his stark white pajamas. As he approached, the old man stood very still and quiet, making Mitch wonder again if the lightning strike had harmed him in some way.

"Mr. Arndt?"

The old man said nothing. He just went on staring in Mitch's direction.

"Mr. Arndt?" Mitch said, a little louder.

He went on staring. Then, just like a hypnotist had snapped his fingers to bring him out of a trance, he opened his mouth and said, "I can't find my glasses."

Mitch breathed a sigh and helped him find his glasses, which he had knocked off the nightstand while fumbling in the dark for them. The old man put them on. "Some storm," he said.

"We've got to get out of here."

Mr. Arndt looked at him, and in the reflection of his glasses Mitch saw the fire burning in the trees outside the window. It had already started to burn the little cabin, just thirty feet away, and it would reach the cottage soon. Mitch thought of his things in the cabin that he would soon lose, especially the photo of Maria and the brooch. After tonight they weren't nearly as important to him, but he was sad just the same.

"Where's your cane?" Mitch asked.

Mr. Arndt pointed to the corner where it leaned against the wall. Mitch retrieved it and handed it to him.

"We have to move as fast as we can. Ready?"

The old man began three-stepping toward the living room. Mitch let out a relieved sigh. Up to now, he hadn't been sure he would be able to get the old guy to move.

But he did move, right out the bedroom door into the living room, without any prodding. There he stopped, and Mitch felt panic rising again. The flames might engulf the cottage at any moment.

"We need to get out fast."

"Get the box on the secretary desk," Mr. Arndt instructed.

"We don't have time!"

"Just the box."

Mitch hurried over to an antique desk against the wall. A burled walnut box sat on top of it. He snatched it and had started back toward Mr. Arndt when something on the wall caught his eye. He stopped and stared at about twenty photos of all sizes, all in black and white and set in old-fashioned frames. Some were of Mr. Arndt's father, but most were of Maria. Mitch hated leaving them, but there was simply no choice. They had to get out now.

He took Mr. Arndt's elbow and hurried him along. They went through the kitchen and out on the porch just as the flames began licking at the corner of the cottage. The heat was intense. A couple minutes later they might have been trapped inside.

He hurried Mr. Arndt down the porch steps, and they made their way out to the trail and started in the direction of the beaches and the Smythe lawn. They had reached the end of the trees and just started onto the grass, when Mitch saw something that made him stop in his tracks. After everything else he had experienced that weekend he should not have been shocked at what he saw, but he was all the same.

Up there on the lawn, spread out on either side of the walkway from one end of the veranda to the other, were at least two hundred ghosts. They stood with their backs to the harbor and only appeared in the light of the fire and an occasional lightning flash, so Mitch wasn't able to make out much of their detail. But their clothing and hairstyles told him these were the victims of the west wing fire back in nineteen-twelve.

"Why are you stopping?" Mr. Arndt said beside him. These were the first words he had uttered since they left the cottage.

"Don't you see them?"

Mr. Arndt turned his gaze up at the apparitions standing on the lawn. "Yes." And he said something which indicated to Mitch that he knew more than he was letting on: "They wouldn't have missed this one for anything."

He started up the grass toward the crowd of souls standing between them and the hotel. Mitch kept pace at his side. He had no clue what had drawn this incredible gathering to the lawn. The electrical storm, maybe? Why they should be there now, whether summoned or by sheer circumstance, was beyond his understanding. He only hoped Mr. Arndt understood better—and that they were doing the right thing by approaching them. Then again, what choice did they have? Mr. Arndt was barely mobile, the dock was destroyed so they couldn't get to a boat, and the fire had spread to the trail behind them cutting off any escape from that direction.

So they went on toward the hotel, and after some time Mr. Arndt finally came out of his stupor. He began talking about nineteen twenty-four, reminiscing in remarkable clarity about events that should have been dulled over the past eight decades.

"That night Maria was murdered, I stood on my porch watching the tower burn," he said, working hard with his cane to make his legs move as quickly as they could. "My Papa had just gone off to the hotel with some neighbors, and he made me stay behind. Back then, the trees and stuff weren't so tall and I could see the hotel and part of the lawn in front. I saw the ghosts there that night, too."

He stopped a moment to catch his breath. Mitch looked up at the apparitions, still with their backs to the water, only fifty feet away now.

"What did they do?"

Mr. Arndt began his three-step walk again. "Nothing. At least nothing I saw. I heard a noise and found Robert Akers hiding in the bushes."

"I know," Mitch interrupted, sparing him the ugly memory. "I saw that tonight."

Mr. Arndt gave a small nod of understanding.

Mitch took another long look up the lawn at the ghosts and shuddered. The gathering of so many dead people, all dressed in their nightclothes, looked like something out of a zombie movie.

"But why would they be here? Why now?"

"Absolution, maybe."

"I don't understand."

"Sorry, can't help you." Mr. Arndt stopped and nodded at the ghosts. "No time right now."

They had drawn to within twenty feet of the gathering. Thankfully, the ghosts appeared as they probably had just before the fire and not after it. Their faces were devoid of any emotion, and Mitch couldn't guess what their intent might be.

"Are you sure about this?" he asked Mr. Arndt.

Mr. Arndt nodded. "Keep going."

They did, and when they were just a few feet away the crowd of spirits began to part, leaving a path wide enough for them to walk through comfortably. Like lords passing among their vassals, Mitch and Mr. Arndt walked between the sad spirit forms of all those tragic people. There were people of every age, children, too, all of their faces ashen, eyes dark and emotionless. Mitch only hoped they would not close the path behind them, trapping them. But they didn't, and the path they made reached up the walkway between the dolphin and seal topiaries, all the way to the veranda steps. The rain had stopped, but the fires still burned and the lightning flickered in the dark clouds overhead. Each time the lightning flashed, the ghosts all around them took on a more solid appearance, much like headlights shining on fog. When it became dark again their transparency returned.

Off to the right side of the hotel some staff dressed in firefighting gear had trained a fire hose on the burning roof. This drew Mitch's attention for a second or two, and when he turned around again, Mr. Arndt had stopped and was staring at him. His expression was that of a man who has just learned he has terminal cancer. Mitch didn't understand at first, and he looked around at the crowd of souls for an answer, but nothing seemed to have changed. When he looked back at Mr. Arndt, the old man's eyes had fixed on the veranda. Following his gaze, he saw Robert Akers at the top of the steps.

CHAPTER THIRTY-SIX

Robert came casually down the veranda steps and stopped in front of Mr. Arndt.

Mitch said, "Leave him alone, Robert," but Robert ignored him. He just stared at Mr. Arndt, his expression a mix of contempt and curiosity.

"So, this is what became of the child whose life I spared that night," he said.

"I've had a good long life, how about you, Robert?"

Robert looked unperturbed, grinning as he gave Mr. Arndt the once over. "If this is what I had to look forward to, I suppose I ought to thank you." He stepped forward and stood face to face with the old man.

"Stay away from him," Mitch warned, but Robert still ignored him.

"Do you want to know how it feels to have a knife stuck in your ear?" Robert said. He reached out and laid his hand over Mr. Arndt's ear. Mr. Arndt let out a cry of agony and fell to his knees. "Something like that."

The old man held his head in both hands, clearly in considerable pain. Still, he managed to say, "It was worth it."

Mitch had seen enough. He kicked out at Robert, trying to knock him away, forgetting just what he was trying to strike. His foot swung through Robert's hip and he lost his balance and fell on his back. The next thing he knew, Robert was standing over him, pointing. "I've had it up to here with you," he growled.

Mitch rolled over on his belly and pushed himself up on his feet. He knew what Robert Akers could do to him, but his contempt for the man was so great, there was no room left for fear. "Leave him alone, take me on."

Robert made a quick step forward and his hand shot out and grabbed Mitch's temples between his thumb and middle finger. He pressed hard, and Mitch felt a buzzing sensation zip through his head. He saw stars, and then everything began to fade. He couldn't hear very well for all the buzzing in his head, but he did hear Mr. Arndt shout something at Robert and saw him point behind him. Robert let go of Mitch and he fell to the ground, his head in agony, his vision blurred.

He heard someone say, "That's better." The voice hadn't come from Robert or Mr. Arndt, but someone else close by.

Robert stared down the walkway. "Well, well, Bertie. Well, well."

Mitch looked in that direction, and even through fuzzy eyes he recognized the piano player. Dressed in his impeccably tailored tuxedo, not a hair out of place despite the strong wind blowing in from the west, Bertie stood on the walkway a short distance from Mitch, looking down his hawkish nose at Robert.

"It's time to go," Bertie said, as though he were talking to a child.

"Stay out of this," Robert growled back.

"I won't, Bobby. One's an old man who can't defend himself, and the other's my friend."

Robert snickered. "Jerry. Right."

"Leave him be." Bertie's face was hard, firm.

"I said stay out of this," Robert warned in a voice low and threatening, like a dog preparing to attack.

Bertie turned his gaze down at Mitch and winked like they were the old buddies he claimed they were. This seemed to aggravate Robert. He took a step toward Mitch, but Bertie quickly moved over to cut him off. Bertie said over his shoulder to Mitch, "You and Teddy head up to the hotel now."

Mitch got to his feet and walked around Robert, keeping his eyes on him the whole way. Robert stared back but didn't move. In his eyes Mitch saw something he hadn't seen before: uncertainty. When he was safely past him, Mitch went for Mr. Arndt who still lay on the ground. He helped him to his feet, and together they walked away toward the wheelchair ramp end of the veranda, which had been spared the flames.

In his head, Mitch heard Bertie say, "You have no business here, Bobby." He waited for Robert's reply, but none came. Suddenly, he sensed a presence to his right, and when he turned that way, Robert was standing beside him.

He ignored Mitch and reached for Mr. Arndt. But before he could touch him, Berties's voice came into Mitch's head again, saying, "I mean what I say, Bobby."

Robert hesitated, glancing back at Bertie where he still stood on the walkway, surrounded by the mob of spirits. A rolling thunder clap—the loudest yet—made the earth beneath Mitch's feet rumble. A fraction of a second later the sky lit up a bright green as a dozen lightning bolts crisscrossed directly over the island. The bolts connected in the middle, and there was a great exploding sound like a bomb had gone off. The sky turned white, and Mitch smelled sulfur and something else that his brain interpreted as burning copper. Instead of fading to black again, the sky stayed lit up, but not by lightning. Something else—something Mitch couldn't even guess at—kept the sky lit from up above the clouds. The atmosphere surrounding him felt electrically charged. It reminded him of the time his cousin dared him to put his tongue over the terminals of a nine-volt battery when he was a little kid. His concern now turned from Robert Akers to this strange electrical storm. If the electricity pulsing through the atmosphere increased to any appreciable degree, he and Mr. Arndt might be electrocuted before Robert could do them any damage. He took Mr. Arndt by the elbow. "Come on, we've got to get inside fast."

As they made their way up the wheelchair ramp, Mr. Arndt's pace agonizingly slow on the incline, a window opened and Wendy stepped through it onto the veranda. She rushed down the ramp and helped Mitch walk the visibly shaken and exhausted old man over to a corner of the veranda deck where he could rest for a moment. After they had helped him into a rocker, Mitch asked Wendy, "Do you see them?"

Wendy looked in the direction of the mob of ghosts and gave a rapid nod, her eyes wide like a child's. Mitch thought she would be delighted to see all these apparitions—the subject she had made a career pursuing—on the Smythe lawn. But she looked positively terrified.

The thunder had died down to a low rumble, but the rumble hadn't stopped. Suddenly, a ball of green-white lightning spun out of the sky to the north, passed low over Forge's Island, and came across the harbor straight at them. Before it reached Sumner's shore it exploded, lighting up the island so brightly that Mitch had to turn his face away for fear of going blind. After a few seconds the brightness died down, like a great light dimmer had been turned down, making it bearable to look again. Mitch turned his eyes back to the lawn and saw Bertie walking toward Robert. When he was within a few feet of him, Bertie stopped and stared, seemingly daring Robert to make a move. Robert glared back, and even from up on the veranda Mitch could sense the contempt pouring out of him, as though all the hatred in his being had flowed out and mixed with the electrical charge in the air. Until tonight, Mitch had never been in the presence of anyone he would have described as evil. Bad, yes, but not evil. Whatever had caused this man, who'd had every advantage in life—great wealth, good looks, Ivy League education—to become so contemptuous of other humans when he was alive, it had stayed with him even after death. No longer was Mitch shocked by the knowledge that Robert had murdered Maria, nor the manner in which he'd done it. Robert Akers would have destroyed *anyone* who challenged his ego. That was the one thing he could never tolerate.

The two ghosts went on staring in silence, Bertie in a relaxed stance, one hand in his jacket pocket, the other holding a lit cigarette which gave off no smoke. In contrast, Robert seemed anything but relaxed. His body looked tensed up, coiled like a cobra ready to strike.

In the middle of this stare-down, Bertie turned and looked up at Mitch and his companions on the veranda. Incredibly, he winked!

Still, there was no movement between the men. Not a word, either. It seemed the two could go on forever staring each other down, waiting for the other to make the first move. And it seemed the storm would go on forever, providing a dramatic backdrop for this battle of nerves.

Yet something was happening, something was about to change. Mitch felt it before he saw it. There was a sudden quelling of the electric buzz that had permeated the atmosphere all around them the past several minutes. At the same exact moment, the rain and hail stopped. The wind followed suit, dying down to nothing, like someone in the heavens had unplugged a fan. And then, incredibly, the fires all went out. The one the firefighters were still battling on the veranda just died down to nothing. As Mitch watched in stunned disbelief, the fire raging from Mr. Arndt's cottage, and everything surrounding it, just died. The charred remains were still there, but no flames, no glowing coals, and only a little smoke.

Mitch looked at the sky. Something about the atmosphere had changed.

Just as this last thought registered, Mitch understood why the fires had stopped. The atmosphere, indeed, *had* changed—there was no oxygen. His last two breaths had drawn in nothing. His lungs had already started to ache. He tried breathing in again, but nothing came. Next to him, Wendy panted as though she'd had the wind knocked out of her. In his rocking chair, Mr. Arndt's hands went to his throat in a choking gesture. Mitch looked at the other end of the grass in front of the veranda and saw that the firefighters had dropped their fire hose and were making similar choking gestures.

Somehow, the oxygen had been sucked from the air all around the resort. They were all going to suffocate out here like fish out of water.

They had to get inside the hotel, which maybe hadn't been affected. But he couldn't leave Mr. Arndt out here, and he doubted he would have the strength to drag him inside when he was rapidly losing strength himself. He looked at Wendy beside him and saw panic in her eyes. Her mouth formed words but nothing came out. She was trying to tell him something, but she might as well have been trying to have a conversation in deep space. Finally, she grabbed his upper arm and pointed with her other hand across the lawn where something black moved toward them from the area of the cart trail. The thing undulated like an amoeba or a drop of oil floating on a rippling body of water. Mitch could not decide whether it was alive or not.

The black thing reached a spot on the grass behind the ghost mob and stopped its progress. It stopped undulating, too, and began to grow in all directions until it was the size of a small car. Still, it had no definite shape, and it might as well have had no color either, because the complete blackness was not solid, but an empty void.

Just then a loud, wrenching sound like huge pieces of steel grinding against each other pierced the quiet. This sound was accompanied by the rapid expansion of the black spot, until it covered everything behind it—the harbor and Forge's Island to the north and east, Lover's Lookout to the west—as though black crepe had been hung over the sky all the way down to the Smythe lawn. Everything in the foreground—grass, topiaries, trees—became white and as opaque as the ghosts themselves, like a photo negative. Mitch raised his hand in front of his face, and it, too, was colorless and transparent. When he looked at Mr. Arndt, who sat just in front of him, the old man appeared the same. But Wendy, standing behind him against the backdrop of the hotel, appeared as solid and colorful as she had before.

This only lasted a few seconds, and then the blackness collapsed in on itself, shrinking to the size of a mere dot above the same patch of grass where it had started. A great and sudden flash of light shot out from the dot in all directions, blinding Mitch for a moment. When his pupils had adjusted again, everything was as it had been just before the black thing showed up. Except for one thing: all the ghosts, Robert and Bertie included, were gone.

And here was another welcome change: Mitch was breathing oxygen again.

On the western horizon the sky had begun to clear. Soon it would be clear over the Angels, too.

CHAPTER THIRTY-SEVEN

Mr. Arndt survived Robert Akers' assault that night, but he didn't have long to live. Three months later he passed away in his sleep at his home in Cambridge near Harvard University. On his dresser stood numerous photos of Maria, Roger and his Papa. Mitch liked to think that the four of them, and Tatiana of course, were reunited in some form of family unit wherever they were. He liked to think there was no need for keeping secrets over there, that they were finally free of that earthly burden.

He was thankful he got to know that strange, but wonderful man who taught him to look beyond the plainly visible to see what was really there. He'd had the good fortune of spending a lot of time with him after they left Sumner Island, and getting to know him much better. That fall he often drove from Fowler over to Cambridge after his last class of the day. They would sit in rockers on Mr. Arndt's porch overlooking a quiet, shady street, watching cars and joggers and bicyclists go by. Most of the time their conversation turned to politics and philosophy, and they would inevitably end up arguing until they were ready to throw Moxie in each other's faces.

That's the way Mitch would always choose to remember Mr. Arndt: sitting on his porch in Cambridge, silhouetted against a backdrop of trees dressed out in brilliant autumn colors, late-afternoon shadows creeping across the porch. He only wished he had met the old guy sooner. There were so many questions, and he only had time to ask a few.

One topic was the murder of Robert Akers in New York in 1933. Ever since that weekend on Sumner Island, Mitch had suspected Mr. Arndt was somehow involved. When he finally mustered up the courage to ask, he was surprised to find Mr. Arndt was only too glad to tell him the whole story.

At the time, Mr. Arndt told Mitch, he was a student at Columbia University. Feeling alone and angry after the death of his beloved Papa two years before, he had gotten into a little drinking habit, and one night he ran into Robert Akers coming out of a bar in the neighborhood where he lived. Thankfully, Robert did not recognize him. Teddy thought maybe it was just a fluke, a one-time occurrence, but each time he peered through the window over the next few nights he saw Robert again, always seated at the same table, surrounded by disreputable-looking people. On the last night a fight broke out and the bartender shoved Robert out the back door. This is what had become of the son of one of America's most powerful business tycoons.

Teddy followed Robert down a dark alleyway and called out his name. When Robert turned around, Teddy—a 19 year-old honors student preparing for a career in medicine—stuck a kitchen knife in Robert's abdomen, then plunged it in his left ear. No one ever guessed who did it. Mitch sensed that Mr. Arndt felt no guilt about what he had done. He also sensed that he derived no satisfaction from it. When he finished his story, he just stared at the darkening sky through sad eyes, saying nothing. Not even killing Robert Akers would bring back the sister he loved so much.

When Mr. Arndt died, Mitch called up Wendy at Longfellow College and asked her to accompany him to the funeral. He sobbed throughout the service; he missed his friend so much. When it was over he asked Wendy to have lunch with him, but she declined, explaining that she already had plans with her fiancé. It seemed that for months she had waited to hear from Mitch, and when he never called, she had given in to her boyfriend's efforts at reuniting. So the wedding was on again. Feeling numb, Mitch kissed her on the cheek and said goodbye, knowing he wouldn't be seeing her again.

After that he threw himself into his work at Fowler where he gave out tougher assignments and harsher grades the rest of the semester. His students nicknamed him Lambert the Horrible, but he didn't care. Work had become his whole life, his sole source of comfort and escape, and he expected everyone around him to work just as hard. It made no difference to him that he was the most unpopular professor on campus.

Then one day he got a call from a lawyer in Boston who asked if he would come to his office to discuss Mr. Arndt's estate. They met in a small, dusty office on Beacon Hill overlooking the Common. The attorney, who looked about as old as Mr. Arndt, pulled a will out of a file and shoved it across his desk at Mitch. The will had been written in August of that year, just weeks after the Sumner Island weekend. In it Mr. Arndt had named Mitch the executor of his estate. He had also left to Mitch everything he owned, including his house in Cambridge and the cottage on Sumner Island.

Stunned, Mitch asked the lawyer why Mr. Arndt had done this. "He has no other family, no friends, everyone's gone," the lawyer wheezed. "You seem to be the only one left."

So Mitch moved out of his little apartment and into Mr. Arndt's four-bedroom house in Cambridge. It was a cozy place and well cared for, but it took some getting used to. Unlike Mitch's apartment, which was all new, Mr. Arndt's place was filled with furniture and appliances that had stood around the house for decades. Even an old Kelvinator, just like the one on Sumner Island. Mitch was sure some of the furniture hailed back to Teddy's childhood. Thankfully, everything was tasteful, but it still didn't feel like home and Mitch considered selling everything and buying all new stuff. But after a few weeks he changed his mind. Somewhere in that time span he began to actually feel like he had been there forever, and he came to enjoy his life on that little street in the Harvard neighborhood where the atmosphere smelled of high academia and liberal politics.

There were a few surprises in that house, too. He found a photo of Teddy and Maria aboard the *Tasha*, with Bar Harbor in the background. He also found a little tuxedo up in the attic, all wrapped in yellowed cellophane. It looked about the same size as the one Teddy wore the night of Maria's birthday party, and Mitch imagined that he'd kept it for just that reason. The most interesting thing he found, though, was his quarter-moon brooch. He had been cleaning out Mr. Arndt's desk drawers when he came upon a small, black velvet bag with string ties, and there it was inside, along with a note from Mr. Arndt. The note read, "Mitch—found this on my kitchen table one night. Thought you might know who it belongs to. Ted." Below that, there was a P.S.: "By the way, it looks a lot like something else that's been kicking around here for a while. You'll find it in the bottom drawer. Good luck." From somewhere far away, or maybe close by, Mitch felt Mr. Arndt's warmth. He opened the bottom drawer, and among a lot of yellowed papers and old folders, he found the box Mr. Arndt had made him carry out of his cottage the night it burned. Inside the box he found a diamond and sapphire quarter-moon pendant, complete with gold chain. How Mr. Arndt came to possess Maria's lost pendant he had no idea, because the old guy left not a single clue.

In that same drawer Mitch found something that settled some other questions he had puzzled over since his time on Sumner Island: a copy of the Last Will and Testament of Roger Boudreau. In it, Roger had left most of his fortune to his siblings in the event Maria died before him or at the same time. This Mitch expected, but not what he read in the next paragraph down: 'To my dear friend and esteemed colleague, Dr. Wolfgang Arndt, I leave a sum adequate to deplete all mortgages and debts of any kind then existing in his name, as well as a sum sufficient to pay all of his child(ren)'s college education expenses up to and including any graduate and professional education they may wish to pursue. In addition, I direct that any sale of my stock in Smythe Resort, Ltd. include the following provision: 'For a period of ninety-nine (99) years following the date of the sale of any stock owned by Roger Boudreau, the fee owner in the cottage presently owned by Dr. Wolfgang Arndt (Lot 1 in a plan entitled Survey of Land of S.R.L. dated Apr. 12, 1898 by Lytle & Pastore Surveyors, Portland, Maine) shall enjoy all club privileges and meal privileges at the Smythe Resort, free of charge.'" What Roger Boudreau had cleverly done is provide for his biological son without ever actually naming him in the Will, most likely out of a chivalric respect for Teddy's mother.

Mitch had finally learned the real reason why Mr. Arndt was given first-class, expense-free service at the Smythe. He also learned how the Boudreau suite and the middle tower came to be renovated then left empty after Maria and Roger died. That was also in Roger's will: "My apartment, sited in the Smythe Hotel on Sumner Island, State of Maine, I leave to my loving daughter, Maria, or to Dr. Wolfgang Arndt should my daughter predecease me or die concurrently." Dr. Arndt had inherited the apartment after Roger died, had it rebuilt to the same specifications, then left it vacant. Probably, he couldn't bear to have it rented out and he did not need it himself since he had the cottage. Dr. Arndt never married, and in his own will he left everything to Teddy. Teddy also had opted to leave the Boudreau apartment as it had been, and he never used it or allowed anyone else to. So, what Mitch once thought to be a brilliant marketing ploy turned out to be nothing more than a legal tie-up that the Smythe owners were helpless to resolve. And now the apartment belonged to Mitch, who decided he would do exactly as Mr. Arndt and his father before him had done: keep it vacant and perfectly preserved.

There was one more surprise waiting in the drawers of that desk, and this one stunned him. It was a Princeton University Yearbook from 1924. When he opened its leather-bound cover, four pieces of paper slid out onto the desktop. The first was a receipt from a vintage book store in Boston dating from just a few weeks ago. The second was a copy of a microfilmed obituary page from the *Chicago Metro-Telegraph* dated September 3, 1924. It read:

OAK PARK MAN STRUCK BY TRAIN

CHICAGO - An Oak Park man was killed early this morning when his car was struck by a train in the lakeside section of Chicago.

Gerald Sande, 22, died when his car stopped on the grade crossing at W. Washington near the intersection of N. Wells. Sande was killed instantly when his crushed 1923 Packard automobile was pushed three hundred feet down the track.

The son of prominent Chicago trial attorney, Bjorn Sande, Gerald Sande was a May graduate of Princeton University and planned to attend Harvard Law School this fall.

According to police, Sande's car had stopped or stalled on the railroad tracks at approximately 3 a.m. as a freight train, traveling to Peoria, approached the crossing. Engineer, Louis Parisi, said he blew the engine's warning horn and applied the brakes but could not stop in time.

The impact caused the automobile to explode into flames. Police said the fire was so intense, everything inside that wasn't metal was completely incinerated.

Police are investigating the reason the car was stopped on the tracks …

Mitch skimmed the rest of the article, but there was nothing else that interested him. All that mattered was that a man named Gerald Sande had lived in the Chicago area, attended Princeton University where Bertie went to school, and had died not long after Maria but before she had appeared to Teddy in the schoolyard. He was sure this was his man. But had he really had a relationship with Maria of any kind? The last piece of paper—another copy taken from a microfilm—settled that question. It was from the May 1924 issue of a magazine called *Society*:

NEWPORT REGATTA BALL A SPLASH

Debutantes and suitors tripped the light fantastic in Newport Saturday at the annual Reggie Regatta Ball. The Ball, which kicks off the annual three-day sailing meet, is a traditional mixer for the just-come-of-age set among the East Coast's most socially prominent families. It also serves as a fundraiser for several charities, including the Beacon House and Bridge House shelters in Boston founded by lumber baron, Roger Boudreau.

Seen together at the party were a number of New York's famous young people. Michael Cord White of the Wall Street brokerage family was seen dancing with Phoebe Hughes, whose recent fling with one of the Rockefeller clan's most eligible would appear to have cooled off. Maria Boudreau, daughter of Roger Boudreau, spent most of the night in the company of Gerald Sande, son of Chicago trial attorney, Bjorn Sande …

So there it was. Now, all that was left to see was Jerry's picture. With trembling fingers he flipped through the fragile pages of the Yearbook faster than he should have, but only one of those pages meant anything to him. And he finally found it: Gerald Sande's image, clear as could be, seated in the front row of a group photo of the fencing team. Gerald Sande, smiling straight into the camera, looking exactly like Mitch. If the name "Gerald Sande" had not appeared under the picture, Mitch would have thought he *was* looking at his own image. In fact, when he looked closely, he could see the same tiny mould that grew on his own face just below the lower lip.

Impossible!

Yet there it was, plain as can be. Just as fascinating was what wasn't there: the small scar above Mitch's left eye where he'd gotten beaned with a baseball as a kid. The scar didn't matter much. Mitch was Jerry. Or Jerry was Mitch. Either way, they were one and the same.

CHAPTER THIRTY-EIGHT

Mitch thought solving the riddle of Gerald Sande would put his mind at ease for a while, but it didn't. Confirming Jerry's existence, the fact that he had met and romanced Maria for a brief time, and the fact Jerry looked exactly like him only raised more questions, the answers to which could not be found in a yearbook.

Besides, he was desperate to contact Maria again.

Christmas came and went and he found himself alone most of the time when he wasn't at work. He didn't realize it, but he had slipped into a deep depression. He lost weight—something he certainly didn't need—and people told him his eyes looked like they had sunk back into their sockets. He hadn't noticed and didn't care much either. When friends tried to get him to go skiing—his favorite sport—he declined. All he wanted to think about was summer and hot weather and being by the ocean.

It seemed like forever, but the warm weather finally did come, and in early May he was on the very first ferry out to the Angels. Upon reaching Longboat Harbor he disembarked at a brand new dock and took the trail to the left. He really had no interest in going up to the hotel at the moment; a dream he'd had the night before compelled him elsewhere.

He walked at a brisk clip, past the swimming beaches and the pavilion, up around the bend to the right where he began to see the damage done by the lightning storm the summer before. Most of the trees had been bulldozed, but some others with minor charring remained standing. Mr. Arndt's cottage and cabin had been torn down and the land cleared so only a bare dirt spot remained. He stopped for a moment, remembering the porch and the rocking chairs, and felt his depression return. He moved down the trail quickly—he hadn't come here to mourn.

Passing through the first tree tunnel, he looked off to the right hoping to see a grassy hill and a flat-top tree at the crest. Instead, he saw the same modern houses he had seen the time he went up there with Wendy. There was even a brand new house under construction. Still, he refused to lose hope. He followed the new trails up to the spot just below the crest of the hill where he and Wendy had stopped in front of the driveway of the topmost house. He saw no sign of life up there. In all probability the owners wouldn't be out to open their summer house until Memorial Day weekend.

He started up the driveway. The farther up he went, the more he relaxed. The house clearly was deserted. The windows were shuttered up with some sort of steel coverings to keep out the winter weather, and the crushed-shell driveway had not been raked and cleared of leaves and twigs that had accumulated in the fall and winter months. The pool in the back of the house was covered with a blue tarp.

He reached the top of the driveway and stopped to have a look around. He had to admit he felt a little foolish trespassing on someone's private property because of a mere dream. There had been a time when he would not have even considered it. The weekend of the séance—which seemed so long ago now—had changed all that for him, and he was willing to chance that he was on a wild goose chase. Besides, if he turned out to be wrong, at least he had spent an afternoon close to Maria, and that made the trip worthwhile.

That was exactly how he expected to justify his trip to Sumner Island that day. It had been more than eighty years since the last time Maria walked the island and maybe stood at the top of Lone Tree Hill. Even if his dream the night before was accurate, so much had changed. So much of the hill had been dug up, graded and covered in concrete. The chances of finding what he was looking for seemed terribly remote. The only landmark he had to work with was no longer even there—the tree with the flat top no longer stood. Probably it had been taken down to build one of these houses or trails, maybe even the swimming pool he now stared at from a picket fence beside the driveway. The pool seemed to have been set into the very crest of the hill, as the land sloped away on at least three sides. The fourth side was where the house stood, and that was built on a slight incline sloping away toward the Smythe Hotel in the distance. Mitch was all but certain he stood in the area where the tree had once stood. Only the area was now covered with just a few small shade trees, not much larger than saplings, most likely planted by some landscape architect.

Mitch opened a gate in the picket fence, went out back and stood near the pool. He imagined a chainsaw cutting through Maria's tree, leaving a stump to be pulled out by a winch and chain. All that would be left were roots, which would lie rotting in the ground on the other side of the pool wall. He walked around the concrete deck, imagining those very roots beneath his feet, knowing that whatever had been there beneath the soil with those roots must now be gone forever. Dejected, but looking forward to seeing Maria's portrait in the Smythe lobby again after all these months, Mitch turned to go back out the gate.

That's when he finally saw it.

It was partially hidden behind a small cabana on the east side of the pool: a tree stump, about three feet in diameter, rising out of the ground to a height of maybe two feet. He went back there and looked up-close. The top of the stump had long ago faded to gray; apparently the tree had been taken down long before the new owner of this hilltop had put in his new home. Mitch guessed that the owner had just left the stump because there was plenty of room to put in the pool and cabana without removing it. He walked around the stump, remembering the wonderful view from this spot, now partially blocked by the cabana but still spectacular to the east, north and south. He knew he had sat against the trunk on the west side, so that's where he went. He sat exactly where he had in his visions and scraped at the packed dirt with his hands. As he did, it occurred to him that there might be layers of dirt on top from eight decades of blowing dust, mud flows, digging, or any other form of earth shifting. To his surprise, he didn't have to dig deep before cutting a finger on something sharp, just as before.

Feeling like an idiot for having cut himself when he knew better, he started thinking about how he was going to dig in the hard earth. In his dream he had found a rock with a natural point and dug with that. He looked around, and sure enough, there was a piece of broken flagstone near the back of the cabana. He went to work with it, digging around the spot where he had cut his finger. Soon, he had uncovered the top of a rusted yellow box about six inches wide and ten inches long. The thing that had cut him was a broken handle on the top. He kept chunking away at the hard dirt until he had uncovered most of the box, then he grabbed the other end of the handle and pulled hard. The box broke free of the earth and he lifted it out of the hole and rested it on the stump. He could now see that it was a toolbox with two locking clasps on the front, just like in his dream. He had no idea what was inside; the dream hadn't taken him that far. Excited to the point of trembling, he unfastened the clasps and flipped the top open. Inside, he found two objects. The first was a gold Spanish doubloon with a cross on the front and some lettering on the back. The gold piece rested on top of the second object, a small, folded-up piece of paper.

Mitch set the doubloon aside and pulled out the paper. He unfolded it and read the few words written in a woman's cursive writing: "Seek and you shall find. Happy hunting."

He read it over four or five times before examining the coin again. Then he read the note once more. With a feeling of warmth in his belly, he placed the note and the coin back in the metal box and carried it under his arm down the hill. His destination: the Smythe hotel's lounge, where he looked forward to toasting Maria and her brother with a scotch on the rocks before catching the ferry back to the mainland.

EPILOGUE

Mitch did seek as the note told him he should. He spent the rest of the summer looking, but came up with nothing. Summer faded into autumn, the leaves changed colors, and soon he was back at Fowler College, buried in his work again, trying to put behind him what he hadn't been able to for more than a year now. It began to dawn on him that he might be searching for a long time. Maybe years, maybe even a lifetime. And so he made up his mind to focus more on what he already had, and stop living for what he did not. It wasn't easy. But he had been reasonably happy in his simple life before that weekend on Sumner Island, and so he threw himself back into that life, concentrating his energies on what he loved best, teaching history.

One Indian summer afternoon he was leaving his last class where he had engaged his students in a vigorous discussion of America's role in the Treaty of Portsmouth. Cutting across the quad to his office, his head was crowded with the words and negotiating strategies of Witte and Komura. Unlike older New England colleges with their ancient stone-and-brick buildings, the Fowler campus had been built in the blocky, sterile style of the fifties, but it looked just as beautiful this day with its groomed lawns and colorful foliage.

On this particular Friday afternoon the quad was mostly deserted. One female student sat, open book in lap, on one of the benches along the walkway on which Mitch now tread. He strolled along, taking his time, and eventually reached the bench. By now he had changed his mind about her status because she was not dressed in the casual clothing a student might wear. Instead she wore a long plaid skirt, white blouse and red cotton sweater. A felt hat with a wide brim obscured her downturned face. Beside her, a lunch bag lay open on its side, an apple spilling out of it. She was reading the book he used in his class, *The American Twentieth Century*, but he didn't believe she was one of his students. As he walked by, her head stayed down, her face still hidden. He walked a few yards past her then turned to look back. She raised her head and met his gaze, although her eyes were concealed behind sunglasses. An uncomfortable moment passed before he mustered up the courage to say something. He went back toward her, looked straight into her dark glasses and said, "Excuse me, are you in my class?"

The woman looked up and smiled warmly. "I'm not a student."

"Oh." Feeling awkward and a little stupid, he searched for something else to say. "I asked because we're using that same book in my course."

"You're Professor Lambert. I've heard a lot about you."

"You have?" This surprised him. He wasn't that well-known around Fowler. Still a mere associate professor, he had yet to make his mark.

"You wrote the book on the Boudreaus. You were out on Sumner Island for that séance."

So that explained it. If anything had made him famous it was the Sumner Island séance. His name had been mentioned in numerous newspapers and magazine articles about it. "Yep, that's me. Too bad you're not a student. You might enjoy the course I'm developing for next semester."

"The one about the supernatural in American culture?"

Again, Mitch was surprised. "How did you know about that? It's not even in the course catalogue yet."

"I kind of overheard Dean Selig talking about it," she explained. "I hope you do something on Washington Irving. That would be exceptional."

Mitch was impressed. And puzzled. The only other person at Fowler familiar with the course was, indeed, the dean of his department, Jacob Selig. But Dr. Selig was away on sabbatical this fall.

Another awkward silence followed, then Mitch said, "Well, it was nice meeting you," and started away from the bench. But before he could take a second step, the woman stuck out her hand. "I'm Elizabeth Turcotte. I just joined the teaching staff in the history department."

So that explained it. Mitch shook her hand and mumbled another "Nice to meet you." Still feeling ill-at-ease, he politely excused himself and continued on his way. He was nearly to the end of the walkway when he heard a voice call out, "Professor!" He ignored it, thinking it had been directed at another teacher coming through the quad. Then he heard "Professor Lambert!" and stopped.

He turned around. Elizabeth Turcotte still sat on the bench in the distance. The only other souls in the quad were a couple of young men who had appeared on the grass with a Frisbee.

Elizabeth stood up and removed her sunglasses, and Mitch's knees went weak. He would have recognized those eyes from a hundred miles away, never mind a hundred feet.

He hurried back to the bench where he stared silently into her lovely green eyes, his mouth unable to form words. She took off her hat, pulled out a barrette in the back and her dark auburn hair fell to just past her shoulders.

"I thought since it's such a nice day and we're going to be colleagues, maybe we should get acquainted." She smiled shyly and gave a little shrug.

Mitch shook his head in wonder, still unable to speak.

"I was going to have a late lunch out here, but if you'd like, I'll buy you a cup of coffee in the cafeteria," she went on.

Finding his voice at last, Mitch croaked, "I'd like that." He hesitated a beat before adding, "Maria."

She turned her head a little to one side and squinted at him. "Elizabeth."

He kept his eyes fixed on hers, but they didn't waver. Still . . . something in her expression . . .

At last he blinked and gave a quick nod. "Elizabeth."

They walked off in the direction of the cafeteria. He looked forward to their coffee break together, which he predicted would be a long one. They had a lot to talk about.

ABOUT THE AUTHOR

Michael Cormier is an attorney with a busy practice ranging up and down the coast of Maine, New Hampshire and Massachusetts. His writing efforts began in sports reporting, and in recent years he has turned to fiction, winning first place in *Prime Time Cape Cod*'s short story competition in 2008. A longtime resident of seacoast New Hampshire and Maine, his interests in local lore and world history are evident in *Sumner Island*, his first novel.